SENTINELS

THE OMEGA SUPERHERO BOOK 3

DARIUS BRASHER

D1564591

To you the reader, who makes writing for a living possible.

Power tends to corrupt, and absolute power corrupts absolutely. Great men are almost always bad men.

— LORD JOHN DALBERG-ACTON, *LETTER TO BISHOP MANDELL CREIGHTON*

Any man who tries to be good all the time is bound to come to ruin among the great number who are not good.

— NICCOLÒ MACHIAVELLI, *THE PRINCE*

1

If you had told me years ago when I was a skinny, bullied farm boy that I would eventually become the licensed superhero known as Kinetic who fought crime in one of the country's biggest cities and that late one night I'd break into the apartment of a mob enforcer named Mad Dog and wait for him to come home so I could scare him to death, I would have laughed in your face and asked what you were smoking.

And, if I had been a lot more adventurous back then, I might have asked you for a hit of it.

But I hadn't been adventurous. Back then I had merely been a small-town farm boy who had never been anywhere or done anything or used any name except the one my parents had given me, Theodore Conley. But now, as a 20-year-old who had operated for over six months in Astor City, Maryland as the licensed Hero Kinetic, I was a lot more adventurous. Developing superpowers at the age of seventeen, discovering you are an Omega-level Metahuman who has the potential to become one of the most powerful Metas in the world, enduring the rigors of Hero Academy, defeating the supervillain who killed your father, being Amazing Man's Apprentice near Washington, D.C., completing the terrifying Hero Trials, being attacked by Mechano of the Sentinels during those Trials, and surviving multiple assassination attempts all tended to make one more adventurous.

Or dead. Fortunately, the former instead of the latter had happened to me.

Then again, the night was young. I was lying in wait for Antonio "Mad Dog" Ricci, after all. He was a leg-breaker for the Esposito crime family. I doubted Mad Dog had gotten his street name because he was a canine lover who was just mad about man's best friend. When he came home to discover me lurking inside, it was unlikely he'd mistake me for a dog, and greet me with a pat on the head and an indulgent "Who's a good boy?" Him trying to cave my skull in with a tire iron was far more likely.

Though my former farming self would never have believed it, waiting to confront a mob enforcer in his high-rise Astor City apartment in the still of the night was not the craziest thing I had done since getting superpowers. Heck, it wasn't even the craziest thing I'd done this month.

Not everyone agreed.

"Have I mentioned how crazy this is?" asked my best friend Isaac Geere for the umpteenth time. Isaac murmured his question in a near whisper. Though alone in Mad Dog's apartment, we kept our voices down. In the stillness of the dark apartment, speaking in a normal tone sounded like a shout.

Isaac was the licensed Hero Myth. He had the Metahuman ability to turn into various mythological creatures. Though he wasn't currently using his powers, he still managed to do a pretty good nagging harpy impersonation without them.

"Not in the last five minutes or so," I responded in a similarly low voice. We had been over this several times. Though Isaac was partly joking around—when was he not?—I knew he was partly serious, too.

"Time for a reminder, then. You've had some horrifically bad ideas in your time, but this one's a doozy. I think it even edges out the time you sucker-punched one of the Hero proctors during the Trials. Intimidate a guy named Mad Dog? The madness of it is right there in the guy's name. Trying to scare a guy named that is like trying to drown a shark. Either his parents named him that, which means Mad Dog is carrying around the genes of lunatics, or people gave him that nickname based on his behavior, which means he acts like a lunatic. Either way, I doubt he scares easily."

"Of course Mad Dog is not his real middle name. Who'd name their kid Mad Dog?"

"A crazy bitch."

I groaned. "How long have you been sitting on that pun?"

"I thought of it thirty minutes ago. I've been waiting for the right time to spring it on you."

I more sensed than saw Isaac grin at me in the darkness of the room we were in. The only illumination was the faint glow of the city's night lights leaking in through the closed blinds of the apartment's windows, especially the floor-to-ceiling glass window directly behind us. Plus, Isaac blended into the dark room because he had on plain dark clothes rather than the colorful costume he normally wore as Myth. Two years older than I, Isaac was also taller. He was toned, but on the wiry side.

Like Isaac, I also wore plain dark clothes instead of the costume I usually wore as Kinetic. We each had on black ski masks and gloves which we had donned after entering Mad Dog's apartment. Wearing my Kinetic costume made me feel ten feet tall and like I was truth and justice personified. My current outfit made me feel about as heroic as a cat burglar.

Isaac said, "On second thought, *we're* the ones who are the lunatics. After all, we're government-sanctioned superheroes sworn to uphold the law, not to mention truth, justice, and the American way. Despite that, we illegally broke into an apartment to frighten a private citizen. I must have been absent from class with the flu the day the Academy taught us that breaking and entering to intimidate someone was A-OK. And, the fever from the flu must've done permanent damage to my brain since I agreed to go along with this cockamamie idea." I faintly saw his head shake. "Do you hate your Hero's cape so much that you're looking to have it taken away from you so soon after earning it?"

"We didn't break into anything," I said. "We opened the door like we own the place and strolled right in."

"Try that argument on the judge who presides over your felony trial. Call me to let me know how it goes. Assuming they let you make phone calls from prison. I wouldn't know. I've never been locked up like you have. Why a salt of the earth Hero like me hangs out with a jailbird like you is a mystery." There was another barely seen head shake.

When we had arrived at Antonio's apartment earlier, I had used my telekinetic powers to unlock the door. The door had opened for us as easily as if we were Antonio's landlord. We discovered once the door was open that Antonio had an alarm system. It beeped at us, demanding attention, as soon as we were inside. Leave it to a criminal to be security conscious.

As its beeping made obvious, the alarm system had been armed. Its luminescent numeric keypad was mounted next to the door. I had been about to reach inside the guts of the alarm with my powers to disconnect the power when Isaac warned me against it. A lot of alarms were designed to go off in a remote location when the local power was killed, he had said. So, I instead had lightly run my telekinetic touch over the keypad. Most of the keys were stiff from disuse. Three of them weren't—the five, the two, and the zero. Surmising those keys weren't stiff like the others because they were the ones Antonio used to deactivate the alarm, I started hitting those keys, hoping to stumble on the correct combination of numbers before the alarm went off. The math that had been drilled repeatedly into my head at the Academy told me I had about a seventeen percent chance of getting the access code right with each attempt if the code was merely three digits.

Fortunately, the guardian angel who protected Heroes turned burglars must have been looking out for us. The access code had been zero-two-five. I had gotten it on my third try.

"With you clearly misunderstanding what constitutes breaking and entering, how you managed to pass the Academy's Hero Law class is beyond me," Isaac was saying. "Maybe you cribbed the correct answers off my test papers. Now, where was I before you interrupted me with your jailhouse lawyer nonsense about how we didn't break into anything? Oh yeah, I remember—I was talking about what a great idea coming here is. It's so great, thinking about it makes me sick to my stomach. We're dressed up like the Hamburglar, sitting in the dark apartment of a sociopath who terrorizes people for a gang of even worse sociopaths, waiting for him to come home so we can beard the lion in his own den. And did I mention this apartment is numbered 1313? Everybody knows the number thirteen is good luck. Nothing but rainbows and butterflies. It's why the Apollo 13 mission went so swimmingly. Everything about this whole situation is just peachy-keen. What could possibly go wrong?"

"Swimmingly? Peachy-keen? Beard the lion in his own den?" I repeated. I grinned. "You sure do talk funny for a black guy from Los Angeles."

"You sure do talk funny for a black guy from Los Angeles," Isaac repeated mockingly in an over-the-top exaggeration of my South Carolina accent. "You're one to talk, Gomer Pyle. You're the hick pot literally calling the sophisticated kettle black. Ironic, not to mention racist. I prefer Melanin American over 'black guy.' Anyway, I take back what I said before. You're not Gomer. You're more like Lucy Ricardo. This is the kind of harebrained scheme she'd come up with. Next you'll suggest we break into the Tropicana Club so you can sneak into Ricky's act."

"No one's got a gun to your head—"

"Yet," Isaac interjected. "No one's got a gun to my head yet. Just wait until Mad Dog gets home. I'm sure he'd be more than happy to rectify that."

"What I was going to say before I was rudely interrupted was that you can always back out and go home. When you get there, maybe watch some modern television shows so your references aren't so dated. While you're bringing yourself up to date on contemporary pop culture, I'll take care of Antonio by myself."

"You're chock-full of both bad ideas and bad taste today, aren't you? Most modern shows are rubbish. Classic TV is the best TV. As for me leaving you here by yourself, you can forget that. You might need backup who'll save you from your own bad ideas. I said I'll help, so I'll help. I'm no welsher. Besides, even though this is a horrifically bad idea, at least we're here for a good cause. Your heart's in the right place. Apparently, you believe that the ends justify the means. I must've also been sick the day they taught that at the Academy."

"If only you had contracted a permanent case of laryngitis." Isaac ignored me as if I hadn't spoken.

"On the plus side, if this thing goes sideways, I'll be on the scene so I can be the first to say, 'I told you so.' Also, someone needs to be around to bail you out of jail."

"If this goes south, you'll likely go to jail with me. You're an accessory before, during, and after the fact."

"Darn it, I hadn't even thought of that." I faintly saw his head shake again. "You see what you've done to me, Lucy? Your bad planning and shaky grasp of the law have rubbed off on me."

I grinned. Isaac would likely be making jokes on his deathbed. "If I'm Lucy, you know that means you're Ethel Mertz, right?"

"That's the one part of these shenanigans that makes me happy. There are far worse people to be. Ethel was kinda hot. I've got a thing for mature white women in frumpy dresses and comfortable shoes."

"Sometimes I think you overshare. Other times—like now—I'm sure of it."

It was well after 2 a.m. Despite my ongoing banter with Isaac, I felt myself getting drowsy, like weights had been attached to my eyelids and they were slowly getting heavier. I fought the temptation to close them. If Isaac was right that this was a bad idea, a worse idea would be for Mad Dog to come home and find me curled up asleep on his couch.

I stood up from the large couch I had been on with Isaac. I was stiff from sitting for so long. I stretched. My shoulders popped. It sounded like a cap pistol being fired in the stillness of the dark apartment. We had been waiting for Antonio to arrive for over two hours. My movement stirred the otherwise still air. I got a fresh nauseating whiff of rotten seafood and decaying Chinese takeout. I had grown so accustomed to the stench of Antonio's overflowing kitchen trash can that I could barely smell it anymore except when I moved around.

In addition to the trash can being in dire need of empty-ing, clothes and other of Antonio's belongings were strewn sloppily all around the apartment. Apparently, he was so busy beating up his girlfriend and terrorizing people for the mob that he was an indifferent housekeeper. Contrary to what the Book of Proverbs said about idle hands, Antonio's busy hands were just as much of the Devil's workshop.

Isaac was in the middle of yammering about how I was his sidekick when my powers alerted me that someone was outside the apartment's door. Isaac was saying, "You're the Ron Weasley to my Harry Potter, the Hodor to my Bran Stark, the Chewbacca to my Han Solo, the—"

"You'll be the Abel to my Cain if you don't pipe down," I hissed. "Someone's outside."

I focused on the presence on the other side of the door. My hands burned a little, as they always did when I exerted my powers. My powers had developed a lot since they had first manifested years ago. They were like a muscle—the more I used them, the stronger they grew. One thing I was now capable of doing was to emit a pulse of telekinetic energy that allowed me to map out my surroundings. It was like the echolocation some bats used to hunt in the dark, only my powers were tactile rather than sound-based like bats' echolo-cation was. If it weren't for the fact DC Comics would sue me into poverty, I'd change my name to Batman.

I sensed a large man on the other side of the door slide a key into the lock.

"He's coming in," I whispered. Isaac got off the couch and stood near me.

The lock turned. The door opened. Light flooded in from

the hallway, making me squint. The light framed a tall, broad man wearing dark pants and an untucked white button-down shirt. His shaved white head was slightly conical. It reminded me of a hollow-point bullet.

Antonio's huge body filled the doorway like he was a giant entering a dollhouse. He was even bigger than he appeared in the pictures my *Astor City Times* co-worker Hannah Kim had shown me. Looking at him, I had no doubt Antonio was good at his job as a mob enforcer. If I didn't have superpowers and a guy Antonio's size showed up to demand the vig on money I'd borrowed from a mobbed-up loan shark, I'd poop my pants and hand over my last dollar so fast it would make George Washington's head spin. Even with super-powers, facing a guy Antonio's size made my sphincter tighten a little.

Antonio stepped inside. He apparently didn't see me and Isaac concealed in the shadows of the room. His keys jangled as he threw them into a bowl on a table by the door. Antonio turned his back partly to us to flip on the lights. I blinked away the abrupt brightness.

Now that I could see him clearly, Antonio's belly swelled out a bit, rounding out the fabric of the shirt above his pants. Though he clearly was overweight, the tightness of his shirt across his barrel-chest indicated there was a lot of muscle underneath the fat. My farming father would have described Antonio as "hard fat." I knew farmers back in South Carolina like Antonio, men who were very strong thanks to lives of physical labor, but who ate what they wanted when they wanted, so they carried a lot of extra weight around. Theirs was a functional strength. They weren't vain gym rats who weighed their food, flexed at themselves admiringly in the mirror, and fretted about sculpting the perfect abs.

I had spent most of my life in terror of guys who looked

like Antonio. I guess old habits die hard because I felt a sudden surge of fear as I stared at Antonio. A guy like me trying to scare a big guy like Antonio was like a mouse trying to scare a water buffalo.

Then I realized how silly I was being. I swallowed my fright. I wasn't a naive, rail-thin farm boy anymore. I was a licensed Hero. I had faced people far worse than a beefy non-Meta like Antonio. So what if he looked like he grabbed smaller guys like me and picked his teeth with us? If he tried to pick his teeth with me, I could knock them out of his mouth and make a necklace from them.

As soon as I felt a surge of confidence brought on by my internal pep talk, I tried to tamp it down. The last time I was overconfident, I had just foiled a bank robbery in Washington, D.C.'s Chinatown and had nearly gotten my swelled head blown off after a hot blonde snuck a bomb into my clothes. Despite having superpowers, maybe it was smart to also have a healthy amount of fear.

Then again, *Kinetic: The Man With Plenty Of Fear* was a less-than-heroic title for a superhero comic book. Perhaps it was why no one had bought the rights to my life story.

Antonio turned toward us. His beady, piggish eyes widened in surprise when he spotted me and Isaac. I used my powers to slam the door shut. I turned the deadbolt. I hoped the click of the lock was ominous to Antonio's ears.

"Welcome home," I greeted Antonio with a cocky smile on my face, and an irrepressible flutter of fear in my heart. I'd said the words with casual confidence, as if I lay in wait for guys named Mad Dog every day of the week and twice on Sundays. Experienced Heroes like Amazing Man and Athena—the senior drill instructor at the Academy—always seemed completely unflappable, as if they would greet Armageddon's Final Trump calmly and with a slight smile of anticipation. I tried to channel my inner Athena. Minus the boobs.

I had to give Antonio credit: it only took a split second for the deer in headlights look to fade from his face. The ski masks we had on made it obvious Isaac and I weren't here to sell Avon. Antonio reached under his shirt, moving faster than I would have thought possible for a big man. Then he froze with his hand inside of his shirt. He didn't move a millimeter further, as if he were a movie someone had hit the pause button on.

Antonio was doing his best statue impersonation due to me. Thanks to my echolocation abilities, I had already run my mind over Antonio's big body—yuck, by the way—and determined he had a holstered pistol hanging from his belt that was concealed by his untucked shirt. I had stopped him with my powers before he could reach it. Though Antonio struggled mightily against my hold on him, he couldn't move a muscle. I could barely feel his struggling. He was no match for my powers. I'd used them to pick up and fling tons before. Me immobilizing Antonio was akin to a man holding a grasshopper in place. The grasshopper didn't stand a chance.

With Antonio still frozen in place by my telekinesis, I pulled his gun free of its holster with my powers. Antonio also had a long folding knife in his front right pocket. I pulled the knife out too. I flung the knife across the room, where it hit the wall with a clatter. It fell to the floor.

As for the gun, I lifted it into the air with my powers. I held it in front of Antonio's unmoving eyes. He had no choice but to stare down the barrel.

"We came here to have a friendly chat with our new chum Antonio here," I said to Isaac, "and the first thing he does is try to pull a gun on us. What do you suppose Miss Manners would say if she heard about this?"

"She'd say it was outrageous. She'd also say we should chastise Antonio for his rudeness by shooting him with his own gun," Isaac said. We had an argument before Antonio's arrival about which of us would get to play bad cop, and who would be forced to play good cop. We had compromised and agreed to play bad cop-bad cop.

"Maybe we will shoot him," I agreed. Running over the contours of the gun with my powers told me it was a Smith and Wesson nine millimeter with a thumb safety mounted on the side. I made a great show of slowly turning the gun in midair so Antonio could clearly see its side. I flicked off the safety inches away from Antonio's eyes. I turned the gun so he once again stared down its barrel. "Whether our boy Antonio comes down with an acute case of lead poisoning all depends on if he does exactly what we tell him.

"Here's the thing, Antonio: We hear through the grapevine that you like to beat up your girlfriend Hannah Kim. Sometimes you rape her, too, when she's not in the mood to sleep with you. Since my friend and I both frown on domestic violence, we thought we'd swing by and express our displeasure. And by displeasure, I mean that we're pretty pissed. And when we get pissed, we tend to do things like shoot woman beaters and rapists in the head."

"After we break their bones and beat them black and blue," Isaac interjected.

"Right. After we break bones and beat them black and blue. I almost forgot."

"How could you? It's the best part." Isaac smiled a smile at Antonio that was a combination of gleeful and ominous. If I hadn't known Isaac as I did, I'd have thought that breaking people's bones was how he spent his weekends at the beach.

Antonio's bald head was now mottled red, either due to frustration at not being able to move, anxiety, fear, or all the above. His body struggled in vain to free itself. Antonio's small, close-set eyes were wild-looking as they stared down his gun's barrel. If a feral pig was injected with a boatload of steroids and started walking upright, I imagined it would look a lot like Antonio.

I said to him, "For some mysterious reason that boggles the mind, Hannah is in love with you despite how you treat her. If she knew we were here, she'd probably step between you and the gun pointed at your ugly face. But, unfortunately for you, she's not here. The only people here are you—a walking argument for abortion if there ever was one—and two pissed off guys with Metahuman powers. Our powers are why there's a gun floating in your face. They are also how we broke in here without leaving a trace.

"Despite being pissed, we're reasonable men. As such, we're going to offer you a deal. You're going to call Hannah today. You're going to break up with her. Tell her you found someone else. Tell her your job busting shopkeepers' kneecaps keeps you too busy to have a girlfriend. Tell her you've realized you're gay and that you're moving to a tropical island to do some dick diving. I don't care what you tell her so long as you end things with her. Then, you'll never see her or get into touch with her again.

"In exchange for you doing that, we won't break every bone in your body, beat you to a pulp, and then shoot you in the head with your own gun." I of course had no intention of doing all that—I was a Hero after all, not a hoodlum like Antonio—but he didn't need to know that my threats were hollow. He just had to believe that they were not. "As I said before, we're Metas. Pretty powerful ones at that. That means there isn't any place on the planet where you can run where we won't find you and end you if you don't cut off all contact with Hannah.

"Which is it going to be, Antonio?" I asked. "Break up with Hannah and live, or refuse and die a painful death?" Isaac cracked his knuckles ominously, which I thought was a nice touch. The cracking sounded like fireworks in the enclosed area.

Antonio didn't say anything.

"Speak up, we haven't got all night," I said sharply. I twisted the gun and slugged Antonio on the temple with its butt. I hit him hard enough that it would really hurt, but not too hard. Despite this guy being a piece of crap, I wasn't trying to kill him.

I brought the gun back down to point the barrel at Antonio's face. Blood streamed down from the gash I had opened at Antonio's temple. It dripped into his left eye. Antonio did not blink it away, which I thought was odd.

Oh! In my fervor to come across as a vicious thug who'd kill as readily as I'd swat a fly, I'd forgotten I had Antonio's body completely frozen. He couldn't speak even if he wanted to.

Feeling like a complete doofus, I released my powers' hold, but only on Antonio's head. He blinked furiously and shook his head as if he were awakening from a dream.

"Well?" I said, trying to keep my embarrassment for my oversight out of my voice. I couldn't imagine that an actual violent thug would sound abashed. If Antonio and I hadn't been on opposing teams, I'd have asked him to find out for sure.

Antonio stared at me with rage in his pig eyes. The blood on the side of his face made him look even more fearsome than he already did, which was plenty.

"I'll rip your heads off and shit down your necks," Antonio rasped in a voice that was surprisingly high for a man his size.

It reminded me of Mike Tyson's. "You don't know who you're fucking with."

So much for scaring Antonio to death.

"Sure we do," I said. "You work for the mob. But your mobster friends aren't here to protect you. Even if they were, we'd stomp them just like we'll stomp you if you don't do as you're told. We're Metas, remember? You don't scare us." *We eat guys like you for breakfast,* I almost added, but that sounded over-the-top cheesy, even to my inner critic.

Antonio opened his mouth again. This time, no bluster came out. Instead Antonio spat out something that looked like a yellow glowing marble. It grew exponentially in size as it shot from his mouth toward us.

It was more instinct and training than conscious thought that made me raise a force field around me and Isaac right before the glowing ball hit us. The ball exploded with an ear deafening boom when it slammed into my field.

It happened too fast for me to brace myself against the concussive force. Isaac and I were blasted backward, off our feet. We hit the back of Antonio's couch as if we had been picked up and thrown there. The heavy couch toppled backward from the force of the impact. Isaac and I hit the vertical blinds that covered the floor-to-ceiling window, then the window itself. The blinds rattled like a nest of rattlesnakes. We bounced off the window and hit the floor below it with a bone-shaking thump. The couch fell on top of us. The upturned couch covered us like a tepee, swallowing us in near darkness. I felt like a well-shaken martini.

"Is now a good time to say I told you so?" Isaac gasped. I could barely hear him as my ears rang from the explosion.

Before I could respond, the couch exploded into smithereens.

Isaac and I were thrown backward once more. We hit the

window again. This time, we collided so hard we smashed right through it.

With a crash and tinkle of breaking glass, we were flung into the cool night air outside.

The wind shrieked in our ears. We plunged toward the ground far below.

2

Isaac and I doing shooting star impersonations outside of Mad Dog's tall apartment building could be directly traced to when I met his girlfriend Hannah Kim during my first day of work at the *Astor City Times* newspaper about six months ago.

I knew there was something amiss with Hannah the moment I laid eyes on her. Maybe it was because my Heroic training had made me good at reading people. Well okay, perhaps "good at reading people" was a stretch. After all, I was the guy who had almost gotten his head blown clean off by the bomb-smuggling hot blonde in Chinatown and who had just been caught flat-footed by the fact Mad Dog was a Meta. My ability to read people was certainly not at a Sherlock Holmes level. Heck, it probably wasn't even at Dr. Watson's level. Thanks to my Heroic training though, I certainly was better at reading people when I met Hannah than I had been when I lived on the farm. Back on the farm, I had been better at reading when sweet potatoes were ready to be dug up than I had been at reading people.

Maybe I knew something was amiss with Hannah because,

as someone who had been pushed around and bullied a lot as a kid, I was hyperaware of the signs of it happening to someone else. Maybe it was the fact Hannah wore a skin-concealing, long-sleeved turtleneck when I met her even though it was warm outside and the *Times'* offices weren't cold. Maybe it was the fact I had volunteered at a dog shelter when I was in high school and had dealt with an abused Rottweiler there named Kiara. Kiara always had a slightly fearful look in her eyes, as if she suspected you'd haul off and hit her when her back was turned. I saw an echo of that same look in Hannah's eyes as I shook hands with her during my tour of the *Times'* offices.

Regardless of why I sensed something was amiss with Hannah when my *Times* supervisor introduced me to her, I did. An educated guess made me reach out with my left hand as my right one shook Hannah's to grab her forearm, as if in an overly enthusiastic greeting. Hannah winced when I lightly squeezed her forearm. Since I certainly had not squeezed hard enough to hurt her, I didn't need to be as smart as my estranged friend Neha Thakore, who under her code name Smoke had been the valedictorian of my Academy class, to deduce that Hanna's long-sleeved sweater concealed some sort of injury.

As I had been sworn in as a licensed Hero the month before I met Hannah shortly after completing the Trials, the words of the Hero's Oath had still been ringing in my ears:

> *No cave so dark,*
> *No pit so deep,*
> *Will hide evil from my arm's sweep.*
> *Those who sow darkness soon shall reap,*
> *For in the pursuit of justice,*
> *I will never sleep.*

I didn't need a graduate degree in poetry to interpret the words to mean I was sworn to protect those who couldn't protect themselves. My oath, plus a healthy dose of nosiness about what had caused the injury I had surmised was on her covered arm, made me try to befriend Hannah in my early days as an employee of the *Times*. I didn't even have to go out of my way to do so as my job duties took me to the art department almost every day. Hannah worked there as a graphic artist. Despite my important sounding title of Assistant Staff Writer, as the newest hire in the paper's editorial division and as someone who had exactly zero newspaper experience, I was in reality a gofer and errand boy who one day in the far distant future might be allowed to write something for publication if I kept my nose clean, demonstrated I could type without breaking the keyboard, and consistently got the reporters' and editors' lunch takeout orders right.

Anyway, I got to know Hannah in my daily visits to her department. At first, she thought I was hitting on her. Maybe I would have if I hadn't still been messed up in the head from Neha rejecting me weeks before when I had told her I loved her. If I had hit on Hannah, I doubted anyone with eyes would have blamed me. Hannah was super cute, and just a few years older than I. She was of Korean descent, with light brown skin and straight glossy black hair worn long. She had rich, dark, and slightly troubled eyes that focused intently on you when you spoke as if you were the only person in the world. She had unmistakably feminine curves despite probably only weighing a hundred pounds dripping wet. She was also smart, having graduated with honors with an art degree from an Ivy League school before getting a job at the *Times*.

Hannah wore a blue and white striped hat that was in the style of the hats train conductors wore. She always had it on, even indoors and even if it clashed with the rest of her outfit.

"My boyfriend Antonio gave it to me," she had said with pride when I asked about it in one of my first trips to the art department. She emphasized the word *boyfriend* slightly, as if to say, "Don't get any ideas." As I had stood over where Hannah sat, I got a flash of a fresh bruise on her throat despite the long neck of her sweater. I had wondered at the time if Antonio had given her that bruise as well as the hat.

When I had persisted in talking to her in my subsequent trips to the art department despite knowing she had a boyfriend, I think Hannah mentally put me into the friend zone. Story of my life. She slowly opened up to me over the course of several conversations, both in the office and over lunch.

At first, she told me that the bruises and injuries she often came to work sporting were caused by her natural clumsiness. "Oh, I tripped and fell while running on the treadmill," she said on one occasion. "I burned my hand ironing," she said on another. Like clockwork, a day or two after Hannah came to work with a fresh injury, she'd show up wearing a brand-new necklace or a bracelet or flowers were sent to the office for her. I didn't have to be a social worker specializing in abuse victims to know Hannah was lying to me and that the gifts she got were someone's way of making things up to her. Not even the Three Stooges were as clumsy as Hannah pretended to be.

Hannah had finally confessed the true cause of her injuries after weeks of me asking about them. It's amazing what people will tell you if you're patient and listen more than you speak. Maybe I should have hung up my Hero's cape and instead become a priest specializing in taking confessions. Thanks to my romantic overtures being rejected by Neha, I already had the celibacy part of priesthood down pat.

"Antonio doesn't mean to hurt me. Sometimes I talk back and it makes him mad. It's mostly my fault really," Hannah had said when she finally confessed to me. Her train conductor's hat had been accessorized with a swollen shut black eye that day. I wondered what gift Antonio would get her to make up for punching her in the eye. Maybe a gem-encrusted eyepatch.

Once Hannah had let the abuse cat out of the bag, it was hard to get her to stop talking about it. She told me I was the only one she had told about what Antonio did to her. I think it was a relief to get what was happening to her off her chest. She told me all about Antonio and their time together, both good and bad. Though she danced around coming right out and admitting it, I was convinced that Antonio also sexually forced himself on Hannah when she wasn't in the mood.

Hannah also told me what Antonio did for a living. He was an enforcer for the Esposito crime family. His street name was Mad Dog. Though I had only been in Astor City for a couple of months at the point Hannah told me this, I knew about the Esposito crime family thanks to my after-work crime-fighting efforts, both alone and alongside Myth. It would have been impossible to not know about the Espositos. Fighting crime in Astor City and not knowing about the Esposito crime family was like fighting global warming and not knowing about greenhouse gases. When it came to illegal activity in Astor City, blacks and Mexicans ran the drug trade, a Metahuman named Brass Knuckle ran the whores, and the Esposito crime family ran pretty much everything else. There was an uneasy balance of power among the various groups that occasionally flared into violence when one group or another overstepped its bounds into someone else's territory.

Despite me urging Hannah to break up with Antonio and go to the police, she refused. "I don't want to get him in trouble," she had said. "Antonio loves me." She always said his name worshipfully, like he was the Jesus Christ or something.

"Must be mighty hard to see that through one eye," I said. If she heard me, she completely ignored me. Her uninjured slanted brown eye had shone almost maniacally.

"And *I* love *him*. We're going to get married one day. He's big and strong and tough and brave. Sure, he does things that aren't exactly legal, but everyone's got to make a living somehow. Besides, even if I went to the police, they wouldn't do anything." She had added with perverse pride, "Antonio tells the cops what to do, not the other way around."

Women. Even with the help of superpowers, I still didn't understand them. It baffled me that an educated, accomplished, and pretty woman like Hannah would be proud of dating an abusive gangster. Then again, if there was one thing my twenty years on the planet had taught me, it was that life wasn't a movie where the nice guy wound up with the girl at the end. More often than not, the jerk walked away with the girl as he laughed and kicked sand in the nice guy's face. Screenwriters who crafted movies where the nerdy guy with the heart of gold walks into the sunset arm-in-arm with the blonde cheerleader who has learned to appreciate the nerd's true value were filthy liars. Or, maybe they were simply nerdy guys deluding themselves. Then again, maybe I was just jaded, bitter over what had happened between me and Neha.

If Hannah had told me when I first moved to Astor City that a gangster could tell cops what to do, I wouldn't have believed her. The brief time I had spent fighting crime at night plus the local news I'd consumed as a part of my job had disabused me of the notion that all Astor City cops had the noble goal of serving and protecting. I'd learned that a lot of the cops here were essentially uniformed criminals with a badge and a license to kill. The problem was there was no easy way to tell the corrupt cops from the good ones. Life wasn't an old western where the good guys wore white and the bad guys wore black. And, even if I found a good cop and reported Antonio to him, he wouldn't be able to do anything if Hannah wasn't willing to press charges against Antonio.

So, me going to the police myself about Antonio's abuse was out. Also out was confronting Antonio as the Hero Kinetic. Licensed Heroes were not vigilantes. Just as the police didn't have the authority to do anything to Mad Dog without Hannah being willing to press charges, a Hero didn't have the authority either. Real life was not a comic book where masked superheroes could go around willy-nilly punching lowlifes in the face. If I accosted Mad Dog as Kinetic without legal justification, he would be well within his rights to call the police on me and have me arrested. The Heroes' Guild, the self-regulating body all Heroes belonged to, would be compelled to investigate my arrest, and would probably punish me for breaking the law. The Guild might even take my Hero's license away. Pitbull, the chief proctor of the Trials whom I had pissed off during the Trials, also served on the Guild's Executive Committee. He would be thrilled to have an excuse to rip my Hero's cape off me.

On top of that, if I confronted Mad Dog as Kinetic after Hannah had confessed to her co-worker Theo that her boyfriend hit her, Hannah wouldn't need her high-priced Ivy League degree to figure out that the masked Hero Kinetic and the only guy she had told about her boyfriend's abuse were one and the same person. A secret identity was supposed to be kept a secret. If it wasn't, it would be called a tell-everyone-and-their-mother identity.

So, as the Hero Kinetic, my hands were tied. If I were being a good little Hero, I'd simply shake my head at Hannah protecting her douchebag boyfriend and turn my attention to something I had the legal authority to do something about.

That's exactly what I did for months. Then, one day

Hannah had come to work with her arm in a sling, broken in two places. Her face was battered as well. She told everyone at the office she had slipped and fallen down the stairs. She couldn't look me in the eye when she tried to sell me on that lie too. She and I both knew what had really happened to her.

That incident had not only broken Hannah's arm, but it was also the straw that broke the camel's back. I knew I had to do something about Hannah's abuse before Mad Dog injured her further or, worse, killed her. If I couldn't do anything as the Hero Kinetic about Antonio, then by God I would do something about him as Theo.

Since I shared a rental house with Isaac and another roommate, Isaac had seen me preparing to go out to confront Antonio the night after Hannah had come to work with a broken arm. Isaac had wormed out of me what I planned to do to Antonio. At first, he had tried to talk me out of it. He had seen that my mind was made up. Though he still didn't approve, here he was now with me, falling out of the night sky like a shooting star after being blasted out of Antonio's apartment.

If a willingness to risk life and limb over something you had advised against wasn't true friendship, I didn't know what was.

3

Antonio blasting me and Isaac through his apartment window was not the first time I had been thrown through glass. You don't get used to it. Then again, if you get to the point where you do get used to it, you probably need to re-evaluate your life choices.

Back when we were at the Academy, Athena had told us more times than I could remember that in an unexpected crisis, you rose or fell to the level of your training. That was why, as silly as it sounded, emergency preparedness experts advised people to practice dialing 911—when the poop hit the fan, you would have a hard time remembering your name, much less how to get into touch with the authorities. That was also why I had been drilled in the use of my powers so thoroughly that using them to save my bacon in an emergency was as automatic as ducking when a baseball was flung at your head.

Endless training was why I had instinctively raised my force field around me and Isaac when Antonio had spat his energy blast at us, or whatever in the heck it was. And, it was why I still had my force field erected around us when we had been flung through the thick glass of Antonio's window. Otherwise we no doubt would have been sliced to ribbons by the breaking glass. Assuming Antonio's energy blast hadn't blown us to bloody bits before we even hit the window.

The city's lights spun like a kaleidoscope around us as we fell down the side of Antonio's apartment building. I felt like a James Bond martini—thoroughly shaken. But despite being rattled, thanks to my training and force field, I seemed uninjured. I was flustered, startled out of a year's growth by the fact Antonio was a Metahuman, and spinning ass over teakettle as we fell, but uninjured. Being unhurt would change all too soon if I didn't shake off being shaken up.

Shake off being shaken up? Huh. One was not as eloquent as one might hope when plunging toward the ground like a duck full of birdshot.

Isaac tumbled in the air near me, close enough to spit on. The fact he hadn't transformed into a flying mythological creature to save himself demonstrated he was even more shaken up than I was.

Preventing the ground from performing the world's most violent cosmetic surgery on our bodies was obviously priority number one. Priority number two was to fly back up to Antonio's place and kick his ass.

I used my powers to slow and then halt both of our descents. We were still several stories up from the ground. We hovered in the air a few feet from the face of Antonio's building like two tethered helium balloons.

Isaac shook his head as if to clear it from cobwebs. He looked as unsettled as I felt.

"Tell me you didn't know Mad Dog was a Meta," he demanded. His voice was raspy. The wind whipped around, making it hard to hear him. "Because if you did know and neglected to share that niggling little detail, I'm going to punch you in the face as soon as I finish punching Mad Dog in his face."

"I had no idea. Honest." I was breathing hard. "If Hannah knows, she didn't tell me. My guess is that she doesn't. She was so proud when she told me Antonio works for the mob. If she knew Antonio is a Meta on top of that, she'd probably shout it from the rooftops."

"Well, the cat's certainly out of the bag now. Let's go back upstairs and do some of that face-punching I mentioned. We need to make it quick, though. Mad Dog's blasts probably woke up half the neighborhood. Surely someone's called the police by now. We need to be long gone by the time they show up. I'm a black man wearing a ski mask in a white neighborhood in the middle of the night. They'll shoot first and ask questions later."

Isaac was right. I had no interest in going to jail again. It hadn't been much fun the first time. I had even less interest in the Guild finding out a Hero was illegally skulking around people's apartments.

I lifted us back up toward Antonio's floor. I slowed as we approached the hole in the glass we had been ejected from. We cautiously peeked inside Antonio's apartment. We didn't want to rush in recklessly and get our asses handed to us again. Once spat at, twice shy.

The only part that remained of the huge glass window we had been blasted through were jagged shards. They lined the perimeter of the hole like shark's teeth. Inside, Antonio spoke animatedly on a cell phone to someone. My first thought was that he had called the police. My second thought called me an idiot. A guy like Antonio didn't call the police; he had the police called about him. He was probably calling for mob reinforcements on the off chance his blasts hadn't already taken care of us.

Antonio looked up and spotted us. His eyes widened in surprise. His mouth began to open. There was a yellow glow between his parted lips.

I had seen this movie before and had no interest in the sequel.

With my force field around me, I rocketed through the gaping hole in the glass. I had the presence of mind to simultaneously drop Isaac inside the apartment.

I hit Antonio like a battering ram right in his fat midsection. He grunted like a wild boar at the impact. The cell phone flew from his hand. I shot forward several feet with my head buried in Antonio's stomach, like a fist that had punched rising bread dough. I slammed Antonio against the wall. His big body collided with it with a satisfying crash.

I bounced back a bit from Antonio, landing on my feet. Antonio slumped off the wall and sank to his knees. He groaned weakly. His eyes were a little crossed. Despite having been rocked, he tried to stand up again. I hated to give the devil his due, but I had to admit Antonio was a tough bastard.

I sealed Antonio's mouth shut with my powers to avoid being blasted again. I could have immobilized his entire body as I had before, but I refused to hit a man who couldn't defend himself, even a piece of crap like Antonio.

I launched a back leg side kick into his ribs. Antonio fell to the side, catching himself with an outstretched arm before he hit the floor. With my force field still up to protect my hands, I swung a flurry of punches at Antonio's head. Antonio's arm slipped from under him. His upper body toppled heavily to the floor like a felled tree.

Since Antonio was out of commission, I should have stopped there. I knew that, but didn't. There was so much I had been frustrated by and mad about since coming to Astor City: I was mad at myself for stupidly getting caught off guard by Antonio being a Metahuman; frustrated by Hannah's stubborn refusal to break up with Antonio; angry and hurt about Neha having rejected me; frustrated about not knowing what to do about the Hero Mechano, who was the main reason I had moved to Astor City; and dismayed about how big city life had taught me that the morality I had grown up believing in few others shared. These days, it seemed like black was white, and up was down. Nothing in my life was going as I had expected or hoped. There was so much I couldn't do anything about, and so much I didn't even know how to go about doing.

I could do something about Antonio's big fat pig face, though. So I did.

Repeatedly.

"Jesus, get off him," I faintly heard Isaac say. I didn't. My arms and shoulders felt loose and easy, like I had found my rhythm while hitting a speed bag.

"I said get off him! You're gonna kill him."

Arms grabbed me from behind, stopping me from punching more. I was roughly pulled to my feet. It wasn't until that moment that I realized I had been on one knee, punching Antonio's supine body over and over like my fists were pile drivers.

As my bloodlust faded and the scales fell from my eyes, I saw that Antonio was barely moving. His fleshy face was busted up, more red than white now. It looked like a raw ribeye steak. Antonio's blood dripped off the force fields surrounding my clenched fists. Crimson blood splatters on the carpet around Antonio's head looked like a Rorschach test. I was glad there wasn't a psychologist around to ask me what the splatters looked like. I would have been forced to admit they looked like I had gone way too far.

Antonio writhed sluggishly on the floor, like a snuff film

stuck in slow motion. His moans reminded me of a hospital patient's whose pain meds had worn off.

Mortified, I shrugged out of Isaac's grasp. Shame stabbed me like a rusty knife. I tried to keep it out of my voice as I spoke to Antonio with a roughness I didn't much feel anymore. My anger and frustration were draining out of me like dirty water out of an unplugged bathtub.

"If you thought that was bad," I said to him, "imagine what I'll do to you if you lay a hand on Hannah again." Antonio's left eye swam red with blood. I wasn't sure if it was from his scalp wound from earlier, or from the beating I had just given him. His remaining good eye looked up at me, partly unfocused, partly a dull basilisk stare of hate. "Break up with her, and do it today. After that, never speak to or see her again. Then you better pray she has a nice long life and dies peacefully in her sleep. Because if she so much as skins her knee or gets a hangnail, I'll assume you were responsible and come looking for you. What I did to you today will look like a kiss on the cheek compared to what I'll do to you then."

I thought I heard the wail of police sirens wafting up from far below through the broken window.

"Come on, let's go," Isaac said impatiently. He pulled insistently on my shoulder. The faint wail of police sirens, now louder than before, was not a figment of my imagination.

"Remember what I said. Don't make me have to come back, Antonio," I told him. He just stared up at me balefully through his one non-bloody eye. He didn't answer. I still had his mouth sealed shut since I had no idea if he could still spit energy blasts at me even when hurt. Antonio let out a noise that was half grunt, half moan. I almost felt sorry for him. Then I remembered all the times I'd seen Hannah limping or wincing in pain. My pity for him died stillborn.

Isaac and I rushed over to the opening in the window. A

couple of police cars with their lights flashing were below, in front of the building. Unless it was the world's biggest coincidence, they had been summoned to investigate all the noise coming from Antonio's apartment. Lingering to have a chat with the cops about why two Heroes out of costume had illegally broken into a man's apartment and beaten him bloody seemed a bad idea.

I launched into the air, pulling Isaac along with me. As soon as I was high enough to avoid the tall buildings around us, I shot off toward the west. Toward home.

"What the hell is wrong with you?" Isaac demanded angrily once we were safely away from Antonio's apartment. He had to shout to be heard over the rushing wind. "The plan was to threaten to beat him to death, not to actually beat him to death."

I didn't respond. I stared straight ahead into the murky night sky. Even though Antonio was a criminal, a bully, a woman beater, and a rapist, I had gone too far. I knew I was in the wrong.

And yet, part of me was satisfied I had finally done something proactive after spending months frustrated and feeling impotent. Not only because of Hannah, but because of everything. That satisfied part of me didn't care that I was in the wrong.

Later, when I'd cooled down some more, I wondered if my frustrations and my life in Astor City were turning me into as much of a thug and bully as Antonio was.

4

The afternoon after my encounter with Mad Dog, I dutifully waited with a small crowd of people at a crosswalk for the light to turn so we could cross Tennessee Avenue. So many races were represented in the throng, it was like standing in the middle of the United Nations building. I had just walked several blocks to here from the Tennessee Heights subway stop with my work messenger bag bouncing against my thigh, its long strap diagonally across my chest. Tennessee Heights was the suburban neighborhood in Astor City Isaac and I rented our house in.

The people at the intersection with me looked simultaneously exhausted and relieved, the look of people who had spent all day slaving away in pursuit of someone else's dreams. I imagined a similar look was on my face. I had just left work at the *Astor City Times*. My fellow rodents and I had been given a temporary reprieve from the rat race. It would resume tomorrow morning, long before we could grow to miss it.

I walked to and from the subway during the work week because I did not have a car. I did not need one. Between walking, Astor City's extensive public transportation system, cabs, and ride-sharing apps, I could get anywhere in the city I needed to go. In fact, I could get to most places in the city just using the subway. Except the northeastern quadrant of the city, which was by far the most affluent part. When the subway had been redesigned and rebuilt after an alien invasion destroyed most of the city in the 1960s, the residents of the northeastern quadrant successfully lobbied to keep subway stops out of the northeast. They wanted to minimize public transportation there to keep the riffraff out. As a college dropout with a pronounced Southern accent and a low-paying, entry-level job, I had no illusions about the fact they would consider me part of that riffraff. I wondered if they would be so quick to call names if a supervillain attacked and they needed me to rescue them. It was hard to look down your nose at someone saving your life.

When I needed to get somewhere in the city really quickly, I could always fly. Flying to and from work, though, would make it far too easy for someone to connect the Hero Kinetic to the riffraff Theodore Conley. Marvel and DC had taught me the key to maintaining a secret identity was to keep it a secret. And people said comic books did not teach you anything.

While we all waited for the light at Tennessee Avenue to change, I turned a bit to gaze at Star Tower, the building I had left less than an hour ago. The UWant Building was next to it. Though they were downtown and miles away from where I stood, the silver-colored Star Tower and the emerald-colored UWant Building poked up out of the trees in the distance like erect phalluses. If my penis, erect or otherwise, were as green as the UWant Building, I'd consult a doctor; if it were big enough to tower over trees, I'd consult with a porn casting director.

Despite having been in Astor City all these months, I still loved to look at the huge buildings. I hadn't gotten used to their size. On the small farm I had grown up on, trees had been the only skyscrapers. Aiken, the small town closest to the farm, hadn't had a building taller than three stories. Even Washington, D.C., the city I had served my Apprenticeship near, didn't have any buildings taller than the Washington Monument, which was only 555 feet tall.

The UWant Building made the Washington Monument look like a child's toy. It was the tallest building in the entire country. Star Tower, where I worked, had been the undisputed king of downtown until the UWant Building's completion over a decade ago. Star Tower had been built by a book publishing company with the help of state and federal funding. It had been the first piece of major construction in the city after the V'Loths destroyed Baltimore in 1966. In addition to the V'Loths mostly leveling the city, they killed hundreds of thousands of its residents. After the Hero Omega Man sacrificed himself to kill the V'Loth queen and end the alien invasion, Baltimore changed its name to Astor City as a symbolic "screw you" to the V'Loths. Their home world orbited a nearby star. "Astor" was a corruption of "aster," the Greek word meaning star. I knew that because training to be a Hero had taught me more than merely how to throw a punch.

When work on Star Tower finished a little under two years after it began, the building had been the tallest in the United States. If naming Astor City after the word for star was saying "screw you" to the V'Loths, naming the country's then tallest building Star Tower and building it in the ruins of the city the V'Loths had destroyed was giving the V'Loths the middle finger.

Now, the UWant Building was the country's tallest. Its emerald color made it look like something out of the city of Oz. It had been built by UWant, the world's dominant Internet search engine. If it wasn't a sign of the times that a building built by an Internet company had eclipsed a building built by a book company and the government, I didn't know what was.

The rise of the Internet and the decline of traditional media were why I worked downtown in the *Times'* annex in Star Tower instead of the *Times'* headquarters on the outskirts of the city. The Star Tower annex housed the *Times'* digital and social media platforms. Though you didn't have to be psychic to foresee that the digital versions of the *Times* would soon overtake the paper version both from a popularity and revenue standpoint, the *Times'* annex was still seen as the redheaded stepchild of the company by most of the graybeards who had worked at the *Times* longer than I'd been alive. Stan Langley, a longtime editor at the paper who had been transferred from headquarters and put in charge of us at the *Times'* annex, was the only member of the *Times'* old guard who didn't treat us youngsters at the annex with utter contempt. Other than Mr. Langley, the graybeards seemed to view the Internet as a passing and quite distasteful fad that was likely responsible for the national debt, terrorism, and their erectile dysfunction.

If they asked me, I could give them the addresses of some websites that could probably help them with that last part. As a healthy young man who hadn't slept with anyone since Neha and I had our falling out before I moved to Astor City, I had more than just a passing familiarity with porn. The good little Catholic boy still living inside of me had been shocked by some of the things I had seen online, but apparently not shocked enough to stop me from seeing them.

While I and my fellow rat race survivors waited for the light to change so we could cross Tennessee Avenue, two teens ambled past us into the busy intersection, talking loudly to one another as if they were miles rather than inches apart. One was white, the other Hispanic. The vulgar slang the guys used was English, but just barely. Their baggy jeans hung halfway down their butts, exposing tight underwear. I wondered what kept the beltless jeans from falling to their ankles. I doubted it was modesty.

Cars honked and slammed on their brakes with loud squeals as they avoided hitting the teens. Completely ignoring the cars who had the green light, the teens slowly swaggered across the road as if they had designed it, cleared it, paved it, and the city had named it after them.

After the teens were out of their way, the cars proceeded through the intersection. No one rolled down his window to tell them to get out of the middle of the street. Life in Astor City had probably taught them that wasn't a good idea. Just yesterday a guy driving through the part of Astor City known as Dog Cellar—which was the kind of bad neighborhood you'd expect it to be from its nickname—had stopped his car to tell three teens who were jaywalking to get out of the road. The three pulled the guy out of his car, beat him unconscious, took his car for a joyride, and then wrecked it. The news had said the guy was from out of town. That was unsurprising. Natives knew to avoid Dog Cellar if they could. They especially knew better than to challenge the young men of various races who aimlessly wandered the city like packs of feral dogs. I had dealt with my fair share of them when I patrolled the city at night as Kinetic. Their amoral opportunism and casual criminality were more than a little scary. And I had superpowers.

Like the towering buildings of downtown Astor City, seeing young men who seemed content with having nothing productive to do was not something I had gotten used to. The way I was raised, if you weren't asleep or sick, you were supposed to be working, studying, or doing something else productive. Idleness was shameful. If you didn't have a job, you went door to door offering to cut people's lawns, or walked up and down the road to pick up glass bottles and aluminum cans to redeem them for recycling money, or any number of other ways to make an honest buck. You did *something*.

Then again, between working during the day and fighting crime at night, I was almost always exhausted. By contrast, the shiftless young men who wandered the city seemed well rested. Maybe they had a better handle on how to live life than I did. Perhaps one day I'd shelve my upbringing, pull my pants down to my thighs to give my junk some fresh air, and give those guys' devil-may-care lifestyle a whirl. After all I'd been through since developing my powers, God knew I needed the rest.

The ambling teens were almost across Tennessee Avenue now. Thanks to Heroic training that had long before now become reflex, I noticed that the sagging pants of the short Hispanic teen hung diagonally, a little lower on the right than on the left, as if the right pocket contained something heavy. Curiosity made me gently probe the inside of that pocket with my powers. My mental touch was met with hard steel and smooth wood made warm by the teen's body heat. A small caliber pistol. Maryland had some of the toughest gun laws in the country. Even if the teen was older than he looked and was an adult, it was unlikely he had a license to carry. It was more likely the teen would one day wave his gun in the face of someone who was more scrupulous than he about following the state's gun laws.

Back at the Academy, Athena had tried to break me of the habit of moving my hands when I used my powers, but she had never been able to do so. Even now I needed to move my hands to use them. I lifted my hand, pretending like I was swatting away a fly. Instead, I unobtrusively used my powers to pull down the jeans of the Hispanic teen, pantsing him like I was a high school bully.

The teen cried out in surprise, grabbing at his falling pants. Too late. The jeans pooled around his legs. I pulled the gun out of the pocket, making it look as if it had bounced out thanks to its collision with the asphalt. I made the gun skitter away from the teen, forcing it to slide into a storm drain a few feet away from him.

The teen cursed, pulled his pants partly back up, and shambled over to the storm drain. He lay down on his belly, stuck his arm into the storm drain up to his shoulder, and groped for the gun. His search was in vain; little did he know I had made sure the gun was well out of his reach. Some of the pedestrians waiting at the intersection with me tittered at the display, but not too loudly, not wanting to be heard laughing at the teen or his friend standing over him. If you drew attention to yourself on the streets of Astor City, you almost always regretted it.

Once the walk sign said we could cross Tennessee, I and my fellow stick-in-the-mud, law-abiding pedestrians did so. We passed the teen jaywalkers. The shorter one still groped for his gun. Though I suspected the stories I heard about there being mutant alligators in the Astor City sewer system were merely urban legends, the devil in me wished one of those gators would happen along and make an hors d'oeuvre of the teen's arm.

Smugness tugged the corners of my mouth into a slight smile. Despite not yet having done anything about Mechano of the Sentinels, at least I had done something about a punk with a gun. Baby steps.

I broke away from most of the pack by taking a left at the corner, and then a right onto Williams Place, the street on which I lived. Row houses lined both sides of the street. Most were well-kept and looked recently renovated. A handful were old and rundown. Tennessee Heights was well on its way down the gentrification road from poor to solidly middle class.

The house I shared with Isaac and a guy named Bertrand Dubois was one of the ones that had seen better days. It was one of the few rental houses on the block. Our landlord, a squat cigar-chomping guy named Mario, had asked, "Do you want to live in a palace, or do you want cheap rent?" when we three roommates had asked him for the umpteenth time that certain repairs be made. Since none of us were swimming in loot—if we had been, we wouldn't need to be roommates—we had opted for the cheap rent. Astor City was an expensive place to live, and an affordable residence wasn't easy to come by. Having it fall down around our ears in slow motion was a trade-off we were willing to accept.

I nodded at Deshaun as I sidestepped his outstretched legs on the walk to my house. He nodded back in acknowledgement. His baseball cap was pulled low over his eyes. He was a very fleshy black guy who carried a lot of his weight in his midsection. When he stood, he looked like a partially melted chocolate bar. He wasn't standing now. He sat in his usual spot on the short stone and concrete wall lining the street. His thick legs stretched out in front of him onto the sidewalk. He wore a red, black and yellow Astor City Stars basketball jersey, so oversized that it looked like a tent even on Deshaun's overweight body. And, just as the two jaywalkers had, Deshaun wore baggy and saggy blue jeans. Jeans dangling at half-mast seemed to be as much of a uniform for young knuckleheads as costumes were for Heroes.

Deshaun was one of several drug dealers operating out of a dilapidated house at the end of the block. The house was owned by a guy named Mitch who had inherited it from his deceased parents. Mr. and Mrs. West, the nice elderly black couple who lived directly across the street from me and had been there since they were dewy-eyed newlyweds, told me Mitch's parents had been teachers who were pillars of the community. Mitch had followed in their teaching footsteps by teaching guys like Deshaun how to sell drugs. Deshaun and another guy named Fidel took turns dealing on my street. Deshaun had the day shift; Fidel had the night shift and would replace Deshaun in a few hours. Deshaun and Fidel dealt drugs on my street twenty-four hours a day, seven days a week, in fair weather or foul. Like the U.S. Post Office, neither snow nor rain nor heat nor gloom of night would stay these poison peddlers from the swift completion of their appointed rounds.

Unfortunately, I knew all too well from life on our block how the drug dealing process worked: People looking to score would approach either Deshaun or Fidel. They'd talk about what the customer wanted, negotiate a price, and then money would change hands. Deshaun or Fidel would go to one of the places on or around the street where they had their supply stashed—they never kept the drugs on their person to guard against the unlikely event the police hassled them—and then return with the goods. The other guys who worked for Mitch had a similar setup all throughout Tennessee Heights.

Tennessee Heights was Mitch's territory. Mitch had carved it out as his area of operation long before I arrived in the neighborhood. From what I'd heard, the guy who ran the Tennessee Heights drug operation before Mitch had objected when Mitch showed up after his parents' death and started dealing in the area. Those objections took the form of pitched gun battles between Mitch's forces and the other guy's. Mitch's adversary one day disappeared. Word on the street was he had taken up residence on the bottom of nearby Astor Bay with his insides well ventilated by bullet holes. Since then, Mitch had ruled the Tennessee Heights drug roost. Mitch apparently paid kickbacks to someone higher up in the city's drug trade hierarchy, but I didn't know who. Or was it supposed to be whom? I didn't know that, either. I was a Hero, not a grammar nazi. I did know though that those kickbacks went in part toward paying the cops to keep them off Mitch's back.

I felt Deshaun's dark eyes on me as I mounted the short steps of our two-story row house. When it was new ages ago, the house probably had been dark red. Now the house was a faded pink, like a dollhouse that had been handed down through generations of careless children. Black ornamental shutters hung sloppily from the dirty windows, reminding me of fake eyelashes on a drunk old lady.

I pulled my house keys out of my pocket. I still felt Deshaun's gaze as a tightness between my shoulder blades. His gaze made me uncomfortable, the way being around a dog who'd bite you if he had a chance would make you uncomfortable. Though we acknowledged each other when we saw one another, I didn't like Deshaun. I didn't know anything about him other than what he did for a living and who he worked for, but that was enough. I was very anti-drug. Sure, I knew there were otherwise law-abiding people who smoked a little weed after work to unwind or did a bit of coke on the weekends to loosen up with no lasting ill effect. I had also seen far too many others in my short time as a Hero whose lives had been ruined by drugs: the mother who rented her underage daughter to men for the night to score a meth fix; the father who spent his last dollar on crack and zoned out on the drug while his crying children went hungry in the next room; the fresh-faced college co-ed who died with a heroin needle in her arm and her dealer's penis in her mouth. Those were just a few of the lives I had seen ruined by drugs. Too many. If every illegal drug in the world were piled up and doused with gasoline, I'd be the first one in line with a lit match.

I knew my dislike of Deshaun was mutual. He had offered me a free sample of his wares the first week I had moved in. With a sly smile, he had called it a "housewarming gift." I had refused it. No dealer could get me hooked with that old "the first one's free" gambit. I'd been forewarned by watching my fair share of ABC Afterschool Special reruns as a kid. My refusal had perhaps been firmer and more impolite than it should have been; I hadn't known at the time I'd be seeing the guy almost every day. Deshaun probably thought I was the world's biggest square. Maybe he was right. You couldn't pay me enough to put a thief into my body that would steal my brains. Drugs and superpowers did not mix. And, though Deshaun obviously didn't know I was a Hero, he might have sensed, if only subconsciously, that we were on opposite sides of the legal tracks. A wolf probably didn't have any great affection for a shepherd either, and for much the same reason.

Though neither Isaac nor I made much money, we had taken some of the money we had saved during our tenure as Amazing Man's Apprentices and splurged on a state-of-the-art alarm system. The system was linked to the watches Isaac and I wore. They were part timepieces and part communicators, relics from our days as Apprentices that the Old Man—what we called Amazing Man—had let us keep. Since my watch was not going off, I assumed no one had broken into our house. Even so, before slipping my key into the lock of our front door, I used my powers to do a quick scan of the house to double check that all was well. After all, Antonio had an alarm system, and look at what had happened to him. Kinetic had made a lot of enemies in Astor City fighting crime at night. As far as I knew, no one knew Kinetic was little ol' me, but it was better to be safe than sorry and wind up walking unexpectedly into the welcoming but deadly arms of a vengeful criminal. Besides, attempts had been made on my life before. Not only had Mechano tried to kill me during the Trials, but there had been that bomb-planting blonde in D.C., not to mention Iceburn's multiple assassination attempts. Though Iceburn was in federal Metahuman prison, whoever had hired him was still out there somewhere, presumably still grinding his ax against me. Though no attempts had been made on my life since I moved to Astor City, I never could shake the feeling that the sword of Damocles hung over my head, dangling by a thread, ready to fall and slice me open.

Yeah, I had mastered the art of paranoia. I was thinking of teaching a class in it.

No one was inside the house according to my powers, including Isaac and Bertrand. Well, no one human. My telekinetic touch felt the bodies of several mice scurrying in the walls of the old house. There were also a couple of rats the size of small dogs. The female rat was in the middle of "doing her wifely duty," as my grandmother might have put it. Despite Nana's folksy phrase, it seemed to me the male rat was doing most of the work.

I suppressed a shudder as my mind brushed over the frenzied rodents. There's nothing like a little rat porn to start the evening off right. It was estimated the number of rodents in Astor City exceeded by a large margin the millions of humans who lived here. Big city life was even more glamorous than I'd dreamed.

I went inside, closing the door behind me, relieved to leave Deshaun's gaze on the other side of it. I sighed in relief. I had survived another day in the big bad city. Actually, I spoke too soon. Since I intended to go out on patrol tonight, the city would get another chance to have a whack at me.

5
_____

W hen Isaac and I first moved into our Tennessee Heights rental and I had come to understand what Deshaun, Fidel, and the rest of Mitch's drug-slinging crew were up to thanks to Deshaun's offer of a housewarming gift, I was in a lather to put my Hero suit on and get rid of Mitch's entire operation root and branch.

"You know what happened when they killed off the cats on Australia's Macquarie Island?" Isaac had asked me.

"Huh? What the heck does that have to do with anything?"

"In the late twentieth century, the cats were eating too many of the island's birds. So, they had the bright idea to shoot all the cats. Any idea what happened?"

"I've got the feeling that even if I don't want to know, you're going to tell me. You're as bad as Neha, Mr. Know-It-All."

"That's Captain Know-It-All. Have you forgotten I'm a superhero? Anyway, when they killed all the cats, they solved the problem of too many birds being killed all right. But they inadvertently caused a new problem. Little did they realize the cats had kept the island's rabbit population under control. Without the cats, the rabbits bred like . . . well, like rabbits, with predictable results. Pretty soon the rabbits were eating everything in sight and causing an ecological disaster."

"And the moral of the story is what? That rabbits like to get it on? No duh. You know I grew up on a farm, right? You're trying to teach Catholicism to the Pope. Let's go find an Eskimo and you can tell him all about snow."

"If I'm Captain Know-It-All, you're my sidekick Offensive Lad. It's Inuit, not Eskimo. Try to show some cultural sensitivity, you redneck cracker. Next you'll be calling me the N-word."

"How come you get to call me names, but if I returned the favor, it would trigger a second Civil War?"

Isaac had smiled smugly. "Reparations. You got years of my people's free labor. I get this."

"Your people?" I snorted. "Your ancestors are from Jamaica, not the Deep South. You're no more descended from slaves than I am."

Isaac had put his hand over his heart. "Whatsoever you do to the least of my brothers, you also do to me," he intoned solemnly. "I learned that from the Bible. Or maybe it was a fortune cookie. I forget. Anyway, we seem to be diverging from the original topic. What were we talking about?"

"The unfairness of reverse racism?"

"Before that. I remember now. We were talking about Australia. The moral of the Australia story is that you shouldn't remove a perceived problem without carefully studying the ecology first. Crime has an ecology just like nature does. We just moved into the neighborhood. Before we blindly bull ahead, let's first make sure taking Mitch and his minions out won't mean he'll get replaced with an equal or worse problem."

Literally the next morning after that conversation, I stood on the front stoop of the house, locking up and about to walk to the subway to go to work. I saw a kid on a bike slowly peddle down the street. He couldn't have been any older than thirteen. Long, lean and lanky, he was big for his age. He had a mini-Afro with a pick peeking out of the top of it. He peered carefully into each parked car as he leisurely pedaled by. His manner reminded me of a patient cat waiting to pounce on a careless mouse. I pretended to fumble with my keys so I could stay on the porch and watch him. Even without Heroic training, I would know the kid was up to no good.

He stopped almost in front of our house, leaning on his bike next to the car owned by my neighbor Saul. Saul was a public school teacher married to another teacher. Their row house shared a wall with ours. The kid pulled a metal rod off his bike. He smashed the rear window of Saul's car. He stuck his hand inside the car, pulling out a laptop that Saul had stupidly left there.

Before pedaling off with the computer tucked under his arm, the kid looked up and locked eyes with me. His unashamed and unafraid eyes held a challenge, as if to say, "What do you think you're gonna do, white boy?"

If he only knew.

I was about to give the kid's bike a discreet sideways push with my powers to send him sprawling when my intervention became unnecessary. Deshaun was on drug-slinging duty that morning, as he was every morning. As the kid approached where Deshaun sat, Deshaun hauled to his feet and took a couple of casual steps forward between two parked cars. Deshaun grabbed Saul's laptop from the crook of the kid's arm as he pedaled past, simultaneously yanking hard on the kid's elbow with his other beefy hand.

The bike went one way and the kid went the other. The kid collided with a loud thump into the back of a parked car. He slid down and sprawled on the ground, yelling bloody murder all the while.

Deshaun looked down at the kid dispassionately. He told the kid to shut up as he'd wake up the entire neighborhood. When the kid didn't, Deshaun kicked him in the ribs a couple of times. The kicks didn't appear to come from a place of anger. Deshaun's manner was more like a doctor administering a needle to a patient who needed a vaccine.

With one arm, Deshaun dragged the kid off the ground. The kid struggled. Deshaun let go of him long enough to smack the back of his head with an open palm a few times until the kid stopped squirming. With Saul's computer in one big hand and the back of the kid's neck in the other, Deshaun then frog-marched the kid down the sidewalk and up the short stairs to Saul's porch. They were now on the same level as I and about ten feet away. The side of the kid's face was already beginning to swell from where he had slammed into the parked car.

Deshaun nodded at me in brief acknowledgement. He pounded on Saul's door with his foot. Since it didn't look like I needed to intervene, I just stood there and gawked. It was like watching a play.

After a few moments, Saul opened the door. He was a Hispanic guy a few years older than I. His surprise at the tableau in front of him was evident on his brown face. The surprise increased when Deshaun thrust the computer into Saul's hands.

"This here's Mr. Saul. Tell him what you did," Deshaun rumbled at the kid.

"I ain't do shit," the kid said sullenly.

Another meaty slap to the back of the head. The kid cried out and recoiled from the blow, only to be jerked upright again by Deshaun's hand, which had quickly resumed its place around the back of his neck.

"Mind your fucking language," Deshaun said. "Show some respect when talking to your elders. Now again, tell Mr. Saul what you did."

The kid said, "I found that computer on the street under the busted window of a car. Picked it up and was gonna turn it into lost and found with the cops."

That tall tale elicited more smacks from Deshaun and more howls from the kid. Saul glanced at me, disbelief at what he was witnessing evident on his face. Finally, the actual story of what the kid had done was loosen by Deshaun's blows. The truth spilled out of the kid's mouth like a waterfall.

"Tell him you're sorry, and that it won't happen again," Deshaun said after the kid finished.

"I'm awful sorry Mr. Saul. I won't do it again. Promise." The kid had been smacked so many times I believed that he actually was sorry.

Saul went out to his car to assess the damage. Meanwhile, Deshaun and the kid spoke for a few moments at the foot of Saul's stairs. I lingered, not even trying to pretend I wasn't listening in. It's only eavesdropping and therefore rude if people don't know you're listening. I think I read that in an etiquette book somewhere.

"What's your name?" Deshaun asked the kid.

"Lamar."

"You new around here, Lamar?"

"Yeah. Mom just moved us here a couple of weeks ago."

"I thought so. If you were from around here, you'd know the deal." Deshaun hesitated. "You got a cell phone, my man?"

The fact Lamar considered lying was written all over his young face. "Yeah," he finally said, no doubt avoiding the temptation to lie by remembering how it had felt when Deshaun had cuffed him.

Deshaun stuck his hand out. "Hand it over."

"Why?" Lamar asked, his voice cracking.

"Because actions have consequences. Unless you got the money to fix that man's window."

"I ain't got no money."

"Big shock. Then hand the phone over."

Reluctantly, Lamar pulled a smartphone out of his back pocket. He gave it to Deshaun. Deshaun dropped it to the concrete sidewalk and ground it underfoot. Lamar looked down at the debris like he was going to cry.

Deshaun said, "Mr. Saul lost a window, now you lost a phone. Karma's a bitch. Remember that the next time you come around here. Tennessee Heights is off limits for any of your foolishness. If you wanna bust up people's windows and steal they shit, do it somewheres else. This is a nice quiet neighborhood, and I'm gonna keep it that way. Now get outta here. Remember what I told you."

Like a student released from the principal's office, Lamar scurried away. He retrieved his bike which lay in the middle of the street. He pedaled away, glancing back at Deshaun sullenly.

Deshaun looked up at where I still stood on the porch.

"Kids these days. If you don't watch em, the whole neighborhood'll go to hell," he said.

"You're doing the Lord's work," I had responded. Deshaun's dark eyes had narrowed dangerously a touch, perhaps suspecting I was making fun of him. Then, with an almost imperceptible shrug of dismissal, he ambled back over to his usual spot. He resumed leaning against the short wall, waiting for a customer to come by to get a fix.

Later Saul told me $400 was in his mailbox the next day

with only the words "For your car window" scrawled on the front of the plain white envelope the cash was in. Though there was no proof the money was from Deshaun, it certainly wasn't from the Tooth Fairy. I guess Deshaun and his boss Mitch figured the money was a small price to pay for people in the neighborhood continuing to overlook the drug deals happening every day right outside our doors.

That incident with Lamar and Deshaun had been my first indication that maybe uprooting Mitch and the people under him would have unintended consequences as Isaac had suggested. My subsequent conversations with the Wests across the street and others who lived in the neighborhood for years made me conclude that doing something about Mitch would be a mistake and might result in his replacement by someone much worse. Apparently, before Mitch had come along and imposed a rough form of peace and justice on the neighborhood to minimize the number of times the police came around, Tennessee Heights had been as dangerous as a warzone. Despite the fact Mitch was a dope dealer, the long-time residents of Tennessee Heights respected him and what he had done for the neighborhood.

So, I had given up on the idea of taking care of Mitch and his crew as Kinetic. It really burned my butt to see people openly flouting the law, though. Back on the farm, life had seemed simpler, more black and white.

Then again, I had just gotten finished lying in wait for Antonio and beating him up. Maybe those of us who illegally broke into glass houses should not throw stones.

WITH DESHAUN SIMULTANEOUSLY WAITING FOR CUSTOMERS AND standing guard over the neighborhood on the other side of the closed front door, I climbed the stairs to the second floor of our house. Out of habit I avoided stepping on the next to the last stair from the top. That stair creaked loudly when you put your weight on it. Though the house had undergone some minor cosmetic renovations since its construction over a hundred years ago, the creaks and groans the house made when you stepped on certain spots indicated the house's age. The noises the house made suited me just fine. Even if an intruder got past our high-tech alarm system, the creakiness would alert us to a stranger's presence.

The second floor consisted of bedrooms for me and Isaac, and a bathroom we shared. Bertrand's bedroom was in the basement, along with a small bathroom he exclusively used. He worked as a freelance translator. He often saw Isaac and me leave the house together late at night, dressed in regular clothes, with our Hero costumes stuffed into a duffel bag. We were usually going out to patrol the city, but Bertrand did not know that. He had no idea we were Heroes. He just thought we were security conscious night owls.

I went into my bedroom. Nothing was on its off-white walls except scuff marks and holes left by a procession of tenants over the years. The room was bigger than the bedroom in the mobile home I had lived in with Dad on the farm, but not by much. It was more than enough for my needs, though. I lived a pretty spartan existence, a habit I picked up from my time in the Academy. It's not like I owned a lot of stuff anyway. My room contained a cheap bed, a chest of drawers with framed pictures of my parents and Neha on top, and a bookcase stuffed full of books. As I hadn't seen or spoken to Neha since she rejected me when I told her I was in love with her, I knew I should take her picture down. I just couldn't bring myself to do it.

The books were my prized possessions. I had bought most

of them since moving to Astor City. As busy as I was, I still loved to read. After all, before I met Isaac and Neha, books had been my best friends. After Mom died when I was twelve, Dad and I were too poor to buy books. I spent a lot of time in public libraries as a kid as a result. Now that I was an adult and had a job, it gave me great pleasure to own books. Though my tastes ran to mostly science fiction and fantasy growing up, my time at the Academy and as an Apprentice had ignited an interest in history. As a result, most of the books in my bedroom's bookcase were biographies and histories.

I opened my small closet and stowed my messenger bag on the top shelf. The inside of the closet appeared smaller than it had when I first moved into the house because I had used the carpentry skills Dad had taught me to build a hiding place on the left side of the closet. I had built a similar hiding place in Isaac's bedroom closet. Just as Isaac's did, my hiding place contained my Heroic paraphernalia: The greenish-black mask whose technology obscured my features when I put it on. My armored Kinetic costume, which was dark green on top and black on the bottom. A police scanner. The thick gold ring with the imprint of a masked man on the face of it that I received along with my Hero's license. My Hero's license, which looked pretty much like a college diploma, except I didn't know any college diplomas that had been signed by the current chairman of the Heroes' Guild's executive committee, Pitbull, the Secretary of the U.S. Department of Metahuman Affairs, and the President of the United States.

My two capes were also in this hiding place—a red one from when I graduated the Academy, and a snow white one I got at my Hero swearing-in ceremony. I usually only wore a cape on ceremonial occasions because a cape was a mighty handy thing for an opponent to grab and choke you with.

The only Hero-related stuff the hidden area didn't contain

was the wrist communicator I already had on and always wore. The door to my Heroic hideaway looked like nothing more than the narrow side wall of my closet. Apply a little pressure here and a little more there, though, and the wall slid open to reveal my hidden things. The hidden area was tiny, barely big enough for me to squeeze inside of. The Batcave it wasn't. Being a somewhat freshly minted Hero, perhaps it was too soon for me to have a full-scale lair. I looked forward to the day when I had a lair containing an Alfred who would cater to my every whim.

Looking at the door to my hideaway caused a fresh stab of guilt to my conscience. The image of Antonio's bloody face staring up at me was still fresh in my mind. What kind of Hero was I to beat Antonio as I had? Yes, I had been trying to protect Hannah. But did the end justify the means? Lawyers said that when a fellow lawyer was appointed to the judiciary, he often came down with an acute case of robe-itis—that is, putting on the judge's robe and all the power it represented went to the lawyer's head, making him behave in ways he never would before he became a judge. Had I contracted the Hero equivalent? Did I have cape-itis? Had I let the authority to use my powers my license granted go to my head? Did being a Hero make me think the rules—both the explicit legal ones and the implicit moral ones—didn't apply to me?

I stared at the hidden door my costume hung behind. My stomach twisted. I had planned on going out on patrol after I ate and once darkness fell. The thought of donning my costume and mask and the high ideals they were supposed to represent so recently after violating those ideals at Antonio's made me sick. Maybe all work and no play made Theo a dull bully.

I needed a break. The city would have to hobble along without Kinetic tonight.

I pulled off my dress shoes, khakis, and button-down shirt. I tossed the clothes into my laundry basket. Already feeling the stress of the workday draining out of me, I put on shorts and a tee shirt instead. I padded back downstairs and into the kitchen.

I examined the contents of the refrigerator with a critical eye, trying to decide what I was in the mood for. I tended to eat both clean and prodigiously. In addition to our almost nightly patrols, Isaac and I both worked out several times a week, and my body constantly needed refueling. The Academy and the Old Man had pounded into my head the importance of being as fit and strong as possible since you never knew when you would have to rely on the strength of your body instead of the strength of your superpowers. Thanks to years of training, though I was not the scrawny kid I used to be, neither was I as big and muscular as I intended to eventually be. As Athena had always admonished us when we didn't give our all during Academy training, "Somewhere out there is someone who's training his tail off while you infants are slacking, whining about how tired you are and how much your body aches. And, when you meet that non-slacker, he will beat you. Battles are won or lost long before they are actually joined by your level of preparation."

Plus, though I was not overly vain, being buff looked much better in tight costumes than being pudgy did. Though almost all Heroes were fit—every two years the Guild required us to pass a rigorous fitness exam to maintain our licenses in active status—I had seen a few costumed supervillains with flabby arms and potbellies. It was not a good look.

Computer programmers had an expression: garbage in, garbage out. The same was true of the human body—if you consistently fed it crap, you would have a crap body. The reverse was also true. That was why our fridge was packed with high-quality foods. In addition to us shopping at organic grocery stores, Isaac and I had pooled our meager salaries to join a community supported agriculture group. Through the CSA, Isaac and I got food from local farmers. There was no farmland in Astor City of course, but the surrounding counties had plenty. Every week the CSA made a delivery to our house of whatever produce, meat, and dairy that was in season. If no one was home, the delivery guy left the food in a cooler we kept on the porch. If it weren't for the watchful eyes of Deshaun and Fidel, I had no doubt the food would disappear shortly after it was delivered. Though I hated to admit it, living on a street with watchful drug dealers had its perks.

With Athena's advice about discipline and preparation ringing in my ears and the form-hugging fabric of my costume on my mind, I considered making a stir-fry with the steak and fresh vegetables delivered by the CSA the day before. The meat was from a grass-fed, antibiotic-free, hormone-free, free-range cow. The cow had lived so well, it was a wonder it had died. The stir-fry would be high protein, high fat, high calorie, and low carbs. The perfect building blocks for growing muscles. I could end the meal with my usual kale shake, composed of a ton of kale, an unpeeled cucumber, an avocado, fresh ginger and garlic, and several strawberries blended together until it was a radioactive green smoothie. I often added some hemp protein powder to the mix, mostly for the protein, but partly in the hopes there was some residual psychoactive marijuana in the hemp to help me forget I was drinking something that tasted like the bottom of a garbage pail. Isaac called the shakes my Hulk Loads. I had never turned into the Incredible Hulk drinking them. They did turn my poops green though. Baby steps.

My stomach recoiled at the thought of yet another healthy meal, and my mind recoiled at the thought of making one.

Screw my muscles, I thought. I instead pulled out some left-over pizza. It was Bertrand's, but he had told me earlier I could have some.

I popped several slices into the microwave. The smell of melted cheese, sausage, and pepperoni soon filled the room. If there was a Heaven, it probably smelled like a pizzeria. If I was going to take a break from patrolling, it seemed only proper to take a break from clean eating too. I was in the mood for comfort food, not utilitarian fuel. I'd return to my strict diet tomorrow. As my father James used to say, "All things in moderation, including moderation." Not all his Jamesisms were draconian.

I took the pizza into the living room. I opened the drapes. The late afternoon sun poured in through the two windows. There were thick metal bars outside the windows, as there were on all the windows of the house. The bars were relics from a time long before I moved in when the neighborhood had been more dangerous than it was now. Through the corner of one window I saw the lower part of Deshaun's legs stretched out on the sidewalk as he waited for a customer and kept watch over the street. Last night a Hero had beaten a civilian up after breaking into his place, and today a drug dealer was protecting that Hero. The whole world was topsy-turvy.

I settled into the couch and turned on the television. I had just missed the local news. I normally watched it before I went out on patrol as it gave a nice summary of the not so nice crime in the city. The fact I watched local news didn't mean I liked it. It was wall-to-wall murders, stabbings, assaults and corruption interspersed by ads for fast food joints, car dealerships, and payday lenders. They should have called the local news Death, Destruction and Desolation Delivered with Delight. Too long and too alliterative, maybe. The newscasters always seemed so thrilled to talk about someone's grisly murder. Maybe they had lived in the big city too long and had lost sight of the fact that every murder victim was someone's child. The fact the local news channels had reported favorably on some of my and Isaac's nocturnal crime-fighting exploits did not make me feel better about them.

I channel surfed as I ate the pizza. Nothing captured my interest. The scripted shows I came across didn't draw me in. When you were used to flying around the city and battling criminals, watching a bunch of actors pretend to do so held little appeal. My reality was far more dramatic than fiction.

Though I had intended to avoid news entirely, I eventually settled on watching CNN. After a while, CNN might as well have been watching me because I stared off into space. Images of what I had done to Mad Dog paraded in front of me. The blood on the carpet around his head looked like a Jackson Pollock painting.

6

———

"Well if it isn't the Ultimate Fighting Championship's middleweight contender," Isaac said after he walked in the front door. "Did you find somebody new to beat senseless today? Or did you switch species and decide to kick puppies instead?"

I was still in front of the television with most of my pizza, now long cold, in front of me on the coffee table. Isaac came into the living room, put his laptop bag on the floor, and plopped down heavily in a chair on my left in front of the windows. He was shaved bald, fully exposing the light brown skin of his head. His lack of hair made the jagged scar on his forehead from our fight with Iceburn years ago even more prominent. The Academy forcing all us males to keep our heads shaved while we were there had turned Isaac onto the benefits of not wrestling with a full head of hair every day. Straight black glossy hair was on his hands and knuckles. Naked, he was hairy everywhere except on his back, like a wolfman with male pattern baldness on his backside.

Isaac wore a crisp white shirt and gray dress slacks. He had just left work. He worked for Pixelate, a company not too far from Star Tower. Pixelate did movie animation. Isaac was an illustrator there. As drawing, painting, and sculpting mythological creatures helped him transform into them—as Isaac often said, "If I can't visualize it, I can't become it"—Isaac had become quite the artist in the years I had known him. His Heroic training had given him marketable artistic skills, helping him to land his job at Pixelate. My own Heroic training hadn't provided me much in the way of job skills, unless juggling telekinetically counted. The main reason I had my *Times* job was because the Old Man was friends with the *Times'* publisher and had pulled some strings for me. When he didn't have his costume on, the Old Man was Raymond Ajax, the uber-wealthy philanthropist and retired industrialist who knew movers and shakers around the world.

I said in response to Isaac, "I see you're launching right into criticizing me again. Whatever happened to 'Hey man, how was your day?' Or, 'Anything interesting on the news?' Instead you're busting my chops. You're worse than a nagging wife. If this is what being married is like, I'm glad I haven't taken the plunge yet." I left unspoken the fact that women were hardly breaking the door down, trying to get to me to marry them. "That reminds me: I'm pretty sure Bertrand thinks we're gay. All the time we spend together, the fact neither of us has ever brought a girl home, the late nights out together, only to return in the wee hours with cuts and bruises. I think he thinks we spend our nights partying at a gay bondage club or something."

Isaac snorted.

"I wish I were gay just so I could come out of the closet," he said. His brown eyes glittered maliciously. "It would give my homophobic mother a heart attack." I had learned during the Trials that Isaac had a love-hate relationship with his mother. Mostly, he loved to hate her. Based on what I knew of her, I could hardly blame him.

"If we were gay, you know I'd be the top, right?" I said. "It's my right as an Omega-level Meta. An Omega like me is named after Omega Man himself. A Beta-level like you is naturally beneath me."

"Nuh-uh. You're crazy. You didn't even know what a top was until I taught you." Isaac hesitated. "That sounded dirtier and gayer than I meant. Anyway, nobody—and I mean nobody, Omega-level or otherwise—gets to peel this brown peach."

"That's a visual I could have gone my whole life without."

"You're the one who brought it up. And yes, pun intended. But don't think you're going to divert me with all your gay talk from the topic of what happened with Mad Dog. I'm the master of changing the subject when I don't want to talk about something. Don't try to pull a me on me. You've been avoiding talking about what happened ever since last night."

"What do you want me to say? That I went too far? That I lost my head? That I never should have pounded on Antonio the way I did?" I was suddenly exasperated. "Okay, I went too far. I lost my head. I should have given Antonio a cookie for abusing Hannah instead of a beating. Happy now?"

Isaac shook his head at me. "I just don't know what's gotten into you lately. It was bad enough that you wanted to break into Antonio's place. I went along with that because the cause was just. And like you, I couldn't think of a better way to stop him from abusing Hannah. But for you to pound on him like you did—" He broke off, his eyes suddenly widening. He leaned forward. "Hey, do you have a thing for Hannah? It would certainly explain your behavior. Trying to scare off the competition?"

"Of course not," I said hotly, offended by the suggestion I'd used my powers to get a girl. Well, I was *mostly* offended. The truth of the matter was that, deep down, I wasn't so sure what my motivations were. When I had originally befriended Hannah it had been to figure out what the deal was with her constant injuries. But now that I had gotten to know her, I felt myself trying to ease out of the friend zone with Hannah despite the fact I was still very much in love with Neha. The few times Hannah had touched me had sent my pulse racing. Etched in my mind, I could close my eyes and visualize those moments as if they had been captured on film. In fact, just two nights ago I had a dream about Hannah. And it wasn't the kind of racial equality dream Dr. Martin Luther King, Jr. had spoken of, either. Rather, it was the kind of dream you could turn into a white-on-Asian interracial porno.

Unmollified suspicion smoldered in Isaac's brown eyes. But thankfully, he let the issue of my complicated feelings for Hannah go. "So why did you go all WWE on Antonio then?"

"I don't want to talk about it."

Isaac shook his head. "If you think I'm going to let you off the hook that easily, Antonio's energy blast must've knocked something loose in your head last night. You haven't been yourself for a while now. Last night was just the starkest example of it. As your friend, if something's troubling you, I want to know about it. As a fellow Hero, if what's bothering you is making you cross the line and beat someone to a pulp, I *need* to know about it. You didn't see your face as you were pummeling Antonio. I did. The way you looked, if I hadn't been there, you might have killed him. I'm not going to let that happen again."

Isaac's face, which normally had a half-grin dangling from it, was dead serious. "So, you've got a choice: either tell me what's bothering you so we can do something about it, or I'll report what happened last night to the Guild and you can tell them what's bothering you."

I was shocked. "You wouldn't dare. I've known you for too long. You wouldn't do that to me. Plus, you broke into Antonio's place with me. You'd be on the hook with the Guild as much as I'd be."

"I don't care. Right now, with you bottling up whatever it is that's bothering you, you're a danger to yourself and others. I'd rather get both of us into a little trouble now than see you in serious trouble later after you badly hurt or kill someone. Plus, like you said, we've known each other a long time. Long enough for me to know that, despite whatever's come over you lately, if you did seriously hurt or kill somebody, you'd never forgive yourself. So what's it gonna be: talk to me, or talk to the Guild?"

Isaac and I stared at each other. The only sound in the room for several long moments was the voice of a CNN reporter dispassionately talking about a fresh atrocity in Peru perpetrated by its dictator, the supervillain Puma. The United Nations was debating a resolution asking the Sentinels to intervene.

After a while, I looked away, breaking our gaze. I let out a long breath.

"Okay, you win. I'll tell you what's bothering me." I paused, not knowing where to begin. "It's everything."

Isaac leaned back, put his feet up on the coffee table, and laced his fingers behind his head. "Everything? You'll have to be a bit more specific."

"Everything. Mechano. Being a Hero. Life in the big city. Neha. Everything."

"All right, we'll tackle them one at a time. Let's start with Mechano. Since you know he was the person who made attempts on your life during the Trials, I still don't understand why you don't report him to the Guild. The Guild has an investigative division devoted to looking into allegations of Hero malfeasance. All us new Heroes were introduced to Ghost, the head of Guild investigations, when we were sworn in." Isaac paused, shuddering at the thought of Ghost. "Remember how he looked during our swearing-in ceremony? Like he had just stepped out of someone's nightmare. He might be the scariest thing I've ever seen, and that's saying something as I've seen my mother without makeup. Ghost has the reputation of being entirely fair and going where the evidence leads him. Even with a Hero of Mechano's prominence, if Ghost concluded that Mechano tried to assassinate you, the Guild would take his cape away and turn him over to the civil authorities for prosecution so fast that his murderous metal head would spin."

"As I've told you before, it's not that simple. If I report what I know about Mechano to the Guild, they'll ask me how I know what I know. And if I tell them that, I'll get someone else into trouble." I shook my head. "I won't do it."

That wasn't the whole truth. The whole truth was that I knew Mechano had tried to murder me because I had cheated on the final test of the Trials. In that test, I had to battle Isaac. Hacker, a fellow Trials participant who had owed me a favor due to me saving her life earlier in the Trials, had at my request used her Metahuman hacking ability to reprogram Overlord before my battle with Isaac. Overlord was the artificially intelligent computer designed by Mechano which oversaw the Trials. Overlord determined who won the duel between potential Heroes that comprised the final Trials test. Before Hacker had monkeyed with its system, Overlord had been programmed to declare just one of the duelists the winner. The winner got his Hero's license; the loser was out of luck and would have to go through the Trials all over again if he wanted to get his license. That hadn't seemed fair to me at the time. It still didn't. So, I had Hacker change Overlord's programming so it would declare a tie and that both Isaac and I were the winners if the result of our battle was close.

When inside of Overlord's system, Hacker had stumbled upon two shocking facts: the world-renowned Hero Mechano had planted nanites into Overlord's system which had tried to kill me earlier during the Trials; and, Mechano had programmed Overlord to allow the planting of a bomb into one of my Trials' tests. That bomb had nearly blown my head off—not to mention other body parts I had grown quite attached to—plus almost killing a bunch of innocent bystanders. As that bomb was a bigger version of the bomb slipped into my pocket by the blonde woman in D.C. before the Trials, perhaps Mechano had been behind that attempt on my life as well. For all I knew, Mechano was also the one who had hired Iceburn to kill me after my powers first manifested, leading to my father's death.

So, after completing the Trials, recuperating from them, and then getting my Hero's license and white cape during the Guild's investiture and swearing-in ceremony, I had known what was next on my to-do list:

Confront Mechano and find out why he had made attempts on my life. Also, figure out if he was behind Iceburn being sent after me and, if so, kick his mechanical butt from here to Pluto for being responsible for Dad's death. Oh, and avoid Mechano throttling me with his super strong robot body, or blasting a hole through me with his energy beams, or doing something even more unpleasant to me. Let's not forget that very important part.

My list of things to do post-Trials had been all too clear. What had been a lot less clear was how to go about crossing all those things off my list.

You could go a bunch of different routes once you got your Hero's license after the Trials. Some Heroes joined the military or went into law enforcement. Other Heroes went into private industries where their powers would prove useful. Hacker, for example, worked for a tech firm in Seattle. Others went into private security. Neha had done that. She had moved to Chicago to work for a famous reality television star. Thinking about Neha made my heart ache, even all these months after our fight.

The most traditional route for Heroes, though, was to use your powers to fight crime and Rogues, the technical word for supervillains. Though some Heroes fought crime out of the goodness of their hearts, many others also leveraged the fame acquired through their crime-fighting efforts to make money. Massive Force, for instance, was a textbook example of how to make crime-fighting lucrative. Before he was murdered here in Astor City, he had made a boatload of money by making paid personal appearances, through television, movie, and book deals, and on toys carrying his likeness. As someone who used to be scrawny, I had a hard time picturing an action figure being made in my likeness. Maybe one day someone would instead make a movie about my life. It could focus on how a small-town farm boy felt overwhelmed by the big city even though he was a Hero. Its title could be *Stranger in a Strange Land*. I hoped Robert Heinlein's estate didn't sue me.

Some Heroes banded together in teams to fight crime. Mechano was a member of such a team. And not just any team. Mechano was part of the Sentinels, Earth's oldest and most preeminent superhero team. The Sentinels were headquartered right outside of Astor City. As Athena had been so fond of saying, every battle was won or lost based on who was better prepared to fight it. In light of that, to prepare to take on Mechano and perhaps all the Sentinels—God help me!—if they too were involved in Mechano's shenanigans, I needed to find out everything I could about him. Not only would such information help me figure out how to take him out if I needed to, but maybe it would also give me a clue as to why Mechano had attacked me.

To find out everything I could about Mechano and the Sentinels, I figured I needed to go where they were. Namely here, in Astor City. That was how a farm boy who grew up intimidated by the size of a Walmart Supercenter found himself living in one of the biggest cities in the world, wrestling with how to confront one of the most prominent Heroes in the world.

The Sentinels were the gold standard for Heroes, which made Mechano's involvement in the attempts on my life even more disturbing and perplexing. When the average person heard the word "Hero," they usually thought of the Sentinels. This was no hyperbole; surveys had been conducted that had amply demonstrated just how ingrained the Sentinels were in the public's consciousness. For good reason. The Sentinels had saved the world more times than I could count. They had fought off alien invasions, defeated Rogues bent on world conquest, destroyed civilization-ending asteroids on a collision course with the Earth, and done a bunch of other things to pull the planet's bacon out of the fire.

I had grown up idolizing the Sentinels. Especially Avatar, one of the team's founding members. He had helped found the team shortly after the passage of the Hero Act of 1945, the federal law mandating that all Metahumans register with the federal government, and that forbade us to use our powers unless we were first licensed. Avatar had formed the Sentinels along with Omega Man, Lady Justice, Millennium, and three other Heroes to deal with menaces that were too formidable for a single Hero to handle alone.

Most people thought of Avatar as the second greatest Hero, right after Omega Man. Though Omega Man had been killed in the V'Loth invasion, there was an urban legend he would return to life if the Earth faced a potentially world-ending crisis again. Avatar had an unusually long life span and had been the Sentinels' leader until he was murdered a couple of months before my own powers manifested.

I didn't like to think about Avatar's murder. Like me, Avatar had been an Omega-level Metahuman and therefore one of the most powerful people in the world. Unlike me and my powers, which still were developing and growing, Avatar had been at the height of his powers when he was killed. If it could happen to him, it certainly could happen to my scraggly ass. In fact, thanks to Mechano, it almost *had* happened to me. Several times. If I were a cat, I'd be on at least life six or seven by now between my encounters with Iceburn and what I had been through in the Trials. It was enough to make me want to lock myself in my room to conserve my remaining lives. I couldn't bring to justice the guy who had hired Iceburn or find out what Mechano's beef with me was while barricaded fearfully behind the door of my room, though. Besides, Coward Man was a less than heroic-sounding name.

In addition to Mechano, the current members of the Sentinels were Seer, Doppelganger, Ninja, Millennium, and Tank. Avatar's spot on the team had been vacant since his murder despite the precedent set by the team's founders that there always be seven members. The Sentinels had said that Avatar's empty spot would be filled once they found a Hero worthy of taking Avatar's place.

The public often called Mechano "The Mechanical Man" because he had an artificial body, but the consciousness of a man. That man's name was Jeffrey Cole. Mechano was the only Sentinel the general public knew the real name of. Cole's Metahuman power was the ability to download his consciousness into mechanical receptacles. Cole's human body was long dead as he had been born in the late 1800s, but the essence of the man lived on in Mechano's robotic body. I had seen a couple of black and white pictures of Cole before his human body had died. He had been a spare man with stringy black hair, a widow's peak, deep-set intelligent eyes, and a moustache trimmed to near invisibility.

Mechano's current robot body was his fourth one. The first of Cole's robot bodies had been mostly destroyed in a battle with the Rogue known as Vengeance long before I was born. The second and third bodies were decommissioned by Cole and put into storage after he built his current one. It was far more powerful than the others. Cole's body du jour was almost seven feet tall, super strong, and had sensors that gave him superhuman senses of smell, touch, sight, and hearing. Also, he could project various forms of energy through the single rectangular red eye his body sported. I had seen television footage where Mechano's energy blast had sheared off the top of a mountain and, on another occasion, reduced a skyscraper to a smoking pile of twisted metal and rubble. There were undoubtedly other things Mechano could do I didn't know about as he was constantly tinkering with and enhancing his mechanical body.

As indicated by him designing and building such powerful robot bodies, Cole was a mechanical and electronics genius. It was not known whether that aptitude was a facet of his Metahuman powers. Regardless of whether his genius was Meta-based or not, Cole held more patents for various inventions than any other person in history. Heck, Mechano had even invented the material that composed the artificial teeth implanted in my jaw by the Guild after the Trials to replace the ones I'd lost in my battle with Isaac. The oral surgeon who put the implants in—an upper and lower incisor, plus a canine—had assured me of their quality after he had performed the procedure.

"Though they look natural, they're as hard as diamonds," he had said, as if he wanted me to chomp down on a steel beam to test them, "and they'll be free of cavities, decay, and discoloration long after your natural teeth have rotted out of your head. The material they are made of was invented by Mechano himself." The doctor had said that last part proudly, as if he had been on hand to shout "Eureka!" when Mechano had come up with the stuff. I also wanted to shout when the doctor told me that, but I had wanted to shout an expletive instead of eureka. Thanks to knowing Mechano had tried to kill me, I had no interest in having anything related to him anywhere near me, much less implanted in my jaw. Unfortunately, the doctor did not tell me Mechano had invented the tooth material until the teeth had already been implanted and it was too late to remove them.

After learning of Mechano's connection to my teeth, I halfway expected that at some point my new teeth would explode in my mouth, or start dripping sulfuric acid, or drill through my skull and into my brain, or something else equally unpleasant. So far, however, they had done nothing more nefarious than biting my tongue so hard blood was drawn. In the teeth's defense, that incident had been the fault of my overly enthusiastic devouring of a hamburger rather than theirs. My tongue had been in my mouth my entire life, and yet I sometimes still bit down on it. It made me wonder how often someone would inadvertently bite down on something they weren't used to having in their mouth. Consequently, the thought of being fellated terrified me. Being a guy, my fears would likely not stop me should the situation arise, which it most definitely had not since my falling out with Neha.

In addition to Mechano's inventions like the material comprising my teeth, he had also commercialized many of his other inventions and made them available to the general public. Other technology he had not commercialized. Those exclusive pieces of tech he only made available to the Sentinels and the Heroes' Guild. Almost all the futuristic tech the Sentinels used was designed by Mechano, not to mention much of the technology the administrative arm of the Guild relied on, including the Guild's holosuites and matter transporters. Cole had even designed the secret space station only Heroes knew about which the Guild maintained in geosynchronous orbit around the Earth. Built by the Guild after the V'Loth invasion in the 1960s had caught Heroes and the rest of humanity by surprise, the space station was part alien invasion early warning system, part world guardhouse, part Guild office complex, and part Hero clubhouse.

If you had told me before I learned I was a Metahuman that the Guild had a top-secret space station, I likely would have called you a liar, and then peed my pants with excitement if you gave me proof. It was a testament to all the crazy things I had seen and been through since developing my powers that I hadn't been even slightly surprised when Pitbull told us new Heroes of the space station's existence at our swearing-in ceremony. These days, if you told me Santa Claus was real, a Hero, and used delivering toys during Christmas as a cover to check people's houses for criminal activity, I wouldn't bat an eye. I had seen too much.

The royalties Mechano raked in for his various commercially available inventions were immense, making Mechano one of the richest men in the world. Much of that money was used to underwrite the Sentinels' expenses. Being the world's preeminent superhero team was not cheap. In addition to them maintaining a sprawling mansion on the outskirts of Astor City that was part headquarters, part residence, part fortress, and part tourist attraction, they used various forms of high-tech transportation to travel around the world to trouble spots. They also paid their members handsomely, something only a handful of other Hero teams in the country like the Heartland Heroes, the Gulf Coast Guardians, and the Sunshine State Warriors could afford to do. As a result, the Sentinels were full-time Heroes, unlike people like me who had to work a regular job to keep bread and butter on the table. Sometimes I couldn't even afford the butter. I was an entry-level employee at a newspaper—hardly a thriving industry—after all.

Famous superhero teams like the Sentinels and the Heartland Heroes were part of the reason why Isaac had moved to Astor City with me. He wanted to get enough crime-fighting experience to eventually apply to join one of the major Hero teams. Being on such a team would give him the biggest platform to help the most people possible, Isaac said. He wanted to follow in the footsteps of his father Herbert, a California state trooper killed in the line of duty when Isaac was fourteen. I suspected that was all true, but only part of the truth. It had been the goal of Isaac's hated stepbrother Frank Hamilton, aka Elemental Man, to join one of those teams. Frank would never be able to do so as I had defeated him during the Trials. Though I was no family psychologist, I thought one of Isaac's motivations for wanting to join an elite Hero team was to rub Frank's nose in it.

The handful of elite Hero teams didn't let just anyone join, of course. They only accepted cream of the crop Heroes with solid track records and tons of experience. Isaac figured moving to Astor City with me would get him the experience he needed. Our months in crime-ridden Astor City had convinced him he had made the right move. "Getting my license was like getting a college degree in being a Hero," Isaac had once said. "Operating as a Hero in Astor City is giving me my PhD."

As a lifetime admirer of the Sentinels generally and Mechano specifically, the fact that a Hero at Mechano's level had tried to kill me would have been almost flattering had it not been for the fact his attempts had nearly been successful. Someone repeatedly trying to murder you tended to knock fanboy adulation right out of you.

The problem with me tattling to the Guild about Mechano as Isaac suggested was that I'd be telling on myself and Hacker as well. If I reported Mechano to the Guild's investigative arm, it would ask me what evidence I had. The only evidence was buried deep inside of Overlord, and the only reason I knew it was there was because I had cheated during the Trials. The Guild would take a dim view of me cheating. Even though I had only cheated because I didn't think the test was fair, there were three things I knew for certain: women liked bad boys more than nice guys (Hannah and Antonio were Exhibit A for the truth of this); Peter O'Toole was a double-phallic name; and, that the Guild could not care less about what I thought was fair. If I told the Guild I knew Mechano was out to get me because I had cheated on the Trials, the Guild would likely not only revoke my license, but those of Hacker and Isaac as well. If it had just been my license on the line, I would have risked it in the interest of getting to the bottom of what Mechano had against me. I would not risk the licenses of Hacker and Isaac, though. Not when they had worked so hard to get them. Plus, Isaac had nothing to do with me cheating.

He still didn't know about it as I hadn't told him. I wasn't planning to. Despite his constant jokes, Isaac was even more of a Boy Scout than I was as indicated by his threat to tell the Guild about our run-in with Antonio. If I told him I'd cheated during the Trials, there was the distinct possibility he'd report it to the Guild. I didn't think he'd do it since it would get me into trouble, but I wasn't willing to take a chance. Not with three people's licenses on the line.

So, reporting Mechano to the Guild was out of the question. Besides, as Dad had often said, "If you have a dog who needs to be put down, you don't farm it out to someone who might botch it. You do it yourself." The older I got, the more I realized Dad and his Jamesisms were on the money more often than not. If Mechano was the one responsible for Dad's death, I wanted to be the one to find that out and take care of Mechano. I didn't want to hand the responsibility over to the Guild's investigators, despite how competent Ghost seemed and how terrifying he was.

If I wasn't going to go to the Guild, then what? Saunter up to the front door of Sentinels Mansion and ask to see Mechano to accuse him of several felonies? What would I say? I could see it now:

Hiya, Mechano. I'm Kinetic. I'm a big fan. Or I used to be before I found out you tried to have me killed during the Trials. I know that because I did a teensy bit of cheating on my final test. Help a brother Hero out and don't tell the Guild about that. I'd hate to have to give up my Hero's cape before I've even broken it in good. It took a month before I could get it to hang just right. Anyhoo, I'd thought I'd pop over and sock you in the metallic jaw for trying to murder me. But before I do that, I wanna ask if you also hired a Rogue assassin named Iceburn to kill me. He killed my Dad instead, so I'm still a little irked about the whole thing. While you're at it, be a good scout and tell me whether the rest of the Sentinels were involved. If they were, even though they're the world's most powerful Heroes, I'll have to kick their asses too. Why are you laughing? I didn't know machines could laugh. Anyway, you pinky swear to tell me the truth about the Sentinels' involvement? That's a good robot. Uh, cyborg. Android? Well, whatever in the hell you are.

I had studied enough military strategy to know, as plans of attack went, that one blew. So, I had spent much of my time since moving to Astor City trying to formulate a better plan. Through exhaustive review of news archives available to me as a *Times* employee and from multiple visits to the public areas of Sentinels Mansion, I now knew more about the Sentinels generally and Mechano specifically than the president of their fan club did. Almost all my time not spent working or fighting crime was spent thinking, planning, and scheming, trying to come up with the best way to deal with Mechano and find out if he was behind my father's death. Even my nighttime crime-fighting I saw as preparation for confronting Mechano. Despite having studied hard in the Academy, I now knew that being a Hero wasn't something you learned how to do from a book. It was something you learned in the skies and on the streets.

Despite studying the Sentinels and preparing to confront them, I felt I had made zero progress. I was no closer to dealing with Mechano than I had been when I first moved to Astor City. I wasn't sure what held me back. Fear? Intimidation? Indecision? Doubt? All the above? After all, Mechano was world-renowned, beloved, and rich. Whereas I was . . . not. Yes, I was just as much of a Hero as Mechano was. That was like saying someone who had just graduated law school was the equal of a Supreme Court Justice. The thought of me going up against Mechano was more than just a little daunting, like being at the base of Mount Everest and staring up at the heights you knew you had to climb. Plus, I was afraid my relative inexperience and less-than-cosmopolitan background would lead me into taking the wrong step against Mechano. After all, I was the guy who had been chomping at the bit to take Mitch and his minions out until Isaac had counseled me —correctly, I now realized—to proceed with caution.

I suffered from paralysis by analysis as I dithered these past few months over the best way to deal with Mechano. I needed to act. As Dad had often said, "If you think too long, you think wrong." But knowing you needed to do something and knowing how to do that something were entirely different things.

"Hello! Earth to Theo."

Startled, I realized Isaac had been speaking while I had checked out, thinking about Mechano and the Sentinels.

"I'm listening," I said.

"Lying is definitely not one of your superpowers," Isaac said. "What I was saying was you're trying to tell me you went postal on Antonio because of your frustrations over Mechano?"

"Not just Mechano. I'm frustrated over the way this whole damned city operates. On that note, did you hear that Silver-back is out of jail?"

Isaac looked startled. "Already? We stopped him from robbing that armored car just last month. Wasn't that his third strike? I figured he'd be cooling his heels the rest of his life in MetaHold." MetaHold was the federal government's primary prison for detaining criminal Metahumans. Iceburn was imprisoned there. It was on Ellis Island in New York, near where the Statue of Liberty had been before Black Plague destroyed the iconic statue in the 1980s. The government official who came up with the idea of imprisoning Metas in the same place millions had once streamed into this country seeking freedom must have had one heck of a sense of ironic humor. *Give me your tired, your poor, your incarcerated superpowered masses yearning to break free.*

"They released him the day after we caught him," I said. "Yesterday he successfully robbed two more armored cars. He got away clean as there weren't Heroes around those times to stop him. I just heard about it today."

"You've got to give the guy credit for consistency, if not for good citizenship, by sticking with robbing armored cars. Maybe a foolish consistency is the hobgoblin of little minds, but apparently it also does wonders for a Rogue's bank account. So why did they let him out? It can't be because of his winning smile." Silverback was a bigger, scarier-looking version of the gorilla he had named himself after. Real silverback gorillas didn't have razor-sharp fangs as long as your forearm and the strength to pick up a tank like it was a paperweight, but Silverback did.

"That's what I wondered. So after hearing today about the new robberies and his earlier release, I went to the police precinct we had turned Silverback over to. I flashed my press badge and told them I was researching a story about Metahuman criminal activity. The cop I spoke to said Silverback had been released because the Heroes who had brought him in had violated Silverback's civil rights in apprehending him. Supposedly we had used excessive force."

Isaac snorted. "That's a load of bull. We captured Silverback by the book. Besides, you didn't hear me complaining about excessive force when Silverback tried to screw my head off like it was a bottle cap."

"You're preaching to the choir. The whole civil rights violation thing is baloney. So, when I got back to the office, I used the *Times'* computer databases to run a few checks on the cop who authorized Silverback's release. A Sergeant Martin O'Donnell. Turns out that, a little over a week after Silverback's release, O'Donnell registered a brand-new sailboat with the Maryland Department of Natural Resources. Now how does a lowly police sergeant afford a six-figure sailboat?"

"Maybe his wife is loaded. I hope she has a cute sister. My retirement plan is to marry into money. Depending on how much money she has, she doesn't even have to be cute. If she has enough loot, she doesn't even have to be a she."

I ignored most of what Isaac said. I did that a lot. "Maybe, but since his wife is a secretary driving a fifteen-year-old car, I doubt it. I checked her out too. I think it's more likely money changed hands between Silverback's attorney and O'Donnell, and a week later O'Donnell goes from being a landlubbing sergeant to a sailboat captain."

Isaac took his feet off the table and leaned forward. He carefully examined my face. "Who is this cynic and what has he done with my innocent friend Theo?"

I shook my head. "This city is killing my innocence. What little was left of it after the Trials."

The funny business that had gone down during the Trials was a recurring conversation between me and Isaac. Not only had Mechano twice tried to kill me by tampering with Overlord, but I strongly suspected Pitbull had broken Trials protocol by pitting me against Isaac in the final test when our opponent was supposed to be picked at random. I had angered Pitbull by mouthing off to him before the final test and by refusing to apologize for punching Lotus, another of the Trials' proctors.

On top of all that, several people had died during the Trials, including our friend Hammer. Though I hadn't thought while I was in the Trials too much about the implications of those deaths—trying to not follow in Hammer's footsteps had afforded little time for philosophical reflection—time and perspective had made me question how the Trials were conducted. Were Heroes who sorted through Hero candidates by killing them worthy of being called "heroes"? That was another reason why I hadn't gone to the Guild about Mechano: I wasn't sure I entirely trusted the Guild anymore after what it had put us through during the Trials.

Was I any better, though? After all, I was the guy who had just beaten Antonio bloody. How far would I have gone had Isaac not stopped me? I was also the guy who cheated during the Trials. Yeah, maybe Pitbull had himself broken the rules by making me go up against Isaac, but my parents didn't raise me to believe two wrongs made a right.

I let out a long sigh. "Silverback, Mitch, Antonio, Mechano, the Trials, life in the big city . . ." I trailed off, shaking my head in frustration. "Being a Hero is not as I expected it to be."

"What were you expecting?" Isaac asked.

"I was expecting there to be a clear right thing to do, and a clear wrong thing to do. A Hero would do the former, and avoid the latter. When I was a kid thinking about what the life of a Hero must be like, I figured they were the good guys who had life figured out. That to them, things were either black or they were white. Now that I'm both an adult and a Hero, nothing seems black and white. Take Deshaun, our friendly neighborhood pharmacist. If the world worked the way I thought it did when I was a kid, he'd either be working an honest job or in jail. Instead, he's lounging around outside, bold as brass, corrupting society one clear baggy at a time. And as crazy as it seems, the neighborhood's probably better off because he's there. Or take Mechano, a renowned inventor who's helped save the world more times than we probably even know about. And yet, he's tried to kill me at least twice. What other nefarious things has he done that we're ignorant of?" I shook my head again. "Makes it mighty hard to figure out who's the bad guy, and who's the good guy."

Not for the first time, I wished Dad were still alive. Though he had not been an educated man, he had wisdom you couldn't get from a book. I just knew he would be able to point me in the right direction. I missed Mom too, but she had been more of a nurturer than an advice dispenser. At least she had been before cancer had hollowed her out, sapping her vitality, making me and Dad her nurturers instead of the other way around.

I started tearing up at the thought of my parents. Feeling like the world's biggest baby, I yawned and stretched, pretending like I was tired so I could rub the tears from my eyes before Isaac saw them. A 20-year-old licensed Hero and I still got misty-eyed over my deceased parents? Maybe I would change my code name to Crybaby.

If Isaac noticed my tears, he had the good grace to not say so.

"People are neither all bad nor all good," he said. "Nobody's just one thing. Take you for example. You're a good guy, but you still lost it with Antonio last night." His gaze was uncharacteristically serious again. "You know that can't happen again, right? We're Heroes. Even if there are some who don't follow the rules, that doesn't give the rest of us the excuse to not follow them too. If we stop following the rules, that means we're no better than Antonio or Silverback."

"Yeah, I hear you. I'll try to not let it happen again."

Isaac sat back, again putting his feet up on the table. "Good. As for all that other stuff, I don't have a good answer for you. I'm not all-wise. Who do I look like, black Buddha?"

"Then what good are you?"

Isaac chewed on that for a few moments. Then he brightened.

He said, "I have a gallon of unopened rocky road ice cream in the freezer."

I grinned. "I withdraw the question."

We went to look for answers in the bottom of Isaac's ice cream. Though we didn't find any, it was still a pretty good time.

7

Hannah did not show up for work the next morning. There was no email to her supervisor, no call, no anything. I did not think much of it. I just assumed Antonio had done as I demanded and had broken up with Hannah, and that she was too upset about it to come to work. Even so, I thought it was weird that Hannah did not contact her boss. She was normally very responsible. I guessed Antonio breaking up with her had really knocked her for a loop. Oh well, I thought. Better to be knocked for a loop than continue to get knocked around.

Hannah did not come to work the following morning, either. When I discovered her absence again during one of my usual trips to the art department, I started to get worried. Like the day before, Hannah had not contacted her supervisor to tell him she was going to be out. None of her other co-workers had heard anything from her, either. I called both her cell and home phones several times during the workday. She didn't answer or return my calls.

As the day dragged on, I progressed from worry to near panic. If it hadn't been for the fact Mr. Langley had given me a research assignment he had emphasized he needed as soon as humanly possible, I would have left during lunch to go check on Hannah to make sure she was okay. As it was, I didn't finish Mr. Langley's assignment until about an hour before quitting time.

Despite the fact he oversaw the *Times'* annex, Mr. Langley didn't have an office. Rather, he had a desk in the middle of the busy press room bullpen just like the reporters and editors under him. He always said it was so he could "try to nip in the bud you youngsters' constant attempts to kill American journalism and replace it with a slang and misspelling-filled Twitter thread."

With the sound of the newsroom's clattering keyboards in my ears, I put the completed project on Mr. Langley's desk. It was a summary I had hastily written about the Corruption Cabal, plus a copy of all the press clippings I could find about them. The Corruption Cabal was a team of Rogues the criminal division of the U.S. Department of Metahuman Affairs had announced this morning were the main suspects in the recent murder of Blaze, one of the Gulf Coast Guardians.

Mr. Langley's fingers flew over his keyboard as I stood there. Thin in the chest, thick at the waist, and skinny in his arms and legs, Mr. Langley looked like a pear with pipe cleaners for limbs. His blue eyes flicked over to the folder I put on his desk, to me, and then back to his computer screen as I lingered, waiting for him to stop typing. He didn't.

After a while he said, "What, do you want a cookie for doing your job? Maybe you've got a Facebook post about how hard you work that you want me to like?" Mr. Langley's tobacco-stained teeth flashed dully in his mouth as he spoke. His eyes were still intent on his screen. He often said his once brown hair had turned gray since coming to the *Times* annex "from riding herd over a bunch of wet behind the ears kids who know more about emojis than about journalism." I didn't mind his tone. I'd learned months ago that his bark was worse than his bite.

"No," I said. "I wanted to ask if I could leave work a little early today."

"Got a hot date?" His eyes still on his screen, his fingers continued to dance.

"Something like that."

"Then get out of here. Never let it be said I stood in the way of a young man's throbbing loins. The fourth estate in general and this newspaper in particular can hobble along without your talents until tomorrow. When you come in tomorrow, be sure to remind me exactly what those talents of yours are. I can't remember."

I gathered my things and beat a hasty retreat to the elevator. It seemed like forever before the elevator made it from the sixty-first floor to the ground floor. If I had simply busted open a window and flown to Hannah's, I would almost be there already. But, I hadn't brought my costume. Since I was costume-free and did not want to risk Theodore Conley being spotted soaring in the Astor City sky, I walked hastily up the block and then down the stairs into the closest subway station. Using my monthly subway pass, I got on the train toward South End, the neighborhood Hannah owned a condominium in. Besides, it was likely that I was overreacting and that Hannah was just fine.

Even though it was only early rush hour, the subway was packed. I stood elbow to elbow with thousands of other commuters in the eight-car train. A stiletto-heeled lady's oversized luxury purse dug into my stomach; a tall man's elbow kept tapping my shoulder; a young Hispanic woman's ample derriere pressed into my groin. Under normal circumstances I might have enjoyed the latter a little. As it was, I wanted to punch all three of them. Even with the subway car's air conditioner running, the air was hot and sticky thanks to the press of people. The smell of mingled perfumes, colognes, ethnic foods, and body odor filled the air. I was used to riding the subway, but since I was in such a rush to get to Hannah's, the sights, smells, and sounds I was so accustomed to annoyed me like they usually never did. Though I knew taking the train was still faster than grabbing a cab during rush hour traffic, I felt a fresh surge of irritated impatience every time the train rumbled to a stop.

After what seemed like forever, the train reached the South End stop. Dozens of people and I spilled out of the subway car, joining hundreds of others from other cars making their way to the exit. As I slowly advanced to the turnstiles leading out of the station, I suppressed the strong urge to use my telekinesis to clear a path through the people in front of me like Moses parting the Red Sea.

Finally, I made it through a turnstile and then onto the escalator leading outside. I rapidly clambered up the left side of the escalator. My damp dress shirt was plastered to my back thanks to mounting anxiety and the heat of the subway car. Three people—no doubt tourists since natives knew you stood on the right and climbed on the left—blocked my path. I impatiently told them to move out of the way. I wasn't overly polite about it, either. My mother, who had oozed Southern charm, would have been horrified.

I exited the escalator. I squinted, blinking at the bright late afternoon sun. Trees lined the sidewalk on both sides of Mulberry Street. Cars zipped by. It took me a moment to orient myself. I had been to Hannah's condominium a couple of times before with some of Hannah's other work friends, but this was the first time I had taken the subway there.

I got my bearings from the landmarks of Star Tower and

the UWant Building which, thanks to their towering heights, were visible from most parts of the city. I set off toward Hannah's building.

Hannah's fine, I assured myself as I hastened toward her address on Hanover Street. I wove through the throng of slower pedestrians. *She probably just got sick from the stress of Antonio breaking up with her and forgot to call in to work.*

Why, then, did I have an increasingly sick feeling in the pit of my stomach? It was with an effort I kept myself from breaking into a run.

I arrived at Hannah's multi-story building on Hanover Street. It was red brick with black metal accents. Flowerpots in full bloom dangled from many of the units' balconies, giving the building a festive look. You needed either an access card or to be buzzed in to get through the front door. I planned to use my powers to open the door if I couldn't get Hannah to answer the intercom mounted next to the door.

I didn't need to. Right as I approached the glass door, a professionally dressed white woman came out. She held the door open for me with a slight smile. I gave her a tight smile in return as I breezed past her. I guess I didn't look like a criminal. If I had been with Isaac, I doubted she would have been so quick to let us in. Hanging out with Isaac so much had taught me racial profiling was all too real even though he was no more a criminal than I was. Less so actually, since I had been to jail and Isaac had not, as he was fond of reminding me. Life in Astor City had opened my eyes to how the wider world often was. It was not always a pretty sight.

I ignored the elevator, rushing past it to enter the stairwell. I pounded up the stairs to the fifth floor. I exited the stairwell and turned the corner, entering the hallway where Hannah's doorway lay.

I took a long breath in front of her door, trying to calm

down. *Everything's fine. Everything's fine. Everything's fine,* I repeated in my head like a mantra.

I knocked on the door and listened intently. There was no answer. I knocked again, harder this time. Still no answer.

I was about to unlock the door with my powers and go inside when I hesitated. What if Hannah was inside taking a bath or something and I barged in on her? I imagined she would enjoy unexpectedly flashing me far less than I would.

I lifted my hand slightly and gave the interior a quick scan with my invisible telekinetic touch. All was still inside.

I glanced around the hallway. No one was around. And, if there was a security camera somewhere, it was hidden so cunningly that I couldn't see it.

I reached out again with my powers, feeling the door's lock. To my surprise, it was already unlocked. I was about to put my hand on the knob to twist it open when some instinct made me hesitate. I instead turned the knob with my powers, opening the door without leaving my fingerprints behind.

The smell hit me as soon as the door was open. The barely suppressed dread I had felt on my way here climbed out of the pit of my stomach and constricted my breathing.

I had smelled something like this before. Though Dad had only grown fruits and vegetables, his brother Charles who had lived up the road from us raised livestock. Every year, Dad had helped Uncle Charles slaughter his pigs. One year I helped too. Under Dad's watchful eye, I had used a small blowtorch to burn the hair off the pig carcasses before Dad and Charles cut them open. The smell of the pigs' dirty hair burning and their skins scorching was one I would never forget—an acrid, foul, and yet somehow sweet smell. It was like the smell of a barbecue restaurant which desperately needed to clean its bathrooms.

That was the smell that hit me as soon as I opened

Hannah's door. It was the sweet smell of cooked meat mingled with the stronger stench of offal and death.

My heart, already pounding, rose to my throat. After again glancing around to make sure there was still no one nearby, I levitated off the ground a few inches and then into Hannah's condo. If I found inside what I feared, I didn't want to contaminate the scene by walking in and touching stuff. I closed the door behind me with my powers.

Though there were no lights on, I could see well enough with the sunlight streaming in from the partially open blinds in front of the glass door that opened to the balcony. Mustiness lay underneath the decaying meat smell, as if the condo had been sealed up for a while. The air was warm, uncomfortably so. Someone needed to turn the air conditioner on. I floated forward, through the condo's short entryway.

Straight ahead was the closed door to Hannah's guest room. To the right was the kitchen. To the left was her sunken living room, decorated in shades of white and light brown. Despite the fact Hannah was a neat freak, the living room was a mess: the coffee table was overturned, the magazines normally on that table were ripped and strewn around the room, all of the couch cushions were on the floor, and the wall-mounted flat-screen television dangled precariously from a single bolt.

On the far side of the living room, against the wall near the dangling television, Hannah sat. One leg was folded under; the other was splayed out in front of her. She wore a plain white tee shirt and gray shorts. Her head was tilted slightly to the side, as if she were studying something from a different angle. Her eyes were open, her Cupid's bow lips slightly parted. She had on that stupid blue and white conductor's hat she always wore that Antonio had given her, though it was askew and on the verge of falling off. A slight breeze would have been enough to jostle it off her head.

There was also a gaping hole, bigger than a softball, right under Hannah's ribcage. Through her charred flesh, I caught a glimpse of the wall behind her.

"Oh my God!" I exclaimed. As the condo was silent as a tomb, my voice sounded like a yell.

I quickly floated over to Hannah and hovered in front of her. Though the hole in her torso and the paleness of her skin made it obvious it was an exercise in futility and wishful thinking, I ran my telekinetic touch over her body to check for a pulse. I felt like a filthy necrophiliac. My stomach churned threateningly as my mouth filled with saliva. I tasted bile in the back of my throat. I swallowed, willing myself to not throw up.

There was, of course, no pulse. The muscles of Hannah's body were stiff. Rigor mortis. Though I was no coroner, I knew enough about how the human body decomposed to know that Hannah's stiffness indicated I was hours and hours too late for there to be a pulse. Today was Friday. Isaac and I had confronted Antonio in the wee hours of Wednesday morning. The extent of the rigor mortis indicated Hannah probably died sometime Wednesday.

Hannah's face was bruised and puffy. There were abrasions and dried blood on her neck and arms. There was so much blood, it looked like magma oozing out of an erupting earth. Blood splatters were on her shirt, like a white canvas paint had been repeatedly flicked on. The edges of the shirt surrounding the hole in her abdomen were charred, like the charred edges formed if you held a piece of paper over a lit candle.

Hannah's lifeless eyes stared at me. They seemed almost accusatory. Her skin, normally a light golden brown, was deathly pale. Except for her legs. Her legs were a dull mottled crimson. Livor mortis, the fourth stage of death that followed rigor mortis. It happened when the heart stopped pumping and gravity pulled on the blood's red cells to make them pool in the bottom of the body. The next stage was putrefaction, where Hannah's body would break down and her organs would liquify. From ashes to ashes, from dust to dust.

On the wall above where Hannah's body sat, there was a pattern at about eye level that marred the otherwise pristine eggshell white color. In the center of the pattern was a scorch mark. Around that black and brown scorch mark was dried blood and a yellowish-green discoloration. The colors trailed down from the largest part of the pattern down to Hannah's body. Bits of Hannah's black hair and something that reminded me of cooked liver dotted the pattern. I realized the stuff was bits of Hannah's flesh and organs.

Antonio must have done this. It *had* to be him. What were the chances of a vicious Metahuman with energy-based powers who wasn't Antonio beating Hannah up and then killing her right after I had a run-in with Antonio?

Close to zero.

It was all my fault.

Though I was no crime scene investigator, I didn't need to be one to figure out what had happened. The scene played out in my mind's eye like a horror movie. At some point after I beat up on him, Antonio came here to confront Hannah, thinking she had put me up to it. Hannah denied it. Antonio didn't believe her. The frustration I had seen in his eyes after I had beaten him he had turned on Hannah. They fought. Antonio knocked her around. Then, perhaps in anger, perhaps on cold-blooded purpose, he had spat one of his Metahuman energy balls at her. The blast from it had flung Hannah through the air, just as it had done to me and Isaac.

The difference was Hannah didn't have one of my force fields to protect her. She had slammed into the wall, with the ball of energy boring a hole through her insides. She had hit the wall with such force that the television was jarred from its mountings. Hannah had then slid to the floor, like a discarded doll a child didn't want to play with anymore. Antonio then fled, not bothering to lock the door behind himself.

It was all my fault.

The hate-filled glare Antonio had given me before Isaac and I left his apartment loomed up in my memory. Since Antonio had not known who I was and therefore couldn't do anything about me, he had directed his fury at Hannah instead. If I had not gone to his place to confront him, none of this would have happened. I was as responsible for Hannah's death as Antonio was.

No, I was even more responsible for her death than he was. Antonio was a piece of shit. Shit was supposed to stink. I was a Hero. I was supposed to know better. To *be* better.

I had intended to help Hannah, to save her from Mad Dog's abuse. I had instead killed her, just as surely as if I had done the deed myself. If I had reported Mad Dog to the authorities as an unregistered Metahuman like I was supposed to and he had been arrested, Hannah would still be alive. If I hadn't gone to Mad Dog's house in the first place, Hannah would still be alive.

It was all my fault.

Hannah's dead eyes still stared at me accusatorily. I couldn't bear the sight of her and what I had done to her anymore.

I turned away in midair, sick at heart and sick to my stomach. The movement stirred the air, bringing my partially acclimated nose a fresh whiff of Hannah's body. It pushed my stomach over the edge. It churned like an erupting volcano.

My throat burned. I threw up so hard, it felt like the vomit came from my feet instead of my belly. Fortunately, I had the presence of mind to activate a force field to avoid contaminating the crime scene. The first thing I'd done right in a while. My force field caught all the foulness as it surged out of me. The sharp stench of it mingled with the smell of decay and death.

I wiped my mouth with the back of my hand once I finished spewing. I had thrown up more than I thought humanly possible. My teeth felt fuzzy, my throat raw, my mouth acrid. My nose ran. I tried hard to not cry. My blurred vision turned the vomit floating in front of me into something out of an impressionist painting. It looked the way I felt. Perhaps I'd call it *Portrait of a Young Man as a Friend-Killing Loser*.

Some Hero I was.

8

I floated near Hannah like a deflated helium balloon for several eternal minutes, full of sorrow and self-loathing and self-pity. With an effort, I tried to shake off this waking nightmare. Moping here wasn't doing anyone any good. Certainly not me, and most definitely not Hannah. She was gone. Though it was my fault and my responsibility, there was nothing I could do about the fact she was dead now.

A sudden surge of anger cut through my sadness like a hot knife through butter. I felt a stab of pain in my hands. My fists had clinched so hard that my nails dug into my skin.

I couldn't do anything about Hannah. There was plenty I could do to Mad Dog, though.

I pulled out my cell phone, intending to call the police. Though I hadn't met Hannah's parents and didn't know how to contact them, Hannah had told me about them. They were still alive. Hannah had a brother as well. He was in graduate school somewhere. The police would track them all down and notify them of Hannah's death. Though I was to blame for her death and by all rights should shoulder the responsibility of notifying her family, I couldn't bear the thought of doing it.

Besides, the first thing I needed to do was find Antonio. I wanted to get to him before the police figured out he was responsible and take him into custody.

I stopped myself right as I was about to hit the last digit of 911. How would I explain to the cops what I was doing inside Hannah's place? I could tell them the truth, namely that I had come to check on her since she had been absent from work. My presence here, however, would almost automatically make me a suspect in her murder. I assumed there would be sufficient forensic evidence indicating I wasn't involved. For example, once the cops determined the exact time of Hannah's death, they would determine I was at work at the time, or maybe with Isaac. Even so, I should be going after Antonio, not fooling around dealing with the cops, waiting for them to clear me of a crime I did not commit. For all I knew, the cops would take me into custody until they ruled me out as a suspect.

No, I wouldn't risk it. My mind racing, I put my phone back into my pocket.

How would I find Antonio? If I were him and I had just killed my girlfriend, I would not lounge in my apartment, waiting for the police to come around to have a not-so-nice chat with me.

No. Antonio was a vicious asshole, not a stupid one. He would try to disappear. With his mob connections, doing so would be easier for him than for a normal person. The sooner I got on his trail, the better.

Though I now itched to get out of here to find Antonio, I suppressed the urge to bolt out the door. This would be the only chance I would get to survey the crime scene before the police got here and sealed it. Maybe there was an indication here of where Antonio would run to. It was worth taking a few minutes to look around.

Still using my powers to avoid leaving fingerprints, I searched Hannah's condo as thoroughly as I could. I carefully put everything I picked up back exactly the way I found it. Other than a hidden cache of sex toys in Hannah's bedroom which made me feel like even more of a filthy voyeur than I already did, I found little of interest and absolutely nothing that gave me any idea of how to locate Antonio if he was not at his apartment. I did see a framed picture of Antonio and Hannah together at the beach on Hannah's nightstand, though. Hannah looked so happy and so full of life in the picture; always the tough guy, Antonio glowered at the camera. The temptation to blast the picture into smithereens was almost irresistible.

During my search, I found a box of plastic trash bags under the kitchen sink. After I completed my futile search, I pulled two of the bags out with my powers, double-bagged them, and emptied my floating pile of puke into them. I pulled the bags' drawstrings tight and twisted the top of them several times for good measure. I then grabbed the bag, and floated toward the front door.

I paused in front of the door. I sighed. I could not leave without saying goodbye. I floated back into the living room, levitating again in front of Hannah's body. Though I didn't want to, I forced myself to look at her one last time.

"I'm so sorry I did this to you, Hannah," I said. My voice cracked. I swallowed hard. "I promise I'll make Antonio pay for it."

Hannah didn't answer. The jaunty angle of the hat Antonio had given her seemed to mock me. Her lifeless stare was more than I could bear. I knew it would be a while before it stopped haunting me. Maybe it never would.

I floated to the front door again. The bag of vomit slung over my shoulder made me feel like a Santa Claus who delivered death and destruction instead of joy and toys. I waited for two people I sensed to pass and for the hallway to clear again.

I opened the door with my powers, landed on the other side of it, and closed the door behind me. I took a deep breath, happy to once again breathe in air that didn't reek of death and vomit. I stared at Hannah's closed door for a long moment, lost in thought and regret.

So much death. First Mom, then Dad, then Hammer, and now Hannah. I wasn't getting used to the people I cared about dying. I didn't want to get used to it.

Still carrying the trash bags, I took the stairs back down to the first floor. I left the building and walked back toward the subway station. I dumped my vomit in the first trash bin I saw on the street.

I got on a train headed toward my house. At Huntington Place, three subway stops from Hannah's, I got off the train again and exited the station. I hurriedly walked to a gas station a couple of blocks away. Thanks to my nightly patrols, I knew there was a pay phone outside it. Mr. Langley often said that a few decades ago in Astor City, pay phones were as common as public urination. The urination had stayed, especially in shadier areas like Dog Cellar, but the pay phones were mostly gone thanks to almost everyone having a cell phone. The one at the gas station was one of the few I knew of that still existed in the city.

There were several security cameras mounted high up on the exterior of the gas station building, right under the roof's overhang. Two of them were on the side of the building the pay phone was on. The gas station was relatively busy, but no one was looking up in the direction of the cameras. I took advantage of that by unobtrusively using my powers to pull a few leaves from the roof's gutters. I levitated the leaves down, hovering them directly in front of the cameras, blocking their view of the pay phone.

I used the pay phone to dial 911. When the operator picked up, I said, "There's been a murder at 616 Hanover Street, Unit 57. The victim is Hannah Kim. The perpetrator is Antonio Ricci, who goes by the street name of Mad Dog. His address is 34 Furman Drive, Unit 1313. He's an unregistered Metahuman, so use caution when you apprehend him."

"Who are you? How do you know all this?" the operator demanded.

"I'm just a guy trying to do the right thing. So far, unsuccessfully." I hung up. The police got a lot of crank calls. They would not go to Antonio's place first on the say-so of an anonymous 911 caller. They would go to Hannah's, though. Once they found her body, they would take my call seriously. They would find and notify Hannah's family. They would pinpoint where the 911 call had come from, see that there were video cameras here, and check the footage. They would only see a closeup of leaves. And eventually, they would go to Antonio's place to question him.

I planned to get to him first.

I had intended to take the subway to my house so I could get my costume. However, I was too impatient to get my hands on Antonio to get on the train again. Besides, no one at the gas station seemed to be paying me any mind.

I sprang into the air, rising quickly so anyone who happened to look up would only see a blur. *It's a bird! It's a plane! It's Stupid Man! He kills his friends faster than a speeding bullet.*

Once I was out of the cameras' view, I dropped the leaves hanging in front of them. The sprawling city spread out under me as I rose higher and higher. Using the landmarks below to orient myself, I shot off in the direction of my house. I planned to land in some unobserved spot close to home, maybe a back alley, and walk the rest of the way. I would then grab my costume, suit up, and go find Antonio. I would check his apartment first. In the likely event he wasn't there, I'd figure out some way to find him.

As usual, I had a force field around me as I flew to protect me from the brunt of the wind and from random debris. The wind screamed around me as I rocketed toward the house. Soon, I thought, Antonio would be screaming too.

I said a silent prayer for Hannah. Having grown up a devout Catholic, prayer came as automatic as blinking when dust was in your eye. I had seen too much senseless death these past few years to be convinced anyone was listening. Regardless, I figured it couldn't hurt.

Then I fixed my thoughts squarely on Antonio. My jaw tightened.

You can run Mad Dog, I thought, *but you can't hide.*

_____

9

As it turned out, I was wrong. Mad Dog could both run and hide.

It was four days after I discovered Hannah's body. I had used what little leave time I had built up at the *Times* to take off work so I could devote all my time and energy to locating Antonio. I was no closer to finding him than I had been when I started.

It was the middle of a cloudless night. I landed on the roof of the UWant Building. Its green glass facade shimmered in the moonlight and the city's lights. I had on my Kinetic costume and mask. I was exhausted. Constantly on the go, I had barely slept since discovering Hannah's body. I felt a tickle in the back of my throat. The beginning of a sore throat? I hoped I was not getting sick. I was already sick at heart.

I came up here a lot. The only way someone could get up here from the building itself was through an access panel on the south side of the roof, which was a small observation deck and parapet surrounding the UWant Building's tall spire. Months ago, I checked and confirmed that the access panel had been welded shut. As a result, I could fly up here to think undisturbed. Being so high on top of the city's tallest building made me feel like I wasn't really in the city anymore, even though I was smack dab in the middle of it.

The wind gusted, whistling like a banshee. This high up, the wind was always cold regardless of how hot it might be down below. Other than the sound of the wind, it was quiet up here. The sounds of the bustling city did not reach this high. Standing up here was like being a god on top of Mount Olympus, surveying from afar the toils and troubles of the mortal men below.

Star Tower was to the left. The twin blinking aircraft warning lights on top of it seemed to look up enviously at the emerald UWant Building that had eclipsed it. The lights of the rest of Astor City sparkled like jewels below. From up here, the city was beautiful, like a mirror image of the sparkling stars above. I knew stars were nothing more than a series of nuclear explosions; they'd burn you with heat and radiation if you got too close. I was beginning to think the same of Astor City— the closer you got to it, the more it burned and tarnished you.

A few minutes after I arrived, I spotted a dot in the sky. It rapidly grew closer, moving from being an indistinct, distant speck to a large, winged animal.

A huge bird, almost man-sized, touched down on the roof near me. It had reddish-brown plumage and a contrasting snow-white head and breast. It was a Garuda, a bird from Hindu mythology that could fly faster than the wind. It was one of the few of Isaac's forms that could come close to keeping up with me when I flew full tilt.

The bird's form shimmered with a slight glow, expanded, and suddenly Isaac stood where the Garuda had been. He had on his Myth costume, a form-fitting, full-body black number with light blue bands on the wrists and ankles. Its cowl covered Isaac's face from the nose up. A ferocious-looking dragon was emblazoned in blood-red on the costume's chest. Like me, Isaac wasn't wearing his cape.

"Any luck?" I asked him. I was grateful he hadn't said *I told you so* at any point since I'd told him what happened to Hannah. I had enlisted his help when I wasn't able to locate Mad Dog on my own. As I had expected, Mad Dog had been nowhere to be found when I went to his place the day I discovered Hannah's body. I had since discovered he was nowhere to be found anywhere else as well.

"No," Isaac said. "I've been in touch with every source I've developed on both the right and the wrong sides of the law." He shook his head. "No dice. You?"

"The same. I'm at the point where I feel like I'm just spinning my wheels, rushing from place to place and person to person, but not really getting anywhere." In addition to my throat not feeling right, my voice was raspy. I needed a good night's sleep. I pushed the thought aside. There would be plenty of time for rest after I caught Antonio.

"There's no guarantee Antonio is still in Astor City," Isaac said. "Maybe he went to Italy to check out the Sistine Chapel and get acquainted with his long-lost ancestors. Heck, he could be in Timbuktu for all we know. If he is, he might as well be on Pluto. I couldn't find Timbuktu if you drew me a map of it, gave me a superpowered bloodhound, and started me off in the right direction."

"It's in Africa. A city in Mali."

Isaac rolled his eyes. "You think I don't know that? I was feigning ignorance for effect. But thanks for trying to teach a black man about the motherland. Next you'll be trying to school me on jazz, teaching me how to dunk a basketball, or telling me how to build a video game console or a pacemaker.

My people invented those last two, you know. Stay in your lane, white devil. And speaking of staying in your lane, there are certain things we're good at. We both are pretty good ass-kickers. I can charm a yolk out of an egg without breaking the shell. I'm sure you can grow a mean rutabaga thanks to your childhood in Mayberry or whatever the name is of the hick town you grew up near. But finding someone who clearly doesn't want to be found? That, my friend, we suck at."

I knew what he was doing. He was trying to make me laugh, to distract me, to take my mind from what I had done to Hannah. It wasn't working. I said, "Tell me something I don't already know. What's your point?"

"My point is that maybe we should leave this up to the professionals. The news says the police consider Antonio a person of interest in Hannah's death. They're already looking for him. They're experts at finding people. Despite our considerable talents, we're not. We should let the pros do their jobs."

"No," I said firmly. "This is my fault, and therefore my responsibility. I'm not going to just sit back and let someone else clean up my mess." I snorted. "Besides, with the police in the city as corrupt as they are and Antonio's association with the Esposito crime family, if the cops do manage to find him, they'll probably pat him on the head, tell him to not be so naughty, and let him go. Assuming they're looking for him at all. Remember what happened with Silverback? Maybe money has changed hands and some police captain miraculously has the money to finally build the addition to his house he's always dreamed of in exchange for Antonio walking away free as a bird. If the Hero Kinetic is the one who captures him, it'll shine so much publicity on Hannah's death that it will make it that much harder for the cops to sweep what Antonio did under the rug."

"You're being too cynical. Not all cops are bad cops."

"And you're being too naive. If every cop was like your father, I'd be less concerned about it. But they're not. You know that. You've seen some of the same shenanigans that go on in this city that I have."

"Okay, so let's say you find Antonio before the cops do. Then what?" Isaac demanded. "Will you hand him right over to the authorities? Or will you indulge in a bit of vigilante justice?"

"If you're asking me if I plan to kill him, the answer is no. You know I'm not a killer. If I couldn't bring myself to kill the Meta who murdered my father, I'm certainly not going to kill Antonio. Which is not to say that Antonio doesn't deserve it. You should have seen what he did to Hannah. He beat her like a piñata before blowing a hole clear through her."

"What will you do if we find him? You'll beat the crap out of him again?" Isaac shook his head. "Like I told you a few days ago, I won't stand for it. I'm all for Antonio being captured, but I'm not for him being brutalized. Even if he is a piece of crap, he's a piece of crap with legal rights. We're Heroes, not gods. We don't get to do whatever we want to whomever we want whenever we want. We're supposed to follow the rules just like everyone else does."

Anger bubbled up within me. "You're talking to me about Antonio's rights? What about Hannah's right to not be beaten up and murdered?" I snorted derisively. "You of all people shouldn't be moralizing. How about stepping out of your hypocritical glass house before throwing stones at me? You're the same guy who encouraged me to kill Frank during the Trials."

"I was wrong then. You were right to not listen to me. I was too emotional about the whole situation due to what Frank had done to my sister, just like you're too emotional now about what Antonio did to Hannah." Isaac shook his head. "Which is another reason why you should let the police handle Antonio. You say you won't kill him, but I wonder if you'll remember that in the heat of the moment if you find him. I remember the look you had in your eye when you were beating his face to a pulp. It's the same look you have now. You're exhausted, mad, upset, and grieving. You're not thinking clearly. For your own good, you should just let this go before you do something you'll regret."

I grew more and more irritated as Isaac spoke. My anger and frustration about the whole situation boiled over. "You know what I regret? Asking you for your help." I rose into the air. The wind was cool against my flushed face. "While we're here jawing, Antonio is likely burrowing further and further underground. We're wasting time. I don't need to be lectured, and I certainly don't need to be told what to do. I'll find Antonio on my own. If you've got a problem with what I'm doing or have done, go tattle on me to the Guild like you threatened to do earlier. Afterward, go home, curl up with the Boy Scout Handbook, and mind your own goddamned business. In the meantime, I've got a homicidal Rogue to find."

"C'mon Theo, don't be like that. I'm trying to look out for you. All I'm saying is . . ."

But I couldn't hear what he was saying. I was too high in the air now, having risen far above where Isaac stood. Before he could transform into a creature to fly after me, I zoomed off into the distance faster than Isaac could follow.

The problem was I didn't know where I was flying. I had already tried everything I could think of to find Antonio. What was I supposed to do now? Go door to door looking for where Antonio might be holed up? I could see it now: *Sorry to bother you ma'am, but are you by any chance harboring a homicidal mob enforcer who spits energy balls? He's a big fat guy with pig eyes and a bald bullet head. Hard to miss. No, you haven't seen him? Okay, thanks for your time. Wait, what's that? Am I crazy? I'm an adult dressed up like a trick-or-treater when it's nowhere close to Halloween. Quite possibly.*

I wasn't opposed to going door to door if that's what it took, but there had to be a faster and more efficient way. Besides, as Isaac correctly pointed out, there was no guarantee Antonio was even still in Astor City. If I had to knock on every door in the world, I'd be dead and buried long before I'd stumble upon Antonio.

As much as I hated to admit it, Isaac was right—we weren't experts at locating people. My Heroic training had prepared me for a lot of things: Fly like a bird? Check. Punch bad guys in the face? Check. Use my powers to do something as crude as picking up and flinging a massive boulder or something as delicate as using a razor to shave with my eyes closed and my hands tied behind my back? Check. But find a bad guy who obviously didn't want to be found so I could punch him in the face or drop a boulder on him? Not so much.

And, though I worked at a newspaper, I was little more than a gopher and clerk, a far cry from an investigative reporter who was skilled at finding people.

I slammed to a stop in the air so suddenly that it was almost like hitting a wall. I was so excited by my realization that I barely felt the ache caused by the abrupt halt of my forward momentum.

I'm such an idiot, I thought. That was it! The *Astor City Times.* I worked for one of the world's most respected newspapers. Surely one of the more seasoned employees would know how to find someone who didn't want to be found. How stupid of me to not have thought of it before now. My anger and exhaustion must have made my brain sluggish. I was scheduled to go back to work tomorrow, anyway. I had been thinking about not going in and risk getting fired to continue looking for Antonio. Now I had a reason other than not being fired to show up.

The next morning when I got to work, I walked up to Mr. Langley's desk. As usual, he was in front of his computer, peering at its screen as his fingers flew over the keyboard. I didn't know how he had avoided glasses considering his age and all the hours he spent staring at a computer. He was always here when I came to work in the morning, and he was always here when I left for the day. Though I knew he smoked from the way he smelled and the heavy stains on his teeth, I had never seen him leave his desk to take a smoke. Sometimes I wondered if he lived here, if he didn't need to sleep, and if he was part chimney who generated smoke without a cigarette.

"Do you have a minute?" I asked.

Mr. Langley's clear blue eyes didn't look up from what he was reading, nor did he stop typing.

"Sure. After all, I'm just lounging here idly by the pool, sipping on a Mai Tai, praying some youngster will happen along and break up the monotony of the day by asking me a fool question."

"Who would you go to for help if someone was missing?"

"It's '*Whom* would you go to.' You work for a newspaper, not a hip-hop website. Proper English is one of the tools of our trade."

I suppressed an eye roll. I knew it was whom, and I knew he knew I knew. I think it gave him a kick to bust the balls of the young people in the office.

"Well, *whom* would you go to?" I asked, emphasizing the correct word.

"The police," he said immediately.

"Let's say you tried the police, and they came up empty. Then whom would you go to?"

Mr. Langley looked up for the first time. He stopped typing. His piercing blue eyes looked at me probingly. I hadn't slept at all last night, and I couldn't remember when I last shaved and showered. Under Mr. Langley's gaze I was abruptly hyperaware of the fact I must have looked like death warmed over.

"Does this have something to do with Hannah Kim's missing boyfriend? I know you two were friends. You leave early the day her body is discovered, you abruptly use all your leave time and disappear, and then you reappear looking like something the cat dragged in asking who is good at finding people. I've been in this business too long to believe in coincidence. As I reminded you earlier, this is a newspaper. If you know something about her murder that's newsworthy, spill it."

I felt like an open book under Mr. Langley's stare. "This has nothing to do with Hannah," I said. If I said it did, Mr. Langley would ask more probing questions, none of which I wanted to answer as their answers all involved me being the Hero Kinetic. I had become quite a facile liar since starting down the road toward being a Hero years ago. I didn't like what that said about the nature of being a Hero. "The daughter of a friend has run away from home, and she's understandably worried sick. She's hoping to hire someone to help find him."

"Find her."

"Huh?"

Mr. Langley's eyes hadn't left my face. "You said your friend's daughter is missing. If that's the case, a daughter is a her, not a him."

"Oh." Perhaps I wasn't as good a liar as I thought. "Her.

That's what I meant. I misspoke. She wants to hire someone to help find her."

Mr. Langley gave me a slight wry smile. I didn't think he believed my cover story. His eyes returned to his computer screen and he resumed typing.

"Well, there's a private investigator on College Avenue not too far from Astor City University named Julian Ward. He's relatively cheap, especially considering the prices around here. He's pretty good when he's not drunk. Unfortunately, he's drunk a lot. That's why he's relatively cheap. Alcohol seems to be an occupational hazard when it comes to PIs."

I shook my head. "I'm not interested in a drunk. I want somebody who's both good and sober. Money is no object." Thanks to having two roommates, I could live in an expensive city like Astor City using just my relatively meager paycheck from the paper. I still had in savings almost all the money from selling Dad's farm, plus the money the Old Man paid me for being his Apprentice. That, along with the accrued interest, amounted to a pretty penny. I'd spend every dime of it if necessary to find Antonio.

"Well if money's not an issue, I've got just the guy for you." Mr. Langley stopped typing. He consulted the old-fashioned rolodex he kept by his telephone, and jotted a name, address, and telephone number on a slip of paper. He handed the paper to me. The clattering of his keyboard resumed.

"That guy is better than he seems," Mr. Langley said. "Maybe even as good as he thinks he is."

"Better than he seems? What's that supposed to mean?"

"You'll see. And remember what I said about how we're in the business of printing what's newsworthy. If you stumble upon something that fits the bill while you're helping your friend find the daughter you for some reason refer to in the masculine, don't keep it to yourself."

I thanked Mr. Langley and hurried away before he asked more questions I didn't want to answer. As I went back to the desk I shared with another low man on the *Times'* totem pole, I looked down at the note Mr. Langley had written.

Truman Lord, Private Detective and Licensed Hero, it read.

10

Truman Lord's office was downtown on Paper Street, within easy walking distance of Star Tower. I walked toward there during my lunch hour.

During the walk, I heard the roar of a jet overhead. I looked up. The distinctive S-shaped logo of the Sentinels was on the bottom of the airplane's wings. One of the Sentinels' jets, just leaving the Sentinels compound on the outskirts of the city based on its low altitude and the direction it traveled. I had the sudden urge to go airborne and rip it into two. My frustration over Antonio had set my temper on a hair trigger. Besides, my beef was with Mechano, not with all the Sentinels. First I would deal with Antonio, then I would turn my attention back to Mechano. One thing at a time.

The address Mr. Langley had given me was for a brick office building painted off-white. A high-rise directly across the street from it dwarfed it. The office building's red brick showed through the faded white paint in spots. Many of the building's windows were dirty. The glass of the front door was cloudy with age and irregular cleaning. It squeaked noisily when I opened it. The vestibule sported old wallpaper that peeled away from the wall in spots. The glass-encased building directory missed several letters. It made finding Lord's name a puzzle to be solved. Clearly the building had seen better days.

My first impression of Lord based on his building? I was not overwhelmed with confidence.

Finally, I found Lord's name. His office was on the third floor. I waited for the elevator, heard ominous groaning noises through the elevator doors, and started up the stairs instead. After the last few days, getting stuck in an elevator on top of everything else would make me flip my lid.

I had heard of Truman Lord before Mr. Langley gave me his name. Anybody who paid even passing attention to the news over the past few years would recognize Lord's name. His name and face had been ubiquitous for a little while. First, Lord had uncovered that one of the Sentinels was a killer. Later, Lord's fifteen minutes of fame got extended when the Sentinels hired Lord to find Avatar's murderer. During that investigation, Lord was framed for Avatar's death. Since Avatar had been beloved the world over, people thinking Lord was responsible for his death turned Lord into an international pariah. When Lord later exposed the true murderer, the people who had been screaming themselves hoarse demanding Lord's head on a silver platter immediately began singing his praises.

Some Heroes wanted to be famous. Isaac for example, in one of his more unguarded moments, had admitted he wanted to be. That was another reason he wanted to join one of the major Hero teams since their members were as famous as rock stars. Not me. If Kinetic became no more famous than he already was thanks to my exploits in Washington, D.C. and here in Astor City, that would suit me just fine. What

Lord had gone through as a suspect in Avatar's murder was proof that fame was too fickle for it to be worth chasing after. As far as I was concerned, fame was like having a pet scorpion—it might not sting you today, and maybe not even tomorrow, but eventually it would. Stinging was in its nature. No thanks.

Lord was the only Hero who was also a private detective, or at least he was the only private detective who was openly also a Hero. Most Heroes kept the fact they had superpowers a secret when they were out of costume to keep their friends and family from becoming targets of the enemies the Heroes made while in costume. Lord never wore a costume and was completely open about the fact he was a Hero.

I exited the stairwell onto the third floor. Lord's office door was in the middle of the hallway, next to an accountant and across from an insurance agent. His dark brown wooden door was closed. I faintly heard music playing on the other side.

Truman Lord, Private Investigations was spelled out in professional, gold-plated letters on the top half of the door. Under that were three small signs, written in black magic marker on yellow pieces of paper ripped from a legal pad.

The first one read: *QUIET!!! A sensational super sleuth, wise worldly wit, groovy gregarious gunslinger, and awesomely alliterative adult works wearilessly within.*

The second one read: *Salesmen, proselytizers, and supervillains are shot on sight, so keep out. If you don't know what proselytizer means, you keep out too. This is a high literacy zone.*

The third sign showed a crude drawing depicting two stick figures. The one on the right wore a fedora and held a gun pointed at the figure on the left. The words "POW! POW!" appeared over the gun. The stick figure on the left wore a black cape and lay on the ground, evidently bleeding based on the dots of red ink that dripped from it. "Curses! Foiled again by Truman the Terrific!" read the speech bubble over the prostrated figure's head.

After seeing the state of disrepair of the building and reading these ridiculous signs, I almost left. I was hardly in a playful mood due to what had happened to Hannah and being exhausted from days of unsuccessfully searching for Antonio. I did not have the time nor the inclination to fool around with someone unserious. Only the knowledge that Lord had been the one to find Avatar's murderer and the fact that Mr. Langley had recommended him made me swallow my annoyance.

I knocked on Lord's door instead of turning around and leaving. A man's voice told me to come in. I opened the door and took a moment to peer inside before entering.

The room beyond the door was square. The carpeting was thin, almost threadbare. A small, ratty, old couch was against the wall. A metal file cabinet was next to it. On top of the cabinet was a coffee maker. The pot was half full. Next to the coffee maker was a small boombox. Music played out of it, something old, jazzy, and croony that my grandparents likely would have enjoyed.

A bunch of the office's ceiling tiles were warped and discolored, as if there had been a major water leak at some point. A window was on the other side of the room from where I stood. Its blinds were open, letting enough sun in that the overhead lights were off. In front of the window was a desk. Its thick, old wood looked like it had been salvaged from Noah's Ark. A desktop computer was on top of it. Though the desktop was ancient, it still looked cutting-edge compared to how old the desk looked. In front of the desk were four battered chairs.

The office was the opposite of ritzy and ostentatious. It

matched the building that housed it. If the office had not been spotless, I would have described it as seedy.

Behind the desk sat Truman Lord. He was a white guy with a battered face wearing a maroon polo shirt. I recognized him from the pictures I had seen when he was in the news a lot due to Avatar's murder. Though I had seen those pictures years ago, Lord looked the same. Though he was much older than I, I was struck by how there was a certain timeless quality to him, as if he had sprung out of his mother fully formed and would go to his grave the same way I saw him now.

Other than that timeless quality, the first thing that struck me about him was his size. Even sitting, he was large and imposing. Not fat, but big-boned and well-muscled. His forearms looked like they could crack unshelled Brazil nuts if he pressed them together. Despite the preppy shirt he wore, there was a vaguely menacing, almost thuggish, air about him.

"Though I know I'm pretty, you gonna just stand there with the door open and admire me, or are you gonna come in?" he said to me, not unkindly. There was a slight, cocky smile on his face. He spoke with a hint of a Southern accent. "I've worked and slaved to accumulate an extensive fly collection. You're letting them all out."

I stepped inside, closing the door behind me. Lord didn't stand or offer to shake hands as I approached his desk. I once read that the tradition of men shaking hands developed as a way of demonstrating peaceful intentions by showing neither man had a weapon. If true, it explained why Lord didn't offer a handshake. His right hand was below the lip of his desk where I could not see it. With my telekinetic touch, I sensed Lord had slid open the desk's top right drawer. There was a large caliber gun inside. Though he didn't pick the gun up, his hand rested on the lip of the open drawer where he could get to the gun in a hurry. My chest tightened. I tried to keep the tension from showing on my face. In his defense, a man like Lord who was both a Hero and private detective had probably made a lot of enemies over the years. If I were him, I would keep a gun handy too.

Notwithstanding my body's automatic stress response, I wasn't too worried. If Lord pulled his gun on me, he was in for a surprise. I could make him eat that gun if I wanted.

With his left hand, Truman raised a small remote control and clicked off the music. There was a large glass bowl on the corner of his desk, like something you might serve punch from at a party. Rather than punch, water filled this bowl. In front of Truman on the desk was a thick open book. It was an English translation of the *Bhagavad Gita*, which was sort of like the Hindu equivalent of the Bible. I only knew of it because I had spent so much time with Neha, who was a practicing Hindu.

Lord saw what I was looking at. He said, "Don't be too impressed with my reading habits. I'm just looking at the pictures."

I was confused. "A friend of mine is Hindu. There aren't any pictures in that edition. I don't know if there are pictures in any edition."

The book thumped as Lord slammed it shut with his free hand. He looked at the book in disgust, as if it had tricked him. "Explains why I haven't found any. The cover art duped me. I wish you had shown up hours ago. You could have saved me a lot of time and trouble. Oh well. I'll try again with a different book later. You know what they say: Liber medicina animi."

"What's that?"

"It's Latin."

"That much I knew," I said.

"It means 'A book is the soul's medicine.' Or maybe it

means, 'Hello, I'm Julius Caesar and I'm lost. Which way to Rome?' I'm not sure. My Latin is rusty."

Lord motioned slightly with his head at the chairs in front of his desk. I sat. There was a framed picture of a woman on the window ledge behind Lord. She was a very attractive redhead with a big toothy smile. Girlfriend or maybe wife, though Lord did not wear a wedding ring. Lord's unseen right hand still rested on the lip of the open drawer containing the gun.

Now that I was closer to him, I saw that his broad nose was slightly misshapen, as if it had been broken on more than one occasion. His knuckles were scarred and calloused. A fighter's hands. There was scar tissue on his face, especially around his eyes. Both ears were slightly cauliflowered. There was something unapologetically masculine about the man. It all enhanced the thuggish vibe Lord had. If I hadn't known he was a Hero and I met him in a dark alley, I would assume I was about to be mugged.

"Mr. Lord, my name is Theodore Conley."

"Congratulations. Call me Truman. Mr. Lord is what you call God when you're being formal. I'm not Him. Easy mistake to make though. Happens all the time."

"I work under Stan Langley at the *Times*."

"Congratulations again. Stan's a big boy. You managing to squeeze from under him to come see me is quite an accomplishment."

"I know you're both a licensed Hero and a private detective. Mr. Langley recommends you highly." I was beginning to wonder why.

"As well he should."

"I need some advice."

"More deadlifts and squats, fewer bench presses and bicep

curls. Your lower body is underdeveloped compared to your upper body."

I shook my head in irritation. "I don't need weightlifting advice."

"That's what you think."

"Mr. Lo—Truman, I'm being serious."

"Me too. Leg day at the gym is a serious matter. It's not to be joked about."

It was getting harder to swallow my irritation. This was the jackass who had solved Avatar's murder? First Mechano, now this joker. Was every Hero in this city a disappointment?

"A friend of mine was murdered several days ago," I said. Truman didn't interrupt to make a stupid joke. If he had, despite his slightly menacing air and hidden gun, I might have slugged him. "Her name is Hannah Kim."

"I remember reading something about that in the newspaper. Graphic artist at the *Times*, discovered in her residence with a hole blown through her?"

"That's her. I want to talk to you about finding her killer. I can pay you."

"I should hope so. I don't work for free. I'd developed a strange habit over the years that requires money to support. It's called eating."

I tried to ignore him. "The killer is Hannah's boyfriend. A guy named Antonio Ricci."

"What makes you so sure he's the killer? Were you there?"

I suddenly realized there was intelligence behind Truman's half-mocking eyes. I felt wary. Truman's idiotic banter had made me careless. I'd forgotten I was talking to a Hero. Though I had been unimpressed by some of the Heroes I had met, I had yet to meet a stupid one. Except maybe me since I caused Hannah's death. I needed to choose my words around Truman more carefully. I wasn't willing to blow my secret identity by telling Truman about my run-in with Antonio before Hannah's murder.

"No. I'm assuming he's the killer based on the police saying he's a person of interest."

"Pretty big leap from him being a person of interest to him being a murderer," Truman said.

"Hannah had confided to me that Antonio abused her. Plus, the news says he's a suspected member of the Esposito crime family. A guy like that is capable of murder."

"And since the police haven't found Mr. Ricci yet, you want to hire me to do it?"

"That's the idea."

Truman leaned back in his chair a little. His hidden hand was still near the gun. "And what's your interest in all this?"

"I already told you. Hannah was my co-worker and my friend."

"I've got a lot of friends. Not too many of them would rush out to hire a private investigator to find a guy who may or may not have killed me and who may or may not be on the run when the police have been looking for him for less than a week."

"What can I say? I'm a good friend."

"Apparently," Truman said. "How long have you been friends with her?"

"About six months."

"About six months," Truman repeated. "You're really going above and beyond the call of duty for someone you've known for only six months." His look was assessing. "Were you in love with this girl?" he asked abruptly.

"What? No, of course not. She had a boyfriend."

"Were you sleeping together?"

"What was it about 'she had a boyfriend' didn't you understand?"

"And I have a girlfriend. That doesn't stop women from beating down the door to get to me."

Now I was really irritated. "Weird. I didn't see any women in the hall clamoring to get inside."

"The day is still young. They're at work. Once it's quitting time, it'll look like the mother of all bachelorette parties in here." Truman still stared at me. His gaze made me uncomfortable, like I was being examined under a microscope. "Do you know anything about Mr. Ricci other than what's being reported in the media?"

"No," I lied.

"What about the circumstances surrounding Ms. Kim's murder?"

"No. Are you going to help me, or are we going to play Twenty Questions?"

"They're not mutually exclusive. Your responses to the latter will determine the former. Let's say I find Mr. Ricci for you. Then what? If you're looking for a little eye for an eye retribution, you're barking up the wrong tree. I'm not that kinda guy. Or would you be looking for me to turn him over to the police?"

"Uh, I was hoping to have a chat with him first."

"You want to have a *chat* with him?" He emphasized the word in disbelief. "You, a guy wearing khakis and penny loafers who works for a newspaper, want to have a chat with a hardened criminal who works for the mafia? To find out the best place to buy brass knuckles that match your ensemble, perhaps?"

"I guess I want to hear from the horse's mouth why he would kill Hannah." I was increasingly uncomfortable under Truman's piercing gaze.

The room fell silent. I heard traffic passing by on Paper

Street below the office window. There was the faint sound of a woman talking in the office next door.

"I've been in this business a long time," Truman finally said. "I've developed certain instincts. Like when someone's lying to me."

"I'm not lying."

"Maybe a lie of omission, then. You're definitely leaving stuff out of your little story. A friend who's only a friend doesn't run out and hire a private investigator when the victim's body is barely cold and the police haven't started investigating in earnest yet. If you had a romantic relationship with Hannah I could wrap my head around it. But just a platonic friend?" Truman shook his head. "There's definitely something going on here you're not telling me. I've found over the years that when I stick my nose into a situation I don't fully understand, it tends to get shot at. My nose isn't much to look at, but it's the only one I've got. I'm trying to hang onto it, not have it blown off thanks to swallowing the half-baked story of a young man I don't know from Adam. Have you seen the Sphinx before? Someone shot its nose off a long time ago, probably because the Sphinx was silly enough to stick its nose where it didn't belong. It's not a good look, and not one I plan on emulating. Unless you start being honest with me, I'm going back to reading my book. The throng of female admirers I told you about will be here in a while. I want them all to myself. So buzz off. Hurry along now. Go. Scat! Vamoose!"

I stood up so abruptly that the chair toppled over. It hit the floor with a loud bang. I didn't pick it up.

"It was a mistake to come here," I said. I turned my back to Truman and stalked toward the door. *Screw this clown,* I thought. *I'll figure out some other way to find Antonio. Truman isn't the only private detective in the city.*

"Hey Theodore!" Truman called out to me right before I opened the door.

I turned my head.

The gun that had been in Truman's drawer was now in his right hand, pointing at me. Looking down the big barrel of the high caliber gun felt like looking down the muzzle of a cannon.

Truman fired.

11

The gun's blast was deafening. The bullet had barely cleared the gun's barrel before I drained it of its kinetic energy with my powers. It froze in the air just a foot or so from the muzzle. Despite my exhaustion, I hadn't been so stupid as to not monitor Truman and the gun with my powers even though I had turned my back to him.

I spun to face Truman. With a small finger flick, I ripped the gun out of his hand. I twisted the gun around in the air to point its muzzle at Truman's head. Turnabout was fair play. I'd find out how Truman liked having a gun pointed at him.

Before the gun was in place in front of Truman, some of the water in the big bowl on the desk exploded out of the glass. As quick as a wink, it surrounded the gun. There were loud cracking and popping sounds as the liquid transformed into solid ice almost instantaneously. The ice-encased gun fell onto Truman's desk with a loud thump.

I tried to break the gun free of the ice. Shockingly, I couldn't. My attempt was met with implacable resistance. It should have been as easy as snapping a dry twig in two.

I had known that Truman's Metahuman power was

hydrokinesis, or the ability to manipulate water. Reading about it in newspaper accounts and seeing it in action were two different kettles of fish, though.

I looked up from the gun, ready to defend myself. Truman did not look like he was about to attack me again. He still sat behind his desk. He clenched and unclenched his gun hand as though I had hurt it when I disarmed him. Otherwise he looked smug, like a man who was watching a movie unfold the way he expected it to. He grinned at me.

His smug grin was my first clue. My second clue was the floating bullet. Thanks to all my Heroic training over the years, I was good at judging angles and trajectories. Now that I had a moment to focus on the path the bullet would have taken had I not stopped it, I realized it would not have hit me. It would have sailed well over me and hit the wall near the ceiling.

I realized it had not been a bad shot. Truman had not been trying to hit me at all. He somehow suspected I was a Metahuman and had tried to get me to expose that fact by shooting at me. Like an idiot, I had fallen for it. The first rule of being a secret super-human was to not expose the fact you were a secret superhuman. Truman was not the clown I had originally taken him for.

Truman's smile faded as he winced and shook his right hand. He said, "You could've been a little gentler in disarming me."

"And you could've not shot at me," I said.

"A good point."

"What gave me away?" My heart pounded. Even though I now knew I was not in danger, it was hard to be blasé about a gun fired anywhere in your direction.

Truman's smile returned, as if I had passed some sort of test by realizing what he had done. "A couple of things. The way you checked out the room before you came in, like you were looking for potential threats. I do something similar. Also, the way you move. There's a certain amount of grace and confidence that goes with being a trained fighter. You've got it. And, though you said you knew I'm a Hero, the fact didn't seem to intimidate you at all. A normal person tends to be nervous around people with superpowers. You weren't. It all pointed to the idea that you are a Metahuman. And not just Metahuman, but a trained Metahuman. Game recognizes game, as the kids say. This," he said, pointing to the still hovering bullet, "just confirmed my suspicions."

"You could have just asked if I was a Meta."

"And have you lie to me?" He shook his head. "I'm not as young as you. Life's too short to waste it asking questions you're likely to not get straight answers to. Besides, this way I'd know, and you'd know I knew. Saves time." He reached out as if to pluck the bullet out of the air, appeared to think better of it, and withdrew his hand.

"Touching it won't hurt you," I said.

"I said the exact same thing to my girlfriend Ginny last night."

I lowered the bullet, bringing it to a rest primer side down on his desk. A sudden knock on Truman's closed door startled me.

"Everything all right in there?" came a woman's voice.

Truman stood. He was tall, probably a couple of inches over six feet. "That's Charity, the accountant next door. She's probably come over to sexually harass me again. Who can blame her?"

He walked past me and opened the door. The middle-aged woman on the other side had bobbed blonde hair, was professionally dressed, and a little on the heavy side. She was attractive, but more handsome than pretty. She glanced at me, then back at Truman.

"Are you all right?" she asked. "I heard a gunshot."

"And you rushed to my side, sweet Charity? My hero. But no need to worry," Truman said, "I was merely swatting a fly."

"With a gun?" Charity's voice was disbelieving.

"It was a mighty scary fly."

"Well, as long as everything's okay," she said dubiously. She started to turn away, then noticed the signs taped to Truman's door. Her eyes scanned them.

"Why in the world would you have these idiotic drawings on your door?" She sniffed disdainfully. "This is supposed to be a professional office building, not an art exhibition at an insane asylum."

"Don't you see what it says there about how certain people should stay away? I'm using these signs to keep the undesirables out."

"And yet, somehow, you're here."

Truman made a long-suffering sigh. "A woman's tongue is sharper than a serpent's tooth. That was in my horoscope this morning. Now I know why."

Charity shook her head in disgust. "You can't take anything seriously, can you?"

"Life's too serious to be taken seriously."

Charity shook her head again. She turned and walked away. Truman stuck his head out the open door and watched her.

"Stop staring at my ass," floated Charity's voice from down the hall.

"Stop putting your ass where I can see it," Truman retorted. "This is supposed to be a professional office building, not a catwalk." He closed the door and went back around his desk to sit down. He looked at me somberly. "I think she's in love with me."

"She hides it well."

"Too many do," he agreed sadly. "So, tell me Mr. Theodore Conley—assuming that's your real name—how'd you stop the bullet in midair and pull off that little disarming trick with my gun? Magnetism? Metal manipulation?"

"I'm telekinetic."

"Well that certainly explains where you got the code name of Kinetic from."

Stunned, I hesitated for the briefest of moments.

"I don't know what you're talking about," I finally managed. It was clear from the sudden smile on Truman's face that my hesitation hadn't been lost on him.

"Ah don't know what you talkin' about," he said, repeating my words in an exaggerated version of my Southern accent. He resumed in his normal voice. "I grew up in Georgia. I know a South Carolina accent when I hear one. Unless my ear for accents betrays me, you grew up in western Carolina, probably near the Georgia border. Edgefield County, maybe?"

Edgefield County was only about a ten-minute drive from the farm I had grown up on. "Aiken County," I admitted cautiously. Though I certainly didn't want to reveal my secret Heroic identity, saying where I was from seemed a safe enough admission. "What's where I grew up got to do with anything?"

"Nothing, if I hadn't seen footage of the Hero Kinetic a couple of months ago. Using his telekinetic powers, he had foiled an attempted warehouse robbery in the wee hours of the night, and the local TV news stuck a camera in his face and asked him for a comment. He didn't say much before he flew off, but he said enough for me to hear his accent. When I heard it, I thought, 'Well I do declare! Someone from the

Palmetto State is a Hero right here in Astor City. He must've come here recently as I've never even heard of him before. Bless his heart. Ain't it a small world.'" Truman had adopted an exaggerated Southern accent again as he recounted his thoughts. "I made a mental note of it. The Heroic community is a relatively small one, after all. I figured I'd run across Kinetic sooner or later, and I'd swap incest jokes and chitlin recipes with my fellow Southerner when I did.

"So, let's recap what I've observed about you today: One, you move and behave like someone who's had Heroic training. Two, you sound like the same Southern gentleman I'd seen on the news. Three, not only are you a Metahuman, but you're a telekinetic, just like the guy on the news. Four—and this one's the clincher—you look like him. You both have the same build. Kinetic also looks like he often skips leg day. Sure, the contours of your face are different than Kinetic's, but that's no doubt because he wears a mask with tech embedded in it that changes his facial features. It's all the rage with Heroes these days." Truman's battered face split into a grin. "You won't catch me sporting one, though. I'm too pretty to obscure my looks with a mask. As I always say, don't hide your light under a bushel basket.

"That all adds up to the conclusion you're the Hero Kinetic. Two plus two makes four." Truman frowned thoughtfully. "Or is it correct to say 'two plus two *make* four' so there's subject-verb agreement?" He shrugged slightly. "I'm not sure. I'm a detective, not a grammar nerd."

I opened my mouth, about to deny it. Truman lifted a restraining hand before I could get a word out. He said, "Before you give me an elaborate song and dance about how I'm mistaken, bear in mind that though I'm no grammarian, I am something of a walking lie detector. As the human body is mostly water, my powers allow me to monitor a man's perspiration rate, blood pressure, and heart rate, among other things. When I suggested you are Kinetic, your vital signs changed. You got as nervous as a mouse at a cat convention. That tells me you were lying when you denied being him."

Truman leaned back in his chair and grinned at me again.

"So now that I've established you are in fact the Hero Kinetic who grew up in the Deep South like me, let's get to the important stuff: I like fresh spring onions and red pepper flakes in my chitlins. What about you? And here's my incest joke: I told my sister I'm into incest. She took it really hard."

The office fell silent.

Truman said, "No good, huh? That didn't even get a chuckle. I guess you're right—one should never joke about having sex with sisters, no matter how much they incest."

Silence again.

Truman shook his head ruefully. "Wow, that one bombed too? I guess your generation of Heroes isn't much into puns."

I was quiet because I was at a loss for words. After all this time in Astor City, no one had made the connection between Theo Conley and Kinetic except for this guy. He came off as a clown, but he had figured out who I was in just a few minutes. I began to understand why Mr. Langley had referred me to Truman and how he managed to solve Avatar's murder. Despite his almost non-stop flippancy, there was more to this guy than met the eye. Heck, when I had come in, he had been reading the *Bhagavad Gita*, hardly an easy read. Nobody who was entirely frivolous read something like that in his free time.

And despite his persona, Truman was still a Hero. As I knew all too well, the Guild didn't hand out a Hero's license to just anybody.

There seemed to be no sense in further denials.

"You won't tell anyone?" I asked. Truman looked hurt at the suggestion.

"Of course not. Snitches get stitches. Besides, it's against the law to reveal the secret identity of a licensed Hero. I have a well-deserved reputation for following the law. It's almost a fetish. 'Lord the Law-Abiding' is what they call me."

"I'm pretty sure it's against the law to shoot a gun at somebody."

"Well, you've got me there. I follow the law, but I'm not a fanatic about it." Truman melted the block of ice surrounding his gun, making the water flow back into the bowl on his desk like it was a slithering snake. After a few seconds, there wasn't so much as a damp spot on his desk. He put the gun back into his drawer and closed it.

"What do you do when your water bowl isn't handy?" I asked.

"I improvise." His eyes flicked up to the water-stained tiles of his ceiling. "Before I started keeping water on my desk, I had to bust open the water pipes in the ceiling a few times. My landlord was less than pleased."

Truman put his forearms on top of his desk and clasped his hands. "So now that I know who you are, are you going to tell me what's really going on with this Antonio Ricci character? Or are you still going to leave in a huff? If that's too soon, you can leave in a minute and a huff. I wish I could take credit for the wordplay, but I borrowed it from Groucho Marx. If you're going to steal, steal from the best."

I hesitated. Though I was still in no mood to appreciate his banter, I was warming up to Truman. If he could figure out I was Kinetic without breaking a sweat, surely he could find Antonio for me.

"Will you keep everything I tell you a secret?" I asked.

"Well, it's not like there's Hero-private detective privilege the way there's attorney-client privilege or priest-penitent privilege, but I can assure you I won't run my mouth about what you tell me. A detective who goes around repeating what a potential client tells him soon has no clients, potential or otherwise."

That settled it. I walked back over to Truman's desk, used my powers to pick up the chair I had knocked over, and sat down again. I told him everything I knew about Hannah and Antonio. I started with how I had suspected Hannah was a victim of abuse when we first met, included my and Isaac's encounter with Antonio in his apartment, and ended with how I had discovered Hannah's body and had been searching for Antonio ever since.

Truman listened intently, interrupting only to ask a few clarifying questions. Honestly, it felt good to talk about all this with someone other than Isaac. I spent a lot of time keeping secrets from people these days: from Isaac, I kept the truth of how we had both passed the Trials and how I knew it was Mechano who had attacked me during them; from Bertrand, I kept the truth of what Isaac and I spent our nights doing; and, I kept from everyone the fact that I was Kinetic. It was a nice change of pace to tell someone the unvarnished truth without evasions or outright lying.

"Now I understand why you've got such a bee in your bonnet over this Mad Dog character," Truman said when I finished. "You feel guilty about Hannah's murder because you think you triggered it by bracing Antonio in his place."

"Don't you think I did?"

"Maybe. Hannah being killed shortly after you confronted Mad Dog is a coincidence that can't be ignored. But assuming you're right that he killed her, it's not like you forced him to do it. We're all responsible for our own actions. If I leave my gun out, that doesn't mean you have to pick it up and shoot someone with it."

"But if I did, wouldn't you feel responsible for stupidly leaving your gun out where I could grab it?"

"A fair point," Truman said. "Now that all your cards are on the table, I'll ask you the same question from before: If you hire me to find Antonio and if I do indeed find him, what are you planning to do with him? And don't tell me again you're just going to have a chat with him. I didn't believe you the first time you told me that tall tale, and I certainly won't believe you now."

I was on an honesty roll, and I wasn't about to stop now. Having someone I could come clean with felt cathartic. "I honestly don't know. I figured I'd find him first, and then cross that bridge when I got to it."

Truman studied my face. For a moment, he looked uncharacteristically serious.

"You want some free advice from an old hand at this Hero business? Don't let anger guide you. It clouds your judgment and makes you do things you shouldn't. We're too powerful to let our emotions sway our decision-making. Anger is a hot coal you hold in your hand while waiting to throw it at someone else. You usually only wind up burning yourself."

"That's quite poetic. Who said that?"

Like a spring shower, Truman's seriousness was gone as quickly as it had come. "Me. Just now. Weren't you listening?" Disbelief must have been on my face because he rolled his eyes. "Fine. You're too young to be this cynical about what your elders tell you. It's a Buddhist saying."

My anger, partly toward Antonio and partly toward myself, was a dull ache in the pit of my stomach. I didn't want it to go away. I wanted it to fuel me until the job was done. "Well I'm not Buddhist."

"And I'm not an electrician. That doesn't prevent me from

using a light switch. You don't have to be something to use the fruits of that something."

I shook my head. "I'm not looking for philosophy or for moral guidance. I'm looking for Antonio. Are you going to help me or not?"

"Now that you're telling me the truth, yes. Assuming you can pay my fee, of course." He told me how much he charged and how much of a retainer he would need for him to begin work. I gulped. Paying him would take a healthy bite out of the money I had saved. I shooed the dismay away as soon as I felt it. I would empty my bank account completely if that meant Antonio was brought to justice.

I pulled out my checkbook and wrote Truman a check. As I wrote out the dollar amount, it occurred to me that working for a newspaper and being a Hero on the side was a sure path to the poorhouse. Being a Heroic private detective was where the money was.

I put the completed check down on Trump's desk and slid it forward toward him. Before taking my fingers off it, I realized I was letting a golden opportunity to kill two birds with one stone pass me by. The Sentinels had hired Truman a few years ago to investigate Avatar's murder. Maybe he could tell me something about them and Mechano that would help me decide what to do about Mechano's attempts on my life.

I pulled my check back. Truman looked at me with amusement.

"Firing me already?" he said. "You wouldn't be the first client to do it, but you're certainly the fastest."

"I may need to hire you for more than just this Mad Dog thing. Rumor has it that you were offered a membership on the Sentinels after you solved the mystery of Avatar's murder. Is that true?"

"It is. And they took their sweet time about it too. You'd

think they would have offered me a spot the moment I passed the Trials. Instead, it was over a decade before they got around to inviting me. They were probably afraid I'd upstage them."

I ignored most of what he had said. If I continued to spend time around Truman, I realized I would have to do that a lot.

"And yet you turned them down." As far as I knew, Truman was the only person to ever have turned down a membership offer from the Sentinels. A Hero turning down an offer from the Sentinels was like a judge turning down a spot on the United States Supreme Court.

"And give up all this?" Truman said, gesturing expansively at his run-down office. I wondered what Truman spent his considerable fees on. It certainly wasn't his decor. "Why are you asking about the Sentinels?"

"Because Antonio Ricci isn't the only person in this city who's a killer." I told him about Mechano's attempts on my life during the Trials and how I needed to find out if he was also connected to my father's death.

And do you know what the strangest thing was about me telling Truman a member of the world's greatest team of Heroes had tried to kill me?

He wasn't even surprised.

12

"I've been quite the busy beaver the past couple of days," Truman said. He was behind the wheel of his car, driving us to someone he said could help me figure out what Mechano had against me.

The city's night lights flicked by as Truman drove. Though it was almost midnight, I was well-rested. I had caught up on some much needed sleep since I'd turned locating Antonio over to Truman.

"I should hope so. I'm certainly paying you enough." Between paying Truman to look for Antonio and to help me untangle why Mechano had tried to kill me, my savings had taken a major hit. We drove through a traffic light. The green lights briefly illuminated Truman's clothing: black jeans, a button-down untucked blue and white dress shirt, and brown cowboy boots. "I thought PIs wore fedoras and trench coats. And whoever heard of a detective tooling around in a Nissan Altima?"

"You watch too many old movies. I don't drink, call women dames, or describe their legs as gams, either."

"One by one, all my cherished illusions are being shattered."

He shrugged. "Welcome to adulthood. Now stop interrupting while your elders are talking about the fruits of their labor. I looked into Antonio's background, hoping it would give me a clue as to where he disappeared to. One thing I found out is that if your boy Antonio isn't in the running for a Bad Guy of the Decade award, he should be."

"That bad, huh?"

"When he was eighteen, he went to prison for a few years for arson and possession with intent to distribute cocaine and PCP. He has a juvie record too, but of course those records are sealed. I wonder what kinds of shenanigans he got into when he was a kid. Setting little girl's pigtails on fire, maybe. Anyway, him going to prison at eighteen apparently is where he got hooked up with the Espositos." Truman shook his head. "The problem with our prison system is that people enter it with a bachelor's degree in crime, and often graduate with a master's or a PhD. Antonio was no different. Him hooking up with the Esposito crime family transformed him from a young knucklehead who slung a little dope and recreationally set fires into an adult douchebag who breaks legs and gouges eyes. Over the years since he left prison, he's been arrested at various times for assault, battery, arson, sexual assault, kidnapping, animal cruelty, obstruction of justice, and murder. His rap sheet is as long as Santa's Christmas list, but it's all naughty, no nice."

"He was arrested all those times, but not convicted?"

"Not once after he started working for the Espositos. His cases never even went to trial. With each arrest, the authorities either dropped the charges because of lack of sufficient evidence or the people who witnessed Antonio's crimes recanted their initial stories, refused to testify at trial, or turned up dead under suspicious circumstances. The Esposito crime family protects its own, especially when one of its soldiers is operating on its behalf, which apparently Antonio was doing in most of the instances he was arrested. The cops and the assistant State's Attorneys I spoke to said the invisible hand of the Esposito family was definitely at work in each instance the evidence against Antonio evaporated. For example, one of those murders Antonio was arrested for a couple of years ago was that of a Maryland judge. Judge Blake. The judge was scheduled to preside over the trial of one of the Esposito family's top lieutenants. The Espositos were looking to tip the scales of justice in their favor by influencing Judge Blake. The problem was, unlike some of our other distinguished jurists, Judge Blake wasn't already in the pocket of the Espositos or any of their allies. And he refused all of the Espositos' subtle and not-so-subtle attempts to bribe him. His personal life was clean as a hound's tooth, so he wasn't susceptible to blackmail either.

"Since the carrots hadn't worked, the Espositos tried the stick. Literally. Judge Blake was beaten to death in his home three days before the trial was scheduled to start. They beat his wife too, but were careless and didn't finish the job. She survived and, from her hospital bed using a photographic lineup, fingered Antonio and another known Esposito enforcer as her husband's murderers."

Hannah's death had erased any guilt I had been nursing over beating Antonio; what Truman said made me wish I had beaten him more. "So why isn't Antonio in prison?"

"Even though the judge's wife and their two small children were placed in protective custody, the Esposito family must've gotten to the wife somehow. Maybe they threatened her kids. Maybe they promised to set her and her kids up for life if she forgot what she saw. A judge doesn't make very much money, you know, not if he's honest like Judge Blake was. Regardless of why, a couple of weeks after she implicated Antonio and his buddy, Mrs. Blake changed her story. She said those two hadn't killed her husband after all. She said she had been in so much pain from her injuries and so distraught over the loss of her husband that she picked Antonio and the other guy out of the lineup by accident. Everybody knew she was lying, but the cops and the prosecutor couldn't get her to admit it and go back to her original story. That, combined with the fact six people came forward and swore up and down they saw Antonio and his buddy in a bar watching the Astor City Stars get their butts stomped at the time the judge was beaten to death meant there was no way the state could get a conviction. So, the charges were dropped and Antonio and the other guy went free."

I felt my jaw clench. "That's not going to happen this time. I'm not going to let Antonio walk away scot-free from Hannah's death."

"Though I understand the sentiment, you might not have much of a choice. I also spoke to the detective in charge of the investigation of Hannah's death. Other than that 911 call you made pointing the finger at Antonio, they have exactly zero leads on who killed Hannah. No one in her building saw anyone coming or going from her unit around the time of her death, nor did they hear anything. There's also no forensic evidence at the scene which points toward Antonio. Like I said, it appears that Antonio has gotten his PhD in crime. Practice makes perfect, I guess."

"No forensic evidence," I scoffed in disbelief. "How about that giant hole in Hannah's chest?"

"Yeah, but there's no proof that Antonio did that. You say he has the power to spit balls of energy, but there's no evidence that Antonio can do that. I checked with the Guild.

Antonio is not registered as a Metahuman, energy-spitting or otherwise."

"A murderous mob enforcer isn't a stickler for following the mandates of the Hero Act?" I asked sarcastically. "I'm shocked. It doesn't matter, though. If the authorities find Antonio, they can test him for the Metahuman gene and discover his powers. That's how the USDMA determined I was telekinetic when I went to register as a Meta. They'll realize Antonio is talking and eating out of the murder weapon."

Truman shook his head. "To draw his blood without his consent, they'll need a court order. To get one, they'll need probable cause connecting Antonio to the crime scene. Like I said before, there isn't any. On top of all that, how much do you want to bet that when I find Antonio and ask him where he was when Hannah was killed, people will come out of the woodwork to swear on a stack of Bibles he was at church with them, praying to the baby Jesus and thinking pious thoughts?"

I felt like punching something. "What you're saying is even if you find Antonio and I turn him over to the cops, he's likely to go free. Again."

"The way things look right now, yes."

The car was silent for a while as I chewed that over. Despite my anger and frustration, it was impossible to not notice that Truman was driving us into Dog Cellar, one of the city's worst neighborhoods. Run-down and boarded-up buildings slowly collapsing in on themselves had taken the place of well-lit and thriving edifices.

"How do you stand it?" I asked.

"How do I stand what?"

"This city. Being a Hero. How dirty and sordid it all is. I used to think being a Hero was a pretty simple matter: Find the bad guy. Punch the bad guy in the face. Take the bad guy to the cops. Thinking about how it really all works makes me want to take a bath."

Truman thought about that for a minute.

"It's not just this city, nor is it just being a Hero. It's the world. You just didn't realize it when you were young and in a small town because you were insulated from it all by age and geography."

My jaw tightened in frustration. "How a smart, educated woman like Hannah could be with an animal like Antonio still boggles my mind."

Truman shrugged. "Hybristophilia," he said.

"Was that a word or a sneeze?"

That got a slight smile out of Truman. "The former. It refers to the concept that a lot of people get off on being with dangerous folks. If that describes your friend Hannah, she's hardly alone. A Rogue I helped put away a few years back named the Pied Piper was responsible for the deaths of hundreds of people. Despite that—or probably because of it —he got more fan mail than a boy band when I put him behind bars. The gallery of the courthouse during his trial was full of so many adoring women, it looked like a teenaged boy's wet dream come true. You'd think they would've been there to see me. I am an intrepid Hero, after all."

"You'd think. There's no accounting for taste."

Truman glanced at me before returning his eyes to the road. "Sarcasm?"

"Maybe. I think you're rubbing off on me."

"You could've emulated my dashing good looks or my flair for modesty, but instead you're imitating one of my worst traits. I hope you stop there. One of me is bad enough. Two would be more than the world can stand. To get back to hybristophilia, you have to remember that though humanity has moved from grunting around a fire to an age of smartphones and satellites in a relatively short amount of time, our genetic evolution hasn't begun to catch up with our technological evolution. Our biological hardware and software are still pretty much the same as that of our cavemen ancestors. Because of that, despite their rational minds telling them it's not a good idea, women are often viscerally attracted to big, strong, dangerous, dominant alphas. Guys like that were great to have around when you needed protection from saber-toothed tigers and the other scary predators that stalked prehistory. Those guys and their dangerous, violent impulses are less great to have around in modern society where the ability to program a computer is more important than lifting a log or outrunning a bear. A lot of the guys who would be tribe chieftains tens of thousands of years ago because they were the biggest, baddest guys around are thugs and criminals now."

"Do you know how fast bears can run?" I interjected. "I used to see black bears every now and then back in South Carolina, and that got me interested in them. They can get up to thirty-five miles an hour for short distances. Grizzlies are even faster. I doubt even the fastest of cavemen could outrun a bear."

"Don't interrupt my theorizing with facts. I'm giving you a brilliant theory explaining attraction and human sexuality, and you're going all *Mutual of Omaha's Wild Kingdom* on me."

"Mutual of what?"

Truman sighed. "Sometimes I forget how young you are. They shouldn't let people become Heroes until they've lived through at least four Presidents and sprouted a couple of gray hairs. Maybe then you all would understand my references."

We passed a bright streetlight which illuminated the interior of the car for a few seconds. Truman's shirt was tight around his big chest and arms. I wondered if he needed to get his shirts specially tailored to accommodate his musculature. Though Truman was dressed like a cowboy turned businessman out for a night on the town, a faint air of menace clung to him. Even when he was doing something as pedestrian as driving a car, something about Truman made you think he was capable of violence at any moment, like he was a coiled spring. That air of potential violence, combined with Truman's battered face and scars, made him seem more than just a little dangerous. He reminded me a little of Antonio that way.

"No offense," I said, "but you're a pretty scary looking guy yourself. Like Antonio, you look like half a caveman. And yet you're not a murderous piece of crap like him."

"True. Then again, I'm more like Antonio and people like him than I'd care to advertise. Frankly, I think I have to be. We're Heroes. To protect society from Antonio and people like him, sometimes we must act more like them than we want to. If you're the sheep dog charged with protecting the sheep, you can't simply appeal to the wolf's better nature when he comes around to jack the sheep. If you do, you're going to wind up with a lot of dead sheep on your hands. Wolves don't have a better nature. They're wolves. You can't lecture or shame or guilt them into behaving like Golden Retrievers. The only thing they understand is a good, hard bite."

Truman's words lightened a bit the guilty load I'd been carrying over Hannah's death. "So you think I did the right thing by confronting Antonio."

"Oh no. That was incredibly stupid. You pissed into the wind, and now it's blowing back into your face. Hannah's face actually, which is infinitely worse. You voluntarily signed up to risk death when you donned a Hero's cape. She didn't."

So much for lightening the load. "Thanks for sugarcoating it for me."

"If you want sugarcoating, go to a confectioner instead of asking me. Look, I get that your heart was in the right place when you went to Antonio's apartment to scare him away from Hannah, but if you had looked before you leapt, you might have realized a guy like Antonio wasn't going to take a threat lying down and just meekly do as you told him. If you had looked into Antonio's background before confronting him, you might have realized a guy with Antonio's history wouldn't back down. He's a professional tough guy. Ninety percent of being a tough guy is making sure everyone thinks you're a tough guy. Otherwise, no one's going to fear you and do what you tell them. A guy like Antonio won't meekly take his ball and go home when you punch him. His first instinct is to punch somebody back. You and your friend Myth weren't available, so Antonio punched back at Hannah instead. Since Hannah was already Antonio's personal punching bag before you lit the match to Antonio's powder keg, it shouldn't have been hard to guess that would happen."

I already had been feeling lower than a snake's belly about Hannah's death. I felt lower still after Truman's mini-lecture.

Perhaps sensing my mood, Truman added, "With that said, try not to beat yourself up too much. You made a mistake. In this business, mistakes come with the job. Hell, they come with being human. Unfortunately, because we have superpowers, our mistakes often have outsized consequences. You're young still, and new at this. You'll learn. Once you know better, you can do better. Assuming you don't get yourself killed beforehand."

"You're saying if I dodge death long enough, I'll have a better idea of what the right thing to do is. Great. Very inspirational. You should quit the detective business and take up motivational speaking." I was annoyed, but more at myself than at Truman. I knew he was right. "Have you made mistakes that have gotten someone killed?"

"Unfortunately, yes."

"How did you cope with it?"

"Well, one time when it happened I consulted with Dr. Feelgood. He prescribed a strict diet of vodka for breakfast, scotch for lunch, bourbon for dinner, and beer for the in-between times when I got thirsty."

"I see. Did drinking help?"

"In the short term, yes. But drinking is like taking a painkiller when you've got cancer—it dulls the pain, but doesn't cure the underlying cause. So in the long term, no. In fact, it made things worse. Drinking led me to make yet another mistake that resulted in another death. It's why I stopped. I don't drink at all now. Guilt is a powerful motivator."

"You know how I'm feeling, then."

"I do."

I felt like a weak swimmer about to drown in a sea of guilt. It was almost more than I could stand. "When does the guilt go away?"

Truman was silent for a moment.

"It doesn't," he said frankly. "Time dulls the sharp edges of it, but you still carry it around inside of you the rest of your life. Like herpes."

Fantastic.

I changed the subject before the impulse to slam my head through the windshield became too much to resist. "If Heroes and people like Antonio are just different sides of the same coin as you say, then what's the difference between them and us?"

"We don't kill. It's what separates us from them. But to be honest, if the dominos of my life had fallen a little differently, perhaps I'd be just like Antonio. After my family was killed, I certainly was on the path toward being like Antonio before I met a Hero named Zookeeper. He helped keep me on the straight and narrow. He sponsored my admission to the Trials, as a matter of fact."

"Your family was killed too?" I had already told Truman about Dad's murder at the hands of Iceburn. "By a supervillain?"

Truman smiled grimly.

"Unless that supervillain's name is Jack Daniels, no," he said. "My father drove drunk with my mother and sister in the car. He plowed into a tree, killing all of them. I was fourteen at the time."

"That's terrible. I'm so sorry."

"Why be sorry? It's not like you poured the liquor down his throat." Truman shrugged. "Besides, it was a long time ago."

In my mind's eye, I saw Dad's charred and smoking body as clearly now as I had over three years ago when I pulled his body out of the fire set by Iceburn. I couldn't imagine that image ever fading or losing its grievous luster. Sadness whirled with anger inside of me, a potent cocktail of emotions over wrongs both past and present. "I don't think it matters how long ago it happened," I said.

Silence.

"You're right," Truman finally said. "It doesn't." His voice was uncharacteristically subdued.

Then, the moment passed, like a swiftly moving dark cloud getting out of the way of the sun. "On the other hand, what kind of superhero doesn't have a tragic backstory? The Flash, Batman, Superman, Spider-Man, Daredevil, you and me. We're in good company."

"Yeah, we're all orphans. What a fantastic thing to have in common."

"It's better to light a candle instead of cursing the darkness," Truman said. "But to go back to how women are often attracted to alpha males. That doesn't apply to just thugs and criminals. Male Heroes get their fair share of admirers. Female Heroes too, for that matter."

"Cape chasers," I said, using the common vernacular for people who were Hero groupies. "Or for women specifically, sometimes Hero hags." There was another two-word alliterative phrase that began with the word "cape" and ended with a vulgar word for female genitalia that was also often used to describe women obsessed with Heroes. I was too much a product of the genteel South to actually say that phrase aloud, though. If I did, my mother would likely crawl out of her grave to wash my mouth out with soap.

"Exactly. In fact, there's even a website called *Hero Hags*. Ever check it out?"

"My friend Myth has told me about it, but no."

"The next time you're feeling low, you should look at it. Ever since you became active in Astor City, there's a section dedicated to you, just as there are sections devoted to just about every Hero in the public spotlight. Fan art, fan fiction, comments on your adventures, that sort of thing." Truman grinned. "There's even a growing collection of erotica describing your . . . how shall I say? . . . exploits. The gist of it is that your powers aren't the only thing about you that are super." He made a big show of looking over to my lap. His teeth flashed in the city's lights as his grin got wider. "If what I've read is true, it's amazing you can walk without tripping over that thing."

My face got hot with embarrassment. I didn't doubt the truth of what Truman said. Since donning a costume, I had noticed women reacted to me much differently as Kinetic than they did when I was just plain old Theo. The first time I had noticed it was during my Apprenticeship when a woman I had just saved from being assaulted near D.C.'s Union Station had flirted with me. I had been so clueless about women at the time I hadn't even realized she had been flirting. I was more worldly now about women than I had been then. That wasn't saying much. I was no Casanova. After all, I still had only slept with one woman. Even so, when women flirted with me now, I usually realized it. They only seemed to do it when I was Kinetic. That told me they were attracted more to the costume and what it represented than to the guy in the costume. It only served to make me more heartsick for Neha, who knew the guy behind the mask.

Truman slowed, and pulled into a parking spot on the street. We were now deep in Dog Cellar, in a part of it I had never been to before.

"I said before I've been a busy beaver," Truman said. "Speaking of busy beavers, we're here." He pointed to the building across the street.

As naive about women as I still was, even I knew the building housed a strip club. I would have to be blind, stupid, and raised in a cave to think otherwise. The windowless, two-story building was painted a garish hot pink. The club's name, Areola 51, flashed in bright neon lights above the illuminated outline of a naked woman with massive breasts and buttocks. A cluster of pink bulbs represented her areolae. Classy. "Girls, Girls, Girls," was also lit up in flashing lights on the left front of the building, as were the words "All Nude, All the Time" on the right side. Two big beefy guys identically dressed in jeans and black leather jackets checked people's IDs before they passed through the front door. The front of the club and the customer line extending from it were lit up like an airfield compared to the surrounding darkness.

"That's a strip club," I said to Truman in disbelief.

"It is. That's a deduction worthy of Hercule Poirot. Are you sure you're not a detective?"

"If this is your idea of a joke, it's not funny. I'm interested in finding out what Mechano has against me and how to deal with him, not in ogling a bunch of strippers."

"Why not do both and kill two birds with one stone? Considering all the bare breasts across the street, I almost said 'Kill two boobies with one stone,' but I didn't know if you know that a booby is a type of bird in addition to a female body part. I hate to waste a booby pun on the ignorant."

Despite the fact Truman was a lot bigger than I, I was tempted to punch him. "I'm paying you to help me, not make stupid puns."

"I am helping you. The puns I throw in for free." Truman jerked his chin toward Areola 51. "The Meta I told you about works here. Her name is Cassandra. She's a clairvoyant whose powers allow her to answer any question asked of her. But, she can only answer one question per person, so choose your question wisely. Short of asking Mechano directly, asking her is the quickest way to find out what Mechano's beef with you is."

"This Cassandra is a stripper?" I couldn't believe my ears.

"She sure ain't a nun. If she is, she's doing it wrong."

"What kind of licensed Hero works as a stripper?" The answer came to me before Truman opened his mouth to respond. "She's not a Hero, is she?"

"Nope."

"Were you drunk the day they taught you in your Heroic training that suborning the use of powers by a non-licensed Meta is a felony? If we were doing our jobs as Heroes, we'd take Cassandra into custody for unauthorized superpower use instead of consulting with her."

"This from the guy who illegally entered Antonio's apartment and beat him up."

"And look how well that turned out. I'm trying to learn from my mistakes."

"Look," Truman said, "I get that you were taught to follow the rules. And that's a good thing as the rules are there for a reason, to keep those of us with powers in check. But if you follow the rules all the time, you'll find yourself outmaneuvered by the people who aren't as scrupulous as you. Look at Mechano. 'Try repeatedly to kill a young Meta named Theodore Conley' is hardly an entry in the How To Be A Hero handbook. If you really want to find out what the deal is with a Hero as prominent and powerful as Mechano, you're going to have to do what you've got to do. What was it Machiavelli wrote in *The Prince*? 'Any man who tries to be good all the time is bound to come to ruin among the great number who are not good.' Besides, Cassandra isn't using her powers to hurt people. If she were, I'd be the first person to turn her in to the Guild and the USDMA. She uses her powers to help people by answering their questions. Well, and to enrich herself. She readily admits the latter motivates her more than the former, but I can hardly blame her for that. She's a businesswoman, not a Hero."

I sighed. I had already broken a bunch of rules since my powers manifested: using my powers without being licensed to defeat Iceburn; cheating during the Trials; and beating up Antonio. There were probably other little things here and there I'd forgotten. Though breaking the rules had seemed to be the best thing to do at the time I broke them, I wanted to get to the point where I walked the straight and narrow path. I didn't want to do something like what I had done to Antonio that would lead to someone else getting hurt or killed. I wanted to be the kind of Hero I thought everyone with powers was when I was a kid.

Maybe Truman was right, though. Maybe, to be effective, you couldn't follow the rules all the time. But how far over the line was too far?

I shoved the thought aside. Cassandra was the only lead I had gotten since moving to Astor City on how to find what Mechano had against me. Tonight, I'd do what I had to do. I'd try to walk the straight and narrow path tomorrow.

I said, "I'm not sure what to make of someone who makes a boob pun one minute, and then quotes Machiavelli the next."

"I'm eclectic."

"That's one word for it. Weird is another. So how does this whole thing with Cassandra work? Do I just walk up to her and ask her about Mechano while trying to not stare at her breasts? That sounds way too easy. The asking part, not the staring part." Since I had seen exactly one woman naked in person, namely Neha, not staring would probably be the hard part. I flushed at the thought. And it was likely to not be the only hard part.

"That's because it is too easy," Truman said. "Cassandra will only tell you what you want to know if you're willing to pay the price for the information. Nothing in life is free. On that note, I hope you brought the money I asked you to. Unlike me, Cassandra doesn't take checks. She's not as trusting as I am. Or as attractive, depending on your glandular bias."

"I did." Between paying Truman and Cassandra, my savings were taking sizable hits. If the money got results, though, I didn't mind. "Why can I only ask one question? If this lady has the power you say she does, she could tell me where Antonio is in addition to what the situation is with Mechano."

"For the same reason you have to move your hands when you activate your powers and I can't turn water into wine despite how hard I've tried." Truman shrugged. "Everyone's powers have limits. I don't know why that's so, I just know that it is. I'm a detective, not a scientist specializing in Metahuman powers."

"How did you know I have to move my hands when I activate my powers? I never told you that."

Truman looked at me like I had asked a stupid question. "Weren't you listening? I'm a detective. Noticing things is kinda my wheelhouse."

Truman reached over, opened the glove compartment, and pulled out a holstered handgun. He pulled his shirt up and shoved the gun down his pants so the gun rested in the small of his back.

"Why do you carry a gun, anyway?" I asked. "You have superpowers."

"Why does a carpenter carry a toolbox? You never know what tool you'll need when. It's better to have a gun and not need it than need a gun and not have it. Besides, you can't wave your superpowers threateningly in someone's face. Sometimes the threat of violence is more effective than actual violence." Truman glanced at the strip club. "Besides, we're about to go into a building full of naked women. I'm in a committed relationship. I've got to keep the girls inside from mobbing me somehow."

"Where's my gun, then? How am I going to keep them off me?"

Truman made a big show of looking me up and down. His eyes met mine. They twinkled.

"I wouldn't worry about it if I were you. Come on, let's go."

He opened his door, got out, made sure his untucked shirt covered his gun, and started to cross the street toward where the bouncers guarded the door to the strip club.

I reluctantly followed him. Though Truman was in my employ, he did not seem to have a problem making fun of me. What they said was true:

It really was hard to find good help these days.

13

Truman and I joined the line to get into Areola 51. Music thumped faintly from inside the building. Though the area immediately around the building was clean, beyond that the sidewalks and street were littered with trash. Even the city's street sweepers were afraid to venture into Dog Cellar.

On either side of Areola 51 were dilapidated buildings that looked like they belonged on the set of a post-apocalyptic movie. Despite the fact it was the dead of the night, scary-looking guys swaggered in and out of view as they ambled along, many in the middle of the street, some holding up their baggy jeans with one hand. They were going God knew where to do God knew what. Maybe they were going to their late-night chess clubs or hoping to catch the last few minutes of midnight mass. I doubted it.

"Here we are," I murmured to Truman in a low voice so the guys ahead of us in line wouldn't hear me, "standing in front of a hot pink building in the wee hours of the morning in the worst neighborhood I've ever seen to consult with a stripper-cum-clairvoyant. And who said big city life wasn't bewitching?"

Truman snickered. "You said cum." I didn't lower myself by responding. I felt low enough just standing here.

Wielding penlights, the big bouncers checked people's IDs before letting them in. Actually, I should say they checked each *man*'s ID because everyone in line was male. They were of various races and ranging from around my age to elderly. They looked normal enough, the kinds of guys you might see shopping at the grocery store or waiting at the doctor's office. They didn't look like degenerates. I for one felt like a degenerate. Nobody had ever told me there was anything wrong with going to a strip club, but the bishop who had presided over my confirmation into the Catholic Church hadn't encouraged me to rush out and start stuffing bills into a stripper's G-string, either. I had been taught that objectifying women and reducing them to their sexuality was wrong. If a strip club wasn't a shrine to objectification, I didn't know what was.

The line surged forward. I got close enough to the front door to read the sign posted there. I nudged Truman.

"The sign says no one under twenty-one is allowed inside," I whispered.

"Yeah, so?" Truman whispered back.

"I'm only twenty. I don't turn twenty-one for a few more weeks." I felt a surge of relief at the fact I wasn't old enough to go inside. Surely there was another way to figure out what I wanted to know about Mechano than to consult an unclothed clairvoyant called Cassandra. Maybe Truman also knew a slut with a sixth sense named Sylvia. I would not have been surprised.

Truman sighed. "Now you tell me," Truman murmured back. "Add twenty-one and up to the list of things you ought to be before the Guild gives you a license." He eyed the two bouncers. One was white, the other Hispanic. Though they looked dim-witted, what they lacked in apparent smarts they made up for in size. They peered carefully at people's IDs, seeming serious about checking dates of birth rather than simply going through the motions. "If I'd known about this sooner, I could've gotten you a fake ID. Now I'll just improvise something. If I can't get you past these two lunkheads, I should retire, surrender my superhero secret decoder ring, and take up knitting. Wait, what are you doing?"

"Improvising," I said. Inspired by Truman's fake ID remark, I had pulled out my Maryland driver's license. Though I hadn't had my own car since leaving South Carolina, I had gotten a Maryland license when I lived with Amazing Man in Chevy Chase as he let his Apprentices use his cars. "Stand in front of me so they can't see what I'm doing."

With Truman's big body blocking my movements from the view of the bouncers and the other guys in line, I looked critically at the hard substance that comprised the license. I looked not only with my eyes but, more importantly, with my powers. I immediately discerned that the license was made of a polycarbonate plastic with a thin laminate coating on top. My photo, date of birth, and name were etched into the plastic with a laser. I had dealt with polycarbonate lots of times before. Plenty of things in our modern society were made of those plastics, such as eyeglass lenses, DVDs, smartphones, and automotive components.

What most people don't realize is that everything around us is made of atoms and molecules that are constantly moving. Generally speaking, the molecules of a solid move less than the molecules of the liquid form of that solid, which in turn move less than the gas form of that liquid. The more the molecules moved, the more heat there was. That was why steam was hot, but if you cooled it, it became liquid water; if you cooled it further still, it became solid ice.

I hovered a hand over the license to help me concentrate my powers on it and, more specifically, the year of my birth. I focused on the six that was the last digit of my birth year. I shrank down in my mind's eye, down to the barely moving lattice structure of the polycarbonate molecules that comprised the "6" on the license. With my powers, I forced those molecules to vibrate slightly more, making the polycarbonate more pliable. I simultaneously kept the molecules of the laminate above the six rigid to keep the now hot plastic underneath from burning a hole through the thin coating.

I gently nudged the now pliable plastic of the digit, lengthening its top and reshaping its bottom, so that it looked like a "5" rather than the "6" it had started off as.

Once it looked as good as I could make it, I slowed down the molecules of the plastic again, cooling and re-hardening what had been semi-liquid moments before.

I released my powers' hold on the plastic. My heart pounded with exertion. Though the whole process had only taken a few seconds, for some reason manipulating matter on a molecular level took a lot out of me, far more so than picking up something massively heavy did.

According to my license, I was now a year older than I had been seconds before. Time sure flew when you were having fun waiting outside of a strip club. I ran a finger over the year of my birth. Though the once perfectly flat laminate covering the license was now a tiny bit raised over the newly formed "5," it was barely noticeable and not visible to the naked eye.

Truman took the license out of my hand and looked at it with a critical eye before handing it back. "Not bad," he murmured.

Once we got to the front of the line, Truman and I handed

our IDs to the large bouncers. My doctored one passed their inspection without so much as a raised eyebrow. One of them held the door open for us. The music from inside blared louder. Truman and I stepped inside. The door closed, plunging us into relative darkness. The inside was ill-lit compared to the bright area outside the club. I blinked, waiting for my eyes to adjust to the dimness.

"You have a bright future as a counterfeiter ahead of you," Truman said. He raised his voice to be heard over the thumping music. Its loudness made my insides vibrate.

"Something to look forward to," I said, suppressing a smile. I still wasn't happy about being in a strip club, but was pleased I had gotten past the bouncers without Truman's help. I had screwed up the situation with Antonio and Hannah so royally that it felt good to know I wasn't completely incompetent.

There was a bar near the front door. Truman and I lingered near it. The song playing when we came in went off, replaced by an equally loud rap song. I didn't recognize it, but based on its oft-repeated refrain, it was titled *Twerk Dat Booty*. Nothing compares to the classics.

My eyes adjusted to the dim light. I peered around. This floor of the club was one giant room. It was crowded despite its size. Smoke swirled like thin fog, a violation of the city ordinance prohibiting smoking inside of businesses. Though some was cigarette smoke, much of it was marijuana. The acrid smell of the drug was one I knew all too well. Though marijuana was illegal in Maryland, there were parts of the city, including my neighborhood, where smoking a joint on the street was as common as littering. Police didn't bother arresting people for weed. They had bigger fish to fry in a place like Astor City.

The inside of the club was a huge rectangle. The door we

had just come in from was in the middle of one of the long sides of the rectangle. Directly across from us on the far side of the club were two brightly lit stages. Each had two brass poles running from the stage to the high ceiling. The stage on the left featured two women who could have been photographic negatives of one another: a very dark-skinned black woman, and a very pale, redheaded white woman. Both were thin, long-haired, attractive in a hardened way, and as naked as the day they were born. Assuming they had been born. I couldn't imagine either of these improbably busty women as babies. Maybe they had been manufactured fully formed by some mad scientist with a breast fetish and a surplus supply of silicone. Using the brass poles as props, both women danced, shimmied, and shook in rhythm to the song blaring from the club's overhead speakers.

The stage to the right featured four or five nude and semi-nude women. They writhed together so closely that it was hard to tell exactly how many there were, where one of them ended, and where another began. My face got hot as I realized what they were doing to each other. It was probably illegal in private; it was definitely illegal in public. Watching them reminded me of the time I had almost tripped over a snake ball when picking peas back on the farm. The mass of entangled, wet-looking, mating reptiles had simultaneously been both obscenely fascinating and disgusting. The mound of women was like that snake ball, only without a ball in sight. There were strap-ons, though. One out of three pieces of masculinity wasn't bad.

To the left of the stages was a closed doorway with a lit-up sign reading *Private Dances* above it. In front of the two stages stood dozens of men, with more in front of the stage on the right than on the left. They looked almost transfixed, like television junkies watching their favorite show. From time to time they flung bills onto the stages. The stages' floors looked like they were carpeted with giant green and white confetti.

Scattered around the room were several smaller, circular stages. They rose out of the club's floor like stalagmites. Each had a brass pole extending from its center to the ceiling. There were strippers on each of these stages in various stages of undress. These smaller stages were also surrounded by men who looked up at the women hungrily. The looks on their faces reminded me of how a pack of dogs looked up at you when they were about to be fed. The large woman featured on the small stage closest to me had climbed to the top of the pole high above, and hung upside down with the pole gripped between one leg's calf and thigh. My first thought was that I hoped she didn't fall and break her neck; my second thought was that her oversized breasts and ample derriere would likely cushion the impact.

In addition to the women on stage, scantily clad women were scattered throughout the club. Tray-laden waitresses, all topless and wearing only silver-colored thong bikini bottoms, flitted among the throng of men, serving drinks and being ogled. The woman mixing drinks behind the bar we stood near was, like the waitresses, topless. Unlike them, she was very obviously pregnant. Her pendulous, veiny breasts hung down, resting on the swell of her pregnant belly. Several men were clustered around the bar, eying the pregnant woman hungrily, which struck me as being like wanting a piece of cake already chewed and swallowed by someone else.

Some of the strippers had on more clothes than the waitresses did. The ones who weren't dancing on the stages sat next to or in the laps of men, flirting so aggressively that I wondered if the men would need a cold shower afterward. I needed one too, and those women were nowhere near me. From time to time one of those women would stand, pulling a guy behind her as she walked toward the private dance doorway. The men always looked eager; the strippers, once their faces were out of view of the men they had in tow, always looked either bored or disgusted, even though they had looked like cats in heat moments before. The strippers who weren't flirting with the customers waited for the women on the stages and poles to finish so they could take their place.

Looking around, the number of women I'd seen naked in my life went from one to dozens of all ethnicities, colors, sizes, and body types in the span of just a few seconds. As I was enthusiastically heterosexual, the sight was more than just a little overwhelming. It was like a starving man walking into the world's biggest all-you-can-eat buffet. But, as someone who had been raised Catholic and taught that sexuality was sacred and not something crass and vulgar to be commercialized, watching these women shimmy, shake, and objectify themselves was as morally repulsive as it was viscerally exciting. The half-naked pregnant bartender was particularly shocking.

Like a decaying fish on the shore glittering with reflected moonlight, this place was at once both rotten and beautiful. My heart raced. My mouth was dry. It was difficult to get air in. I was torn between bolting back outside and grabbing the closest strippers and taking them to the private area.

"First time in a strip club?"

Startled, I realized it was Truman who had spoken, and not for the first time. I had been too transfixed with all the flesh on display to notice before. He looked at me with amusement. I flushed, this time with embarrassment instead of arousal mixed with repulsion. Not trusting myself to speak, I nodded in answer to his question.

"Can I interest you gentlemen in a private dance?" came a voice from my right, startling me again. I turned to see a young woman with vampire white skin and long, golden blonde hair standing next to me. She wore toweringly high heels of clear plastic, bringing her almost up to eye level with me. There was a large tattoo of a red apple with a bite taken out of it on the side of her neck. Her dark red lipstick matched the apple's color. Her electric blue dress looked like it had been painted on. Though it covered her from the bottom of her neck to right above her knees, it was so tight it revealed more than it concealed. It made her look more indecent than if she wasn't wearing anything at all.

"No thanks," Truman said, rejecting the woman's offer. "If you try to dance in that outfit you're liable to cut off your blood flow. I won't have your death on my hands. Or my lap."

If the woman heard any of that other than the word *no*, she gave no indication. She leaned toward me. I got a glimpse of milky-white cleavage. "How about you, big boy? My name's Lilith. I'll show you a good time." Her voice was low, breathy, and slightly slurred. Her perfume, strong and cheap, hit me like a hammer. The cheeks of her otherwise white face were almost as red as her lips and tattoo. It wasn't the flush of health or even rouge. It was an unhealthy, mottled red. The pupils of her eyes were unfocused and unnaturally huge; her irises were but narrow blue halos around them. I wondered what drugs she was on to make her sound and look like this. All of them, maybe.

Lilith's braless chest pressed against my arm. Her body radiated heat like an oven. I opened my mouth to respond. Nothing came out. I had been struck dumb by her body's proximity and blatant sexuality. She wasn't my usual type, but it had been so long since I'd been touched by a woman that anyone with a vagina would be my type at that moment. My body responded strongly to her.

Lilith looked down, smiled hazily, and reached down to

grab my crotch. My throat tightened, like I was having an allergic reaction. In my wildest dreams, I never would have predicted that the second person ever to touch me like this and the first person since Neha would be a stripper. Part of me wanted to pull the woman's hand off me. The rest of me called that other part a killjoy and didn't move. Not that I could have, anyway. I was frozen in place, like a mouse transfixed by an approaching snake.

"What's the matter, baby? Cat got your tongue?" Lilith purred. She stroked and tugged on me through my pants. Primal need tugged at me even more insistently. Blood pounded in my ears like a jungle drum.

"Yeah, a pussy cat," Truman said. If I could do more than struggle to breathe, I would have used my powers to fling him across the room. Him speaking, though, just feet from where this stranger fondled me, was enough to snap me out of my paralysis.

"I'm not interested in a dance either," I croaked.

"Your mouth says no, but this says yes," Lilith said, giving me another squeeze. It almost made me moan. Her lips brushed my ear, sending chills up and down my spine. "If you pay a little extra, I'll do more than just dance for you."

I shocked myself by being tempted. It had been so long since I had touched and been touched. Cassandra could wait. If I had put off dealing with Mechano this long, surely he could wait an hour or so more. Lilith's breasts pressed harder against me. Sexual need bubbled up inside of me, like a volcano about to explode. Oh, who was I kidding? Cassandra and Mechano wouldn't be put off for an hour. My carnal desires had been pent up for too long. It would be a few minutes at the most. If that long.

My sudden ache for this woman was so strong it was almost painful. Even Lilith's apple tattoo seemed alluringly sexy, though I normally was not a fan of tattoos on women. I wanted to take a bite of that apple. Temptation, an apple, and a blue dress . . . maybe that classic song I had often heard the Old Man play, *Devil With A Blue Dress*, was based on this woman.

I had grown up believing what this woman proposed was wrong. But, if there was one thing Astor City had taught me, it was that small-town values weren't always compatible with the big city. Besides, people paid for massages all the time, and I never saw priests and nuns picketing massage parlors. If paying a woman to rub you during a massage was morally fine, what was so different about paying her to rub you where the sun didn't shine?

I looked at Lilith hungrily, teetering toward saying yes. Even with the dramatic dilation of her pupils, I saw eagerness in her eyes. It made me hesitate. It was not the same eagerness I felt, the eagerness of a man for a woman. Hers was a mercenary eagerness, the eagerness of a fisherman who had hooked a fish and was reeling him in, or a con artist who had found a naive mark.

Sudden disgust twisted in my stomach where there had only been naked lust before. I didn't want to be touched by someone I paid to do it. I was reminded of the Hero hags, who only had their erotic fantasies about me and people like me because of the power we represented. I wanted to be touched by someone because she wanted to do it, because she liked and wanted me, not because she liked my cape or wanted my money.

I grabbed Lilith's wrist and pulled her hand off me. "I said that I'm not interested," I said, more firmly than before. It would sound more convincing had my body not visibly disputed me.

Lilith pouted sexily. "Are you sure? It'll feel real good. For both of us. You're awfully cute."

"I'm tempted, but I have to say no. The truth of the matter is I don't have any money." The first part was true enough. I was lying about that last part; I was trying to spare her feelings.

The sex kitten look on Lilith's face slid off as if it had been a mask. "Then what you doin' in here, you broke ass muther-fucka?" Her voice, before alluring, was now harsh and ghetto. It was as if I was looking at a completely different person than the one who had her hand on my private parts seconds before.

"Studying your elocution," Truman said.

"Ain't nobody touchin' my elocution unless you got money. You gotta pay to play." Lilith gave me a hard look, and then a snort of disgust. She flounced off. Her perfume lingered behind like a ghost. Moments later, she was across the room with her arms wrapped around a middle-aged guy sporting dad jeans and a comb-over. The seductive look she had beguiled me with before was back on her face. The man said something to her. She threw back her head and laughed, as if whatever he had said was the wittiest thing she had ever heard. The man's hand slid down to her butt and stayed there. I felt a hot irrational surge of jealousy.

Truman said, "Though the strippers get tipped when they dance out here, they make their real money in the private area. That's why that woman came onto you so aggressively." Truman's voice went up a few octaves and became breathy. "That, and the fact you are so *dreaaaaamy*," he added, stretching out the last word in a bad imitation of Lilith's voice. He smirked, then looked back over at Lilith. She was now touching the middle-aged man as aggressively and intimately as she had me. The smirk faded from Truman's face, replaced by a touch of sadness.

"I feel sorry for people like that," he said.

"Why? He seems to be having a good enough time," I said as I mentally chided myself for being jealous. When a stripper paid attention to you, it wasn't as though she was yours—it was just your turn. In a sudden flash of what I hoped was cynicism and not insight, I wondered if the same was true with all romantic relationships.

"Not him. He's just an idiot who's liable to get the contents of his wallet sucked out through the contents of his pants. I feel sorry for her. Hers is no kind of life to be living, even if she's too blinded by youth and drugs to realize it just yet. Nobody ever became a stripper because her daddy loved her too much or because she got tired of being a rocket scientist. If you work here, it's because your life took a wrong turn somewhere. There aren't a bunch of little girls whose ambition in life is to grow up and take their clothes off for a living. Or prostitute themselves. A lot more than just dancing goes on in those private rooms, after all. As your new friend implied, she would've let you do just about anything to her if you paid her enough."

With Lilith no longer pressed against me, the fever she had triggered within me was subsiding. How quickly her true nature had been revealed when I told her I didn't have any money cast a different light on all the gyrating bodies around me. Though I won't lie and say I didn't still find the women arousing, they no longer transfixed me. It was like a high fever breaking. Yes, I was still hot and bothered, but I was no longer mesmerized to the point of paralysis. I now saw the women's dancing for what it was: advertisement for a product I did not need.

I said to Truman, "I'm glad to hear you think strip clubs are wrong, too. I was beginning to think my upbringing had made me a prude."

"Oh, I don't think they're morally wrong. I don't think prostitution is wrong, either. If two consenting adults agree to get naked or swap bodily fluids in exchange for money, what business is it of mine? The fact that it's not my business doesn't mean I must like it, though. The stories of women like the ones in here usually don't end well. If I could, I'd wave my magic wand and create a different life for every woman in here." For a moment, Truman looked sad and tired. "Unfortunately, my wand is in the shop for repairs. Besides, nobody here asked me to save them, and would likely spit in my face if I suggested they needed saving. I love a naked woman as much as the next guy, but standing here makes me feel dirty. I wanna go home and take a hot bath."

The tired look on Truman's face faded as quickly as it had appeared. He looked his old jocular self again. He pointed down at the part of me that I was mortified to see pointed back at him. He said, "Whereas you need to go home and take a cold shower. Your magic wand seems to be working just fine."

As it turned out, you cannot die of embarrassment. If you could, I would have done so right then and there. Where was a fig leaf when you needed one?

"Where's Cassandra?" I asked, as much to change the subject as to move things along. Now that the spell these women had cast over me was broken, I wanted to get out of here as soon as possible. All this jiggling flesh made me uncomfortable.

"I have no idea. You can always use your divining rod to find her. Though it's currently pointing at me, I can assure you I'm not her."

I tried to ignore both my so-called divining rod and Truman's remark about it. I could've taken a page out of the book of almost every woman I had ever known since they had ignored my divining rod all my life. "What do you mean, you have no idea?" I demanded. "You said she worked here."

"I did and she does. Doesn't mean I know where she is. She assumes a different form after every time she answers someone's question. Figuring out who she is is the first step in getting her to answer your question. 'It cuts down on the riffraff and the unserious,' she had said when I asked her why she makes people jump through that hoop. She said otherwise she'd be overrun with people asking her questions, which would be great for her bank balance, but terrible for her free time."

"Have you asked her a question before?"

"I have."

"Good. Then you can tell me how to find her."

"Nope. It doesn't work that way. If I help you find her, her powers won't work on you. Besides, I don't even know if how I found her before would work more than once."

"What question did you ask her?"

The dark cloud returned to Truman's face. "Not that it's any of your business, but I asked if it's possible to resurrect a young Meta who died while under my protection."

"And is it?"

"I'm working on it," Truman snapped. I clearly had hit a touchy subject. "Look, quit stalling. Are you going to look for Cassandra or are we going to continue to play this rousing game of Nosy Questions?" It was hard to remember that Truman worked for me instead of vice versa. I wondered if Henry Ford's employees had been this mouthy.

Truman was right, though. I *was* stalling. I didn't know where to begin. I had no idea how to go about finding Cassandra. Then again, just a few short years ago, I had no idea how to do all the Hero-related stuff I now did without a second thought.

I stood up straighter. I was a licensed Hero. I had been to other dimensions, other planets, fought off supervillains, and survived more deadly scrapes than I wanted to remember. After all that, how hard could finding a woman be? Yeah, maybe my people-finding track record had been less than exemplary lately, but surely finding a Metahuman stripper was easier than finding a Metahuman murderer. At least it promised to be easier on the eyes.

My pep talk seemed a lot less peppy when I turned my attention away from Truman back to the strippers. There were dozens of them, each different, yet somehow luridly all the same. Finding a stripper in a building chock-full of them when you didn't have any idea who you were looking for was worse than looking for a needle in a haystack. It was looking for a needle in a needlestack. Considering how drugged up Lilith had been, I suspected finding a needle in this place would be easier than finding Cassandra.

The thumping music coming from the loudspeakers made it hard to think. The secondhand marijuana smoke I breathed in did not help. What was it they called getting high from someone else's weed smoke? Hotboxing? The word had a double-meaning when all this female flesh surrounded you.

With effort, I forced myself to concentrate. I cast my eyes over the people in the room. No one stood out. Well, that's not true. The employees definitely stood out from the patrons. The women on the stage on the right stood out due to the perverted things they did to one another. The stripper dancing on the small stage a few feet away stood out because she looked like she was smuggling two hams in the bottom half of her tight dress. The waitress who just walked past me stood out because she had nipples that jutted out like miniature Star Towers.

Each woman stood out for one reason or another that was

uniquely her own. However, no one stood out in a way that made me think she was Cassandra. Unfortunately, no one had a neon sign over her head identifying her as *Cassandra: The Stripping Clairvoyant*.

Could Cassandra be Lilith? She had come up to me, after all. Maybe her clairvoyance had told her I had come to see her and she had pointed herself out to me. Maybe giving me a genital handshake was her way of saying, "Hi, I'm Cassandra. I'm as pleased to meet you as you obviously are to meet me." If Lilith had the power of prophecy, though, she hid it awfully well. When I thought of an oracle, I thought of someone ancient with wise eyes who wore robes. I didn't think of someone like Lilith.

I looked over at Lilith again. She led the middle-aged man she had previously been groping toward the door to the private area. Now that I was no longer gripped by lust, I saw that she had an unfocused and hazy look, the way people who were high and liked to stay high often did. How many men would she need to objectify herself for tonight, I wondered, to get enough money for her next series of fixes? I understood why Truman felt sorry for her. It was hard to believe she was the Meta who could give me the answers I needed. She looked like she needed answers to life's problems, not like she dispensed them.

I glanced at Truman, hoping he would help me despite what he said earlier. True to his word, he was not helping me look for Cassandra. Rather, he leaned over the bar, talking to the pregnant bartender. He might have been trying to convince her to get a different job in the best interests of her unborn child. Or, he might have been asking if he could get a glass of milk straight from her built-in taps. You never knew with him.

Truman clearly was going to be no help. Since no one

leapt forward and announced herself to be Cassandra, I needed to try something other than staring at everyone like someone who had never seen a woman before. If I couldn't find Cassandra with my eyes, maybe I could find her with my powers.

I closed my eyes and lifted my hands a bit. Normally I tried to be subtler when I used my powers. Here, no one paid me any attention. There were far too many other, jigglier, things to pay attention to.

As I had when I used my powers to sense Antonio about to enter his apartment to find me and Isaac inside, I emitted pulses of my telekinetic touch. Like a submarine using sonar to find what was around it in the depths of the dark ocean, I used my telekinetic touch to feel everyone and everything in the club. I did it gently, not wanting people to feel me probing them. Though I could hit someone so hard with my telekinesis that it felt like a punch from a pile driver, I could also touch someone so gently to count the hair on their head without mussing it. With the soft touch I now used, the people in the club would feel nothing consequential, like a weak puff of breath on the back of their necks, except all over.

I concentrated on finding something unusual, something that would indicate who Cassandra was. It was an effort to not get distracted by all the flesh I ran my mind over. My powers confirmed what Truman had said about how more than just dancing went on in the private area. Some of the positions the people there sweatily engaged in I had never even heard of, much less tried. At this rate, I would be the most experienced guy who had only slept with one woman in the history of mankind. I wondered if there was an award for that. I shuddered to think what the award statuette must be shaped like.

There! I found something unusual. A woman who sat on a man's lap on the other side of the club from me didn't feel like everybody else. Though the inner core of her was flesh and bone, the outer surfaces of her body didn't feel like flesh. Touching her versus touching the other women in the room was like touching soft Styrofoam versus touching human flesh —something was there, but whatever that something was, it was artificial. It reminded me of using my powers to run my mind over the holographic characters which had been used during the Trials—something was there, but it was not what it appeared to the naked eye to be.

If this wasn't a clue, I didn't know what was. I opened my eyes and lowered my hands. I strode through the club toward the woman I had identified. When I finally navigated through the throng of people, I found a woman with blonde bobbed hair dressed in pink hot pants and a matching halter top. The guy whose lap she sat on was burly, which was good for him because she was a big girl. A small man might not have been able to support her weight. She was not fat exactly, but thick, with ample hips, big thighs, plump arms, a muffin top, and a prominent chest. "Thicker than a snickers," I had heard Deshaun, my friendly neighborhood drug dealer, say appreciatively about women built like this when they walked by his usual perch on the sidewalk. Standing, this woman would look like the letter S, all boobs and butt.

She had an arm around the man's shoulder while her other hand stroked the man's chest through his shirt. The man was doing a good octopus impersonation as his hands were everywhere. The woman's face was turned away from me and snuggled up against the man's. She murmured something in the man's ear. He half-moaned, half-growled, and squeezed her butt. Maybe she had shared with him her secret angel food cake recipe, but I doubted it. A tall glass half full of an amber liquid was on the pub table next to the man's elbow. A partially smoked joint was in the ashtray.

I tapped the woman on the shoulder. She turned to me. Her lips were a thick, blood red slash in her face. She had dark brown eyes under thick dark eyebrows. I didn't have to be a detective like Truman to surmise her platinum blonde bob was a dye job. I wondered how much I would have to pay this woman to confirm that the carpet did not match the drapes. Then again, the woman's hot pants were so tight it was clear she did not have carpeting at all. She appeared to be a fan of hardwood floors.

"Are you Cassandra?" I said, half yelling to be heard over the music. Another hip-hop song was playing, something with a thumping bassline.

The woman gave me a quick head to toe look-over. It felt as though she was expertly assessing my net worth, like a banker determining a loan applicant's creditworthiness.

"No," she said curtly. The tone of dismissal was obvious. She turned away to bury her head in the crook of the man's neck again, ignoring me like I was invisible. Something in the woman's eyes belied her answer, though. I didn't need Truman's lie detecting abilities to know when I was being lied to. Besides, my powers certainly hadn't been lying when they told me something was weird about this woman.

I felt a hot surge of anger at being dismissed. I was fed up. I was sick of the stench of weed, sick of this loud music, sick of strippers, sick of jumping through hoops, and sick of looking for people who didn't want to be found like Cassandra and Antonio. I wanted to talk to Cassandra, find out what I could about Mechano, and get out of here. I felt dirty. I wanted to go home and soak in a hot tub. I wanted to find Neha waiting in that tub, eager to touch me, not because I paid her to, but because she wanted to. But I knew I would not go home to find Neha. That made me even more angry.

I grabbed the woman's wrist. All the time I had spent in

the gym the past few years getting stronger had not been in vain. I hauled the big woman off the man's lap and to her feet. She yelped in surprise. She stumbled in her high heels before regaining her balance.

"Hey!" the man cried in protest, his tongue thick with weed and alcohol. He unsuccessfully tried to stand.

"I don't care what you say, I think you're Cassandra," I said to the woman. In her heels, she was a little taller than I. Now that I saw her more clearly in the dim lighting, she was not white as I had first supposed. Her tan skin and the shape of her nose indicated a non-Caucasian ancestry. Middle Eastern, maybe. "I need to talk to you. I'll pay you."

"Plenty other girls here. This one's mine," the man said, his anger evident despite his slurred voice. He still struggled to stand. To an outside observer, it probably looked like he couldn't get up because he was too drunk or high. In reality, he could not get up because I held him down with my powers. Avatar with his Omega-level super strength surely could have stood up despite my telekinetic hold, but not this guy. He looked like a fat cockroach on its back with its limbs flailing. I did not want to let him up. I was in no mood to get into a fist-fight with him over a woman I didn't even know. Actually, that's not right—I was in such a sour mood from still being in this godforsaken place that I *was* in the mood to get into a fist-fight, which is exactly the wrong time to get into a fistfight. Anger clouds your judgment. I especially had no business getting into a fight with a non-Meta who was no match for me.

Looking down at me, the woman stared straight into my eyes, her face flushed with anger. Her pupils dilated, like a camera's shutter. The world seemed to come to a stop and distort, centering on the woman's eyes. As if hypnotized, I could not look away. I could not move at all. I heard a dull roar, like the sound you hear when you put your ear to a seashell. Only this sound I didn't hear with my ears. I heard it in my mind. The nape of my neck prickled, the same sort of feeling I got when someone was looking at me when my back was turned. Unbidden, I found myself thinking about why and how I had come to Areola 51. A kaleidoscope of images from the last few days formed in my mind, like a picture book whose pages were being rapidly flipped.

The woman's eyes widened in surprise. Though I didn't know how I knew, I knew she had seen the pictures that had flashed through my mind.

As quickly as it started, it was over. The woman's dilated pupils returned to normal. The world restarted, like a needle on a record player had momentarily skipped and now played normally again. I blinked several times, able to move once more. Though I was fully dressed and this woman was not, I felt more exposed to her than she was to me.

Cassandra—for it was obvious now who this woman was —leaned over the stout man who still struggled to stand. "I need to talk to this guy for a few minutes," she said into his ear, though I could barely hear her over the music. "I'll be right back. Then we'll pick up where we left off."

Without waiting for a response from the man, Cassandra grabbed my hand and led me toward the door to the private dance area. Since I knew she could peer into my mind, I did not take the opportunity to admire her ample backside.

Well, okay, maybe I did peek a little. I was a Hero looking for answers. Not a monk.

14

The door to the private area opened to a flight of stairs leading down. The stairs were ill-lit by several red lights. It had been hot enough in the club proper due to the heat of all the bodies there. It got hotter still as I followed Cassandra down the stairs. Between the red lights and the heat, this must have been what descending into Hell was like. The moans and groans that got louder the lower we went helped with that impression. Feminine wails mingled with masculine grunts. Sounds of pleasure, not pain. Further proof that more than just dancing went on in this private area. If Hell was like this, maybe it was not such a bad place after all. Besides, being from the South, I was used to hot places. Perhaps I would reconsider my plans for the afterlife.

By the time we got to the bottom of the stairs, the sounds of the club above us were completely gone, swallowed up by the moaning and music that filled the long hall we were now in. Thankfully, the smell of weed and cigarettes was mostly gone down here, though the stench lingered on my clothes.

Well over a dozen doors lined the hallway, each numbered. Most were closed. As I followed Cassandra down the hall, I heard different songs coming from behind each closed door. Between the music and the moaning, it sounded like a porno soundtrack.

When we got to the middle of the hall, a door to my right opened. A topless, dark-skinned stripper with watermelon breasts came out, hand-in-hand with a gray-haired old man. The man averted his gaze in embarrassment when he saw me. He wore a wedding ring. His hair was askew, his shirt was partially untucked, and his fly was half zipped. Somehow I doubted the stripper was his lawfully wedded wife. Not only was he old enough to be her father, he was old enough to be her grandfather. I didn't know whether I should chastise him, or high five him. I did neither, instead brushing silently past the two in the narrow hall. Judge not, lest ye be judged.

Cassandra led me toward the end of the hall to one of the open doors. Door number fourteen. If it had been door thirteen, I might have refused to go in. I was not superstitious, but my encounter with Antonio in apartment 1313 had not gone well. Once blasted through a window by an unexpected Meta, twice shy.

Cassandra closed the door behind me once I followed her inside. The small, windowless room was quiet. The moans and music from the surrounding rooms trickled in faintly. The room was empty except for a couch, a small wooden table next to it, and a black speaker mounted on a wall near the ceiling. The lumpy couch had seen better days. A small remote control I supposed controlled the music was chained to the table. In addition to the remote, the table contained several bottles of lotion and lubrication, a box of Kleenex, and a large glass bowl half full of condoms. Though the room was not particularly dirty, once I got a look at the contents of the table, it seemed filthy. The thought of all the people who had done God knew what in this room made my skin crawl. I didn't want to touch anything. You could not get a sexually transmitted disease that easily, but better safe than sorry.

"Truman Lord sent you," Cassandra said. Her tone was businesslike, not at all the seductive cooing she had favored the big man upstairs with.

I nodded yes, though I knew I did not need to. Her words had been a statement, not a question. How much had she seen when she glimpsed my thoughts before?

As if in response to my question, Cassandra asked, "Aren't you a little young to be a Hero?" First Truman, now a stripper I did not know from Adam. Uh, Eve, I mean, since this voluptuous woman couldn't be mistaken for a man even if you suffered from glaucoma and spotted her in the dead of night. At the rate my secret identity was being exposed, maybe I should just fly to the top of the UWant Building again and shout my identity to all the city's residents. Save some time.

"Aren't you a little big to be a stripper?" I retorted, irritated. The words were out of my mouth before I could stop them. Maybe it wasn't the best move to insult a woman I needed information from. That's me, Theo Conley, diplomat extraordinaire. I should get a job with the United Nations.

Cassandra shrugged slightly, making her chest move interestingly. "Different men like different things." If she was insulted, she did not show it. "You brought the money I require." Again a statement, not a question.

I fished the wad of cash out of my pocket and handed it over. Cassandra shoved it down her cleavage and the money disappeared. She had not even bothered to count it. Maybe her breasts would count it. That would be a neat trick I would not mind seeing.

Cassandra directed me to have a seat on the couch. Reluctantly, I did so. The back of my neck immediately started to itch. Though I knew it was psychosomatic, I could not fight the feeling that countless cooties from countless dirtbags were leaping from the couch onto me. Most of me did not want to think about all the action this couch must have seen. A small part of me wished there was a video of it.

Cassandra straddled my legs, and started to sit. Startled, I tried to stand.

"I want information, not a dance," I yelped.

Cassandra shoved me back down by my shoulders.

"Stop being such a shrinking violet." She settled down on my lap with her legs straddling mine. "This is my process. Do you want my help, or don't you?"

I tried to relax. When a stranger's big boobs were in your face, that was easier said than done. I took a long calming breath.

Cassandra was heavy on my lap, but not unpleasantly so. She put her hand over my ears, with her fingertips splayed over the sides of my skull. Her long nails, painted to match her red lipstick, dug into my skin. Her skin was hot against my ears. Her smell filled my nostrils. Her perfume was musky and, unlike Lilith's, seemed expensive. I liked it. Inhaling it made my heart thump faster. I felt the hardness of Cassandra's thigh muscles underneath her plumpness. Her big chest and prominent nipples were right in front of my face. If I leaned forward a little, I could—

Cassandra removed one of her hands from my skull. She clouted me upside the head, hard enough to make my ear ring.

"Ow!"

"Stop perving on me, then," she said matter-of-factly. Her hand returned to cover my ear again. "Lust is one of the most powerful emotions. It distracts me from what I'm trying to do. Look up, away from my chest. Try to empty your mind. Pretend like I'm not even here."

That's easy for you to say, I thought. *You're not the one with big headlights shining in your eyes, blinding you.*

I looked up, into Cassandra's eyes. I tried to shove the thought of headlights away before she smacked me again. My ear still stung. She had a lot of muscle under that flab.

Cassandra's brown eyes bored into mine. I focused on them and not on all the flesh in my lap. As I stared at her eyes, their pupils expanded, much as they had when Cassandra had looked at me upstairs. This time, though, they continued to spread out, like ink spilled on a piece of paper. Their blackness expanded to encompass her brown irises, and then the whites of her eyes, until her eyes were like pools of the darkest oil. My scalp tingled where Cassandra's fingernails dug into it, as if a low-level electric current arced through Cassandra and into me.

Bit by bit, the world fell away like pieces of broken glass. No longer could I smell the smoke in my clothes, or the musk of Cassandra's perfume. The music and moaning stopped, or at least I stopped being aware of them. The only thing left was Cassandra.

She felt lighter in my lap. No longer was she a zaftig woman with dyed blonde hair. Now she was a small-boned old lady with a narrow, pinched face and long stringy gray hair. Her loose, crinkled skin was freckled with liver spots. She still wore a tight pink halter top and matching hot pants. They looked like bandages instead of clothes on this old lady. She was flat-chested. The wad of cash under her top bulged out like a deformed third breast.

Soon, even most of Cassandra faded away. I stopped being aware of her weight, her appearance, and the burning of my scalp where her long nails dug into me. The only things left were Cassandra's eyes. They seemed to have swallowed the rest of the world whole.

The external world, that is. Internally, in my mind, it was as if countless doors were opening, revealing a new world that had been hidden before. Through them I could see . . . well, everything.

I could only see the images hazily, though, as if I viewed them through a thick glass bottle. Though it was hard to be sure, I thought I caught glimpses of my parents when they were young and full of life. Here was Neha, looking so beautiful even with the distortion. There was Isaac, Truman, Mad Dog, Hannah, the Old Man, Hammer, Iceburn, the Three Horseman, the blonde who had planted the bomb on me, the old lady whose tire I changed in Washington, D.C. right before Iceburn attacked me, Athena, Elemental Man, Pitbull, Mechano and the other Sentinels, Avatar, Omega Man, and countless others. Hero and Rogue, Meta and non-Meta, friend and foe flashed before me. Some I recognized. Most I did not. But I knew I was connected to all these people, even the ones I didn't know, in ways I could almost but not quite understand. It was as if we were all suspended in one massive spiderweb, with each movement we made affecting everyone else, some strongly, others faintly.

I knew without knowing how I knew that everything I sought, everything I wanted to know—everything I could *ever* know, no matter how big or small—was all right here. But despite how much I concentrated to bring the distorted images into clear view, I couldn't. Everything was just beyond my grasp, like a chased rainbow.

"You have but a single question, and a single answer," came a voice that echoed in my mind. It did not sound like Cassandra. The voice held an ancient, timeless quality the stripper's voice had not. Even so, I knew it was her. "What is your question?"

I had prepared for this, of course. Ever since Truman had

told me I could only ask Cassandra one question, I had turned over in my mind how I should ask about Mechano. Now that I knew with visceral certainty that anything I wanted to know was at Cassandra's fingertips, I hesitated. Should I ask something else? There were so many things I wanted to know: Where was Antonio? If I found him, what should I do with him? How could I make Neha love me the way I loved her? When would I die? When would my friends die? Would I ever be happy? Was time travel possible? Could I go back in time and keep Hammer from being killed in the Trials? Could I prevent Hannah's murder? Save my father from Iceburn? Prevent my mother from ever getting cancer and dying?

Compared to some of those questions, why Mechano had tried to kill me seemed trivial.

My thoughts kept leading me back to my parents, Hannah, and Hammer. Over the past few years I had seen and done things I never would have dreamed were possible before I entered the world of Heroes and Rogues. I had flown faster than the fastest bird, gone to other dimensions, and seen creatures that were supposed to be myths. I had seen the impossible made not only possible, but into a hard reality. What else was possible that I did not yet know about? I realized as I equivocated over what to ask Cassandra that, in the back of my mind, I had been subconsciously harboring the hope that someday I would find a way to go back into the past and fix things, to make sure that the people who had died did not die. Dad's and Hannah's deaths had been caused by me. They would be alive today if I had made better decisions. If I could go back in time, I could do things differently, make different choices. I could make sure they lived. And, though I did not cause Hammer's and Mom's deaths, they still had been so unnecessary. So unfair. Neither of them had deserved to have their lives cut short.

Maybe I would one day meet a Meta who could time travel and who would be willing to take me into the past with him to make sure no one I cared about died.

Or, maybe I would one day meet a scientist who was working on time travel technology. Yes, time travel tech sounded like something out of science fiction, but not too long ago so did computers you could fit into your pocket. And yet almost everyone had a smartphone with more computing power than the computers that put a man on the Moon. Yesterday's science fiction was often today's science fact. Perhaps time travel was the same.

Maybe, as an Omega-level Metahuman, I myself would one day become powerful enough that I would figure out a way to use my powers to time travel. Maybe there was some twist on how to use my powers I had not yet thought of.

Or, maybe there was some other way to travel back in time that did not involve technology or Metahuman powers.

Maybe time travel was possible. Maybe saving the lives of all the people I cared about was possible. Maybe, as Faulkner wrote, "The past is never dead. It's not even past." I did not know.

But Cassandra did. And even if time travel was not possible, Cassandra would know if resurrection was. If a carpenter from Nazareth could pull off resurrection millennia ago, surely a husband and wife from South Carolina could today.

But, what if I asked Cassandra if I could travel back in time to save Hammer, Hannah, Dad, and Mom or resurrect them somehow and the answer was *No*? I would've wasted my one shot at asking Cassandra a question. More importantly, I would kill off the hope that they all could be saved. It was a hope I had not even been aware I harbored, a hope that kept me going when times were tough. If I didn't have hope that tomorrow could be better than yesterday, what was the point of living?

I remembered something Dad once said, one of his Jamesisms: "The past can be the wind in your sails. It can also be an anchor." I knew if Cassandra told me there was no way the people I cared about could be saved, it would be an anchor that would mire me in a sea of despair, perhaps forever.

I wrestled with the subject of the question I should ask. Mechano, or my friends and family?

Seconds passed. Or maybe it was hours. I could not tell. Time seemed to have little meaning in the internal world Cassandra had sucked me into.

I made up my mind. I needed to know if there was some way to save Hammer, Hannah, and my parents. It didn't matter if Cassandra's answer was no. I had to know for sure. Mechano could wait. I had put off dealing with him this long. Besides, as Isaac had suggested days before, I could simply turn what I knew about him over to the Heroes' Guild and let it handle him. My family and friends should take precedence.

Unbidden, the words of the Hero's Oath I had sworn during my cape investiture ceremony bubbled up to the forefront of my mind. Saying those words along with the other five people who had passed the Trials—Isaac, Neha, Hacker, Hardcase, and Zephyr—had been one of the biggest moments of my life:

> *No cave so dark,*
> *No pit so deep,*
> *Will hide evil from my arm's sweep.*
> *Those who sow darkness soon shall reap,*
> *For in the pursuit of justice,*
> *I will never sleep.*

The words echoed in my mind. Their meaning sank in in a way they had not before.

I could not simply report Mechano to the Guild and let it deal with him. I *was* the Guild. Even though I was inexperienced compared to Heroes like Truman, Athena, the Old Man, and Ghost, I was as much of a Hero and a member of the Guild as they were. According to the oath I had sworn, it was my job to deal with people like Mechano, not to foist him off on someone else. I knew he had tried to kill me during the Trials, both with nanites and with a bomb. With the latter, he had nearly killed and injured others as well. What else had he done wrong that I did not even know about? How else had he violated his own Oath? It was my responsibility to bring him to justice.

If not me, who? Truman and Isaac only knew about what Mechano had done because I told them. Other than me, the only other person with direct, non-hearsay knowledge of Mechano's foul deeds was Hacker. I would not hold my breath on her acting against Mechano. She didn't use her powers to fight crime. She worked for some big tech firm in Seattle. Though she had never come right out and said so, I was under the strong impression that the only reason Hacker had pursued her license was so she could legally cash in on the use of her Metahuman ability to communicate with computers. Besides, maybe it was just as well Hacker did not plan on being a crime-fighter. She had not even known who Spider-Man was until I told her during the Trials. Though Spider-Man was not real, a Hero really ought to know something about the mythology of superheroes. A Hero not knowing about Spider-Man was like a writer not knowing about Shakespeare's plays.

Though Hacker was not interested in the justice-seeking component of being a Hero, I was. With that being the case, how could I let this opportunity to act against Mechano pass me by? How had the Old Man put it years ago when I had been in his Heroic Feats, Ethics, and Theory class at the Academy? "A hero is someone who sees what must be done, and he or she tries to do it regardless of the personal cost." That definition had sounded right to me then, and it still sounded right to me now.

As much as it pained me, trying to bring Hannah, Hammer, and my parents back to life would have to wait. I had an oath to live up to, and a responsibility to shoulder.

"Why has Mechano tried to kill me?" I finally asked Cassandra.

The images in my mind reordered themselves, like a deck of rapidly shuffled cards. I caught quick glimpses of them. Though they started off blurry and out of focus, each became clearer as it flashed by. I saw Omega Man, the greatest Hero the world has ever known, flying straight through the side of the V'Loth mothership in his successful attempt to kill the aliens' queen and stop their invasion in the 1960s. I saw Omega Man's statue on top of the Heroes' Guild National Headquarters building in Washington, D.C. I saw me and Neha flying toward the building years ago for the Trials and talking about the legend that Omega Man would return when the planet faced another great threat. I saw Avatar being shot and killed, the bullet somehow piercing his impenetrable skin. I saw a group of costumed Rogues sitting around a conference table, planning and scheming about something with worldwide implications. I saw me and the Three Horsemen in the college bathroom the day my powers first manifested. The football players were flung violently off me and through the air thanks to my telekinesis. I saw Millennium, Seer, and Mechano talking inside Sentinels Mansion.

They were talking about me. I saw my father, consumed by the fire Iceburn had set.

Finally, I saw Omega Man's smoldering body after he sacrificed himself to destroy the V'Loth queen. The omega symbol emblazoned on his costumed chest rose from his body, white hot, like a phoenix from ashes. It zoomed toward my mind's eye, blotting out everything else with its brightness.

With the omega symbol burning in my mind, Cassandra spoke, answering my question about Mechano.

"Because you are the reincarnation of Omega Man," she said.

15

The cold wind blew in my face as I stood alone on top of the UWant Building. I wore my Kinetic costume and mask. I was supposed to be on patrol. What I was actually doing was being in a funk.

The beauty of nighttime Astor City stretched out below me. The view barely registered. My mind was too busy reeling from what Cassandra had told me yesterday. Since then, I had been in a stupefied haze of shock and disbelief.

You are the reincarnation of Omega Man. Cassandra's words rang in my head like a clarion call.

How could it be true? I did not feel like someone's reincarnation. I just felt like me, the same jumble of doubts and insecurities and uncertainty. I was nothing special. I was just a farm boy from South Carolina. A farm boy with superpowers, sure, but a farm boy nonetheless. Omega Man was the greatest Hero the world had ever known. Omega Man and Theodore Conley did not belong in the same sentence, much less in the same person. Yes, we were both Heroes, but that was where the similarities ended. The fact a mouse and a lion were both animals did not mean they were the same thing.

The whole idea was ludicrous. Cassandra must be wrong. It must be a mistake.

"I don't make mistakes," she had sniffed when I suggested that to her yesterday. After she dropped her Omega Man bombshell, her eyes had immediately turned back to normal, as if a switch had been flipped. I had been abruptly pulled back into reality and out of the image-rich dreamland I had been in. Cassandra was still in my lap, again as big, busty, and young as she had been when I first laid eyes on her. She had no memory of what she had seen and told me during the time her eyes had gone black. She still knew I was a Hero, of course, having gleaned that with her rudimentary telepathic powers before we had even gone downstairs. She said she would not tell anyone. "It's part of the service," she had said when I asked her to keep my secret. She seemed insulted I would even ask.

Regardless of Cassandra's assurances that her powers were never wrong, all day I had tried to convince myself there was a mistake, a glitch in the matrix somewhere. But, despite my efforts to talk myself into believing otherwise, in my heart I knew there was no mistake. The images Cassandra had conjured up in my mind, while bizarre, had been real. I knew in my gut they were. They were what Cassandra had based her answer to my question on. And if those images were real, that meant Cassandra was right about me.

I had not told either Truman or Isaac what Cassandra said. I was too busy processing the shock of it to go around telling people about it. Besides, maybe they would not believe me. I could scarcely believe it myself.

I had gone to Cassandra looking for answers. The answer I got had led to a slew of brand-new questions.

If I really was Omega Man, what did that mean? Urban legend said that Omega Man would return if the Earth faced an existential crisis again. If I was the return of Omega Man, did that mean the Earth was in danger? The world was certainly in a mess. Climate change, pollution of the air and water, Rogues like Puma running amok, people exploiting, subjugating, and killing others because they looked or worshipped differently . . . the list of problems went on and on. However, based on all the history I had studied during my Heroic training, the world did not seem like a bigger mess now than it always had been. Men have always been men, with all the savagery interspersed with moments of brilliance and transcendental beauty that entailed. Evolutionarily speaking, we modern humans were no different than our ancient ancestors. Like Truman had said on the drive to Areola 51, our bodies and minds were Stone Age hardware and software in an Information Age setting. If I, as Omega Man, was supposed to save the planet, what in the world was I supposed to save it from that was new? Reality television?

I had a hard enough time running my own life. Dad was dead because of me. I had completely botched handling Antonio, leading to Hannah's death. If the fate of the world rested on my shoulders, I should get a tombstone and carve on it *Planet Earth: Rest In Peace* right now.

So many unanswered questions. If I was Omega Man, what did Mechano have against him/me? In addition to being the greatest Hero of all time, Omega Man had been one of the founding members of the Sentinels in the 1940s. I would think that Mechano, one of the modern Sentinels, would want to shake the hand of one of the team's founders, not try to kill him.

The biggest unanswered question of them all: If I really was the reincarnation of Omega Man, why me? Why not someone worthier? I was just a guy from the sticks with an unfortunate tendency to screw the pooch. I had gotten Dad and Hannah killed. I had cheated on the Trials. I couldn't even get Neha to love me. If I were to pick someone to be Omega Man, I certainly would not pick me. The Old Man was wise; Athena was a badass; Truman was tough and experienced; Isaac had a heart of gold; and Neha was ruthless. The world was chock-full of better candidates to be Omega Man than I was.

"Why me?" I asked aloud. The gusting wind picked up in intensity, as if in response. Unfortunately for me, I could only break wind. I didn't speak it too.

Add thinking of stupid fart jokes to the list of reasons why me being Omega Man was ridiculous.

I had tried to ask Cassandra all the questions I had about being the reincarnation of Omega Man. She had cut me off.

"I couldn't answer any of your questions even if you owned the UWant Building and signed its deed over to me," she had said. "My powers have strict limits. Think of them as a well that goes dry after you drink from it. No double-dipping. If you want a lap dance, on the other hand, that I can accommodate you with."

I took a pass on the lap dance, of course. Areola 51 had completely turned me off the strip club experience. Besides, what Cassandra had revealed to me had driven women and sex completely out of my mind. That was a feat I would have thought impossible before yesterday. Then again, I would also have thought me being Omega Man was impossible before yesterday. What a difference a single day could make. Who would have guessed that discovering you were a reincarnated version of a Hero who had been dead for over fifty years would turn your libido completely off? I didn't recommend it as a form of birth control. The shock of it was too hard on your heart.

Why me? I thought again.

Why not you? came the immediate response from my subconscious. It sounded like a Jamesism, though I had never heard him say that particular one before. Perhaps it was my own creation. I was channeling Dad more than I was channeling Omega Man. Perhaps Cassandra had gotten her wires crossed and the correct answer scrambled. Maybe that was understandable. Communicating with people in the afterlife had to be the longest possible long-distance call.

I needed answers. Standing on top of this building, brooding, and making unfunny jokes about communicating with the dead were not providing any. The problem was I did not know who had the answers I wanted.

No, that was not right. I knew exactly whom I could ask. What was it Truman had said about Cassandra before we went inside Areola 51? "Short of asking Mechano directly, asking her is the quickest way to find out what Mechano's beef with you is," he had said.

Mechano. I could ask Mechano. At a minimum, he could tell me what he had against Omega Man. The best-case scenario was that he could answer every single one of my questions. If he was not willing to answer my questions voluntarily, I could turn his metallic body into a junk heap until he did. He was long overdue for a good pounding. He had tried to kill me, after all.

I shook my head at my sudden chutzpah. I had let all these months pass being too fearful to confront Mechano directly. Suddenly, after one conversation with a stripper, I was thinking about swaggering into Sentinels Mansion like I owned the place and beating on Mechano like he was a street punk instead of a world-renowned Hero and inventor. What crazy idea would get into my head if I made it a habit to hang out with strippers? I'd challenge Satan to a wrestling match, probably.

The UWant Building's aircraft warning light behind me blinked on and off. It bathed me in red as I thought.

I tried to talk myself out of the birdbrained idea of confronting Mechano. Even if I was Omega Man, that did not mean I was somehow miraculously as powerful as he had been. I had the same power set and power levels today that I had before I even heard of Cassandra. Mechano was still a member of the world's greatest Hero team. I had seen televised footage of him in action. Before I learned he had tried to kill me, watching his exploits had been inspirational. Now, the thought of them was terrifying. Learning I was Omega Man had not deluded me into thinking I could take Mechano on and prevail. Years from now maybe, once my powers reached their full potential and I had more experience. But now? Despite my earlier bravado, Mechano was far more likely to turn me into a junk heap than the other way around.

On the other hand, if it was true that Omega Man would return when the world was at risk again, didn't I have an obligation as a duly sworn licensed Hero to find out as much as I could about the potential threat? I had failed Dad and Hannah already. I had no interest in failing everybody else as well.

Besides, it was not as though I had a better idea. I had obsessed about Mechano for months. After all that thinking about him, it was unlikely I would suddenly have an eureka moment later and come up with a better plan than the one I had now. And even if I somehow came up with the perfect plan in the future, I wanted answers now. If the world really was at risk, perhaps I *needed* them now. What was it General Patton had said? "A good plan, violently executed now, is better than a perfect plan next week."

Then again, Patton was the same guy who slapped a wounded soldier and accused him of cowardice while the soldier was in his hospital bed. Maybe Patton wasn't the best of role models. Maybe the more relevant question was *What would Omega Man do?* WWOMD. It didn't roll off the tongue. I needed to step up my acronym game.

Though I did not know how to create good acronyms about Omega Man, I did know he would not stand up here doing his best indecisive gargoyle impersonation like I was. Based on everything I knew about the man, I knew what he would do.

He would do what he needed to do to get answers.

I rose into the air, off the roof of the UWant Building. I moved quickly, before my quaking insides talked me into changing my mind.

I rocketed off to the north, toward the outskirts of town.

Toward Sentinels Mansion.

16

A short while later, I cautiously slowed to a stop high in the air above the sprawling property just outside of Astor City that contained Sentinels Mansion.

I took stock. Sentinels Way, the road leading to the mansion, was directly below. The face of the mansion was lit up by spotlights so brightly that the four-story white edifice was hard to look at.

Nothing had happened since I entered the mansion's restricted airspace. In continuation of the nothing happening, the grounds in front of the mansion were completely quiet, devoid of all activity. Though the grounds were closed to the public now because it was nighttime and after touring hours, I had expected to see armed guards on patrol. However, the usually ever-present white and blue uniformed guards that made up the Sentinels' security force were nowhere to be seen.

I had a force field up around myself, ready for any and everything. My mind was ready to lash out with my powers at the slightest hint of an attack. All my senses were at high alert. The hair on the back of my neck stood up as I surveyed the complete and unbroken stillness below and around me. Not a creature was stirring, not even a mouse. And it was not even the night before Christmas.

I was wrong before when I thought I was ready for anything. I was not ready for this—the complete absence of anything. The fact that nothing had happened since I entered Sentinels' airspace unnerved me more than if missiles were being lobbed at me. Everyone who knew anything about the Sentinels knew that violation of their property's restricted airspace was usually met with swift and blinding violence. Sentinels Mansion was said to be better defended than any other structure in the country except for the White House, whose defenses had been beefed up to make it perhaps the most secure building in the world after the Rogue Trident assassinated President Greenleaf a few years ago.

The last Rogue who had thought it was a good idea to mount an assault on Sentinels Mansion from the air had gotten a rude awakening. Almost a decade ago, Scimitar had been shot at by gun turrets, surface-to-air missiles, and lasers. Deciding the juice wasn't worth the squeeze, he had retreated to lick his wounds and regrow the hair the lasers had singed off. The Sentinels had released online the footage of Scimitar being repulsed by the mansion's defenses. A video was worth a thousand warnings. No one had dared to fly into the mansion's airspace without permission since then. The Scimitar video was a very violent reminder to everyone that you encroached on the Sentinels' property at your peril. It was rumored that even nuclear weapons protected Sentinels Mansion, but no one outside the Sentinels knew for sure. I always thought those rumors were baloney. Sentinels Mansion was way too close to Astor City for the team to risk setting off a nuclear blast.

None of the property's defenses, nuclear or otherwise,

attacked me. If I had not seen the footage of Scimitar being blasted with my own eyes, I might have thought the reports of the Sentinels' defenses were as much of an urban legend as the nuclear weapons were. No alarms wailed at my presence. No one's voice was raised in alarm. The lack of a response to my presence was unnerving. The only sounds were the insistent chirping of cicadas and the faint hooting of owls from the large forest adjoining the mansion.

I once read that hearing an owl's hoot meant that bad luck and death were ahead. I knew it was just a silly superstition. Nonetheless, a sense of foreboding started in the pit of my stomach and spread through the rest of my body like a fevered chill. Sometimes I wished I had never learned to read.

The woods surrounding the mansion stretched out for miles. The wooded area that composed much of the Sentinels' property was one of the largest urban forests in the country. Thick, tall, black metal fencing enclosed the non-wooded part of the property containing the mansion itself. The fencing stretched between dark granite pillars which were sunk into the ground every thirty feet or so.

A small guardhouse and security checkpoint was next to the fence's only entrance, which was directly across Sentinels Park from the front door of the mansion. As Sentinels Mansion was a major tourist attraction, during the day members of the public waited in line outside the fence's entrance to be cleared by security to tour Sentinels Park and the small portion of the mansion itself which was open to the public. I had stood in that line a few times myself. I had previously visited the mansion in civilian garb in the hopes of learning something that would help me figure out what action to take against Mechano. During the day there would also be protesters picketing and yelling in a designated protest area on the other side of Sentinels Way, just as there had been at Guild headquarters in Washington, D.C. when I had shown up for the Trials. Some people thought Heroes were more public menaces than public protectors. Maybe Mechano had tried to kill them too. We should form a support group.

Behind the mansion was a hidden, underground aircraft hangar. Between the fence around the mansion and the mansion itself was Sentinels Park. Open to the public, the park was a large, immaculately maintained green space. Statues of all the Sentinels, past and present, were positioned throughout the park. Almost all of them were made of marble. The only one that was not was made of bronze and positioned near the front of the mansion. It depicted the six current Sentinels. At the base of the statue were the words of the team's motto: *Those who sow darkness soon shall reap.* The motto was an excerpt from the Hero's Oath, but the general public did not know that. The fact there even was a Hero's Oath was a secret, like a secret handshake between lodge members.

Even from up here, I saw the part of the bronze statue that represented Mechano. His bronze body gleamed in the spotlight shining on the statue. If I were a bird, I would have pooped on it. But I wasn't, so I didn't. I did not want to risk being the Hero caught, with his costume's pants around his ankles, defecating on a statue in Sentinels Park. What a shitty way to become famous.

A massive marble statue of Omega Man loomed up from the middle of the park, dwarfing the rest of the statues. Like the mansion, spotlights lit the gleaming white statue. It was shorter than the four-story mansion, but not by a lot. Omega Man's Metahuman power had been to control gravitons, the particles that comprised gravity. He had been so powerful that people thought he could split the Earth into two had he been so inclined. Fortunately, he never would have done such a thing. His powers were equaled only by his wisdom in using them.

Omega Man's head was positioned so that he looked off into the horizon. As coincidence would have it, I had flown in at an angle so that Omega Man seemed to now be staring directly at me. Watching to see if I screwed up my visit to the Sentinels, no doubt. There was a big omega symbol on the ornate clasp holding his cape together around his neck. Even wrought in marble, Omega Man's cape seemed to billow out behind him heroically. His hair had been so artfully carved that it almost seemed to blow in the breeze. His muscular torso was V-shaped, tapering down to a waist against which his clenched fists were pressed in determination. He had high cheek bones, a dimple in his chin, and a square jaw. If he was not male model handsome, it was a near thing. Even in marble form, Omega Man looked like he was about to spring into action to succor the afflicted and strike a mighty blow against the wicked. I wouldn't be surprised to find a picture of Omega Man if I opened a dictionary and looked up the word "hero." I knew I wouldn't find a picture of me there. I'd already looked.

And I was supposed to be the reincarnation of this guy? Hah! Whoever oversaw reincarnations had neglected to give me Omega Man's good looks and impressive muscles. I wanted to return the product as being defective, but I feared I was twenty years too late for that. Though I was too far away to see it, I knew from prior visits to the mansion that a bronze plaque was next to Omega Man summarizing his accomplishments. I couldn't imagine him becoming me was listed as one of them.

I let out the long breath I had been holding. I was procrastinating, and I knew it. WWOMD? Not hover up here in the air like a confused dragonfly, staring at statuary, thinking about taking a dump on one of them, and letting his imagination run wild with all the terrible things that could possibly happen, that's for sure. And yeah, I definitely needed to come up with a better acronym.

I tried to shake off my fears and foreboding. I descended, landing in the park in front of the mansion. The statue of Omega Man was now at my back. The grass had recently been watered. My boots sank down into the wet ground a tad. A landmine did not explode under me, I was not ensnared in an electrified net, and a bear trap didn't clamp down around my ankle. Something like that would almost be welcome at this point. A threat I could deal with. The complete absence of anything or anyone when I had been all keyed up to deal with the opposite was really freaking me out.

I looked up at the big mansion. A chill ran down my spine. It was part apprehension, part awe at where I stood. Made of white sandstone and featuring soaring columns, turrets, spires, and battlements, Sentinels Mansion looked like the bastard child of an ancient Greek temple and a medieval English castle. Most of the Sentinels lived here, so the sprawling edifice also functioned as a residence.

A large portico extended from the front of the mansion. The stairs to the portico were in front of me. Normally there were guards posted next to the columns supporting the portico's roof. They were nowhere to be seen. Not that I needed it, but the guards' absence was further proof something was amiss. The Sentinels had made a lot of enemies over the years. As far as I knew, the mansion was never left unguarded with the defenses turned off.

Though no one was visible, I could not shake the feeling I was being watched. I felt like a nervous antelope walking in the Serengeti with lions lying in wait in the tall grass. I did not have Spider-Man's Spidey-sense, but that didn't stop me from feeling like I was in danger.

I lifted my hands a little and let out a pulse of my tele-kinetic touch, like the one I had used to locate Cassandra in Areola 51. The pulse confirmed there was no one around outside with me, which made me feel better. My pulse could not penetrate the walls of the mansion though, which made me feel worse. I had no way of knowing if any of the Sentinels were home, much less Mechano. There could be a horde of demon-possessed Rogues waiting for me inside, and I would be none the wiser. I had never encountered something my telekinetic touch could not penetrate. Running across that something the night I decided to confront Mechano did not make me jump for joy.

I climbed up the stairs to the portico. Once on it, I face a stained, dark wooden door that was closed. A doorbell was next to it. This was the main entrance. The entrance people used to tour the part of the mansion that was open to the public was on the east side of the building. I knew from my Sentinels research that normally the only way a non-Sentinel was allowed through this main entrance was if he was expected, if he had already passed a security clearance, and if a retinal and handprint scan confirmed his identity.

I had come too far to be thwarted by a closed door. I was thinking about how much trouble I would get into by forcing my way in when something strange happened:

The front door swung open silently. Quiet darkness lay within.

Yeah, this wasn't at all creepy.

It's a trap! exclaimed Admiral Ackbar's voice in my head from *Return of the Jedi*. If this were a movie, this was the part where the audience would yell at the screen, warning me to not go inside. In the movies, a guy walking into a dark, seem-ingly abandoned house in the middle of the night after its door magically opened to him *never* ended well. I kinda wished Isaac were with me. In the movies, when creepy stuff went down, the black guy always got the shaft first. It would give my cowardly white ass a chance to get away.

Though I knew it was just my nerves talking, I still felt shame at my throw Isaac under the bus thought. Besides, this wasn't a movie, *Star Wars* or otherwise. I've always been more of a *Star Trek* fan, anyway.

What was there to be afraid off? I was a Hero. History had shown I could handle myself. I wasn't scared.

My insides quivered. My instincts shrieked at me to turn around and fly far, far away.

Okay, maybe I was a little scared.

What would Omega Man do? Not fear his own shadow, that's for sure.

I screwed my courage to the sticking place, as the Bard would say. I stood up straight and squared my shoulders. I took a deep breath and puffed my chest out. What was there to be worried about? I was an Omega-level Metahuman, and the reincarnation of Omega Man to boot. I was the very model of a modern licensed Hero.

First Shakespeare, now Gilbert and Sullivan. Apparently, my brain took solace in the classics when I was nervous.

I was procrastinating again.

Trying to channel my inner Omega Man, I strode through the open door. It closed behind me with an ominous click. I was engulfed in darkness as if I had been swallowed by a whale.

17

It was quiet inside of Sentinels Mansion. It smelled the way some old people's houses did, of antique furniture, moldering books, and being closed for too long. It took my eyes a few moments to adjust from the spotlight-illuminated brightness of the outside.

Once they did, I realized my surroundings were not as dark as I had first supposed. There was an orb about four feet in front of me, hovering slightly off the ground like a balloon which had lost most of its helium. The orb was a tad smaller than my fist. It glowed very faintly, like a firefly's bioluminescence. It dimly illuminated the foyer I was in.

I was immediately suspicious of it. A glowing ball had exploded in my face after that foiled bank robbery in D.C. Another had exploded during my third Trials' test and would have killed me had I not absorbed and redirected the energy from the explosion. Fool me once with an exploding ball, shame on you; fool me three times with an exploding ball, shame on me.

With my personal shield up to protect me if the past was prologue, I poked tentatively at the glowing orb with my telekinetic touch. Fortunately, whatever had prevented me from scanning the interior of the mansion from outside of it did not seem to affect my powers here. I halfway expected the orb to explode as soon as my telekinetic touch contacted it. Instead, nothing happened. Though my telekinesis was operating normally, my telekinetic touch passed right through the orb like there was nothing there. There was no resistance to my touch, no pushback, no movement of the orb, no anything. It was as if I probed thin air. Thin air did not glow like this, though. I had never seen anything like it.

Encouraged that my powers were behaving normally again, I tried to use them to probe beyond this room and further into the mansion. I could not reach beyond this room, though. Maybe there was something built into the walls of the mansion that blocked my powers.

Still wary of the glowing orb despite its seeming insubstantiality, I used its light to look around. The parquet floor of the foyer I was in gleamed with polish even in the dim lighting. Straight ahead, on the other side of the glowing ball, was an open doorway. There was an old-fashioned wooden hat rack in the corner by the door I had just passed through. It was the only piece of furniture in the room.

Some instinct made me try the door which had closed behind me. Though the knob twisted in my hand, I could not open it. I braced myself and really put my back into it. The door did not budge so much as a millimeter. I stopped straining at it before I pulled a muscle. Maybe Avatar and his super strength could have forced the door open again, but I could not seem to. I tried to latch onto the door with my powers and open it. I was as unable to grab onto it with my powers as I had been unable to probe beyond the walls of this room.

Clearly, someone had wanted me to come inside, but they

were not eager to have me leave. Though I did not plan on leaving before finding out if Mechano was here, I did not like the fact I could not simply walk back out if I wanted to.

Feeling a little like a mouse in a trap, I turned away from the sealed door. Several framed pictures hung in two vertical columns on either side of the open doorway ahead of me. I stepped forward to get a better look at them. The glowing orb moved as well, staying the same distance from me it had started off at. I froze as soon as the orb moved. I thought my skittishness was understandable. Again, my experiences with strange glowing objects had not been particularly positive.

The orb did not move again until I stepped toward the open doorway once more. It stopped again when I stopped. *Hmmm, interesting.* I did a little experimenting. I stepped to the side. The light did not move. I stepped backward, toward the closed front door. No movement. When I stepped toward the open doorway again, the light started moving as soon as I was about four feet away from it.

"What, am I supposed to follow you?" My voice sounded like a shout in the quiet of the mansion.

There was no answer. Not that I expected one. I was, after all, talking to a glowing ball. What did it say about how weird tonight was that trying to converse with a glowing ball was not the strangest part of it?

If I tried to search this massive place on my own without the benefit of my powers, it would take forever. If somebody had sent this ball to guide me somewhere, maybe I should let it in the interest of saving time. I would keep my shield up and my wits about me, though. The lack of guards, the property's defenses being down, the door opening to admit me but refusing to let me out, the haunted house feel of the mansion, an orb that was invisible to my powers leading me down a potential rabbit hole . . . everything about tonight gave me the heebie-jeebies.

"Lead on, MacDuff," I said to the ball. It glided away from me as I walked toward it and the open doorway. I hoped the ball appreciated my Shakespearean erudition. If it did, it gave no sign.

I paused before passing through the doorway to check out the pictures mounted on either side of it. They were group shots of each Sentinels' team from the group's founding in the 1940s until now. Each one contained Millennium, the only current Sentinel who had also been one of the team's founders. Each picture except the last contained seven Heroes. Since Omega Man, Lady Justice, Avatar, Millennium, and three other Heroes had founded the team, thereafter it was Sentinels' tradition that seven Heroes were on the team. From time to time there would be vacancies due to death, retirement and, in one infamous incident years ago Truman had been involved in, arrest and imprisonment, but the team always brought its members back up to seven as soon as it could find an appropriate Hero to fill the vacancy.

Except, that is, in the case of Avatar. His empty spot on the team had not been filled after his murder. That was why the last picture of the Sentinels contained six Heroes rather than the traditional seven. Seer, who had taken over as chairman of the team after Avatar died, once said at a press conference that Avatar's spot would remain vacant until the team found a Hero worthy of taking his place. *Good luck with that*, I thought as I looked at the six-member picture, the only one Avatar was not in. Avatar had been an Omega-level Hero with the strength of a god and the morals of a monk. Replacing him was not a simple matter of picking a new one out at Heroes R Us.

In these pictures of the Sentinels, there were no cheesy

grins like there often were in group portraits. Each Hero captured in these pictures looked as serious as a heart attack. I guess world-saving was grim work.

The glowing orb waited patiently for me in the next room. It started moving again once I stepped through the doorway toward it. I kept walking, following the ball's glowing guidance. Anytime I did not go where the ball apparently wanted me to go, it froze in place until I started walking in the right direction again.

With the ball as my guide and only source of illumination, I made my way deeper into the dark mansion, twisting and turning through a multitude of rooms. Though I could see but faintly, the rooms I passed through seemed like they belonged in a castle a couple of centuries ago, not in the headquarters of a modern Hero team. They were full of heavy furniture, tapestries, old-fashioned weapons, relics, and antiques, each one labelled. Before long, I had lost all sense of direction. It was like wandering through a building that was part maze, part museum, and part haunted house full of shadowy objects. I doubted I could make my way back to the front entrance without help. It was a shame I had not thought to unwind a ball of string behind me à la Theseus. I hoped the glowing orb was not taking me to see the Minotaur. Isaac had turned into the Minotaur during our battle in the Trials. It had been terrifying. I had no interest in tangling with the creature again.

Though I did not see the Minotaur, I saw things equally fantastic as the ball led me through the bowels of the mansion. I hardly believed some of them were real. In one huge room we passed through, I made out the dim outlines of a twin-engine, metal monoplane suspended overhead. A metal plaque on a pedestal under it read *Lockheed Model 10 Electra, "The Flying Laboratory," piloted by Amelia Earhart when she disappeared in 1937.* I had always heard that neither Earhart nor her plane had ever been recovered.

In another room, above a thick mantelpiece, hung a painting I recognized. It was Vincent Van Gogh's masterpiece *The Starry Night.* The painting was supposed to be in the collection of the Museum of Modern Art in New York City. I had seen it there when Isaac, Neha and I had taken a trip to New York back when we were the Old Man's Apprentices. Maybe the painting and Earhart's plane were mere replicas. I had a feeling they were not.

Though many of the things I saw made my eyes wide with wonder, two things in particular made my heart skip a beat. They were both in a large room full of animal trophies. Some of the trophies were stuffed, others were merely skeletons. The room was like a miniature museum of natural history. There was nothing as common as elephants and pigs in here, though. At the far end of the room was a Triceratops, which somehow managed to looked fearsome even in its skeletal form. Around the perimeter of the room was a snake's skeleton. Well, it would be a snake's skeleton if a snake was the size of a row of subway cars.

There were even live animals. In a large cage were perhaps a dozen birds, though it was hard to count them since they flapped around so much. Each over a foot long, the birds flew wildly around inside their cage. It was hard to make out their exact coloration between the dim light and their rapid movements. They made loud, harsh sounds that set my teeth on edge. If they were supposed to be songbirds, they were tone-deaf.

Passenger Pigeons (Ectopistes Migratorius): Extinct, read the plaque next to the cage. The birds were once so plentiful in North America that their annual migration blotted out the sun. Thanks to over-hunting and the destruction of their habitats, they had gone extinct in the early 1900s. At least they were supposed to be extinct. It said so right here on the plaque. If these raucous birds knew they were extinct, they gave no sign of it. Maybe they couldn't read. I could only hope to be as sprightly as these birds when I was dead.

The two things that made my heart stop were near the exit to the huge animal room. I froze when I saw them, as of course did the ball I had followed.

Mounted high up on the wall was an animal head. It was not a tiger, but could have been a modern tiger's great-great-great-great granddaddy. Its fur was brown with streaks of red, orange, and gold. Its eyes seemed almost alive. They looked down at me hungrily, glittering in the light emitted by the still orb. The way it seemed to look at me, it was as though raw Theo with a side of Kinetic was its favorite food. It had two unbelievably long fangs poking down from its upper jaw. Rows of razor-sharp incisors completed the killing machine that was the animal's mouth. Even dead and decapitated, the animal was so scary, it made my butt cheeks clench. I had to smother the irrational impulse to run.

Saber-Toothed Tiger (Smilodon Fatalis): Extinct. Captured in North America by Millennium during the Pleistocene Epoch, read the plaque under the animal's head. The fact the head was from a saber-toothed tiger was pretty obvious from the animal's appearance, particularly the two huge fangs. This certainly wasn't Sylvester the Cat.

The taxidermied animal to the right of the saber-toothed tiger made my heart palpitate even more than the tiger had. Though clearly in the bear family, it was unlike any bear I had ever seen. For one thing, it was massive, much bigger than the black bears I had seen on the farm or the grizzly bears I had seen in zoos. Even if I discounted the short platform the animal was mounted on, the animal on all fours was still taller than I and had a broad, well-muscled body. If it stood on its hind legs, it would be nearly ten feet tall. Its snout was much shorter than the usual bear's. It was as if someone had taken a grizzly's snout and mashed it down into its skull, like a push switch depressed in the "on" position. The animal's shaggy coat was black with flecks of brown. The lips of its snout were curled in a snarl, exposing teeth clearly designed by Mother Nature to break bones and rip flesh.

Short-faced Bear (Arctodus simus): Extinct. Captured in the area that would become California by Millennium during the Pleistocene Epoch, read the plaque fixed to the platform the bear stood on. I understood why honey companies put their product into cute bear bottles instead of bottles shaped like this monster. If they did, people would be too scared to buy it.

What the plaques for the tiger and the bear said about them being captured during the Pleistocene Epoch was what had gotten me so excited about seeing the animals. I was hardly a paleontologist, but I had learned enough about Earth's history during my training to know that the Pleistocene Epoch ended over ten thousand years ago. How had two animals which had gone extinct thousands of years ago been captured by Millennium and then stuffed and mounted? The implication was obvious. Millennium, an Omega-level Hero whose powers were said to be magic-based, must be capable of time travel.

Maybe Millennium could send me back in time to correct the mistakes I had made. I could save Hannah's life. I could prevent Iceburn from killing Dad. I could make sure Hammer wasn't killed by those robots during the Trials. Maybe I could even stop Mom from dying of brain cancer, though that was a tougher nut to crack. Unlike the bastards who had killed Hannah and Dad, you could not stop cancer by punching it in the face. In Mom's case, maybe I could travel to the future first to see if they had found a cancer cure. With the way medicine advanced by leaps and bounds these days, surely scientists finding a cure was just a matter of time. Once I got the cure from the future, I could then go back into the past and save Mom.

Though I had of course come here to confront Mechano, I was now excited about the prospect of perhaps meeting Millennium as well. He had been a Sentinel longer than anyone else. Helping people was his business. Surely he would help me.

With thoughts of time travel swirling in my head, I glanced at the glowing orb. It seemed to wait patiently for me. It was time to move on. I would not meet Millennium or Mechano standing here staring at extinct animals. I wondered if I would spot lions somewhere in the mansion too. Lions and tigers and bears. I had my "Oh my!" all ready.

I again stepped toward the orb. It resumed its journey to lead me through the house. Though I saw more things that blew my mind, nothing else inflamed my imagination the way seeing the tiger and the bear had. Maybe the past was not written in stone. Maybe it was written on an Etch A Sketch—one good shake and everything could be different. Better.

Eventually, the orb led me to a shiny silver door. It was closed, with a shoulder-high metal and glass scanner on the right of it. The orb floated right through the silver door as if it did not exist, and disappeared. I couldn't follow. The ability to phase through doors was not in my power set.

I need not have worried. When I approached the door, it slid open noiselessly. Bright lights spilled out of the other side. I stepped through the open doorway. I stopped, unable to see. I blinked away the sudden brightness.

My eyes adjusted. Whereas the rest of the house looked like the set from a British period piece, this enormous room looked like the bridge of a starship. It was as if I had stepped out of the eighteenth century into the twenty-fourth. Everything was bright, shiny, glassy or metallic, and high-tech.

"Welcome to Sentinels Mansion, Mr. Conley," came a booming masculine voice. I almost jumped out of my skin, both at the unexpected sound and the use of my supposedly secret identity.

My head snapped toward the voice. Mechano's big robot body sat at a large transparent table in the middle of the huge room. Seer and Millennium sat with him. All three Heroes looked at me. As none of them looked quite human, it was like being stared at by aliens. Since all three were living legends, it was intimidating to say the least.

"We have been expecting you," Mechano said.

18

"We have much to discuss, Mr. Conley. Please come have a seat," Mechano said. His voice emanated from a circular, gold-colored metal grate located on his robot head where a human's mouth would be. I presumed the grate covered a speaker.

Fear clawed its way from the pit of my stomach up to the top of my throat as the three Heroes stared at me. Being afraid of Mechano was understandable. He had tried to kill me, after all. One shouldn't run up to one's attempted murderer to give him a hug and a kiss. Not unless one wanted one's ability to hug and kiss in the future to come to an abrupt and permanent end. Being afraid of Millennium and Seer seemed irrational, though. They were respected Heroes. I had admired them and the rest of the Sentinels for years. They helped people, not hurt them. Besides, after discovering the saber-toothed tiger and the short-faced bear, I should have been particularly delighted to see Millennium and have the chance to talk to him about time travel.

Why then did my gut shriek at me to get the hell out of

here without bothering to say "goodbye, nice to meet you, I'm a big fan" first?

Your gut is the voice of your subconscious mind, the Old Man used to say. *Ignore it at your peril.*

This would not be the first time I didn't listen to him or my gut. Despite wanting to, I was not going to flee. I had come here for answers, not to cut and run the moment someone looked at me hard. I did not sit as Mechano asked, though. Considering his past attempts on my life, I had no interest in getting within easy throttling range of his robot body.

"How do you know my name?" I demanded instead of beating a hasty retreat. First Truman, then Cassandra, now these three Sentinels. At the rate people were learning my secret identity, I should've saved everyone time and trouble and put it on a billboard in big bright letters. As I spoke, the glowing orb which had led me here floated over to Millennium. It disappeared inside his body like a raindrop hitting a pond.

"We know just about everything there is to know about you. We have been closely monitoring you with great interest for quite some time," Mechano said.

Oh no, that doesn't sound at all stalkerish, I thought, though I kept the sentiment to myself.

Now that I was recovering from the shock of being in the presence of these three Heroes, I could hear that Mechano's deep masculine voice had a slightly artificial quality to it, like it was computer generated. As I supposed it was. He said, "Even if I did not already know who you are behind the mask, the feature-camouflaging technology it contains is based on my patents. I can see through it to the real you as easily as looking through a clear window. I could then run your face through my facial recognition software and come up with your real name faster than the time it takes to tell you about it."

"Brag about what you're capable of later," Seer said impatiently. Her clear, strong voice was in stark contrast to her almost frail appearance. "We'll be here all night if you don't cut to the chase."

While the two bickered like an unhappily married couple, I scrutinized all three of them. It was not every day I was face to face with famous people I had watched on television and read about for years.

Seer was not wearing a mask. She never did. Her white skin was pale and tinted slightly blue, like that of a drowning victim. Her long, straight hair was albino white and pulled back into a ponytail. Her face was completely unwrinkled. It made her look both very young and timeless, though I knew she was middle-aged. Her pupils and irises were creamy white. Looking into her eyes was like looking into pools of milk. She wore a robe-like garment that shimmered iridescently, like a soap bubble catching the light. It was partially translucent, giving tantalizing near glimpses of her naked alabaster body underneath. Her figure was willowy, suggestive of a tall adolescent girl whose body had not filled out yet.

Like me, Seer was telekinetic. I had seen footage of her picking up and throwing a jumbo jet with her powers like it was a dart. As I was Omega-level, my telekinesis had the capacity to be far more powerful than hers, but it was not there yet as I did not have the lifetime of developing and strengthening my powers that she had.

In addition to her telekinesis, Seer also had precognitive abilities. Her ability to look into the future was said to be like the vision of a near-sighted person: If someone with near-sightedness looked at a car dozens of yards away, the car would be nothing more than a blur. He would be able to tell it was a car, but wouldn't be able to make out the details of it. If he walked closer to the car, though, he would see the car more and more clearly until it became crystal clear when he was right on top of it. The same was true of Seer's precognition: events in the distant future were hazy, ill-defined, and could change. But as time passed and those events came closer to happening, Seer could see them more and more clearly. I had seen footage of battles where Seer had stepped out of the way of a Rogue's attack with unerring accuracy, seeing the attack coming before it had even been launched.

Millennium was so slim he was almost skinny, though there was something about his presence which made him seem large and imposing. He wore a light brown, shiny metal helmet with a flat top. It reminded me of an upended bucket. Its surface was an unbroken smoothness except for tiny slits for his eyes. There were no openings for his nose or mouth. I could not see his eyes behind his eye slits, only darkness. Looking into his eye slits, even from this distance, was like peering into a bottomless well. It gave me the creeps. He wore gauntlets, cavalier boots, a belt, and a floor-length cape that all matched the brown color of his helmet. The loose tunic and leggings that covered the rest of him were royal blue.

The press often called Millennium the Thousand Year Man. Legend had it that his body was frozen in time, unable to age or change, until he lived a thousand years, at which point he would die. I did not know if that was true, but it certainly was true that Millennium had an exceptionally long lifespan. He was one of the Sentinels' founders after all, and he was still on the team over half a century later. Other than me, Millennium was the sole living Omega-level Hero, and one of only four Omega-level Metas in the world. The other two were Chaos, the Rogue serving multiple life sentences in MetaHold, and Lim Qiaolian, a telepath and super-genius in China who put herself into a self-induced trance when she was five-years-old over seventy years ago. God only knew what she had been thinking about all this time. Maybe she was busy unraveling the secrets of the universe. Maybe she was trying to puzzle out why some people were foolish enough to worship her as a god. Or, maybe she was trying to remember where she had hidden her candy from her brother. If she wound up going through some of the hair-raising stuff I had been through as an Omega-level Meta, for her sake I hoped she never woke.

Millennium's powers were the least understood of the Sentinels, at least by the public. They were said to be magic-based, with his Metahuman ability allowing him to tap into the mystical plane. I would have scoffed at talk of magic and mystical planes before my powers developed. Since then, I've seen too much to not keep my skeptical mouth shut about what was possible and impossible. Regardless of exactly how they worked, like me, Millennium channeled his powers through his hands. And there was no doubt they were formidable. He could teleport halfway across the planet in one moment, and reduce a skyscraper to rubble the next.

Mechano's long, thin, single rectangular eye glowed at me disconcertingly. It was like being stared at by a mechanical cyclops. It was worse, actually, as no cyclops I had ever heard of had the ability to blast you into smithereens with its eye the way Mechano did. Maybe he stared at me like this because he was scanning me with his x-ray vision. I hoped I was wearing clean underwear. It would be hard to seem intimidating to Mechano if I was confronting him with pee-pee stains in the front and skid marks in the back.

Though I knew Mechano's burnished silver body was about seven feet tall, he seemed taller than that, even seated. Though his mechanical muscles were obviously merely for show, he looked like the beefiest of Mr. Olympia competitors painted silver. His head was earless and hairless. His cranium was shaped like a billiard ball with the top loped off, leaving a flat plane at the apex. He had no nose or mouth, with three small holes in the place of the former and a circular gold-colored metal grate in the place of the latter.

The large transparent table the three Sentinels sat at was heptagonally shaped, with tall silver-colored chairs positioned at each of the seven sides. A large golden "S" was stenciled into the middle of the table. The table made me realize where I was. I was in the Sentinels' Situation Room, the fabled room where the team held formal meetings and monitored what was going on in the world, looking for issues the Sentinels needed to deal with. Despite my fear, I felt a surge of awe and wonder. As a longtime Hero fanboy, being here was like a *Star Trek* junkie being transported to the bridge of the starship Enterprise.

On the back and front of each chair around the table was a symbol representing the Sentinel the seat was reserved for: a black and white amorphous pattern that looked like a Rorschach test for Doppelganger; a katana glowing red for Ninja; a metallic blue clenched fist for Tank; and a blood red capital A for Avatar. A black sash ran diagonally around Avatar's chair, presumably to signify and honor his death. Though I could not see the emblems for Seer, Millennium, and Mechano as the Heroes' seated bodies obscured them, I knew they consisted of a wide-open eye with energy rays shooting from its perimeter for Seer, an hourglass with most of its sand in the top hemisphere for Millennium, and a large metal nut with a yellow lightning bolt passing through it for Mechano.

On the other side of the table, against the far wall, was a massive bank of dozens of large video monitors. They flick-ered with various images. Stacked on top of one another to form a semi-circle, the monitors rose from a futuristic-looking, waist-high control panel all the way up to the top of the room's high ceiling. You had to crane your neck to see what was on the monitors at the very top. From the control panel extended a mass of thick metal cables that were silver in color. The ends of the cables tapered down to connect to a silver helmet which rested on top of the big chair in front of the control panel.

I recognized the bank of monitors as well from my research on the Sentinels. Known collectively as Sentry—yet another of Mechano's inventions—the monitors drew from satellite imagery and security feeds from around the globe to keep the Sentinels aware of threats, Rogue-related or otherwise, the Sentinels might need to deal with. The silver helmet resting in the chair fed data from Sentry directly into its wearer's brain. A Sentinel was supposed to be on Sentry duty almost all the time. The fact the three Sentinels sat at the table looking at me rather than one of them wearing the Sentry helmet was further proof something I did not understand was afoot. As if me being allowed to stroll unimpeded into one of the most secure rooms in the world in one of the most secure buildings in the world wasn't proof enough of that.

While keeping a cautious eye on the seated Heroes, I checked out some of the images on the monitors. Some of them were of high-security and high-risk areas I would expect to see under surveillance: the grounds of the White House; the Guild space station; MetaHold on Ellis Island; the supervillain Puma's palace in Lima; the temple that had been constructed around Lim Qiaolian's small comatose body; a mass protest outside the Kremlin; and a riot in Monrovia, Liberia led by a masked black man the size of a small house. Other footage was more surprising and made me wonder how in the world the Sentinels had gotten it.

On one monitor was an orgy. The participants were several

male United States Senators from both political parties and a roomful of girls. None of the Senators were in particularly good shape, which made the footage hard to watch. The fact none of the girls looked older than sixteen made watching it harder still. On another monitor was the mayor of Astor City, sitting back in a leather recliner. His eyes were open, and partially rolled back in his head. His sleeve was rolled up, and a needle was impaled high up on his forearm. I doubted the needle contained civic pride.

As shocking as those and other images were, two others chilled me to my marrow. At about eye level was a monitor showing the nighttime exterior of my house on Williams Place. The way the camera that recorded the image was angled, no one could come or go unnoticed. Isaac's second floor bedroom faced the street. His room's lights leaked out around the window's blinds, indicating he was still up despite the late hour. I wondered where the camera was located. Discreetly mounted on top of a nearby power line, maybe.

The second disturbing image was on the monitor next to the one showing my house. It was of a glitzy nightclub packed with drinkers and dancers. Neha stood next to the dance floor. My heart fluttered as I looked at her. This was the first time I had laid eyes on her since the night I told her I was in love with her.

Neha wore the Smoke costume the Old Man had given her, the form-fitting gray and white one with the shifting curls of smoke on it. Even at a time like this, I couldn't help but admire how great Neha looked in her tight costume. Twenty-one years old, she had the build of a dancer, toned yet feminine. I missed touching her. My sudden yearning for her was as strong as the jonesing of a cokehead for a hit. Her costume's cowl covered her whole face except her mouth, eyes, and nostrils. As Neha was of Indian descent, her skin was olive-colored.

The clubgoers were apparently too cool to make a big deal about the fact there was a costumed Hero in their midst, but they still gave Neha a wide berth. Despite their surface nonchalance, you could tell many of them checked her out from the corner of their eyes.

Neha watched her employer Willow Wilde, the reality television star, dance with three men. Neha was obviously still on the clock as Willow's head of security. The men Willow danced with were dressed like they had just left a GQ photo shoot. They were so handsome, they made me look like a turd with eyes. I felt a hot stab of jealousy at the thought these were the types of men Neha was around these days.

Willow's dress—what there was of it—was so tight it was a wonder she could walk, much less dance. Her artificially large gyrating butt looked like two alley cats fighting to get free of the bag they'd been stuffed in. I wondered what Willow would do for a living once she got a little older and her looks and popularity faded. Pop out a few kids, make them get plastic surgery, and continue the Wilde get rich from doing nothing dynasty, probably.

It was impossible for me to tell from this raw footage where Willow and Neha were. Astor City, New York, Los Angeles, Paris, Rome, Moscow . . . any major city would have clubs like this one with the sort of clientele this one did. Besides, Willow was an international superstar who didn't let moss grow under her feet; she would be welcomed as a celebrity wherever she went. Neha's arms were crossed as she watched Willow. She somehow looked simultaneously bored and alert to any threats. A woman as rich and famous as Willow attracted a lot of attention, often of the unsavory kind. I knew Neha well enough to read more into the expression on her face than mere boredom and alertness, though. There was contempt for Willow and the other clubbers carefully hidden in her expression which seemed to say, "If I slit my wrists right now, how long would it take me to bleed out and be done with this frivolous nonsense?" I wondered if she regretted taking the job with Willow. Maybe if I'd read her emails and texts or listened to the voicemails she had sent me since I'd moved to Astor City instead of ignoring them all, I would know.

I was not so naive as to think Sentry showing images of my friends at my eye level was coincidence. The Sentinels were sending me a message as clear as it would be if they had written it out: We know who your friends are, and we know where they are. If it wasn't an unspoken threat, I didn't know what was. But to what end?

"Please, come closer," Mechano said, his voice jarring my reeling mind. "Join us. I promise we will not bite." His tone was a combination of patronizing and amused. Though I knew Mechano was the consciousness of a man in robot form, it was still weird to hear him use an idiom like "we will not bite." It seemed more natural for a robot to say something, well, robotic.

I walked closer to the three. Not because Mechano asked me to, but to keep from having to shout in the huge room. I stopped short of the table.

Mechano said, "Please do have a seat. You can sit in Avatar's chair. It is really quite an honor, being asked to sit in the chair of one of the greatest Heroes the world has ever known. You would be only the second person to sit in his chair since his unfortunate demise."

'Will you walk into my parlor?' said the spider to the fly, I thought. "I'm good right here," I said.

"Come now. You are too young to be so suspicious." My face must have betrayed my wariness. Unlike mine, Mechano's metal face was immobile and didn't display emotions. His face was as animated as a mannequin's. His voice sounded amused though, as if he spoke to a child who had done something funny. "We mean you no harm, Theo. May I call you Theo?"

"No. My friends call me Theo. Someone who has tried to kill me and is spying on my real friends is not my friend."

Mechano barked out a laugh. Its slightly artificial quality made it seem mocking. His head swiveled toward Seer. "So full of single-minded devotion and righteous indignation. Ah, to be young again." The fact he didn't deny to his teammates that he had tried to kill me wasn't lost on me. Were all the Sentinels in on the attempts on my life, or just these three? And why?

"As old as you are, you'd think you'd have fallen out of love with the sound of your own voice by now," Seer said to Mechano. I got the impression there wasn't any love lost between the two. "Let's get down to business. We have many other matters to attend to."

"The fact I am as old as I am is why I have learned to enjoy the simple pleasures of life when they are presented to me," Mechano said. His head silently swiveled back to me. "In any event, despite her unseemly impatience, Seer is quite right. Let us get down to brass tacks. We let you in here unmolested because we understand you have questions. We have answers. You say we are not your friends, but we want to be. Friends should not have secrets from one another. So shoot. We will tell you any and everything you want to know."

Why beat around the bush? "Did you try to kill me during my Trials by programming nanites to attack me?"

"Of course I did. But you already knew that thanks to your friend Hacker," Mechano said. "Oh, do not look so surprised I know she hacked into Overlord. Actually, on the surface, you do not look particularly surprised. You have a decent poker face for one so young. My systems let me see past your deadpan expression, though. When I mentioned Hacker, I heard your heart rate increase, my infrared vision noted the increased blood flow to your face, and your perspiration rate jumped. All clear indications of surprise. But I digress. I was talking about Hacker. Overlord is my creation. Did you really think someone could force her way into it without me knowing about it? Hacker's power and talents are impressive, but not as impressive as mine. To analogize to the Christian mythology you were raised to believe in, it would be like Jehovah not knowing Eve had taken a bite of the fruit of the tree of knowledge." I wished God would smite Mechano for calling Christianity mythology. If He was too busy to do it, I would happily try my hand at it instead.

I tried to smother my anger. Though Mechano was of course right that I already knew about the nanites, hearing him admit it without a trace of shame, proudly even, made me want to dismantle him piece by piece. Maybe later.

"And did you also plant the bomb in the baby stroller in the holographic mall during the Trials?" I demanded.

"Me personally? No. I was here in the mansion at the time. However, the bomb was my design. And, I circumvented Overlord's security protocols to permit the bomb to be placed in the mall without alerting the Trials' proctors."

My fists balled up in anger. "You could have killed dozens of people."

"Could have. Did not. Thanks to you. Well done, by the way."

I was as interested in Mechano's compliments as I was in eating a plate of puke. The casualness with which he dismissed endangering others' lives infuriated me. And this sociopath was a Hero? "Who planted the bomb, then?"

"Brown Recluse." Brown Recluse was a Trials' proctor, one

I had liked. I'd have to drop him from my Christmas card list and add him to my enemies' list. "I paid him quite handsomely to do it," Mechano said. "Not directly, of course. It would never do for him to know of my involvement. A man as profligate in his personal life as he is cannot be trusted to keep a secret. The payment to Brown Recluse and the delivery of the bomb to him was through a discreet third party, one of the non-Metas I sometimes use to handle unpleasant tasks. It had come to my attention some time ago that Brown Recluse is an inveterate gambler. Since he is as unsuccessful at it as he is dedicated to it, he had accumulated substantial debts to some unforgiving and unsavory people who do not accept excuses as a form of payment. They are so unsavory that Brown Recluse had grown quite alarmed over what they might do to him even though he is a Hero. The money I offered him in exchange for sneaking the bomb into the Trials gave him the financial lifeline he was so desperate for. Let his example be a lesson to you, Mr. Conley: if you insist on playing poker, it really does not pay to draw to inside straights. You would think a Hero like Brown Recluse would have a better grasp of finite math and probabilities." Mechano sighed, which was a bizarre sound coming from a robot. "Addiction really does defy common sense and reasoning. How such an undisciplined man lacking in self-control ever became a Hero is beyond me."

"You're hardly one to judge someone's worthiness to be a Hero." I was in disbelief over how blasé he was about trying to assassinate me. "You're an admitted attempted murderer."

"Yes, but in the pursuit of the greater good. After all, my attempts on your life have resulted in you coming here."

"So you trying to kill me was what? An invitation to come visit? You could have sent me an Evite instead."

The smug sonofabitch had the nerve to laugh. The slightly inhuman sound was worse than nails on a blackboard.

"Your sense of humor is perhaps what I like the most about you. No, the nanites and the bomb were not an invitation. They were a test of your worthiness."

"Worthiness for what? To get my Hero's license? Aren't the Trials enough to do that without you sticking your nose in?"

"No, not of your worthiness to become a Hero. As you say, the Trials do an adequate job of that. Of your worthiness to be a vessel for the spirit of Omega Man."

The Situation Room was quiet for a few beats as the Sentinels and I looked at each other silently.

"Based on our young friend's steady vital signs, he already knew that," Mechano said to Seer, breaking the silence. "He really is full of surprises. How did you find out?" he asked me.

"A little birdie told me," I said. I wasn't about to volunteer information to someone who had tried to kill me. If knowledge was power, it would be like handing more bullets to a sniper so he could shoot at me more. Clearly the Sentinels did not know I had consulted with Cassandra. Maybe they also didn't know I had hired Truman. It was good to see they didn't know everything. With the reputation and history the Sentinels had, it was all too easy to forget I faced men and women, not all-knowing gods. "Why do you care if I'm worthy to carry around the spirit of Omega Man? What business is it of yours?"

"Because protecting the world is our business, Mr. Conley," Seer said. "Omega Man is the key to that. There is a legend about how Omega Man will return to protect the world when it faces an existential threat. Have you heard of it?"

"I have."

"Like most legends, it is not entirely true, though there is a nugget of truth at the heart of it," Seer said. "Omega Man does not need to return because he never died. Yes, his body was destroyed in his successful attack on the V'Loths decades ago. His spirit lives on, though. The Omega spirit was born with mankind, and will exist as long as he does. The Omega spirit walked the Earth amidst the earliest humans, and it will be here after we're all dead and gone."

"Speak for yourself," Mechano interjected. "I will still be here, hale and hearty in another state-of-the-art robot body, centuries after you three are worm food."

Seer ignored Mechano as if he hadn't spoken. Yeah, there definitely was no love lost between the two. Maybe he had tried to kill her at some point too. As for Millennium, he had not said a word since I entered the Situation Room. If it was true he operated on mystical planes, perhaps a hellcat had gotten his tongue.

Seer continued by saying, "The Omega spirit will live on as long as humanity does, trying to protect it and the world he inhabits from harm. It moves from host to host, finding a new host to inhabit when its old one dies. Only it knows for certain exactly how it chooses the people it uses as hosts. But, I can say that it has inhabited some of the most consequential men and women the world has ever known, helping them to avert threats to humanity. King Arthur, Gilgamesh, Lady Mu Guiying, Hercules, Sampson, Joan of Arc, Rama, Beowulf . . . these are but a handful of the men and women through the course of mankind's existence, both famous and lost to history, the Omega spirit has inhabited."

"King Arthur? Hercules?" I scoffed. "Myths and legends. Many of the people you named aren't even real."

Mechano laughed his harsh tinny laugh. "You can lift a boulder without touching it and fly faster than the fastest projectile. You even have a friend named Myth who can turn into dragons and other mythical creatures. Do you realize the irony of you of all people being so dismissive of myths, legends, and extraordinary deeds and people? Many ancient myths are grounded in actual people who possessed powers beyond the ken of ordinary men. Namely, Metahumans. Did you really think Metas were a creation of the modern world? There have been Metas sprinkled throughout history. Some legends are merely that—tales to astonish and amaze, created out of whole cloth, with no foundation in fact. Others have the deeds of Metahumans at the root of them. Distorted by time and exaggeration, yes, but based on actual events and people. Hercules' Twelve Labors, Icarus flying too close to the sun, Noah building the Ark . . . all are based on Metahuman feats."

I could understand why Seer did not seem to like Mechano overly much. He was one of those annoying know-it-alls who used three words where one would do just as well, and a SAT word where a more common one would do. If it weren't for the fact he was giving me the information I wanted, I'd want to slap a muzzle on him. If he had a mouth, that is.

"You're saying I've been walking around all my life, carrying inside of me a spirit as old as time, whose purpose is to protect the world?" I could hardly believe my ears. If it hadn't been for what Cassandra had told me, I would have called the Sentinels imaginative liars. What they were saying was just too absurd. I was the latest in a long line of possessed Metas which stretched back in time as far as Gilgamesh and God only knew who else? Maybe I should talk to an exorcist instead of these three.

"No, you have not been a vessel for the Omega spirit your entire life," Mechano said. "When Omega Man died, the Omega spirit then inhabited Avatar. Before then, Avatar had been a formidable Meta, but certainly not Omega-level. The Omega spirit augmented his powers, transforming him into an Omega-level Meta. That is the effect being inhabited by the

Omega spirit has: it augments the Metahuman abilities—whether latent or already existing—of the person it possesses. When Avatar was murdered, the Omega spirit sought out and entered a new host." Mechano pointed a metal finger at me. "You. Think about it—your powers did not manifest until shortly after Avatar's death. That was no coincidence. If Avatar had never died, leading to the Omega spirit inhabiting you, your latent Metahuman abilities would likely never have been triggered. After all, only a tiny sliver of the world population has powers. Even if you had beaten the odds and developed powers on your own, they almost certainly would not be Omega-level without the Omega spirit. That level of power is exceedingly rare. The odds of it are less likely than rolling a thousand dice at once and having all of them come up snake eyes."

I glanced at Millennium, the other Omega-level Meta in the room. Though he still appeared to stare at me, he had not said a word or moved a muscle since I entered the room. It was weird, like being stared at by a mannequin with black holes for eyes. It felt as though I would be swept off my feet and sucked into those eyes if I looked at them too long.

"You will have to forgive my taciturn colleague," Mechano said of Millennium, perhaps reading my expression. "Though part of him can hear us, most of his consciousness is on another astral plane right now, tending to another matter. Though it is pressing, it is of no concern to you." He said "on another astral plane" casually, the way I might say someone had gone to the bathroom.

With effort, I tore my eyes away from Millennium. Looking at him made me shiver. I said, "Though I get that the Department of Metahuman Affairs' tests say I'm an Omega-level Meta, I'm nowhere near as powerful as someone like Avatar." *Or Millennium,* I added silently, *if he really can do things like travel back in time.* "People say Avatar could've moved the Moon out of its orbit if he had wanted to. If I have the Omega spirit inside me, why don't I have the same level of power Omega Man or Avatar did?"

"Think of it this way," Mechano said, "if someone has the genetic capacity to become a championship level weightlifter, does he slide out of his mother flexing, with his muscles rippling? Of course not. A lot of time, energy, nutrition, and training must be invested before that person reaches his full genetic potential as a bodybuilder, potential that will not be reached if he never curls a barbell or he does not step foot into a gym. The same is true of you and your Omega-level powers. They must be developed and cultivated. In the time we have observed you, we have seen how much your powers have advanced. You are still in the adolescent stage of your development. Just imagine what you will be able to do given more time and training."

"Or if he has the Omega weapon," Seer interjected.

"Unless he has the Omega weapon," Mechano agreed. He sounded irritated at being interrupted. "I was getting to that."

"What in the world is an 'Omega weapon'?" I demanded. Oh goody, more surprises. My mind was already awhirl as it was.

"Legend has it that the first host of the Omega spirit infused part of the spirit into a weapon that can help each new Omega host fulfill his mission of protecting mankind," Mechano said. "I have no idea if the legend is true. Nonetheless, the weapon is real enough. It takes different forms depending on the Omega host who wields it. In King Arthur's case, it was Excalibur; with Hercules, it was the impenetrable lion pelt he draped around his shoulders; with Rama it was his bow; and with Beowulf it was his sword Nægling. Omega Man wore it as the clasp with the omega symbol on it that fastened his cape around his neck. With Avatar, it was his cape itself. The Omega weapon augments the Metahuman power of its wielder. Any Meta can use the weapon, but it is particularly potent when it is coupled with the Omega-level power of the Omega host. To go back to my bodybuilding analogy, the Omega weapon is to a Meta what the most potent of steroids is to a bodybuilder." Mechano paused. "Since you came here already knowing you are Omega, do you also know where the Omega weapon is?"

The eagerness in Mechano's voice was obvious. Even if I did know where this so-called Omega weapon was, I sure as hell wouldn't pass that knowledge on to the guy who had tried to kill me.

"I have no idea. Never even heard of it until now," I said honestly.

Mechano sighed and turned his head slightly to Seer. "Alas, it appears he tells the truth." Being spoken of in the third person when I was standing right in front of someone was my all-time favorite thing. "A shame. Think of what we could accomplish with access to the Omega weapon."

"Obviously Avatar hid it somewhere," Seer said to him. "The cape we buried him in was just an ordinary cape and not the weapon. Now that we have the boy, we'll redouble our efforts to locate it. If the weapon did not somehow nullify my precognition, we would have found it already." Ooops, I was wrong. Being spoken of in the third person was only my second favorite thing. Being referred to as "boy" was my favorite thing.

"Why would the Omega spirit pick me?" I asked, changing the subject before I lost both my temper and my chance to get answers to the questions I've had for so long.

"The criteria the Omega spirit has for picking a new host is unclear to us," Seer said. "If there is any rhyme or reason behind whom it selects, we can't decipher it. It going from Omega Man to Avatar made sense. After all, even before becoming a vessel for the Omega spirit, Avatar was an experienced Hero. However, why it would go from someone like Avatar to an inexperienced farm boy is . . . puzzling." I found it puzzling too, but it was still hard not to be insulted by her tone.

"Especially at a time such as this," Seer added gravely.

"A time such as this?" Maybe being ominous was another of Seer's superpowers. "What's that supposed to mean?"

Seer's milky eyes suddenly seemed to burn with a white-hot flame. "Darkness is coming. Good and evil will soon clash. The fate of the world itself is in the balance. Though much is hidden from me by forces not even I understand, I can foresee bits and pieces of the coming reckoning, like a gathering storm viewed through a dirty windowpane. Millennium and his mystic arts agree with my assessment. There have been signs of the coming conflict for decades, but they now indicate the battle is imminent. The carrier of the Omega spirit holds the key to either victory or defeat. For years we had assumed Avatar would be the carrier at the time of the great reckoning." Her voice turned bitter. "Until his unexpected naivete got him killed. Now, you have the Omega spirit."

She sounded less than enthused about that fact. Truth be told, I wasn't wild about it myself.

Why me? I thought. Though I knew I sounded like a broken record thinking that same question over and over, if there ever was a time for it to be asked, it was when you found out people expected you to save the world. How was I supposed to save the world? I couldn't even save Hannah or find Antonio.

"That is why I turned the nanites against you and used that explosive during the Trials, Mr. Conley," Mechano interjected. "Whoever has the Omega spirit is the key to the coming conflict. We had to make sure you were up to the task. You can understand our concern. When we first became aware of you, you were but a naive child, living in a backwater, getting an indifferent education at a third-rate school. Or so we thought at the time. It turns out you are more resourceful and worthier of the Omega spirit than we had at first supposed."

My mind raced. I connected the dots. "And if I did not survive your attacks, the Omega spirit would pass to someone else. Perhaps someone more worthy, at least in your eyes," I added bitterly. I could hardly believe my ears. These ruthless people were the ones I had so admired ever since I was a kid? This was like finding out that not only was Santa not a jolly old elf, but he had a nasty habit of climbing down the chimney, stealing all your presents, molesting your mother, and poisoning the cookies and milk.

My face grew hot as I realized the truth. The Trials were not the first time someone had tried to kill me. "You're the ones who hired Iceburn to kill me, aren't you?"

"Yes," Mechano admitted flatly. There was no trace of shame in his voice. "Decades ago I designed the Guild's computer system. I left in it backdoors permitting me access without alerting the Guild's computer personnel. Knowing the Omega spirit would seek another host after Avatar's death, I used my backdoor access to have the Guild's Metahuman Registry computers alert me when the Department of Metahuman Affairs registered a new Omega-level Meta. Since Omega-levels are so rare and since your powers manifested so soon after Avatar's death, we knew you had to be the new Omega host when you registered with the DMA. After we examined your background, we were concerned that you were too young, inexperienced, and unsophisticated to be the vessel for the Omega spirit in this most critical of times. Through intermediaries, we dispatched Iceburn to kill you. We are gratified to see he was not successful."

"That murderer killed my father." It was all I could do to not launch myself at Mechano and tear him apart piece by piece. I was so mad I shook.

"An unfortunate incident," Mechano said. "One we deeply regret. You were the target, not your father. He was collateral damage. As were the eleven people who died in the fire Iceburn set to lure you and the other trainees out of Hero Academy."

"Collateral damage?" I repeated the words bitterly. To have Dad's and all those others' lives reduced to two words was a slap in the face. "And the bomb that girl slipped into my pocket in the bank in D.C.? That was you too, wasn't it?"

"It was."

"And you and Millennium went along with all this?" I demanded angrily of Seer.

"We did," she said. The casualness with which these so-called Heroes admitted to murder and attempted murder was both shocking and dismaying.

I said, "What of the other Sentinels? Were they aboard the let's-kill-Theo train too?"

"No," Mechano said. "They know nothing of the steps we took regarding you. The other three are far too idealistic to have acquiesced had we told them. They are often woefully unwilling to do what needs to be done to accomplish the greater good. That is why they are not here tonight. Over a month ago Seer's precognition alerted her you would be coming tonight. In addition to deactivating most of the mansion's defenses and dismissing our security detail to let you come to us tonight unmolested, we made sure Tank, Ninja and Doppelganger were out of the country for the next few days so the three of us could speak to you privately. They are in Peru, finally putting an end to the Puma regime there now that we have a United Nations resolution giving us legal justification to intercede. You should be flattered. It took quite a bit of string-pulling at the UN to get the resolution passed in advance of your visit."

I felt more and more like a pawn in an elaborate chess game the existence of which I had once been happily ignorant of.

"Tank, Ninja and Doppelganger are of little consequence, anyway," Mechano added. "Now that Avatar is gone, the people in this room *are* the Sentinels." Mechano's arrogant voice turned disdainful. "The others are little more than our lackeys, whether they admit that to themselves or not. With me and my wealth and inventions, Millennium with his raw power, and Seer with her precognition that lets us prepare for threats on the horizon, we are the only members of this team who matter. With me as the first among equals, of course. Now that Avatar is dead, I am the driving force behind the Sentinels. You have heard of the Golden Rule? It is 'He who has the gold makes the rules.' Despite Millennium's and Seer's considerable abilities, my wealth is what keeps the Sentinels going. That means I am in charge, despite the fact Seer holds the title of chairwoman." Seer shifted in her seat, visibly irritated by Mechano's smugness. If Mechano noticed, he didn't seem to care.

It was good to hear the rest of the Sentinels weren't sociopathic killers. Three of them were bad enough.

"Why would you tell me all this stuff?" I asked. I was in shocked disbelief. Not only was I carrying around some ancient spirit, but three of the most admired Heroes in existence were killers. With a man as inventive as Edison, as rich as Croesus, and as diabolical as Vlad the Impaler as their ringleader. The blasé way they had recounted their misdeeds made me suspect this wasn't the first time they had done things no Hero had any business doing.

"We want you to trust us, Mr. Conley," Mechano said in answer to my question. *Yeah, good luck with that,* I thought. "We are being forthright with you about what we have done because we do not want there to be any secrets between us. We want you to join us. Here, as a member of the Sentinels. You would be the youngest Sentinel in history. Consider the honor of it. You will be famous, respected all around the world, at an age where you cannot even legally drink in some states. You will be paid handsomely, of course, more money than you have ever seen before. You could move out of that rathole you live in.

"We left Avatar's spot on the roster vacant all these years in the hopes you would one day prove your worthiness to fill it. The fact you survived the challenges we threw at you and made your way here shows you are indeed worthy. Worthy, but not yet ready for the crisis on the horizon. As Seer said, the greatest threat the world has ever known grows closer. The world needs you to be ready for it. And you need us to help you become ready. We can help you find the Omega weapon. We can help you reach your full potential. We can help you become the world's champion. We can help you be the Hero you were meant to be. The Hero the world *needs* you to be."

"Are you insane?" I couldn't stop myself from yelling. "You killed my father. You tried to kill me. You're just a bunch of murderous thugs! And now you want me to forget about all that and train under you? For what? Because of some save the world fairy tale you might have made up to trick me? Because of fame? Money? You want me to betray the memory of my father for thirty pieces of silver?"

Mechano's clenched fist hit the table. The blow was so

hard I felt the vibration of the impact through the floor. As one of the world's richest men and a Sentinel, he likely wasn't used to someone speaking to him in any way other than worshipfully.

"We did what we had to do," Mechano exclaimed in a raised voice. "There are forces afoot in the world that would annihilate every man, woman and child if they had the means to do so. Chaos, Doctor Alchemy, and others you likely have not even heard of would set fire to the world just to watch it burn. The Sentinels stand against them. We will continue to do what it takes to safeguard the world and the people in it. Even if it means killing a thousand fathers. The lives of the many outweigh the lives of the few."

Mechano stopped, perhaps composing himself. With his unmoving inhuman face, it was impossible to tell. I hated him at that moment more than I have hated anyone or anything.

Mechano continued in a more measured tone. "The world needed a champion, not a semi-literate scared boy afraid of his own shadow who had barely stepped foot off his family's farm. Because of what we did, what we needed to do, you stand here, a licensed Hero. If we hadn't taken the decisive actions we did, you undoubtedly would still live in the boondocks, pulling up weeds and picking ticks out of your belly button."

Despite his insulting tone, I had to admit he had me there. I never wanted to be a superhero, even after my powers manifested. If Iceburn killing Dad hadn't provided the catalyst for me to pursue Heroic training, I likely would still be in South Carolina, as far from the world of Heroes and Rogues as imaginable, cowering from bullies and trying to figure out how to get girls to like me.

If it was true that the world faced some huge threat and that the host of the Omega spirit was the key to combating it, then either killing me to make way for a more likely world-saver or forcing me to step up and prove my capacity to be that world-saver had a certain ruthless, icy logic to it. Viewed through that prism, I could understand why the Sentinels acted as they had.

On the other hand, the Sentinels had taken the same Hero's Oath I did. I was certain I'd remember if the words *feel free to murder in pursuit of the greater good* were in the Oath. I would never do what they had done. Isaac, Neha, the Old Man, Athena . . . no Hero I respected would. The bloodthirsty way the Trials had been conducted had made me suspect there was something rotten in the world of Heroes, and the callous behavior of these three Heroic paragons confirmed it. The Sentinels were so focused on the big picture they seemed to have lost all sense of right and wrong. In pursuit of protecting mankind, they had lost sight of protecting individual men.

Mechano steepled his metal fingers in front of himself. It was an odd mannerism coming from a robot. "Allow me to sweeten the pot of joining us a little. Millennium is an Omega-level Meta like you, only in his case because he had the good fortune to be born with the right and exceedingly rare combination of genetics instead of because he is infused with the Omega spirit. Among his many other talents is the ability to time travel. If you cooperate with us in averting the coming threat, after it is all over he can take you back in time. You can save the life of your father." His words confirmed my earlier suspicions—the Sentinels had led me through the mansion so I would be sure to see the stuffed saber-toothed tiger and the short-faced bear. They had been setting me up to believe time travel was possible.

"How do I know you're not lying to me?" I asked, hopeful despite myself at the possibility of saving Dad's life.

"Because we have been so forthcoming to you about what we have done to you and your family. Why would we suddenly start lying now? You can trust us."

Hah! I trusted these murderers as much as I would a nest of rattlesnakes. Less actually, since rattlesnakes only struck when they were hunting or defending themselves. These three vipers used violence as a tool of manipulation. "How about we save my father first, and then the world second?" I suggested.

"No," Mechano said firmly. "To be frank, the prospect of saving your father is a carrot to ensure your compliance with our wishes. Without it, you are likely to pretend to comply, gather evidence against us, and report us to the Guild at the earliest opportunity."

"What's to stop me from reporting you to the Guild right this instant?"

"You have no proof of the things we told you today. I scanned you quite thoroughly when you came in. You are not concealing any recording devices. Iceburn, the blonde woman in the Washington bank, Brown Recluse—all were hired through a string of intermediaries and third parties. Even if they told the Guild everything they know, the trail would never lead back to us. We have been Heroes at the highest levels for a long time. I can assure you we were quite careful to cover our tracks. In short, if you report what we have told you today to the Guild, it would be your word against ours. The word of a young man who just recently donned his cape versus the word of three of the preeminent Heroes in the world?" Mechano's voice was amused.

"Put yourself in the shoes of the Guild's investigation unit. Whom would you believe? The Guild will conclude that you're defaming the good name of three respected Heroes and punish you instead. You might even lose your license over it.

You certainly will if I anonymously provide evidence to the Guild that you cheated during the Trials. Yes, of course I know all about that. As I said before, Hacker is quite good, but not good enough to completely shield from me what she accomplished when she went rooting around in Overlord's system. Not only would you lose your license, but Hacker and Myth would as well. They might even go to jail over it. Cheating to obtain a Hero's license is a very serious matter and a crime. You would ruin their lives as well as your own.

"With that said, I cannot help but add I admire how you handled that supposedly no-win situation to give both you and your friend a chance to get your licenses. It reminds me of something I might do." I supposed he meant it as a compliment, but he couldn't have insulted me more had he tried. I didn't want to be like this metallic dirtbag in any way, shape, or form.

"What do you say, Mr. Conley?" Mechano asked. "Join us. Together, we will save the world. And then your father."

"And if I refuse?"

"Regrettably, I must admit we cannot take no for an answer. The stakes are simply too high. Not only for the world, but for you and your friends. If you do not cooperate, I can assure you it will not go well for either you or them. Though we would prefer to deal with you as you are now a known quantity, we will deal with your successor host to the Omega spirit if we must."

Well, there it was: As explicit a threat to my life as if Mechano had said he'd slit my throat if I didn't go along with the Sentinels' plans. He was threatening Neha's and Isaac's lives, too. I knew Sentry showing footage of them had been no accident. Not that I needed to hear Mechano threaten me to know the threat was there. I wasn't so stupid as to think the Sentinels would simply let me walk out of here with a pat on the back and a hearty handshake if I turned their proposal down.

The Situation Room was quiet as a tomb as my mind grappled with this dilemma. Maybe the Sentinels had told the truth. Maybe there was a massive threat on the horizon I could help thwart. They certainly were right about me being the new Omega host. Cassandra was confirmation of that. If they were also right about an approaching threat, didn't I have an obligation as a sworn Hero to try to protect the world, even if it meant I would throw my lot in for a while with these manipulative murderers? I could bring them to justice as soon as the threat had abated. I'd be even more powerful by then and be better able to do so. And, Mechano was right: Right now, I had no hard evidence of the Sentinels' misdeeds. Later, maybe I would have enough evidence to prove their guilt to the rest of the Guild.

Plus, if I did cooperate, maybe Millennium really could use his powers to help me go back in time and save Dad. Maybe I could save Mom, Hannah and Hammer, too. The saber-toothed tiger and the short-faced bear I'd seen had been tangible evidence of Millennium's abilities. I didn't understand how saving Dad would work as I likely never would have become a Hero if Dad hadn't died, but I was no expert on time travel. If the Academy had a class on time travel paradoxes, I missed it.

Here's what was in the pro join the Sentinels column:

Save the world. Save Dad. Save Mom. Save Hannah. Save Hammer. Don't be murdered so the Omega spirit would be forced into someone else. Don't get my friends murdered.

Those were all some pretty good pros.

On the other hand was a giant con:

The thought of working with these scheming murderers made my stomach churn and my skin crawl. Why should I reward their bad behavior by doing as they wished? I had no desire to associate further with these scumbags. Dad had been fond of telling me to be careful of the company I kept because you picked up the habits of the people you hung around with. *You become who you associate with*, came the words of his Jamesism to my mind. I didn't want to become like these three, who manipulated people like they were merely pieces on a chessboard and sacrificed them like their lives didn't matter.

No! Screw the Sentinels. I would not join them. These socalled Heroes were nothing but overpowered bullies. As bad as the Three Horsemen, Elemental Man, Antonio, and the other bullies I'd dealt with all my life were, they paled in comparison to these three Sentinels. The Sentinels should've been on the Mount Rushmore of bullies. They had killed my father, a good man who did the best he could all his life. He had done nothing wrong other than have a son who inexplicably was chosen to be the Omega. I would not hitch my wagon to these tarnished stars. If the world really was threatened and I was the key to saving it—God help us!—I would have to find a way to deal with it without these three. They weren't the only Heroes in the world who could help me. Isaac, Neha, Amazing Man, Truman, Athena, perhaps even the other Sentinels . . . there were far better Heroes to associate with. I had a hard time imagining worse.

That all was what I thought.

What I said was, "You're right. You did what you needed to do to make sure I'm the right person to help you deal with the upcoming threat. I can't say I'm happy about what you did to my father, but I can understand it. Besides, after this is all over, perhaps we'll go back in time and save him." I sighed. "I'll join you. I want you to help me save the world."

The room was silent as a tomb again for a few moments. I felt my heart beating.

Mechano's head swiveled slightly toward Seer.

"His vital signs indicate he is attempting to mislead us," he said. "Your thoughts?"

Seer's white eyes burned into mine for a moment.

"He's lying," she said definitively. "He will betray us to the Guild as soon as he is able. Though the boy is our best hope to combat the upcoming threat, we will have to take our chances with the next Omega. Hopefully he or she will be more pliable than this one." Seer shook her head sadly. "Kill him."

Mechano's head swiveled back to me.

"A shame," he said. "I rather liked this one. He is far less sanctimonious than Avatar was."

His single eye glowed bright red, like an exploding sun.

19

An energy blast from Mechano's eye hit me like a Mack truck. Though I had my personal shield up already—if you're foolish enough to walk into the lion's den, you'd better have your chair and whip ready—the force of the blast was still enough to sling me far across the Situation Room. I slammed against the far wall with a massive, bone-rattling thud.

Mechano's energy blast continued to push against the spherical contours of my force field, pinning me against the wall. I felt like a bug caught in the pressurized spray of a water hose. The force of it began to push me into the metal wall, like a pressing thumb making an ever-expanding dent in a soda can.

In movies, fights were always loud. Between the soaring soundtrack and the sounds of the fight itself, you could barely hear yourself think when you watched them. It's understandable they should be loud. Movies were supposed to hold your interest, not lull you to sleep. But real fights often weren't like movies. There were often sounds of exertion and smacks of impact, but not nearly the kinds or levels of sound you heard in movie fights. Sometimes real fights were so quiet, you could almost hear a pin drop.

This one was like that. The fact it was relatively quiet did not make it less terrifying.

The sustained blast of energy from Mechano's eye didn't make a sound, either as it passed through the air or as it pressed implacably against my force field. The only sound was that of the metal of the wall behind me as it crunched and twisted, beginning to warp around me like a custom-made coffin.

There wasn't much noise, but my other senses were over-whelmed. I felt a mounting pressure all over, but especially on my forehead and chest, like someone had stepped on top of me while I'd been lying down, and he was getting heavier and heavier by the second. The brightness of the sustained energy blast was blinding. It was like being inside a fireworks display. There was the smell of burning ozone as Mechano's blast cut through the air. The smell was so sharp, I could taste it. Was it a laser? Something electricity based? Something else entirely? It didn't matter. Whether you were burned to death or shocked to death, either way you were just as dead.

I fought to maintain my shield as Mechano's energy blast pummeled it with a force unlike any I had ever felt before. I struggled to absorb the massive energy of the blast. I felt like a kitchen sponge trying to absorb all the water in a swimming pool.

"I will find the right frequency to pierce your force field soon enough," I heard Mechano say over the harsh sounds of metal twisting and rending around me. "Stop resisting, and I will end this painlessly."

My mind was too preoccupied and my teeth were too clenched for me to tell him to go screw himself. My eyes squeezed tight against the blinding light, which still stabbed at them like knitting needles despite being closed. My will started to flag, like an exhausted swimmer who wants to give into the violent current he struggled against.

Hold on! Just a little longer! I told myself. The absorbed energy filled every cell of my body, threatening to slop over and make me explode like an overcharged battery.

"Stop!" Seer said sharply. "You're playing into his hands!"

Too late, I thought. The words were barely out of Seer's mouth before Mechano's energy beam managed to pierce my shielding. For a split second, my body was bathed in the energy completely unprotected by my force field. I likely would have burned to ash instantaneously had the energy I had absorbed not given me a tiny bit of protection. Even so, it felt like I had plunged into a vat of boiling oil. *Time to go.*

With a thought, I reformed my force field that was now useless against Mechano's energy blast. I turned it from spherical to cylindrical with a tapered end. It went from being like a shield to being like a bullet casing. Using the energy I had absorbed from Mechano as propellant, I shot straight up, faster and more forcefully than I ever could have without Mechano's absorbed energy.

I sliced through the wall I'd been pushed into like a hot knife cutting through butter. I rose like a rocket, leaving a deep groove from top to bottom in the tall metal wall. I punched through the Situation Room's reinforced ceiling as quickly as a wink, leaving the Sentinels behind. Blurred images of the mansion raced by faster than my mind could process as I punched through one floor of the mansion after another. It was eerily quiet inside my force field despite the pandemonium I must have caused in the mansion. I realized I was traveling faster than the speed of sound, hence the silence within my personal shield.

The night sky filled my field of vision. I slowed to a halt as quickly as I could without risking turning my internal organs into pâté by stopping too abruptly.

I quickly took stock as I hung high in the night air over Sentinels Mansion. I had gotten the answers I'd sought. I was in pain and hurt badly, but I was alive. When facing people like the Sentinels, I'd count surviving as a victory. The escape plan I had formulated when I first entered the Situation Room had worked. Even though I was apparently the Omega, I had known the moment I laid eyes on the three Sentinels I would be outclassed if a fight broke out. They were simply too experienced and too powerful for me to take them down on my own. I'd known that, if push came to shove, I shouldn't try to shove back. I should run. He who fights and runs away lives to fight another day.

The problem was, there was no way I would be able to make it from the Situation Room back to the mansion's front door. I had simply gotten too twisted around in the maze-like mansion. Using my telekinesis to penetrate the walls and ceiling of the mansion to escape were out too, as they had proved immune to my powers. Besides, I had suspected they were too reinforced against possible Rogue attacks for me to pierce them at my usual power level.

That was why I had deliberately let Mechano blast me with his energy beam, to give me the chance to absorb the additional energy I needed to escape. It was like Metahuman judo, using my opponent's strength against him. I'd cut it closer than I'd meant to, though, in letting Mechano pierce my shielding. Everything on me felt burnt, even my insides. I felt like a charred steak.

I would have to assess my injuries later. This was not over. All three Sentinels could fly. They would be on me like flies on rotten meat in moments if I didn't do something to stop them.

I had not used all the energy absorbed from Mechano in

making my escape. A substantial amount of it remained, making my body tingle and crackle with barely contained energy. I bent over in the air, clenched my fists, and aimed them down toward the hole far below in the mansion's roof I had just burst out of. I unleashed the energy the cells of my body had absorbed from Mechano. It surged forth from inside me like water from countless breached dams. I channeled it through my arms, down through my fists, and out of my body.

A massive bolt of energy, glowing white-yellow, burst out of me like a fired artillery shell. It hit the roof of the mansion and exploded like a thunderclap. For an instant, night turned into day. It blinded me. The shock wave from the blast hit me, knocking the wind out of me. It sent me tumbling through the air.

Once I righted myself, I looked down at the damage I had caused. There was now a massive gaping hole, smoking and jagged, in the roof of the mansion. There was more empty space than roof, now. Though I couldn't see how far down the damage extended, I had punched through at least the first few floors of the structure.

As I watched, part of the mansion caved in on itself, like a collapsing house of cards.

"Holy shit," I whispered, shocked and awed by what I had done. Though I had intended to do it, meaning to do something and looking at that something were entirely two different things. Despite all the three Sentinels had done to me, that did not change the fact Sentinels Mansion was a symbolic, almost sacred building. I felt like I had just set fire to the White House.

My nose dripped. I reached up with a shaking hand and wiped the wetness away. Blood. The sight of it brought on a sudden wave of vertigo, weakness, and pain. Between Mechano's attack and regurgitating all that energy in one big blast, I felt like a runner who'd been hit by a car at the end of a marathon. I needed a nap, a painkiller, and a pretty nurse to tend to me. I wouldn't have turned my nose up at an ugly one either.

Maybe later. Right now, I needed to get out of here. I was under no illusion that the Sentinels had not survived my attack on the mansion. They had survived far worse in the past. I had just wanted to slow them down.

I started flying south back toward the city as fast as my throbbing mind and aching body would let me. Sentinels Mansion faded into darkness behind me. Though it hurt my head to do it, I sent telekinetic pulses out around me, like an airplane in a combat zone checking for missiles.

I was not being followed. Maybe dropping part of the mansion on the Sentinels' murderous heads had done the trick.

I needed to get into touch with Isaac. I had my cell phone with me, tucked into one of my suit's unobtrusive pockets. I didn't dare use it. The only thing I knew about cell phone technology was how to spell it, but monitoring cell phone calls struck me as child's play for someone like Mechano. Besides, maybe my phone had gotten fried in Mechano's attack after he pierced my force field.

I activated my wrist communicator instead. Isaac and I had a long-standing agreement to always answer our communicators. Even so, it seemed like forever before he answered his.

"Yo," came his sleepy voice. "This had better be good. I was having a dream about the cheerleaders for the Astor City Supernovas. Just me and a bunch of bouncing pom-poms."

"I just left Sentinels Mansion. They attacked me."

"They did what?!" The sleepiness was gone from his voice.

"I can't come home." My tongue felt thick. I was having a hard time speaking. My lips were painfully cracked. Blood trickled into my mouth. "They'll come looking for me. You and Smoke too, probably. You and Bertrand need to get out of the house now. Call Neha and tell her to make herself scarce." I was having a hard time focusing. A building loomed up in front of me, taking me by surprise. I swerved to avoid it.

"What in the world have you done?"

"Not winning friends and influencing people, that's for sure." I swerved again, narrowly missing another building. "Gotta go. These buildings are cagey. They keep tryin' to crash into me." I shut off the communicator, cutting Isaac off.

My brain felt increasingly sluggish. My eyelids got heavier and heavier, desperately wanting to close. It was as clear as the bleeding nose on my face I needed medical attention. I couldn't go to a hospital though. In addition to risking exposing my secret identity by passing out in an emergency room, more importantly, I had little doubt Mechano would monitor the area hospitals' computer systems for new admissions that fit my description. If I had his technological savvy and resources, that was what I'd do. Surely his sensors had picked up he injured me before I made good on my escape.

Getting help at a hospital was out. If I survived the night, I'd be sure to befriend a doctor who was not afraid of murderous Heroes and who made house calls. It was a shame I hadn't already done it. Hindsight really was twenty-twenty.

I needed to hole up somewhere. I was in no condition to go another round with the Sentinels. Even at my best they outmatched me, and I was not at my best. I needed to hide, regroup, recover, and plan my next move. But where could I go? Home and hospitals were out. So was work. The Sentinels surely would look for me there. Besides, I did not want to endanger the workers in Star Tower. I could go to Amazing Man's mansion in Chevy Chase, but there was no way I'd make the flight all the way down there. I was having a hard enough time getting back to Astor City without slamming into something.

Where could I go where the Sentinels would not look for me?

The answer came to me like a thrown lifeline:

Truman.

The Sentinels had not known I knew I was the Omega. Maybe they also didn't know I had hired Truman. Plus, Truman was a Hero who had dealt with the Sentinels before. If there was anyone I could go to who could help me deal with them, it was him.

It was the wee hours of the morning. Unless he was working a case, surely Truman was at home asleep instead of in his office. Truman mentioned he owned a condo not far from his office, but I had no idea where it was.

His office it was, then.

I altered my trajectory, making my way toward Paper Street. If it weren't for the fact I knew the streets of Astor City like the back of my hand thanks to my night patrols, I doubted I could navigate there in the condition I was in. Fortunately, I could make my way there, though I was only faintly consciously aware of doing so.

Before I knew it, Truman's mid-rise office building came into sight. I focused on it like a drowning man dog-paddling toward a life preserver. Normally, if I needed to get into Truman's office after hours, I would have landed on the sidewalk, walked to the front door, used my powers to defeat any security systems and locks, and then strolled into Truman's office like I owned the place.

This was not normally. I was in no condition to do all that. If I landed on the sidewalk, I was likely to pass out there.

I took as careful aim as my lethargic mind would let me. I

fuzzily gathered my personal shield around me. I shot forward.

I crashed through Truman's third floor window like a thrown baseball. Glass exploded and fell around me. I hit the top of Truman's desk with a crash. Items went flying. I caromed off the desk like a bounced ball. I smashed into the wall on the other side of the room, and then hit the floor. I rolled until I came to rest on the threadbare carpet against Truman's couch.

The floor was hard. What carpeting remained smelled, of age and years of foot traffic. There was a nice comfy couch right above me. I wanted to get up and onto it, but couldn't seem to will my body to do it. I couldn't breathe. I apparently had knocked the wind out of myself, having dropped my shield at some point after smashing through the window. Other than the city's lights coming in through the broken window, the room was dark.

"Dude, you suck at landings," came a raspy voice. It wasn't until later I realized it was mine. A breeze from the broken window blew papers from Truman's desk and onto me. A few grew dark with my blood. I would have brushed the papers off, but they seemed too far away. Besides, I was too distracted by the pool of inky blackness expanding in front of my eyes. It beckoned me invitingly. "First Iceburn throws you through a window in Adams Morgan, then Mad Dog blasts you through one, now this. What in the world do you have against doors?"

No one answered. Rude.

The floor seemed far more comfortable with each passing second. Who needed a bed and sheets with a high thread count when you had a nice, comfy floor to relax on?

The pool of darkness descended like a blanket, enveloping me whole.

20

I opened my eyes. I immediately regretted it.

The room was bright. The light gouged painfully at me, like a dagger slashing through my eyes into my brain. I squinted. Squinting made it better. The slashing dagger shrunk to a jabbing needle. Progress. Having your eyes wide open was overrated anyway. No intrepid hero I had ever heard of looked at the world with wide-eyed innocence. Besides, if squinting worked for Clint Eastwood, surely it would work for me. Maybe I would look more like a badass this way.

Even if I looked more formidable squinting, my badass ass felt bad. It felt as though I had gone five rounds with Mike Tyson in his prime with my arms tied behind my back. I wondered if I looked as bad as I felt. It would be hard to look worse.

Blurred images swam hazily in front of me, slowly coming into focus. The first thing I saw was Isaac's unmasked face, looking down at me with obvious concern.

"The bomb that exploded in my face before the Trials, our fight during the Trials, and now this," I whispered hoarsely. "How come every time I pass out, I wake up to see you?"

"You're just lucky, I guess," Isaac said.

Isaac's face was fuzzy. I blinked hard, trying to bring it into sharper focus. "I thought earlier I'd settle for an ugly nurse, but this is going too far," I croaked. I had what felt like a combination of a flu and a hangover. I felt weak and awful. "Beggars can't be choosers, I suppose. Give it to me straight, Nurse Ratched: Will the patient survive?"

Isaac didn't even crack a smile. "Maybe if he gets a brain transplant. What possessed you to confront the Sentinels all by yourself?"

"Seemed like a good idea at the time."

"And now?"

I struggled to sit up. My head threatened to slide off my neck and bounce off the floor like a rotten melon. I willed it to stay in place. My Clint-like squinting likely scared it into submission.

"Now it seems like less than a good idea," I rasped. Now that I was sitting up, all I wanted was to just lie back down.

"That's the smartest thing you've said in a while." Isaac grinned. Relief was evident on his face. "Maybe you don't need that brain transplant after all."

My surroundings fitfully came into focus. We were in Truman's office. The door was closed. I was on his couch. The only source of light was the overhead fluorescents. The window I had flown through was now covered with particleboard, making it impossible for me to tell if it was night or day.

Truman was behind his desk with his feet up and a paperback book in his hand. It was an Agatha Christie mystery. Was he scrounging for tips? Truman closed the book on a thick finger and looked at me as I focused on him.

"Sorry about the window," I said. "I couldn't think of where else to go." My voice sounded marginally stronger.

"It's the ladies in the office across the street you really should be apologizing to. Now they can't look over here and see me flexing. Their lost eye candy notwithstanding, it's no big deal. Worse things have happened in this office. Windows can be replaced." He looked me up and down critically. "You, on the other hand, can't be. You look like you lost a wrestling match with a hot stove."

I looked down at myself. I was out of my Kinetic costume and dressed in only a tee shirt and loose athletic shorts. They appeared to be mine. My skin was red, as if I had spent far too long in the sun, with all the pain and itchiness that accompanied a bad sunburn. My skin was blistered in a few spots. The blisters all were where my Kinetic costume hadn't covered me. Evidently it had afforded me some protection from Mechano's energy blast after my force field failed.

"You tripped an alarm at Truman's house when you flew through his window," Isaac said. Obviously the two had gotten past the *pleased to meet you, I'm a Hero too* stage while I was unconscious since Isaac was walking around unmasked. "He got here shortly before I did. I tracked you here from the GPS on your communicator. Truman had a doctor friend of his come check you out. I packed some clothes for both of us before leaving home, and changed you out of your costume so the doctor wouldn't suspect you're a Hero. Aside from radiation burns, pain, and you exponentially increasing your chances of getting cancer down the road, the doctor said you'll be fine in a couple of weeks. He also advised that whatever you had done to get you into this condition, stop doing it."

My brain played conga drums against my skull. "Sound advice," I said. Like a bad dream resurfacing, I thought of the Sentinels. They likely were scouring the world, looking for me right now. I'd have to figure out how to deal with them. It was like a Cub Scout thinking he'd have to figure out a way to deal with the United States Marines. "Though I can't make any promises. Are Bertrand and Ne—I mean Smoke—safe?" The fact Truman knew Isaac and my secret identities didn't mean I should put Neha's on blast too. Though I thought Truman could be trusted, I had no right to share her secret identity without permission.

"Bertrand I put up in a hotel for a while," Isaac said. "I paid cash for it so it couldn't be traced to me. I gave him a song and dance about how you pissed off a criminal with your work at the *Times*, so it wouldn't be safe for us at the house for a while. Neha I can't get ahold of. I've left messages for her, though."

I felt a surge of apprehension about Neha. I tried to suppress it. She was the smartest of all of us. *She can take care of herself*, I told myself. Still, I wished she were here. I wished I had made up with her before now.

"Also, when I got here and saw the condition you were in, I got in touch with your supervisor at the *Times* and called in sick for you." Isaac hesitated. A slight smile played around his lips. "I think he got the impression I'm your boyfriend, so if you've got your eye on a cutie at work, you're probably out of luck."

"Why would he have gotten that impression?"

"Probably because I told the guy 'I'm Theo's boyfriend.' It had amused me at the time. Besides, I owed you one for calling me a tattletale a few days ago."

"Thanks a lot. With friends like you, who needs the Sentinels?" I stretched out my arms and legs and winced. In addition to the pain, everything was stiff. "How long have I been out?"

"Over a day and a half," Isaac said. "Doctor Hastings gave

you a light sedative to help you sleep. He wanted to give you something even stronger, but I knew you'd want me to tell him no. If the news is any indication, we've got too much on our plate for you to be doing a Rip Van Winkle impersonation right now."

"The news? What do you mean?"

"Truman, can I borrow your phone? Since I'm a known associate of Lobster Lad over there, mine is off with the battery unplugged. I did the same with your phone, Theo. I didn't want someone to ping our phones' GPS to figure out where we are." Despite his jocular facade, Isaac was no dummy.

Truman handed his smartphone over. Isaac sat next to me and used the phone's browser to go to UWant Video. He went to one of the trending videos. It was from one of the cable news channels and titled "Hero or Menace?" The tinny sound of the video from the phone's small speaker soon filled Truman's office:

"The Sentinels, who many consider the greatest Heroes in the world, are dealing with the fallout from an attack on their headquarters outside of Astor City, Maryland early this morning. Sentinels Mansion is internationally recognized as a symbol of the heroic spirit," said a Vixen News anchor. Blonde, busty, and perfectly made up and coiffed with pearly white teeth, she looked like a sex doll come to life. Her sultry look was designed to make the network's mostly gray-haired audience go weak in the knees and hard in the penis. She sat behind a transparent desk. The camera afforded a perfect view of her crossed, tanned, high-heeled legs. If her neckline were a teensy bit deeper and her skirt a tiny bit shorter, she would look like she was about to mount one of the poles at Areola 51.

She continued, "The attack on Sentinels Mansion came,

not from a Rogue as might be expected, but rather, one of the Sentinels' fellow licensed Heroes. This footage was captured by the security cameras on the grounds of Sentinels Mansion."

The woman's perfectly symmetrical features were replaced by a video of me in costume, floating high up in the dark sky over Sentinels Mansion. The video showed me shooting my energy blast into the mansion, the resulting terrific explosion, part of the mansion collapsing, and then me flying away. The video shut off, replaced with a still close-up of my masked face from the video.

The voice of the anchor said, "Both the Sentinels and the Heroes' Guild have confirmed the Metahuman who perpetrated the attack is Kinetic, a licensed Hero who has been active in Astor City the past several months. Three of the Sentinels were in Peru contending with the supervillain Puma at the request of the United Nations at the time of the attack. Millennium, Mechano, and Seer, the remaining three Sentinels, were inside of the mansion when the attack came. No one was injured. Kinetic's attack did cause millions of dollars in damage, however, in addition to destroying priceless artifacts housed in the mansion. Both the Sentinels and the investigative arm of the Heroes' Guild are searching for Kinetic for committing what the Sentinels call 'an inexplicable and senseless terrorist attack.' Here is Sentinels' chairwoman Seer, making a statement a short while ago from the world-famous Situation Room."

The video cut away from my picture, replaced by a recording of Seer. She was in the Situation Room. Part of the room had collapsed, no doubt because of my attack.

"We have no idea why Kinetic launched this unprovoked assault on Sentinels' headquarters," Seer said. "Clearly he is a very troubled young man to attack us without reason or warning. We are just grateful that no one was injured in this dastardly attack. Rest assured that the Sentinels are devoting our considerable resources to locating Kinetic before he lashes out again and hurts or kills an innocent member of the public. Kinetic is unstable and obviously dangerous. Anyone who spots him should avoid all contact with him and immediately report his sighting to us. We have set up a hotline for that purpose. Kinetic, if you are listening to this, please turn yourself in. You have my personal assurance you will be treated fairly." The number for the hotline flashed on the bottom of the screen.

The leggy anchor filled the screen again. "We have sought a comment on Kinetic's behavior from the Heroes' Guild. Other than also encouraging Kinetic to turn himself in and stating that it had opened an investigation into his behavior, the Guild had no comment."

The video shut off. I glanced at the number next to the video's icon. It had millions of views. I took the phone out of Isaac's hand and scrolled through some of the comments about the video. The gist of them was that I should not only be thrown in jail, but castrated, drawn and quartered, burned at the stake, and then buried under the jail. So much for innocent until proven guilty and keeping an open mind until you heard the other guy's side of the story.

A wave of weariness washed over me. Life had given me tons of experience in not being well-liked, but being universally hated even by people I hadn't met was a new experience. I didn't like it. "Tell me Vixen is the only network reporting this story," I said hopefully.

"Nope," Truman said. "Every television news network is playing the footage of the attack on almost a constant loop, including the major international networks. Not to mention it being discussed to death on talk radio and getting above-the-fold coverage in the major newspapers. Including your employer, by the way."

Disgusted, I leaned back on the couch. I regretted it. I grimaced in pain. The pressure against my aching back made it hurt worse. "I'm famous. Or rather, infamous. Fantastic. Not only are the Sentinels looking for me, but every Tom, Dick and Harry in the world who pays attention to the news will have his eyes peeled for me too."

"On the plus side," Truman said cheerily, "you take a real good picture."

"You should call yourself Silver Lining Man," I said.

Still leaning back, I closed my eyes against the brightness of the light. Knowing the world thought I was a crazed terrorist wasn't doing my pounding headache any favors. I hadn't even been a licensed Hero for a year and I was already a household name. And not in a good way. From obscurity to infamy in just a few hours. It must be some sort of record. The enemies I'd made since becoming a Meta like Pitbull and Elemental Man must be having a good chuckle at my expense right about now. What's that German word meaning taking pleasure from someone else's pain? Oh yeah—schadenfreude. People like Pitbull must have been luxuriating in schadenfreude right about now. The Germans were probably pissed at me too.

"You're not going to turn me in to the Guild, are you?" I asked Truman.

"Of course not." He sounded offended. "Remember, I've had less than positive experiences with the Sentinels in the past. If you blew up their mansion, I'm guessing they deserved it."

"Are you going to tell us what happened between you and the Sentinels, or am I going to have to be the one who turns you in to find out?" Isaac asked impatiently.

I reluctantly pried my eyes open. I told them everything, beginning with the revelation Cassandra had made to me up through me crashing into Truman's office. Well, almost everything. I still left out the fact I had cheated during the Trials and Hacker's role in it. Isaac would flip his lid if he knew he had his cape because of cheating.

Once I finished, Isaac leaned back on the couch along with me. His eyes were wide.

He said, "So not only did Mechano try to kill you during the Trials, but he and two Sentinels have been trying to kill you ever since you developed your powers? And now that you've refused to become their protege, they're looking to kill you so this Omega spirit thingamajig will pass to another host? If I didn't know you like I do, I'd think you had been hallucinating, smoking crack, or both. And thanks to your pyrotechnics at the mansion, anybody who pays any kind of attention to current events is going to be looking for you too." He shook his head in wonder and disbelief. "Well, here's another nice mess you've gotten us into."

Truman blinked in surprise. He said, "I would've thought you were too young to quote Laurel and Hardy. Hell, *I'm* too young to quote Laurel and Hardy and I'm older than both of you."

"Isaac and I had the same Hero sponsor. He had a taste for the classics," I said. I turned to look at Isaac, wincing as I did so. My aching body told me to quit moving around so much, but my body wasn't the boss of me. "*We're* in a mess? I didn't see a picture of you on the news."

"You're my brother. If you're in trouble, I'm in trouble." Isaac said it matter-of-factly, as if he had said water was wet or the sky was blue. I felt the same way about him, but to hear him express the sentiment made me a little misty-eyed.

Apparently, being seared like a steak and being a wanted man made me maudlin.

"Please tell me you two lovebirds aren't going to start making out on my couch," Truman said.

"I can't kiss him," Isaac said, sounding shocked. He dropped his voice to a whisper, as if afraid Truman's neighbors might hear a terrible secret. "Theo's a honky."

"So am I," Truman said. "Nobody's perfect."

Sweet Jesus, I thought. *There's two of them.* I blinked away my forming tears and cleared my throat in embarrassment. "I wonder why the Sentinels didn't release my real name and likeness to the public. It would be a lot easier for them to locate and dispose of me if everyone in the world was on the lookout for not only Kinetic but also Theodore Conley."

"It's against the law to expose the secret identity of a licensed Hero," Truman said. "The Sentinels probably don't want to face a bunch of awkward questions from the Guild about why they're breaking the law by exposing it. Not even the Sentinels are above the law. At least that's how it's supposed to work. Clearly the Sentinels haven't gotten the memo saying they aren't above the law. Plus, them releasing your real name and face would beg the question of how they got that information. The Guild's computer records are supposed to be secure and confidential. The Guild would have a fit if it knew Mechano used them as his personal address book."

"That makes sense. Thank goodness for small favors. I'm in a big enough fix as it is without having to put a bag over my head every time I go outside." I shook my head, which didn't do my headache any favors. "We need to figure a way out of this mess and how to bring the Sentinels to justice. Well, Isaac and I do. You didn't sign up for Sentinel wrangling when I hired you, Truman."

"True, but I'm signing up for it anyway," he said firmly. "As much as it would pain my accountant to hear me say it, I'm a Hero first and a businessman second. If a villain needs to be thrashed, I've got an obligation to try to thrash him. As Heroes sworn to protect people and yet who are guilty of multiple counts of murder, felony murder, and attempted murder, the Sentinels certainly qualify as villains." He shook his head in disgust. Then he sighed. "But at the risk of jeopardizing my daredevil reputation, I must admit that if the three of us go up against these three Sentinels, we're more likely to be the thrashees than the thrashers."

"Well that's awfully pessimistic," Isaac said.

"Nope. It's realistic. Lying to yourself about what you're up against doesn't help you figure out what to do about it. We're talking about three of the world's most powerful and experienced Heroes with nearly unlimited resources. No offense, but you two are freshly minted Heroes, even if Theo has this so-called Omega spirit. If I checked behind your ears, you're likely still wet back there. I'm a lot more experienced than you, but I usually deal with street crime. I'm not going to kid myself by pretending that the Sentinels and I are in the same league."

I sank lower into the couch. My headache was getting worse. "That's quite a pep talk. You really should become a motivational speaker," I said.

"Just calling a spade a spade."

The office fell quiet as the enormity of the odds against us sank in.

"Truman's right," Isaac finally said. "If I had to bet on who would win a fight between the Sentinels and us, I wouldn't flush my money down the toilet by betting on us. At the risk of you calling me a tattletale again Theo, maybe the right play here is to turn this whole thing over to the Guild and let it sort it out."

I shook my head. "I hate to agree with Mechano on anything, but he was right about what he said in the Situation Room—I have absolutely no proof the Sentinels did anything wrong other than what they told me. I'll bet Mechano has by now scrubbed from Overlord any trace of him tampering with it. Without that, it's my word against the Sentinels. I know who I'd believe if I were the Guild. Here's a hint: not me. I know I'm telling the truth about all this, yet I can barely believe it myself. How can I expect the Guild to? If I go to the Guild, the only thing I'll accomplish will be to tell the Sentinels where I am so they can try to kill me again."

Isaac said, "We could go to the Old Man. He'd believe us. What he says carries a lot a weight in the Guild. He's on the Guild's Executive Committee after all."

"Who's the Old Man?" Truman interjected. "If you say me, I'll pull my gun out and shoot you."

"The Old Man is Amazing Man," Isaac said. "He was our Hero sponsor. He's the guy who taught us Laurel and Hardy weren't Ed Hardy's less fashionable brothers."

I shook my head. "The Old Man is just one voice among many on the Executive Committee. Even with him in our corner, the Guild isn't going to believe our accusations about the Sentinels without proof." I left out the other reason why I didn't want to go to the Guild: I had no doubt Mechano would carry out his threat to expose me cheating during the Trials. Though I had no interest in being defrocked and losing my Hero's license—I had worked too hard and been through too much to get it—if my license was the only one on the line I would give it up with a whistle on my lips and a song in my heart to bring Dad's killers to justice. My license was not the only one on the line, though. Hacker's and Isaac's were too. I would not snatch from them something they had worked so hard to get. I would not risk them going to prison, either.

"Going to the Guild is out," I said firmly. "We have to figure out a way to deal with this ourselves. I think the key to this whole thing is me being the Omega. The Sentinels said there is an Omega weapon out there that will help me fulfill my power's potential. If we can find it, maybe it will give us a fighting chance against them."

Isaac said, "This Omega thing is the most incredible part of all this. Theo, do you really buy the whole savior of the world stuff the Sentinels are peddling? No offense, but the idea of you carrying around some ancient, world-protecting spirit like Dr. McCoy lugging around Spock's katra in *The Search For Spock* sounds like woo-woo, crystal healing nonsense. Maybe the Sentinels are lying about that, manipulating you for reasons we don't understand."

"I wouldn't believe the Sentinels if they told me water was wet. But Cassandra also told me that I'm the Omega. What do you think, Truman?"

He said, "While I agree the whole Omega thing sounds incredible, the fact that people like us with superpowers exist is pretty incredible all by itself. I've seen too much to think that anything is impossible. Besides, I've known Cassandra a long time. I've never known her to be wrong."

"Okay, let's assume for the sake of discussion that Theo is this world-protecting Omega," Isaac said. "Let's further assume that the Omega weapon is not a made-up red herring. How are we three not-on-the-level-of-the-Sentinels knuckle-heads supposed to find something they have already looked for? Especially when their teammate Avatar was the last one to have it? As you said Truman, they have nearly limitless resources. What can we do that they can't? Rub a lamp and ask a genie where it is?"

"Maybe you don't need a lamp," Truman said. He tapped the corner of his book on his desk thoughtfully. "Maybe you just need me. And if one of you gets up and tries to rub my belly, I swear to God I really will shoot you this time. I know where Avatar may have hidden the Omega weapon. Years ago, back when the Sentinels hired me to find Avatar's killer, I started by trying to figure out Avatar's secret identity. The fact he hadn't told the rest of the Sentinels his real name says something right there about how he didn't fully trust them. For good reason, as we now know. Anyway, while figuring out his secret identity, I stumbled on a hidey-hole he maintained. He called it 'The Mountain.' If there is an Omega weapon, it's liable to be there. I didn't see anything that fit the bill the times I was there, but I wasn't looking for it, either."

"Surely that was the first place the Sentinels looked for it," I objected.

"They don't know about it," Truman said. "Avatar didn't tell them about The Mountain, so I sure as hell didn't either. I figured if not telling them about The Mountain was good enough for a paragon like Avatar, it was good enough for me. Besides, I didn't trust them any further than I could throw them considering how shabbily they treated me during my investigation of Avatar's death."

A spark of hope ignited within me. Maybe things weren't as hopeless as they had first seemed. "The first thing we'll do is go to this Mountain place and look for the Omega weapon."

"Let me see if I've got this straight," Isaac said, sounding incredulous. "We need to go to Avatar's secret hideout, find the Omega weapon which may or may not exist and may or may not be hidden at The Mountain, figure out how to utilize it, use it to defeat three of the most powerful Heroes in the world, bring them to justice, and clear Theo's name. And, after that, there remains the little matter of Theo saving the world."

He scratched his bald head with a look of bemusement on his face. "Oh, is that all?" he said sarcastically. "I'm surprised we haven't done it already since it'll surely be a cakewalk. Did I miss something? Anything else we need to do?"

"No," Truman said. "Once we're finished, on the seventh day, we'll rest."

21

Isaac and I rode the escalator to the top of the exit of the Bladenburg Avenue subway stop in southwest Astor City. We both wore civilian clothes. Since the public had been alerted to be on the lookout for Kinetic, flying in costume to where we needed to go was out of the question.

Also, we had paid cash to ride the subway instead of utilizing the monthly passes both Isaac and I normally used on the subway. The passes were registered in our real names, and we had figured that it would be easy for Mechano to hack into the Maryland Transit Administration's computers to see if we had taken public transportation somewhere. For the same reason, we were afraid to use our ATM cards to get cash. Truman had spotted us our subway fare. Being on the run from a group of murderous Metahumans was putting a real damper on my ability to get around.

After leaving the subway station, we walked on Bladenburg Avenue toward the EZ Keep self-storage facility Truman had told us about. We were in a commercial area full of strip malls and fast food restaurants. Truman wasn't with us. He was off chasing down a fresh lead he had gotten about Antonio's location.

"A Hero has to be able to walk and chew gum at the same time," he had said when I questioned him pursuing Antonio at a time like this. While I appreciated his dedication to my case, it had seemed like the Sentinels should take priority. "A hot lead tends to cool off pretty quickly. You have to pursue it while it's fresh. Besides," Truman had added, his eyes twinkling, "surely the mighty Omega isn't afraid to go to a scary old storage facility without a chaperone."

"Bite me," I had said.

It felt like everyone we passed stared at me as Isaac and I walked down the street. Since I was not in costume, the stares were likely because I was only a couple of shades away from being beet red thanks to Mechano's energy blast rather than because people thought I was Kinetic, terrorist and iconic building ruiner. If being a Hero continued to go this disastrously, maybe I could switch gigs and hire myself out as a one-man mansion demolisher.

A young boy walked by, hand in hand with his mother. His mouth fell open as he stared at me. His tongue was purple from sucking on candy. He pointed at me, his eyes big and round as his embarrassed mother pulled him past me.

I pulled my baseball cap down lower on my head, uncomfortable with all the attention. Walking was a chore. The pain I was still in helped keep my mind off all the looks I got. What a crappy silver lining. Thank goodness Isaac had thought to pack me some long-sleeved shirts. I was glad my burned arms were covered despite the warm weather.

"I feel like a circus freak," I said to Isaac.

"You look like one too."

"Talking to you never fails to boost my self-esteem."

Isaac shrugged modestly. "It's a God-given gift."

EZ Keep was a fenced-in, three-story building next to a gas station. Though I had never been here, I had walked or driven past self-storage places like this one hundreds of times. Real estate prices in Astor City were sky-high and, unless you were wealthy or had roommates like I did, you could not afford very much living space. A lot of people who moved here from less expensive areas stored their extra stuff in places like EZ Keep. Self-storage businesses were as much a part of big city life as panhandlers and muggings were.

During non-business hours, we would have needed to use the access code Truman had given us to get inside. Since it was business hours, we simply walked through the door of EZ Keep's front office. A young, pretty brunette behind the counter looked up. She smiled brightly at Isaac. Her smile faltered when her eyes fell on me. Pity mixed with disgust on her face. Now I knew how Frankenstein's monster felt.

"Can I help you gentlemen?" she said, though she only looked at Isaac when she said it. *Look away, I'm hideous.*

"We're just going to our unit," Isaac said. We breezed past the counter toward a glass door secured with a numeric code access panel on the far side of the office. I punched Truman's access code into the panel. The door buzzed unlocked. Isaac said to the employee, "When we come back, let's talk about what you can do to help me. I can think of a few things." Isaac winked at her. She blushed and giggled.

We passed through the door into a large loading area with two closed commercial bay doors. I hit the button for the elevator. The girl behind the counter looked at Isaac with obvious interest through the glass door we had just passed through.

"I like you better as a wingman when you look like this," Isaac said. "You make me look even more handsome than usual by comparison."

"As a matter of fact, when Mechano tried to cook me alive, all I could think was, 'Gosh, I hope this helps Isaac with the ladies.'"

"I've always said selflessness is your greatest virtue. You're a prince among men."

I changed the subject. "I'm starting to get worried you haven't heard back from Neha." It was the understatement of the century. I had a sickening feeling in my stomach that seemed to get worse with each passing moment. "You've left her several messages and we haven't heard a peep from her."

"I'm sure she's fine. Besides, she's a big girl. She can take care of herself." Despite his words, Isaac looked as worried as I felt.

We rode the elevator to the third floor. We walked through the wide corridors of the storage space, passing dozens of spaces of various sizes secured behind corrugated metal doors painted blue. Our footsteps on the bare cement floor echoed off the closed doors. The lights, controlled by motion detectors, clicked on and off as we made our way deeper into the facility. We saw only one other person, a middle-aged lady. The door to her storage unit was open. Her unit, the size of a medium-sized walk-in closet, was filled from floor to ceiling with furniture and bric-a-brac. She struggled to squeeze a wooden chair inside. I feared the unit's contents, already packed tight, would explode under the pressure of the addition, like one of those toy snakes in a can that shoots out when its lid is opened. I happily would have traded my problems for hers.

Each unit was numbered. We found the one we were looking for, Unit 357. Leave it to Truman to store the portal to The Mountain in a storage unit with the same number as a bullet round. I glanced around. A circle of light shone down on us from the overhead automatic lights. Beyond that was darkness. No one was around. I faintly heard the middle-aged woman grunt with exertion as she continued to try to shove her chair into her overstuffed unit. Hope sprang eternal. I admired her optimism, if not her sense of spatial relationships.

I unlocked the padlock securing Unit 357 using the key Truman had given us. I unlatched the door, leaving the open padlock hanging from it. I swung the unit's door open.

Inside the large unit was a single item in the center of the space. It was a brushed metal cylinder, dull silver in color, much wider and taller than I. The top of it almost touched the ceiling of the unit. A man-sized, rounded rectangular opening on the object faced us, letting us see the object was hollow. More brushed metal was inside of it.

This was the portal to The Mountain, just as Truman had described it to us. He had told us he had his super strong Metahuman friend Shadow break into the apartment Avatar leased under the name of his civilian secret identity once Truman grew to distrust the Sentinels. Since Truman did not want them to access The Mountain using the portal, he had Shadow carry it out of Avatar's apartment and hide it here. When I asked how Shadow had gotten the big portal out of Avatar's apartment and into this unit without being observed, Truman had said he didn't know the precise details, but that he did know it could not have been too hard because, as he put it, "Shadow could steal the pulp out of an orange without breaking the skin." Apparently, Shadow was a professional thief. Between Cassandra and Shadow, clearly Truman kept interesting company.

We stepped inside the storage unit. Despite the portal's size, there was so much room left inside the storage unit that several more people could have joined us without us jostling each other. I closed the door behind us and darkness swallowed us until Isaac flicked on the small penlight he'd brought.

Between the dim light and moving shadows, I felt like we'd stepped into a haunted house. After first using my telekinetic touch to ensure no one was around, I used my powers to lift the padlock on the other side of the door, snapping it shut. The point was not to lock us in, but to keep a passerby out. I could unlock the padlock readily enough again with my powers.

Isaac shined the light directly on the portal. We stared up at it in silence.

"What if something goes wrong and one of us gets stuck in that thing and suffocates? The longer I look at it, the more it looks like an oversized coffin," Isaac finally whispered.

"It does at that," I whispered back. "Don't let that stop you from hopping right on in."

"Me? You're the Omega. If you really are the latest in a long line of dashing heroes, leaping before you look and derring-do is right up your alley. You should go first. I'm just along for the ride to keep you from doing something more stupid than usual, provide comic relief, and hit on the pretty girls. There aren't any girls, pretty or otherwise, in that thing."

"Coward."

"I'd rather be a live jackal than a dead lion."

"Truman says it's perfectly safe."

"If it's so safe, why isn't he here with us letting his actions speak louder than his words by being the first to climb in?"

"You make a solid point." I sighed, and then stepped forward into the portal. The moment I was inside, a panel slid down from the top of the portal. I turned in time to see the portal snick closed. Isaac and his light disappeared.

I felt a surge of claustrophobia in the enclosed, totally dark space. Before my eyes could adjust to the darkness, the curved walls of the portal glowed slightly. I could see again. Not that there was much to see; the portal's interior walls were perfectly smooth and featureless, as if the metal structure had been carved rather than constructed.

The glow from the walls dimmed for a moment. My hair stood on end, as if static electricity had built up in my body after walking on thick carpet. The portal was scanning me. The sensation would have freaked me out more than it did had Truman not told me to expect it.

"Unidentified entity," a computerized voice said, making me jump even though I had been expecting it too, "please state the Hero's password to gain admittance." As there was no visible speaker, I had no idea where the voice came from. It seemed to come from all around me. Due to both nerves and my lingering injuries, my mind went completely blank. It was like that time a couple of months ago when a woman on the subway asked me where I worked. Made witless by the fact a cute girl was talking to me, for the life of me I couldn't remember the name of the newspaper. The girl had looked at me like I was soft in the head, and slowly backed away when I eventually stammered that I couldn't remember. I knew thanks to Truman that the portal would do more than give me a weird look and treat me like I had cooties if I didn't enter the password in time. It would hit me with knockout gas.

Fortunately, my brain fog lifted right as the portal demanded the password for the second time. I quickly recited the Hero's Oath, stumbling over the words a little in my haste: "No cave so dark, no pit so deep, will hide evil from my arm's sweep. Those who sow darkness soon shall reap, for in the pursuit of justice, I will never sleep."

"Password accepted. Please stand by for transport," spoke the computer voice.

It suddenly felt like there were bugs crawling on me, as if I had stuck both feet into an anthill and the ants were swarming all over. Despite the fact I knew to expect this too, reflex made me glance at my body, looking to see what made me itch. There was nothing to see of course. Well, on my body, at least. The walls of the portal soundlessly melted, like I had been dosed with LSD and reality was dissolving around me. I felt nauseous.

Soon after the portal's walls had started melting, they suddenly snapped back into place, as if the melting had been nothing more than a figment of my imagination. The nausea ended and the crawling bug sensation stopped.

The portal's entrance slid open again. Instead of the dark interior of the storage unit and Isaac being revealed, Isaac was gone and the area outside the portal was well-lit.

"Welcome to The Mountain, Hero," the portal's voice said. "When you wish to return to Astor City, simply step inside again. Enjoy your visit."

Feeling like Captain Kirk who had just used the Enterprise's transporters to beam down to an alien planet, I stepped out of the portal. Unlike Kirk, I was not confronted by an alien landscape and scantily clad Orion slave girls I would inevitably have sex with. Unfortunately. Rather, I was confronted with a massive cavern composed of gray rock marbled with veins of white and gold. The veins of white luminesced, making the cavern as bright as Las Vegas at noon. The cavern was so big, I felt like an ant by comparison.

The portal I exited was sunk into the rock face of the cavern. The rock face was curved, extending high above and to either side of me. The only gap in the rock face was far off to the right. Over there was a big hole, like the entrance to a massive cave. The hole was about the size of an opening to an airplane hangar. Through that huge gap was a breathtaking view down on clouds and snowcapped mountains of varying heights. The mountain range extended out for as far as I could see.

The Mountain was in the middle of the Himalayas according to Truman, who had determined that using GPS the last time he had visited here. Thanks to the portal's matter transport technology, I had traveled over seven thousand miles in the blink of an eye. Transporters were another technology Mechano had invented. Unlike most of Mechano's other tech which he had commercialized, the existence of transporters was a tightly guarded secret only members of the Guild knew about, much like the Guild's space station. Politicians would lose their minds if they knew Heroes withheld from the public technology that would revolutionize travel in a way the world had not seen since the introduction of the airplane.

The air at the gap showing the mountain range shimmered momentarily and turned slightly blue before becoming perfectly clear and transparent again. It was indicative of the force field which kept out the harsh cold and elements of the outside. The cavern was as warm and comfortable as my house's living room. More comfortable, actually, since the cavern was so much bigger—it had more square footage than our entire house did. Force field projectors like the ones here that kept the elements out were also Mechano's inventions according to Truman. As much as I hated to admit it, I had to give the devil his due: Mechano really was a latter-day Edison. It was a shame he was a Machiavellian murderous maniac in addition to one of the greatest technological geniuses of all time.

Isaac came out of the portal. He stood next to me. The cavern was completely silent, so much so that the only thing I heard was us breathing. With our mouths agape in wonder, we stood transfixed and looked around.

Directly ahead of us on the other side of the cavern was a curved computer monitor that was somehow suspended from the rock wall. It was massive. It clearly would tower over us if we stood directly in front of it. It was even wider than it was tall. It was angled slightly downward, toward the smooth stone that served as The Mountain's floor. Directly below the monitor was a long, curved, waist-high computer panel that looked like something on the bridge of a navy vessel a hundred years in the future. A single large black chair rested at the focus of the parabola formed by the curved computer monitor.

To the right of the computer panel were several headless mannequins. On each was mounted a copy of the iconic costume Avatar had always worn that was famous and instantly recognized the world over: blood red gloves, matching red shin-high boots, and a gray bodysuit with a utility belt around its waist. The utility belt's color matched that of the gloves and the boots. A bright red *A* was on the center of the chest of the bodysuit. A cape matching the red of the *A* was around the neck of each mannequin.

Mechano had said Avatar wore the Omega weapon in the form of a cape. Could one of these capes be it?

Suspended from the cavern's ceiling and on display throughout the cavern were various artifacts. As a big admirer of Avatar's who had followed his adventures ever since I had been old enough to know the difference between a licensed Hero and a hero sandwich, I knew they were mementos from Avatar's exploits over the years: the gigantic robot exoskeleton Doctor Diabolical had used to level the White House and the United States Capitol in 1971 before Avatar subdued him; the torch from the Statue of Liberty, destroyed in 1985 by the Rogue Black Plague when he threw the statue at Avatar; the originally normal-sized but now man-sized glass tumbler that

Magnifier had tried to brain the British Prime Minister with in 1982; and remnants of the V'Loth alien mothership Omega Man had destroyed in 1966 when he, Avatar, and a bunch of other Heroes attacked the alien fleet hovering in the skies of Baltimore. There were many other artifacts from Avatar's adventures here, some of which I did not even recognize.

After gawking in silence for a bit, Isaac and I looked at each other. His eyes were wide.

"You have a lair!" he said with wonder. "I'm jealous. I always wanted a lair."

"I don't have a lair," I protested. "Avatar had a lair."

"Avatar had a lair. Avatar was the Omega. Avatar is dead. Now you are the Omega. Therefore, you have a lair."

"I'm not sure I agree with your logic, but we'll argue about syllogisms later. Right now, the sooner we find the Omega weapon the better. Assuming it's even here."

"While we look, give some thought as to changing your lair's name from The Mountain. It's too Game of Thronesy."

With Isaac in my wake, I strode across the cavern to the mannequins adorned with Avatar costumes. Despite the fact the rock floor was so shiny and smooth it looked like it had been polished, it was not at all slippery. My shoes had no problem with traction.

We stood in front of the broad-chested costumed mannequins. Each of the five mannequins had on seemingly identical costumes. Just looking at them, nothing was remarkable about the capes on each headless figure. Well, other than the fact they had belonged to one of the world's greatest Heroes. These costumes and everything else in the cavern really belonged in a museum where admirers of Avatar could see them instead of them gathering dust here. If I got out of this fix with the Sentinels with my neck intact, I would make sure everything here got a good home.

But, first things first. Holding my breath nervously, I reached toward the cape on the first mannequin. My hands were clammy. I was anxious. I had no idea what would happen when the Omega weapon came into contact with the host of the Omega spirit. Whatever did happen, I expected it to be something dramatic.

My fingers met the cape's fabric.

Nothing happened.

I waited expectantly.

More nothing happened.

"Maybe you need to say 'Shazam!' or 'It's clobberin' time!'" Isaac suggested.

"You're not helping," I said. "Maybe this cape isn't the right one. Or, maybe it needs to be worn to be activated."

I pulled the cape off the mannequin, undoing the heavy gray metal clasp which held it together around the neck. I draped it around myself, redoing the clasp to secure the cape. The cape's fabric was so heavy I felt its weight on my shoulders. As Avatar had been much taller and broader than I, the cape dragged on the ground and enveloped me like a robe.

Now that the cape was on me, I again waited expectantly. And again, nothing happened. Other than me feeling like a grave robber for wearing a dead Hero's cape, that is.

Isaac eyed me critically. "You look like a trick-or-treater who can't afford a costume other than a bedsheet."

"You're still not helping."

I took the cape off, put it back on the mannequin, and went through the same process with the next cape. And then the next one, the next one, and the next one. With each attempt resulting in nothing happening, I felt increasingly frustrated and foolish, like a ghost hunter looking for a ghost in a haunted house that probably wasn't even haunted.

"So much for hiding the Omega weapon in plain sight," I said as I pulled the last cape off.

"Assuming it's in the form of a cape. Assuming it's here. And, assuming it really exists and wasn't made up by the Sentinels to send you on a wild goose chase for reasons we don't understand."

"Well aren't you a ray of sunshine and optimism today."

"Being told that the guy you routinely crush in chess, *Civilization*, and *Call of Duty* is possessed by some eternal, world-saving incubus makes me skeptical. Call me crazy."

I put the cape back on the last mannequin. I was plenty skeptical myself, but that did not mean I would stop looking for a way to fight back against the Sentinels. "C'mon," I said, moving away from the mannequins, "there are plenty other places to look before we throw in the towel."

Isaac followed. "Since the capes are apparently a no-go, what should we be looking for? Something in a case that reads 'Break glass in the event of the Sentinels trying to kill you?'"

"Heck if I know. I'm hoping we'll know it when we see it."

We started to systematically search the contents of The Mountain. It was hard to shake the feeling we were doing something profane by going through a dead man's things. I felt like a tour guide as I told Isaac what each item represented in the history of Avatar's adventures. Though Isaac knew of Avatar—who didn't?—he was not the Avatar fanboy that I was.

The first thing we ran across that stumped me as to what it was was in the far corner of the cavern from where we came through the portal at. It was a cube-shaped enclosure made of thick, almost transparent glass on four of its sides. Its back wall and floor were the cavern's rock face. The enclosure was big enough to comfortably contain several people. It was completely empty. Its only opening was a door-shaped hole in one of the cube's clear sides. A gold-colored round switch that looked like a dimmer switch was mounted on the enclosure by the door.

I tapped experimentally on a clear wall of the enclosure with a knuckle. It felt as solid as a rock. "Could this thing be it?" I asked.

"What do I look like, the Omega whisperer?" Isaac said. "Hell if I know."

Feeling like a guinea pig with a death wish, I stepped into the enclosure through its door. Nothing happened. I felt the same as I always did, except for more frustrated. So much nothing was happening, I would have been more surprised had something happened.

"You want me to hit the switch?" Isaac asked from the other side of the enclosure.

I sighed in resignation, then steeled myself. "Sure. If this thing happens to be a gas chamber, I bequeath to you what little remains in my bank account."

"I'll try to not spend it all in one place. Here goes." Isaac pressed down on the switch.

This time, something actually did happen: the door I had walked through soundlessly shrank in on itself and then disappeared, like an ameba twisting itself into a different shape. The opening I had stepped through was now filled with the same nearly transparent material that surrounded me. I immediately felt different, and not in a good way. The slight burning sensation I had felt in my hands ever since my powers first manifested was gone. I had grown so accustomed to the feeling over the years that its absence was very disconcerting. I felt naked and vulnerable, as if I had been stripped of my clothes in the middle of a crowd. I had experienced this feeling only once before, during the Trials when Hacker's powers and mine were nullified on the planet Hephaestus.

I lifted my hands slightly and tried to pick myself off the ground with my powers. I did not budge. What had become as second nature to me as breathing now felt impossible.

"Can you hear me?" I said to Isaac, trying to keep the panic of being without my powers out of my voice. I would have given my left nut to be rid of my powers when I first got them. What a difference a few years could make.

"Clear as a bell," he said, the look on his face indicating he was as surprised as I that he could hear me through the thick but nearly transparent walls. It was as if thin air rather than the thick material separated us.

"I think being in here has shut my powers off. Hit the switch again."

Isaac did so. As if by magic, the door dilated open again. The burning in my hands resumed. I levitated slightly off the ground. I was relieved my powers were back. I was so used to them, the thought of losing them was like losing an arm or a leg.

I used my telekinetic touch to probe the enclosure's clear material. Whatever it was made of, it was dense, denser than even the solid rock that was the cube's floor and back wall. I doubted a jackhammer could even scratch the clear material.

"You know what I think this is?" I said. "I think it's a Metahuman holding cell."

"You mean Avatar had his own personal mini-MetaHold? I don't know whether to be impressed or appalled. How often do you suppose he used this thing on somebody?"

"I have no idea. If he kept someone in here, I'm guessing he didn't do it for long. There's obviously no toilet, running water, or food in here."

After playing around with the enclosure for a while, we determined that fresh air got inside it even when the door was closed, though we couldn't figure out how. Pressing and depressing the switch turned the Metahuman dampening field inside the enclosure on and off; turning the knob of the switch controlled the size of the door, from it being a tiny fist-sized opening to it being a full-sized door. But, as interesting as the enclosure and how its technology might work was, fooling around with it was not bringing us closer to finding the Omega weapon. We moved on to examine other items in the cavern.

"What the heck is this thing?" Isaac demanded in front of one of them. "It looks like the Washington Monument's biracial little brother."

"This?" I said absentmindedly, my concentration on where I would hide a cape if I were Avatar. By this time, we had searched most of the cavern. Maybe we'd try the remains of the V'Loth mothership next, which was suspended from the cavern's ceiling from struts directly above us. "This is the neutronium spear Star Czar threw at Avatar years ago." Isaac was right—the object did look more like an obelisk like the Washington Monument than like the spear Star Czar had called it. Dull black in color, its point came up to about as high as my chin. Its base, which rested flat on the cavern's smooth rock floor, was slightly bigger than an extra-large pizza box.

"Neutronium?" Isaac frowned. "What's that?"

If I hadn't been so distracted with thoughts of the Omega weapon, I would have been more smug about knowing something Isaac didn't. He had graduated from the Academy second in our class, right behind Neha. He usually schooled me on things, not vice versa. "It's composed solely of neutrons. Highly dense and once thought to only exist inside of neutron stars, it's the heaviest substance known to man. Avatar with his Omega-level super strength was said to be the only person who could pick this neutronium spear up. Well, other than Star Czar, but that's just because his powers allowed him to create and control neutronium. Since Star Czar is as dead as Avatar, I imagine the neutronium spear will sit here undisturbed for millennia until the earth swallows this mountain again." I pointed upward impatiently. "We're wasting time. Come on, let's check inside the V'Loth spaceship."

I launched myself into the air, coming to a stop abreast the gaping hole in the side of the V'Loth mothership. Isaac joined me in the form of a large golden-hued eagle that glowed faintly. His wings beat powerfully in the air as he hovered next to me. I did not know what this creature was, but I did not have the encyclopedic knowledge of mythological creatures Isaac did.

The original V'Loth mothership had been smashed to pieces when Omega Man had killed the alien queen inside. The pieces that remained of it had been assembled together up here like a giant jigsaw puzzle, with the pieces held in place by thick cables extending from the cavern's ceiling. About the length of an eighteen-wheeled truck, the spaceship looked like a stereotypical UFO, as if a giant silver pie pan had been flipped over and welded on top of another one. Scientists speculated that this iconic UFO shape was associated with aliens even before the V'Loths' arrival in the 1960s because the V'Loths had visited Earth before at some point in man's distant history. I had no idea if that theory was correct. I was a Hero, not an astrobiologist. Between botching the situation with Hannah and my apparent inability to find the Omega weapon, I had not been doing such a hot job of merely being a Hero lately. I had no business speculating on the origins of the UFO trope. I needed to stay in my lane.

We entered the spaceship through the hole on its side. The inside of it was mostly empty space, except for a few large pieces of equipment. I could not even begin to guess at their purpose. Perhaps the ship had been stripped mostly clean over the years. Or, maybe the V'Loths simply traveled light. I had no idea and, frankly, didn't care.

With Isaac still in his bird form, together we searched what little remained in the spaceship as carefully as we could. If the Omega weapon was hidden up here, we sure as heck did not recognize it as such.

We were running out of places to look in the cavern. I was beyond frustrated. Maybe Isaac was right—maybe the Omega weapon was not here. Maybe it didn't exist at all, and the Sentinels had been lying to me. I certainly would not put it past them.

We exited the spaceship from the same hole we entered it. I hovered in the air for a few moments, trying to think of something we might have missed. Isaac flapped in the air next to me. Suddenly, he let out a squawk. It sounded like a squawk of excitement. It just as easily could have been him saying, "I really wanna poop on a car right now." Just like I wasn't an astrobiologist, I wasn't an ornithologist either.

Isaac dove toward the cavern floor as if his eagle form was about to kill a mouse. Curious as to what he was making a fuss about, I too descended. By the time I landed near the neutronium spear, Isaac had already transformed into his normal self. He was on one knee next to the black obelisk.

"What kind of eagle was that?" I asked.

"Aetos Dios," he said absentmindedly, preoccupied by whatever he was looking at. His finger traced a pattern on the floor next to the obelisk.

"In English. I'm not bilingual."

He looked up. "Huh? Oh. It means Eagle of Zeus. And guess what my eagle eyes spotted from up above?"

"My impatience?" I was in no mood for guessing games.

"No. I saw an indentation in the rock floor next to the neutronium spear. It's hard to see it with human eyes, but you can feel it. Come here. Give me your hand. See?" Isaac guided my hand up, across, and then down again, like it was the planchette on a Ouija board. I knew what a planchette was, but not how to find the Omega weapon. Marvelous.

Isaac was right—there was a big square indentation in the surface of the rock next to the neutronium spear. I couldn't see it, but I could feel it.

"So the floor is not as perfectly smooth as it looks," I said. "I don't get why you're so excited."

Isaac shook his head at me. "I think Mechano's energy blast cooked your brains a little. The indentation on the floor is square, and seems to be the same size as the base of the spear. If the spear is as heavy as you say it is, it could've caused the indentation in the floor. It's as if Avatar moved it from where it left this indentation to where it rests now."

"So Avatar moved the spear. I still don't get why you're making a federal case out of it."

"Don't you see? If Avatar is the only person who can lift this thing, maybe he moved it because he hid something under it. Something like the Omega weapon."

I was dubious. "You're making a mighty big deal over Avatar moving the spear a couple of feet. Maybe he simply thought the cavern's feng shui was better with the spear here."

"Well, there's one way to find out." Isaac moved over to the spear and got on both knees in front of it. His body glowed slightly as it always did when he underwent a transformation. His body became translucent. He had assumed his ghost form, something I had seen him do many times before. He shoved his hand down toward the base of the neutronium spear. Part of his arm sank through the floor as if the floor was made of air instead of solid rock.

His face grew excited. "There's a small cavity in the floor right underneath the spear. Something's in here. I can't touch it like this, of course, but I know it's there. A solid feels different when my hand passes through it than empty space does."

I was getting excited too. "Can you pull it out?"

Isaac retracted his arm. He was empty-handed. His body became solid again. "I can't go solid while I'm phased through something."

"What would happen if you tried?"

"Two solids trying to occupy the same space at the same time?" Isaac put his fists together, then spread them out while making an exploding sound. "A massive explosion would happen, flavored with bits of Isaac. You wouldn't be around to enjoy the fireworks display as the blast would likely kill you too."

"Oh," I said.

"Yeah, oh."

I was now as disappointed as I had been excited moments before. What had Avatar hidden under the neutronium spear if not the Omega weapon? If Isaac couldn't phase it out, it might as well be on the far side of the moon for all the good it would do us under the impossibly heavy obelisk. If the Omega weapon really had been stashed under the obelisk, it was so close, and yet still so far away.

Isaac squatted down a bit with his legs straddling the spear. He wrapped his arms around it.

"What in the world are you doing?" I asked.

"Since the EZ Keep clerk isn't handy, I'm making love to the neutronium spear," he said. "What's it look like I'm doing? Trying to pick this damned thing up, of course." He heaved up. Well, he tried to. Despite Isaac straining against it, the spear didn't move so much as a millimeter.

"Weren't you listening before when I told you Avatar is the only one strong enough to move it?"

Isaac continued to strain. The cords stood out on his neck. After struggling vainly, he gave up.

"The *Hero Hags* website says I have my powers because I'm half-demon," he gasped. "It also says that naked you look like a human tripod. The fact urban legend says something, that doesn't mean it's true. I'll try again, only I'll kick the horse-power up some."

Isaac's form shimmered again, becoming larger and more imposing. A huge, bare-chested, burly man with a black bull's horned head took Isaac's place. He had turned into the Minotaur, one of Isaac's forms that had super strength.

I would have said that Isaac was full of bull if he really thought he could lift the obelisk even in his Minotaur form, but making puns did not seem terribly helpful. Since lighting a candle was more useful than cursing the darkness, I said "I'll help," as Isaac squatted down around the obelisk again. I extended my hands, latching onto the obelisk with my powers. "We'll lift together on three."

On the count of three, the muscles of Isaac's Minotaur form rippled dramatically, like a bodybuilder doing a clean and press with a loaded barbell. He grunted and snorted like a bull fighting a matador as he heaved on the spear. I too tried to lift it with my powers, envisioning it as a thimble I was trying to pluck off someone's thumb.

To be honest, my heart wasn't entirely in the effort. I had already done a quick calculation of how much the spear weighed by taking how much a cubic inch of neutronium was said to weigh and doing a rough extrapolation from that based on how big the spear was. The answer had so many zeroes I thought we wouldn't be able to lift the spear even if we had a few dozen Heroes here to help us.

It gave me no pleasure to see that I was right. Despite us straining to lift it, the neutronium spear did not budge even the tiniest bit. We did not come up with an answer to that classic paradox of what happens when an unstoppable force is met with an immovable object because, though we seemed to have found an immovable object, Isaac and I combined were hardly an unstoppable force.

Isaac gave up. He fell backward to the floor, transforming back into his human form as he sprawled there. His chest heaved; his face was red. I lowered my arms and also desisted. I sat down heavily on the hard floor. I felt the way Isaac looked.

"If Avatar hid his diary under this thing and not the Omega weapon, I'm going to be awfully pissed," Isaac gasped.

"Not that we're likely to find out."

"I've lifted a locomotive in my Minotaur form, but the neutronium spear might as well have laughed at our combined efforts. What was it Archimedes said? 'Give me a lever long enough and a fulcrum on which to place it, and I shall move the world.' I defy that old fraud to move this thing. It goes to show that just because you're dead and distinguished, it doesn't mean you know what in the heck you're talking about."

I stood up so abruptly that I got light-headed.

I said, "Maybe you were right about Mechano having cooked my brain. Good God, I'm stupid."

"And you're just now realizing it? To what do those of us who've known it for a while owe this epiphany?"

"You're stupid too for not having thought of it either," I said. "We don't need to be strong enough to pick the spear up. We just need to lever it over so we expose whatever is buried in the cavity underneath it."

Isaac thought about that for a moment. Then he stood up and brushed his hands off. Still breathing hard, he looked disgusted. "As much as it pains me to admit it, you're right—I *am* stupid for not having thought of it. As soon as I catch my breath, we'll try again."

I let out a long breath and ran a hand over my head. I was sweating, from both exertion and my Mechano-induced injuries.

"No, we won't try again," I said. "I need to try by myself. You'll just be in the way."

Isaac blinked. "Excuse me?"

"That sounded harsher than I meant it to. I just mean that I really have to let loose if I'm going to even come close to tipping the spear over. If I'm worrying about not crushing you in the process, I'm not going to be able to apply maximum pressure."

Isaac frowned thoughtfully.

"As much as it bothers me to admit twice you're right, you are right again," he finally concluded. "We both know you have a lot more raw power than I do. If one of us is going to pull this off, it'll be you. Don't mind me. I'll just stand here, look pretty, and cheer you on." Isaac pursed his lips. "If I'd known this would be my role in this craziness, I'd have brought some pom-poms along."

"I'm just grateful you left your cheerleading skirt at home."

"Don't be jealous of my sexy bow legs."

"All right," I said, realizing I was procrastinating, "back up some and give me room." As Isaac did so, I started to focus on what I needed to do. Part of my brain supplied me with how many newtons, or units of force, I needed to tip the neutronium spear over based on my earlier estimate of how much it weighed. The number was massive. I had never generated that much force before in my life. Nor did I think I could. The task seemed impossible.

Then again, what was it Nelson Mandela had said? "It always seems impossible until someone does it." Easy for him to say. I was no transformative figure the way he was. If he were here, maybe a great man like him could come up with a way to get the job done.

Unfortunately, Mandela wasn't here for me to foist the job off on. All I could do was my best.

I faced the neutronium spear head-on. I raised my personal force field to help protect my body from the external pressure I would soon exert on it. I gathered my will, picturing clearly in my mind what I wanted to do.

I wanted to apply a narrow beam of pressure to the top of the spear, like using a pencil to tip over a liter of soda. Simultaneous with applying pressure to the obelisk, I would need to apply an equal amount of force to my body in the opposite direction. It was Newton's Third Law of Motion in action: To every action, there was an equal and opposite reaction. Newton's law was why rockets worked even in the vacuum of space—their rocket engines applied thrust, pushing the rocket in the opposite direction of the thrust even though there was no air to push off of. If I applied the tremendous amount of force I needed to the obelisk without simultaneously applying the exact same amount of force to my body in the opposite direction, I'd shove myself into the cavern wall behind me and be smeared like a bug on a windshield.

I took a deep, calming breath. I was as ready as I was going to be.

To help me concentrate, I extended my arms toward the neutronium spear. I unleashed the invisible beam of pressure I had visualized in my mind on the top of the spear. At the exact same time, I carefully exerted the same amount of force against the back of my personal shield.

Phew! I was not thrown backward through the cavern wall like a shot cannonball. So, I had at least done this part successfully. The obelisk still hadn't budged an inch, of course, but this small success was heartening considering my disastrous track record recently. Baby steps.

Time to ramp the force up. I pushed harder and harder against the obelisk, while of course pushing equally hard against myself. It was like slowly turning a faucet handle and unleashing more and more water pressure.

Soon the faucet was all the way open. I pushed as hard against the spear as I was capable.

From Isaac's perspective, my struggle against the spear was no doubt soundless. From my perspective, things were anything but. My heart pounded so hard, it felt like it would burst right out of my chest. My head, already hurting from my encounter with Mechano, ached even more painfully, as if I had stuck it into an ever-tightening vise. My blood roared in my ears. My body started to shake, as if I stood in the epicenter of an earthquake. I pushed against the obelisk as hard as I thought I could, exerting more of my power against it than I had ever used on anything before. The amount of force I brought to bear on the neutronium spear would swat a jumbo jet out of the air like it was a paper airplane.

The obelisk did not move one iota. I could have been tickling the damned thing with a feather for all the good I was doing.

It was no use. I had failed. Again. You would think I would be used to it by now. I'd been getting lots of practice lately.

I was about to give up.

But then, I got mad. Being rejected by Neha, getting Hannah killed, not being able to find Antonio, not knowing how to deal with the Sentinels and then having to run from them when I finally found the balls to confront them, feeling overwhelmed by life in the big city . . . I was heartily sick of being a loser, of feeling like I was too small of a person to deal with the big issues I had to grapple with. Was I just some dumb hick from South Carolina who was incapable of rising to the occasion? Or, was I the Omega? How was I supposed to save the world if I couldn't knock over a stupid rock?

No! No more failures. No more running away. No more being a loser. It would end today. One way or another.

I knew my body couldn't take much more of this stress. My outstretched arms hurt, as if someone who got heavier by the second sat on top of them. They felt like they'd snap under the strain. It didn't matter. Pain didn't matter. The pressure and stress on my body didn't matter. If I couldn't best an inanimate object, what chance did I have against the Sentinels? I was going to either move this damned neutronium spear, or die trying. If the latter, maybe the Omega spirit would find a worthier host the next time. Good luck to him or her, plus my most heartfelt condolences. I hoped the next Omega knew better than to let his father and friends be killed.

I dug deeper. I hit reserves of strength that, frankly, I didn't even know I had.

The pressure against the obelisk increased. The pressure on my body increased as well. My head throbbed, feeling like it would explode. My ears popped with sharp stabs of pain. Wetness trickled out of them and down my neck. Isaac yelled something, wanting me to stop. I could only faintly hear him, like he was shouting down to me after I had fallen into a deep, dark well. I tasted blood. My nose bled, making it hard to breathe. It was just as well. My lungs were on fire anyway. Who cared? Not me. Everybody knew oxygen was overrated.

I had zoomed right past exhaustion, and rapidly approached collapse. My body cried uncle.

Screw you, I thought to my body. *You're not the boss of me.*

I kept going. I shut out the shrieks and complaints of my flesh. The Mountain, Isaac, everything around me, the entire universe seemed to fade out of existence. There was only me and the neutronium spear. My dark nemesis.

My power surged out of me at levels like I had never experienced before.

Move, I demanded of my nemesis.

It didn't. My jaw clenched so tight, I was vaguely aware of teeth cracking. Mine, I guess. Not the indestructible Mechano ones, presumably. He could go screw himself too. My too-eager-to-throw-in-the-towel, bitch-ass body and Mechano could have a go screw yourself orgy together. As long as they kept me out of it, I didn't care.

Move!

My dark nemesis still didn't. It was proving to be as stubborn as I was. Maybe it would be the new Omega.

Move!!! It had become a mantra. My vision blurred and darkened, like a computer screen that was about to die.

I couldn't see it, but I felt it—the tiniest bit of movement in the neutronium spear. A slight tremor, like when the guy you're arm wrestling is weakening.

Move!!!

Finally, incredibly, unexpectedly, it did. The neutronium spear slowly tipped out of the vertical like a falling domino. Once it was clear it was going to fall, I shut off my powers, relieving the skull-crushing pressure on my mind. I slumped to my knees, hunched over, feeling like a melted candle. I hadn't realized that only my powers had been holding me up toward the end of my struggle.

Son of a bitch! I had pulled it off.

The neutronium spear hit the floor with a crash they might have heard back in Astor City. A crack split open in the rock floor from the point of impact all the way to the far wall. It was as if a giant had come along and pulled the floor apart like it was two halves of a grapefruit. The entire cavern shook, as if a monstrous earthquake had hit. The rock under and around us rumbled. I more felt the rumbles than heard them. Though not completely deaf, my ears weren't working correctly. Isaac shouted something. I couldn't figure out what between my defective ears and the rumbling.

Isaac in his angel form dove into me, shoulder first, like a football player tackling a defenseless receiver. Something inside of me cracked. A rib maybe. I was flung to the side, hitting the ground back first. My body exploded with fresh pain, proving that you could make water wetter. I slid for a bit on the smooth rock surface with Isaac on top of me. An instant later, one of the fragments of the V'Loth ship hit the floor right where I had just been kneeling. If I had still been there, it would've brained me. Obviously it had been shaken loose from its mooring by the faux earthquake.

Isaac lay on top of me with his huge white wings folded around me, shielding me from falling bits of rock from the cavern's ceiling. He stayed there, wrapped around me protectively, until the rumbling around us lessened and then finally died off entirely.

"If someone walked in on us right now, we'd have a hard time convincing them we're not actually boyfriends like I told your boss," Isaac said into my ear once the shaking and rattling ended. Thanks to whatever was wrong with my ears, I barely heard him.

"You saved my life. Thanks." I spit out a tooth chip. My throat felt like I had gargled with glass shards. It hurt to talk. It hurt to everything.

"No. I saved your life *again*. I've done it before, remember?"

Isaac's weight was on my chest. "Grateful, but can't breathe," I rasped.

"Oh! Sorry." Isaac scrambled to his feet. Bits of rock and other debris sloughed off his broad wings and back, pattering like rain on the hard floor. The pressure on my chest lessened, but didn't disappear. Something deep inside my body wasn't right. Every breath was agonizing.

Isaac shimmered and changed from his bare-chested angel form back into his usual self. Other than a gash on his cheek, he seemed none the worse for wear. I wished I could say the same. I felt like a dishrag that had been wrung dry, had holes shot through it, and then set on fire, with the resulting ashes then ground to a fine powder.

"Myth's my name, saving Omegas is my game," Isaac said as he brushed himself off. Despite his flippant words, Isaac seemed awestruck by what I had managed to do to the neutronium spear. The look on his face told me he was for the first time taking seriously the notion that I was the Omega. "You okay? You look worse than you did when we came here, and that's saying something."

"Been better." This was one of those times I wished Isaac didn't talk so much. My ears hurt, not to mention everything else. It was hard to hear. It was hard concentrating on anything other than breathing. If it weren't for the fact moving hurt too much, I would be writhing in pain right now. "Think you broke a rib."

"Better a broken rib than a broken neck." Isaac glanced over at the fallen neutronium spear. "I've gotta admit I'm pretty impressed with you right now. You moved the damned thing. Shall we go see what awaits us under the Christmas tree?"

Since I could not get up on my own, all I could do was nod weakly. Isaac bent over and helped me to my feet. Though I felt like I had been broken and then pieced back together again by a five-year-old with string and Silly Putty, with assistance, I could walk.

Supported by Isaac, I hobbled over to where the neutronium spear lay on its side. A zigzagging crack a couple of feet deep and several inches wide ran from where the spear had fallen all the way to the distant wall the tip of it pointed at. The crack looked like the Grand Canyon in miniature.

With the spear overturned, a cavity was revealed. It was several inches deep and right under where the flat base of the spear had once rested. Lying inside the cavity was a red cape, folded into a square with military precision. Though it looked just like the capes hanging from the mannequins, this had to be what we were looking for. Why else would Avatar hide it under the neutronium spear?

"Help me down," I said weakly to Isaac. He lowered me to my knees. Blood dripped from my face, splattering the floor. A wave of nausea and vertigo washed over me, almost making me topple, before I steadied myself against Isaac's leg.

My hand shook with a combination of nerves, excitement, and pain as I extended it toward the folded cape. Though my experiences with the other capes made me halfway expect nothing to happen, I still felt the way King Arthur must have felt when he tried to pull Excalibur from the stone. Assuming Arthur had been shoved into a burlap bag and beaten with sticks first.

My hand touched the cape.

The light of a thousand suns exploded right in front of my eyes. Isaac, The Mountain, and everything else were swept away like dust before a broom.

I fell over, into oblivion.

22

The plan had gone to complete shit.

The smoke from Baltimore's burning buildings rose from below in thick, dark, hot, toxic plumes. It got into my eyes, partly blinding me. I tried to blink away my sweat and the smoke-induced irritation. My hard blinks almost made me miss a silver V'Loth spaceship emerging from the smoke right in front of me, like a shark out of the murky depths of the ocean.

Knowing from prior experience my force fields would protect me from direct impacts with the ships but were entirely useless against the V'Loths' energy missiles, I darted down and to the left in the air. A glowing energy pulse from the ship missed me by inches, and was swallowed by the surrounding smoke. The near miss singed my right side, even with my protective Kinetic suit on. A howl of pain escaped my lips. It was like being branded by a giant red-hot poker.

The tiny device lodged in my ear buzzed with angry static, setting my teeth on edge. It was a combination transmitter and receiver designed by Mechano which was supposed to allow us Heroes to coordinate our attack on the V'Loths. Its frequencies were no doubt being jammed by the aliens. Though there were Heroes all around me in the smoke, with our communications down, I might as well have been alone.

The buzzing in my ear mingled with the faint screams of other Heroes, the high-pitched whines of countless V'Loth ships as they cut through the air in pursuit of us, the bone-rattling explosions all around me, and the crackling fires below. It was a scene out of Dante's *Inferno*.

Yeah, there was no doubt about it:

The plan had gone to complete shit.

NOTHING HAD GONE WELL EVER SINCE THE V'LOTH SHIPS HAD unexpectedly appeared in the sky over every major city on the planet weeks ago. The date they had shown up—August 12, 1966—would no doubt be a date which would live in infamy. Assuming humanity itself lived.

For fifteen days the V'Loth ships had hung in the sky, completely motionless, like they had been painted there. None of us knew at the time that V'Loth was the name of their species. That knowledge came later. When they appeared, the V'Loths had ignored all attempts at communication by the United Nations and the world's governments. Even when the Soviet Union's fighter jets opened fire on the spaceships hovering over Moscow—a proud people, the Soviets always have had more machismo than prudence—the spaceships ignored the jets' missiles like a sleeping giant would ignore gnats. The missiles did no more damage to the spaceships than a water balloon would do to a tank.

After the initial excitement and fear wore off, people got

used to the alien ships hanging in the sky. They became as much of a fixture there as the sun, the moon, or the stars from whence the V'Loths had apparently come. Politicians debated endlessly about what to do. They wound up doing nothing. That was hardly new. For most of humanity, life returned to normal.

Humanity's endless adaptability was why we had become the dominant species on Earth. I and many other Heroes were still nervous every time we looked up at the spaceships, though. We had seen too much over the years to be blasé about the hovering objects. There was talk about banding together into some sort of Heroes' Guild for the purpose of building a space station to warn us if another group of aliens approached Earth. Mechano apparently had even begun the design work on it. Though it wasn't a bad idea, building a space station after the V'Loths' arrival struck me as being like locking the barn door after the horse had already been stolen.

No one knew what the V'Loths were doing as their still ships hovered silently. Napping, perhaps, tired after their journey across the stars. Monitoring American television and trying to make heads or tails out of *The Beverly Hillbillies*, maybe.

Or, more likely as it turned out, deciding on the best way to wipe out humanity root and branch.

Humanity's reign as the world's dominant species ended abruptly sixteen days after the V'Loth ships appeared. Like a switch had been flipped, all the ships around the world abruptly came to life. They launched surgically precise yet devastating energy blasts at the cities below them. Millions were killed, including several Heroes. Millions more were injured.

In a matter of minutes, the world's great cities were incapacitated. As the cities were the centers of government, technology, culture, and finance, humanity itself was largely incapacitated. Fortunately, thanks to the United States' Hero Act of 1945 and similar laws enacted in other countries, the world had Heroes to defend it. Unfortunately, the V'Loths easily defeated the Heroes who took them on. With the world's various governments crippled, our Heroic counterattacks against the V'Loths were too haphazard and uncoordinated. A guild of Heroes which could organize our defense efforts looked like an even better idea than before, but it was too late for that now. The milk had already been spilled.

It took several days, far longer than it would have if we had some sort of centralized organization, but many of the surviving Heroes from around the world met to try to figure out what to do about the V'Loth threat. I and my wife Neha, aka the Hero Smoke, of course attended. While there, Laser Lass told us all she had heard of a kid in Nebraska whose telepathic powers had recently manifested thanks to him hitting puberty. He allegedly had tapped into the V'Loths' minds and could provide intelligence on them.

Being desperate to find anything that would help us combat the V'Loths, a couple of Heroes were dispatched to look into the kid. It turned out that the 13-year-old boy wasn't a dead end as we suspected he might be. Telepaths were as uncommon as hen's teeth, after all. The vast majority of people who claimed they were telepathic were either frauds, con men, or crazy. But this kid was the real deal. His name was Vaughn Hope. Fitting, because Vaughn was our last, best hope to defeat the alien menace.

Technically, it was of course illegal for Vaughn to use his powers as he was not licensed to do so. As humanity was under an existential threat, none of us Heroes quibbled about encouraging Vaughn to use his powers to help us. We needed to do what had to be done.

Thanks to Vaughn's powers and him burrowing into the aliens' minds, we learned much about the menace we faced:

The aliens called themselves the V'Loths. In English, their name translated into "The People," which says just about all that needs to be said as to how the V'Loths viewed every race that was not them. To them, humans were little more than mold that needed to be cut off the loaf of bread that was Earth.

Like many wasps and ants here on Earth, V'Loth society had a hive-based hierarchical structure. When a new V'Loth queen was born, she left the world she was born on along with a V'Loth armada under her telepathic control. The V'Loth queens were the only V'Loths with any real intelligence; the drones in their armadas were little more than cannon fodder, as intelligent as fingers moving at the command of a brain. A newly born V'Loth queen would then find a suitable new world to make her own. In that fashion, the V'Loths had conquered numerous worlds through the galaxy. Unfortunately, Earth was the planet this particular V'Loth queen had set her colonizing sights on even though our atmosphere was toxic to her. If she left her spacecraft, she would have to wear an elaborate life support suit to survive. The V'Loths planned on terraforming Earth to make its atmosphere more palatable to them after humanity was taken care of.

If you killed the queen, the rest of the V'Loths would be crippled, Vaughn's powers told us. It would be like cutting the head off a snake—the rest of the snake's body might continue to twitch, but it would no longer be a threat.

Based on what we learned from Vaughn, what we needed to do was clear: Find the V'Loth queen and kill her. With the rest of the V'Loth fleet around the world rendered impotent, we could then mop them up at our leisure. Heroes normally didn't kill, of course, but this was not a normal situation. The information we gleaned from Vaughn about the V'Loths made it apparent there was no way to resolve this situation peacefully. You couldn't negotiate with a race of people who did not even view you as a sentient person. If a gnat buzzed around your head, did you try to reason with it, or did you simply swat it? That's how the V'Loths saw us—annoying gnats to be swatted.

Vaughn sensed that the V'Loth queen was in one of the ships hovering over Baltimore, Maryland, but he could not tell exactly which ship without getting closer to her. So, the plan was to take Vaughn to Baltimore. His parents did not even blink at us putting him in danger this way. As James Conley II —my and Neha's son—was about Vaughn's age, I could appreciate how terrified his parents must have been at us needing to take Vaughn to Baltimore and put him in harm's way. But, they were both former Marines. They knew both what was at stake and about making sacrifices for the greater good.

Once Vaughn pinpointed the ship the V'Loth queen was in, we planned to take it out. We assembled the greatest Metahuman force the world had ever known to do so. Every Hero we could get a hold of participated, along with several Rogues who were deemed trustworthy enough.

As plans went, it seemed a good one. It was nice and simple, as all the best plans were, since that meant there were less things to go wrong. Step One of the V'Loth plan: Go to Baltimore. Step Two: Find the V'Loth queen. Step Three: Kill the queen. Step Four: High-five each other.

The plan went to hell the moment Wormhole simultaneously transported all of us to various points in Baltimore near the alien ships. An energy pulse from one of the spaceships vaporized Vaughn the instant he materialized. I knew because I was one of the Heroes assigned to guard him. I witnessed the

13-year-old's death with my own horrified eyes. The pulse had sailed through the force field I had erected around Vaughn as if it did not exist. Vaughn was reduced to flecks of ash in an instant. I couldn't inform the rest of the Metahuman assault force because the communications system Mechano had designed was useless, presumably jammed by the V'Loths.

After Vaughn was killed, the next energy pulse killed Wormhole, another of the bodyguards assigned to Vaughn. Wormhole was supposed to transport us all out of Baltimore if things went sideways.

They most definitely had.

I wasn't sure what had happened. My best guess was that the whole thing had been a trap, and that the V'Loth queen had let Vaughn into her thoughts to lure us to Baltimore so the aliens could eliminate most of the world's Heroes in one fell swoop. With us gone, no one would be able to stand between the V'Loths and world domination. But that was just a guess. It was not as though the V'Loth queen would have me over for a spot of tea so we could braid each other's hair—assuming she even had hair—and gab about world-conquering strategies.

At any rate, that was why I was swooping around the skies of Baltimore, surrounded by total chaos, trying to avoid the fate Vaughn, Wormhole, and too many others had suffered.

I wondered if Neha was still alive. My side, singed by the energy pulse I had just dodged, felt like it was on fire. Teeth gritted, I tried to put the pain out of my mind and focus on evading the continuing blasts from the V'Loth ship that pursued me. It chased me the way a cat chases a mouse, matching my shifting path through the sky. Despite the fact it was as big as a box truck, it was as agile a flier as I was. It was as hard to shake as a bad cold.

Normally, in a situation like this, I would use my telekinesis to immobilize or crush the object that pursued me. I couldn't get a solid lock on the spaceship following me, though. Whatever super-dense material the silver ship was made of resisted my powers. Trying to grab onto it was like trying to cling to a fistful of air.

Everything around me was a blur. I dodged and weaved, trying to shake the pursuing craft so I could take stock of the overall situation and help my fellow embattled Metahumans. I spotted another V'Loth ship ahead and above me. Though I could see it only hazily through the smoke, that didn't prevent me from seeing it blast an airborne Hero out of existence with an energy pulse.

A few Heroes had managed to destroy or incapacitate some of the ships, but there were far more of them than there were of us. They were killing us at a greater rate than we were killing them. It was a battle of attrition we were most definitely losing. Somebody had to do something, and do it soon before all was lost.

Since communications were down and I couldn't coordinate strategy with anyone, I guess I didn't have a choice:

That somebody was going to have to be me.

Fantastic.

Before I could step back and look at the big picture though, I'd have to deal with the ship on my tail. It clung to me like a dog's tick, matching my aerial maneuvers with disheartening ease, spitting energy pulses at me all the while. In fact, the ship matched my movements so precisely, I wondered how much intelligence went into the ship following me. The V'Loth queen was the only one with real intelligence and the drone ships were essentially dumb brutes. Maybe this drone staying on my tail like this wasn't the result of deliberate thought but instead instinctual, like a dog chasing a car.

It gave me an idea.

I knew from a previous collision that, though my force field was ineffective against the ships' energy blasts, it would protect me from a direct impact with the ships. I changed my trajectory, arcing up at full speed toward the ship that had just vaporized the other Hero. The spaceship pursuing me of course followed.

I slammed into the ship above. It felt like driving a speeding car into a wall. Thanks to my force field, I did not turn into smeared Theo on the ship's hull. Rather, I bounced off it like a smashed tennis ball.

As I hoped it would, the spaceship on my tail followed my flight path. It collided with the other ship I had just bounced off. There was a terrific crunching sound. The ships exploded. A shockwave hit me like a brick wall. I fell out of the sky. My tattered cape fluttered around me like the broken wings of a falling bird.

Seconds later, I crashed through the roof of an already damaged mid-rise building. I tore through its floors like a bullet through a house of cards. I hit the bottom floor like a dropped bomb. The floor cratered around me.

Debris fell around and on me. I lay in the crater's center like a dead fish. Like a dead fish, but I was not in fact dead. Though I felt like a half-gutted catfish, I had managed to keep my force field up all this while. It had prevented me from turning into Theo-flavored pâté. I was playing possum, hoping the V'Loths would think the collision and explosion had killed me and they didn't need to pursue me further. I needed breathing room to take stock of the overall strategic situation before the V'Loths exterminated every one of us Metas on the scene.

I closed my eyes and raised my hands a little. Using all the energy I had absorbed from my impact with the V'Loth ship and the collisions since then to boost my normal telekinetic touch range, I used my powers to survey the massive battle raging outside.

The Metas I sensed were far fewer than the ones I had initially shown up here with. I prayed one of the survivors was Neha. I shoved thoughts of her aside. If something wasn't done soon, there would be no survivors at all. First things first.

Since killing the queen was the key to ending this whole thing, I used my powers to look for any sign of her in the chaos swirling around me outside. My touch couldn't penetrate the ships' hulls, but maybe I could figure out what ship she was in simply from how it behaved. I figured someone as important as she was in the V'Loth hierarchy would not be in a ship directly engaging in combat.

Minutes that seemed like eternity passed. Finally, I thought I'd found what I looked for. A V'Loth ship was on the periphery of the main battle, accompanied by a small phalanx of other ships that moved when it moved. It was the only V'Loth ship behaving this way. There was no way I would have spotted the pattern of its movements with the naked eye due to all the smoke and chaos swirling about outside. This had to be her.

But what to do with my newfound knowledge? My powers had no direct effect on the spaceships. What was I supposed to do to the queen? Wag my finger at her and give her a piece of my mind? There were probably Heroes still alive who had offensive powers that could pierce the hull of the V'Loth queen's ship. Laser Lass, for example, probably could. I feared by the time I found such a Hero in all the confusion outside, it would be too late.

A flash of inspiration hit me. My powers could not directly

affect the V'Loth queen's ship. But, my personal force field still worked when I collided with the ships. I could use my body itself as a weapon.

My mind locked onto what I suspected was the V'Loth queen's ship. With my force field around me, I zoomed up, back through the floors I had crashed through before.

In seconds, I had cleared the building. Choking smoke swirled around me. I rose straight up like a rocket, hoping the V'Loths would be so busy with the remaining Heroes that they wouldn't notice me.

In moments, I was so high up in the sky, the smoke from the burning city thinned and then cleared. I glanced down as I continued to shoot straight up. The city got smaller and smaller underneath me. Soon the dark smoke rising from it made it look like a scabbed-over wound on the landscape. No V'Loths were in hot pursuit of me.

Seconds later, the blue of the sky changed, deepening to shades of violet and purple. The blackness of space appeared overhead.

I slowed to a stop. It was freezing this high up. The air was thin. Fortunately, there was enough oxygen and warmth trapped in my force field to sustain me for now.

I took a quick moment to savor the view. Even at a time like this, I got a lump in my throat at the beauty of the world. My world.

For a moment, I had second thoughts about my plan. I didn't want to die. If Neha was already dead, I didn't want James to finish growing up as an orphan. Sure, his Uncle Isaac would take care of him. Isaac, though he was not James' biological uncle and not related to us at all, was my brother in all the ways that mattered. Other than James, Isaac was the only non-Meta who knew Neha and I were Heroes. Though I knew Isaac would take good care of James, an honorary uncle was no substitute for an actual father.

I pushed the selfish thought to the side as soon as I had it. I would not have the heart to look my son in the eye ever again if I turned tail now and ran. There were worse fates than death.

My resolve hardened. Even at this vast distance, I still had a lock on the V'Loth mothership with my powers. With my force field still around me, I started to fly back down to Baltimore. The queen's spaceship was centered in my mind's eye like a bull's-eye.

Faster, faster, and faster I dropped. Gravity helped me achieve a velocity I never would have been able to reach with just my powers. My experience bouncing off the V'Loth spaceship earlier had taught me that I and my powers alone couldn't pierce the tough, otherworldly metal of the V'Loths' ships. But maybe, with gravity helping me fly exponentially faster, I could pierce the hull of the V'Loth queen's ship and kill her. Kill the queen, save the world.

Whether I succeeded or failed, I was under no illusion that I would survive this. The physics of the situation were clear. Force equaled mass times acceleration. Though my mass was relatively small, the speed I was traveling was immense. I would hit the queen's ship with enormous force. My powers wouldn't be enough to shield me from the monstrous forces at play. If the impact with the V'Loth ship didn't kill me, the impact with the ground an instant later surely would.

I still didn't want to die. But better for me to die than for another kid like Vaughn to die. The world was full of kids like Vaughn and my son James. It was my job to protect them.

Almost there. I was vaguely aware of the ship I shot toward scrambling to get out of the way. Its escorts moved to block my path. Mute evidence my target was the correct one. I adjusted my course a tad. The ships weren't moving fast enough to stop me. It was too late for my target to avoid me. Too late for *her*. If I weren't concentrating so fiercely, I might have smiled.

My last thought was of James and Neha. Collectively and separately, they were my everything. I had lived a good life. I had loved and been loved. Who could ask for anything more?

I hit the V'Loth queen's ship like a bullet hitting a watermelon.

23

So this is what Heaven is like, I thought. *Pretty dark. You'd think there would be better lighting. Why wouldn't a god who created the sun, moon, and all the stars spring for some fluorescents? Oh well. At least the joint's quiet. I'm glad to see all that stuff about harps, hymn singing, and non-stop hosannaing is made up bullsh—uh, malarkey. Most people can't stand that stuff on Earth. Why in the world would a loving god make it such a prominent part of the afterlife?*

I had opened my eyes moments before. I was lying down, flat on my back on a hard, waist-high platform. There were no lights other than two torches which guttered and hissed. They were mounted in torch holders attached to bluish-gray brick walls that looked like they belonged in a medieval castle. The walls were tall, swallowed by the darkness above. If there was a ceiling, it was somewhere high above, far from the reach of the sputtering torches' light. The light from the torches dimly illuminated only a small part of the area I was in. The air was foggy and thick. There was a hint of incense in the air, far more pleasant than the acrid smoke smell I had just left behind in Baltimore.

The afterlife isn't so bad, I decided as I stared up into dark nothingness. Boring though, if this was all there was to it. Maybe some harp music wouldn't be so bad after all, to break up the monotony of the silence. I really wished I knew if I had succeeded in killing the V'Loth queen. If she had been killed, I wondered if the world would know I was the one who had done it. Not that I sought acclaim. Nevertheless, I had to admit that *Kinetic Kills Queen* made for a nice headline. Maybe Mr. Langley would use it or something similar in the digital edition of the *Astor City Times*. He had a flair for coming up with punchy headlines.

I blinked, suddenly confused. Wait. How had I just been fighting the V'Loths in Baltimore in 1966? I wasn't even alive back then. Omega Man had killed the V'Loth queen, not me. Neha and I weren't married. She wasn't even in love with me. And we certainly didn't have a teenaged son named after my father.

The last thing I remembered before I had inexplicably found myself fighting the V'Loths was searching for the Omega weapon with Isaac. I had touched the cape hidden under the neutronium spear. Then I suddenly found myself in the skies over Baltimore, with my head full of memories of a life that wasn't really mine. Also, I had been injured badly before I had touched the cape. Yet I seemed perfectly fine now.

What the hell was going on?

I sat up. I was shocked to find that I was suddenly standing. I didn't remember getting to my feet. The hard platform I had just been lying on was gone, as if it had never existed.

Two rows of ornate chairs were before me. The chairs faced each other across a narrow aisle that I stood at the head of. The rows of chairs extended far off into the distance, well past the dim illumination afforded by the torches. Each chair was occupied. Despite the dim light, I recognized some of the seated men and women. Avatar and Omega Man sat in full costume in opposing chairs closest to me. There were a couple of other people sitting here I knew from historical pictures. Most I did not. And yet I somehow knew, without knowing how I knew, that each person here had been a vessel for the Omega spirit.

Everyone in the chairs had their heads turned, facing me. I felt the weight of countless eyes. It was though they peered straight into my soul.

"You have proven yourself worthy of wielding the Omega weapon," they all said at once, filling the room with thousands of voices. Their words came through as clear as a bell despite what I thought would be a babel of noise from so many people speaking simultaneously. "The Omega weapon and the Omega spirit will once again be combined in one host, as is only meet. We chose wisely when we imbued you with our spirit."

If I didn't already know about the Omega spirit, I would think I was on a bad acid trip.

"Are you all the Omega spirit?" I asked.

"We are," returned the countless voices.

I realized now what was going on. My fight against the V'Loths, my marriage to Neha, having a son with her . . . none of it had been real. Well, there were aspects of it that had actually happened back in 1966. Trying to use the telepathic 13-year-old Vaughn to take down the V'Loths had really occurred, as had Vaughn's death when he was transported to Baltimore. A bunch of Heroes dying had really happened too, as had Mechano designing a futuristic communications system that was jammed by the V'Loths. But my own involvement in the battle with the V'Loths was a complete fantasy. Real historical events from the

20th century had been mixed with people from my life in the 21st century to create an immersive illusion, like a virtual reality construct that had seemed one hundred percent real.

It had all been a test to see if I was worthy of wielding the Omega weapon. First the Lotus-induced fantasy during the Trials where my parents were still alive and I had a girlfriend who loved me, now this fantasy where I was happily married to Neha with a son. Why were my dream worlds always so much better than my real world? I was heartily sick of people testing me and my resolve. I thought I had left tests behind when I completed the Trials.

"Life is a test, Theodore. You should know that by now," the voices of the Omega spirit said, as if they had read my mind. Maybe mind reading was as common as breathing here. Wherever here was.

"We are in your subconscious," the voices said in answer to my unspoken thought. "Your struggle against the V'Loths played out entirely in your mind. Your corporeal body still lies on the floor of The Mountain."

"So you're saying I'm talking to myself right now?"

"In a fashion. You are us, and we are you," the Omega spirit said. "Now it is time for you to return to your world. Darkness unlike the world has ever known approaches. The world will need the protection of the Omega like never before. Go forth and serve it wisely."

The room and all the figures it contained began to fall apart and disappear, like a house of Legos rapidly torn apart piece by piece.

"Wait!" I cried out. "I have so many questions. Why me? Why did you choose me for the Omega spirit?"

"Because despite your flaws, youth, inexperience, lapses in judgment, spotty pre-Heroic education—"

"I hope something positive is coming sometime soon," I interjected. Sometimes I couldn't help myself.

"Despite all those things, you try to do the right thing. The trying is all." The countless faces smiled at me fondly. "Besides, why not you?"

Before I could ask the Omega spirit exactly what darkness was approaching and what in blazes I was supposed to do about it, the seated figures and the room winked out of existence. I floated alone in an inky black void.

MY EYES SNAPPED OPEN LIKE MY EYELIDS HAD BEEN YANKED ON. I lay face up on the hard rock floor of The Mountain. Who knew being a Hero would entail so much being flat on your back? You would think Heroing would be more restful than it was.

My right hand clutched the cape that had been hidden in the cavity under the neutronium spear. I faintly heard a moan. It came from me. I tried to stop, but couldn't. Moaning seemed the right thing to do right now. I had felt no pain in the room I had spoken to the Omega spirit in. I felt plenty now. All the pain I had been in from my encounter with the Sentinels and me overextending myself to move the neutronium spear was back with a vengeance.

Isaac knelt over me. His face was streaked with tears. It showed anguish mixed with astonishment. His eyes were red. He said, "You touched the cape a few minutes ago, and passed out. Then, you stopped breathing. I did CPR, but you wouldn't revive. I thought you were dead."

"Death would be a mercy," I croaked weakly. I was joking, yet it wasn't far from the truth. How was I supposed to protect the world from some sort of encroaching darkness in this condition? I doubted I could protect it from an anemic butterfly feeling like this.

Isaac's eyes left my face and got very wide, like he was watching a dog stand upright and recite poetry. "What in the world is happening?"

I tilted my aching head to see what he stared at. Avatar's cape was moving, writhing like a snake. It seeped slowly into my hand, like water being soaked up by a thirsty sponge.

"I think this is supposed to happen," I said, not even knowing myself how I knew that. I was strangely calm despite the fact a long piece of fabric burrowed into me like a worm into an apple.

My hand tingled. Then my arm. Then my entire body as the cape entered me. Soon its fabric had entirely disappeared.

I burst into flames, as if I had been doused in gasoline and lit.

"Jesus!" Isaac exclaimed. He jumped back in shock. He shimmered slightly and leveled his arms at me, no doubt planning to drench me using one of his water-generating forms.

"No!" I said sharply. "I'm fine."

I was more than fine. The fire didn't hurt at all. If anything, it was pleasant, like soaking in a hot bath after an exhausting day. My clothes burned off me as I watched in wonder. Their ashes floated heavenward like motes of disturbed dust.

The flames abruptly extinguished themselves. Now I was as naked as a newborn baby. But not only that. I was as healthy as a newborn too. All the burning and discoloration of my skin caused by Mechano's attack were gone, along with all my aches, pains, and injuries. My hearing and vision were back to normal. My cracked teeth were healed. I felt good enough to wrestle a bear. I would have even been willing to give the bear the first swipe at me.

Choose, something deep inside of me whispered. It was the same combination of countless voices I had spoken to earlier. I heard them not with my ears, but with the essence of my being. That sounds strange because it was. And yet, at the same time, it seemed the most natural thing in the world.

I instinctually knew what the voices meant. They wanted me to choose how the Omega weapon would manifest for me. King Arthur had the sword Excalibur, Rama had his bow Pinaka, Beowulf had his sword Nægling. Toting a sword, a bow, or a similar weapon did not seem appropriate in the modern world, however. I was not Robin Hood or one of his Merry Men.

Omega Man had the clasp that secured his cape around his neck. Avatar had the cape I had just absorbed. Something more along the lines of how those Heroes had manifested the Omega weapon seemed more sensible than wielding an actual weapon like King Arthur or Beowulf had.

I made my decision. In response, the surface of my skin began to feel ticklish, as if a giant feather rubbed lightly against me. Dark blue specks swam up from inside of me to the surface of my skin. There they rapidly expanded, like numerous pools of spilled blue ink. They connected with each other, coating all of my naked body like a second skin from the neck down. Then they thickened and hardened, forming a flexible but incredibly strong body armor. A ghost white omega symbol crystallized on my chest.

I knew the importance of symbols thanks to my studies at the Academy. That was why I had made my new costume look this way. I had picked blue because psychological studies indicated that someone wearing it was viewed as trustworthy and dependable. It was no accident police departments often clothed their officers in blue. I had picked the omega symbol for the obvious reason: I was the Omega. Cassandra and the

Sentinels had told me that before. Now I knew it with every fiber of my being.

It is done, said the voices from within me, this time in a deafening roar. *All hail the new Omega.*

My costume complete, I levitated to my feet. In addition to being completely healthy again, I felt an exhilarating rush, like I could do absolutely anything. I stared down at my suit-covered hands. Normally I saw faint waves of power emanating from them. Now the waves were so thick and intense, it almost made me dizzy to look at them. Also, my hands' normal burning sensation now felt like the burning of a supernova. It was not painful though. It felt like the most natural thing in the world.

I clenched my fist, almost drunk with the power coursing through me. I sensed the rumbling of a distant mountain many miles away. Startled, I realized I caused it. I unclenched my fist and relaxed my will. I felt the distant rumbling stop. Dealing with all this power from the Omega weapon being reunited with the Omega spirit would take some getting used to.

I looked up. Isaac stared at me with bulging eyes, like I had sprouted a second head that spoke Aramaic. Proving he was never at a loss for words, he said, "Not that I'm criticizing your snazzy new threads, but what about sticking with your Kinetic suit's design? I kinda liked it."

"Kinetic is dead," I declared. "I am Omega now."

24

"Omega, eh?" Truman said. He pursed his lips thoughtfully. "I like it. I'm just glad you didn't opt for a code name like Godling or Demigod. Too pretentious."

"I'm so happy you approve," I said.

Isaac and I sat in Truman's office. It was mid-morning. As a repairman had fixed Truman's window, the morning sun streamed in. We were strategizing how we would try to defeat the Sentinels now that I had the Omega weapon. Though my power level had increased exponentially, having the Omega weapon made me no smarter or wiser. I felt like a child who had been handed a loaded howitzer and told to go fight the U.S. Marines.

Though I appeared to sit in Truman's office in normal clothes, in fact I wore the Omega weapon. I would have to start thinking of it as the Omega suit. I had found I could alter its appearance with a thought. It promised to really cut down on my clothing expenses. The Omega suit was now a part of me until I either gave it up or was killed. I had no plans to do either anytime soon.

It turned out that while Isaac and I had been retrieving the Omega weapon, Truman had been productive as well. He had determined that Antonio was hiding in a small village in southern Italy, having been shipped out of the country by the Esposito crime family to keep American authorities from questioning him about Hannah's murder. The Espositos were likely afraid Antonio would spill the beans regarding all the illegal things he had done for them over the years if he cracked under pressure from the authorities. According to Truman's sources, Antonio was having a grand old time banging the local girls and bullying the local boys while he cooled his heels. Antonio having the time of his life while Hannah moldered in her grave made my blood boil.

Now that I knew where Antonio was, I would have to deal with him. But first, the Sentinels. Because of the power they possessed, they were the more pressing matter.

As if on cue, a man in a dark business suit abruptly appeared in front of Truman's desk between where Isaac and I sat. He appeared out of nowhere. One moment he was not there, and the next instant he was.

Before either Isaac or I could react, a column of water from the large bowl on Truman's desk sprang out of the bowl like a striking snake. It whipped toward the interloper's head. It sailed right through his head as if he didn't exist, and splashed against the opposite wall.

Though I barely saw him move, Truman's gun was now in his hand. He pointed it at the man.

"Aside from that neat little intangibility trick, you certainly don't look like Casper the Ghost," Truman said to the besuited, middle-aged man. "You don't look that friendly, either. You want to tell me who you are and what you're doing here? If you're looking for a place to haunt, I'm not interested.

I'm already wrestling with a bunch of demons from my past. I don't need to add ghosts to the mix."

Isaac and I were on our feet now. Isaac looked ready to pounce on the man.

"I know who he is," I said, though I had no idea how he was here. He had a thin black moustache and stringy black hair that receded in the front corners. He was of medium build and looked fit and trim in his dark suit. The suit was well-tailored but dated, as if it had been designed a couple of generations ago. I poked at him experimentally with my telekinetic touch. My touch met with no resistance whatsoever. Even with holographic projections I could feel *something*. It was as if the man was not really here. "This is Jeffrey Cole." Isaac looked at me blankly. "Mechano. I recognize him from the pictures taken of him before his human body died."

Cole beamed at me as if he were *Jeopardy*'s Alex Trebek and I had just doubled my money by answering a Daily Double correctly.

"You're quite right, Mr. Conley," he said. "I see you've done your homework on me. Admirable." His voice was like Mechano's, only without the electronic distortion.

"Okay, now I know who you are," Truman said. "I still want to know what you're doing in my office. And how you're here when your human body is dead. I'm as uninterested in zombies hanging around here as I am in ghosts."

Cole looked at Truman. "Mr. Lord, I have not seen you since we hired you to find Avatar's murderer. I see you have not changed."

"Why mess with perfection?" Truman replied.

"You are obviously working with our young friends here. You have a habit of turning up in the most unexpected places."

"Me?" Truman's gun still pointed at Cole, though I didn't

know what good it would do. "You're the dead man standing in my office doing a poltergeist impersonation."

Cole pursed his lips in amusement. "You are quite right. A few words of explanation. I am here thanks to the talents of my colleague Millennium. What you see before you is an astral projection of my essence." He shook his head slightly in bemusement. "I was an engineer long before I was a Hero. As such, I once believed only in what I could touch and objectively measure. Before I met Millennium, I would have scoffed if you spoke to me of 'astral projections' and 'essences.' And yet, here I am."

"Don't let the door hit your astral ass on the way out," Truman said. "We're having a private meeting about the joy of doing good deeds. Since you wouldn't know anything about that, three's company but four's a crowd. If we decide to murder innocent people instead of do-gooding, we'll give you a ring for some tips. Until then . . ." Truman made a shooing motion with his gun.

Cole laughed mockingly. As self-assured as he sounded in his robot form, he seemed even more so now. A self-satisfied smirk seemed permanently etched on his face. If his form weren't insubstantial, I likely would have wiped the smug look off his face with a hot poker. "Murdering innocent people? Such slanderous allegations. You should not believe everything you hear," Cole said to Truman in a mocking tone. "You would think that the only man in history to turn down a Sentinels' membership would be less gullible."

Truman said, "You'd think a man made of tin would kill less and hang out with lions and scarecrows and girls named Dorothy more. Actually, I take that back about Dorothy. Since you're just a bucket of bolts these days, you don't have the necessary equipment to be interested in girls anymore."

Cole's cocky smirk faltered a bit. "You are as deluded of

your wittiness as ever. To paraphrase Twain, I would challenge you to a battle of wits, but I see you are unarmed. Except for that gun, of course. Put it away before you hurt yourself. Like the water you flung at me, I assure you it would be most ineffective against me in this form."

Truman's computer screen flickered, and then shut off. So did the overhead lights, startling me. Cole looked amused by my reaction. "Never fear," he said. "It is merely a reaction to my appearance here. Magic and technology do not mix well together." Fortunately, enough daylight came in through Truman's new window for us to still see.

Truman looked stubborn for a moment, then put his gun back into his open desk drawer. He no doubt realized Cole was right about the gun being useless. I noticed he did not close the drawer back.

"Okay, we know who you are and how you are here," Truman said. "The question of why you're here remains. To confess your multiple sins and crimes and turn yourself in, I hope. Truman 'The Eternal Optimist' Lord is what they call me. Maybe I'll take the code name Pollyanna, instead. It's shorter."

That got a slight smile out of Cole. He looked like he was enjoying himself immensely. "Hardly. You will hear no confession from me. Any alleged sins I may have committed have been in pursuit of the greater good. They require no absolution." Cole looked at me. "Rather, I'm here to demand that you turn over the Omega weapon."

I hoped the surprise I felt didn't register on my face. "I told you before, I don't know anything about it."

Cole's smile got broader. "Mr. Conley, you have proven yourself to be many things. A good liar is not one of them. The Omega spirit's reunion with the Omega weapon sent shockwaves through the mystical realm. Or so Millennium tells me.

I am a man of engineering and science. I do not understand such things. The fact I do not understand them does not mean they do not exist. My presence here in this form is proof enough of that. Once Millennium sensed the Omega spirit and weapon were together again, it was a simple enough matter for him to pinpoint the locus of the shockwaves and send me here to have this chat with you. You I was expecting to see, Mr. Geere. You and Mr. Conley seem inseparable. However, I did not realize you were mixed up in this as well, Mr. Lord."

"A bad penny always turns up," Truman said. "You being here is proof enough of that."

"Even if Theo did have the Omega weapon," Isaac said to Cole, "why in the world would he be stupid enough to hand it over to you after all you've done?"

"Because he is too young and inexperienced to use it wisely. My colleagues and I will use it wisely."

I didn't see the point of continuing to pretend that I didn't have it. "Avatar hid it from you for a reason. He must have known or at least suspected that you weren't trustworthy. I'd destroy it before I'd give it to you."

"I cannot say I am terribly surprised to hear you say that," Cole said. "We anticipated this would be your response. Unfortunately for you, we are always a few steps ahead of you. It is why we should be in possession of the Omega weapon rather than you. You simply cannot be trusted with it. You are too weak-minded and do not think far enough ahead. If the Sentinels do not take it from you and safeguard it, some Rogue, sooner or later, will wrest it from you. And they will not take it for the purpose of safeguarding it.

"Since you will not hand over the weapon voluntarily, I will instead offer you this quid pro quo: In exchange for you giving me the Omega weapon, I will in return give you Neha

Thakore. Smoke, I believe her Heroic code name is. Descriptive, if unimaginative."

My stomach rose to my throat. My fists involuntarily clenched. "What have you done to her?" I demanded. I wanted to squeeze the life out of him.

Cole smiled the smile of a child on Christmas Day.

"She is unhurt. Well, mostly. She resisted when we took her into custody. She is quite the spitfire, that one. Nonetheless, she is alive and mostly well. That will change if you do not produce the Omega weapon. You have until tonight. Come to the mansion. When you hand over the weapon, we will release Ms. Thakore to you."

"After all you've done, why in the world should we believe you have Neha?" Isaac said. He looked as mad as I felt. "A murderer like you would have no problem lying too."

Cole looked at Truman, shaking his head at Isaac's words with mock regret. "So young, and yet so cynical." He had the nerve to wink at Truman. "Perhaps there is hope for them yet."

"More for them than for you," Truman said.

Cole ignored that. "When I leave here, an email will be sent to Mr. Conley. Attached will be proof we have Ms. Thakore and that she is alive."

I had a sick feeling in the pit of my stomach the Sentinels really had Neha. Why else hadn't she gotten back to Isaac? I shook with frustration and anger. "If you hurt her—"

Cole cut me off. "You will do what?" He smiled at me indulgently, the way an adult would at a child. "Do not make threats you are completely incapable of carrying out. Oh, I have no doubt you and your friends here will mull over all kinds of plans once I leave as to how to rescue your friend while still retaining the Omega weapon. I am confident you will eventually decide to do the right thing, the only option available to you that will ensure the safety of your friend. You are thoroughly outclassed here, Mr. Conley. That is why you will do as I say and hand over the Omega weapon. Further, it is why you *should* hand over the Omega weapon. If the Sentinels do not take it from you, someone else surely will.

"The exchange will take place at Sentinels Mansion at ten p.m. sharp. Come alone, and be prepared to hand over the weapon. If you don't . . ." He trailed off. He shrugged. "Such a pretty young thing, Ms. Thakore is. She has a promising career ahead of her as a Hero. It would be a shame if something happened to her."

"And what of your attempt to kill Theo to force the Omega spirit into someone else?" Isaac said. "You expect us to believe you won't still try to kill him the instant you have what you want?"

"I have discussed that matter with my colleagues," Cole said, as if he were a banker thinking about offering a customer a lower interest rate. "We have decided that access to the Omega weapon will be all that we will need to protect the world. Once Mr. Conley gives it to us, he will be of no further interest to us."

"And why should we believe you?" Isaac said. Scorn was in his voice. "Because of your sterling reputation for honesty and forthrightness?"

"If you wish to have your friend returned unharmed, what choice do you have but to trust me?" Cole said bluntly.

Cole turned as if he was going to walk out the door. He caught himself, snapped his fingers as if he remembered something, and turned back around.

"Oh, one more thing. I said before the electronics failed as a side effect of my astral presence here. That was a tiny bit of a white lie. The truth of the matter is that once I saw where I was, I dispatched one of the drones I have scattered around the city here. It hovers above this building as we speak. It is projecting a dampening field to prevent one of you from recording our lovely conversation." He smiled broadly. I wished he was actually here in the flesh so I could punch his teeth down his throat. "Truman, that strikes me as being something you would be quick-witted enough to think to do. I would hate for the Guild to have evidence of my proposal. The members of the executive committee would be positively shocked to hear me threaten the life of a young Hero. I pride myself on protecting the innocent delusions of others."

Cole smiled his smug smile. "As I said before, you are thoroughly outclassed. Do as I tell you to do, and all will be well." He disappeared as abruptly and soundlessly as he had arrived.

Moments after he was gone, Truman's lights flickered, and then came back on. If only I could get Neha back as easily. I slumped back into my chair, feeling sick to my stomach.

"We'll check out the email that jackass mentioned," Truman said. "In the meantime . . ." Truman pulled his hand out of the drawer he had put his gun back into. A small electronic recorder was in his fist. With my powers, I had sensed that Truman had picked the recorder up and clicked it on when he had put his gun back into the drawer. We listened to the playback. The sound shut off right after Cole had told Truman to put his gun away, when Truman's computer and lights had shut off. The recorder had not captured anything incriminating.

Truman shut the recorder off in disgust. He looked like he wanted to throw it against the wall.

"So much for us having proof of the Sentinels holding your friend hostage," he said. "Without more than just our say so, the Guild would never turn against the Sentinels. And certainly not—" He paused, looking embarrassed.

"You can say it," I said. I was thoroughly deflated and despondent. I had the Omega weapon and Mechano had still made me feel as helpless as a baby. "And certainly not in time to save Neha."

"Maybe they don't really have her," Isaac said, though he didn't look like he believed his own words. He moved around Truman's desk. "Let's check out that email."

Isaac turned Truman's computer back on, and logged into my email account after I gave him my password. An email with *Neha Thakore* as the subject line had come into my inbox minutes before. We opened the email's attachment. A soundless video began to play.

It showed Neha sitting in a simple wooden chair in a plain white room. My heart raced at the sight of her. She was in costume, just as she had been when I saw the nightclub footage of her in the Sentinels' Situation Room. Her costume's cowl had been pulled off her face; it dangled below the nape of her costumed neck. A gold-colored metal encircled her mouth and head, with some of the metal in her mouth. It looked like a futuristic ball gag. Her hands were behind her back, presumably bound there. Her ankles were secured to the chair with manacles made of the same metal that was around her head. The left side of her hair, normally straight and shoulder-length, was a mess of a bird's nest. It was matted against her head with what appeared to be dried blood. Her face was bruised, with much of her skin mottled purplish-red rather than its usual olive color. There was a shiner on her right eye that would probably swell her eye shut in a few more hours.

On her lap was a newspaper, propped up against her torso so the video camera could see its front page. The video zoomed in on the newspaper. It was a copy of the *Astor City Times* bearing today's date. I would have bet any amount of money that the use of the paper I worked for was a deliberate slap in my face.

Then the video panned up to Neha's face. Despite being bound and injured, Neha did not look frightened or in pain. The emotion on her face was pure fury. She glared at the unseen person making the video. If looks could kill, whoever had made the recording was surely dead. I had seen her mad before, but nothing like this.

The video faded to black after less than a minute. I had Isaac play the video again a few more times. It almost physically hurt to watch it, but I forced myself. I wanted to see if there was proof in the video indicating it was the Sentinels who had taken her so we could hand the video over to the Guild. I did not spot anything. Neither did Truman or Isaac. The video could have been shot by absolutely anybody. Even the email address the video had been sent from was not a Sentinels' address. The video had been sent from the email address of the chairman of the Guild's executive committee. Obviously Mechano had hacked into the chairman's email to send me this video. It must have given Mechano quite a chuckle at our expense.

I went back around Truman's desk and slumped into the chair there.

"Neha must hate being held prisoner like this," I said. I felt old and impossibly tired.

"Who wouldn't?" Truman asked.

"Neha in particular hates this. Being helpless and needing someone to come rescue her?" I shook my head at how Neha must feel, knowing her as I did. "It's eating her up inside. She doesn't like feeling weak. She hates being forced into the role of damsel in distress."

"Speaking of being helpless," Isaac said, "how do you suppose they're preventing her from turning into gas and freeing herself?"

"It must be the metal binding her," I said. "A similar

looking metal was used on me during the Trials to suppress my powers. I wouldn't be surprised to find out that Metahuman suppression technology had been invented by Mechano. So much tech the Guild relies on was."

"We've established the Sentinels do indeed have your friend. The question now becomes, what do we do about it?" Truman said.

"There's no time to go to the Guild," Isaac said. "Even if we had evidence to convince the Guild of the Sentinels' crimes—and we don't—by the time the Guild acted, Neha would be dead." Isaac turned to look at me. "You have to give them the Omega weapon. At least for now. Once we have Neha back, we can figure out what to do next."

"Do you really think the Sentinels will simply hand your friend over in exchange for the Omega weapon, say 'So long, and be sure to not talk about all the kidnapping and murdering we've been doing,' and let the four of us go on our merry way?" Truman shook his head. "It's far more likely that once they have the Omega weapon in their possession, they'll kill both Theo and Neha, both to keep them quiet and to free the Omega spirit up to enter someone who might be more compliant than Theo is. I don't believe for a second they'll leave him alone. He knows too much. As do you and I. Once they dispose of Neha and Theo, they'll come after us. Even if we don't have proof of what they have done, I can't imagine the Sentinels letting Heroes with direct knowledge of their wrongdoing continue to walk around, potentially making trouble for them."

"We're going to have to take that risk," Isaac insisted. "If we don't, Neha will die for sure. How these three Sentinels have behaved in the past indicates they're not bluffing about killing her if we don't do what they say."

"Enough," I said, tired of all the yammering. I had said it

low, almost to myself. I was so mad at the Sentinels, so afraid of what they might do to Neha, and so sick of evil people getting away with being evil.

"Let her die," Truman said. Isaac looked at him like Truman had gone crazy. "I know it sounds harsh, but you're letting the fact she's your friend cloud your thinking. Smoke is a Hero. She knows the risk of putting on a cape and costume. It's better to let one person die than let something as powerful as the Omega weapon fall into the hands of these Sentinels. The kind of mischief they're already capable of is considerable. What terrible things would they do with the Omega weapon to boost their already considerable power? Even the rest of the Sentinels combined with the Guild might not be able to stand against them. We have to look at the big picture, not focus exclusively on the welfare of a single person."

"Enough," I said, louder this time. My anger was a grumbling volcano that threatened to erupt. First Dad, then Hannah, now Neha. I was sick and tired of people being hurt because of me.

"Are you insane?" Isaac shouted. His face was red. He thrust it into Truman's in anger. "We're not going to just sit here and let them kill her. If you knew her, you wouldn't be so eager to throw her to the wolves."

Truman did not recoil from Isaac's indignation. "The welfare of the many is more important than the welfare of a single person," he insisted firmly but calmly.

My anger churned in my stomach like lava. The volcano mounting within me exploded. I shot to my feet.

"I said enough!" I shouted. I wasn't sure if I was talking to Isaac and Truman, or to the wider world that allowed innocents to be hurt and killed. I slapped my hand on top of Truman's desk in anger. It boomed like a clap of thunder. Truman's thick wooden desk split in two. It collapsed in on itself with a crash like a demolished building. The computer, books, and files on his desk fell. It all made a racket as it hit the floor. Papers went flying like confetti.

Inadvertently, I had obviously let a bit of my new power slip out of me, like an adolescent boy who's not yet accustomed to his growing body's newfound strength.

Isaac took a step back. He stared at me as if he had never seen me before. Even Truman, normally unflappable, was startled. He looked at me, down at his ruined desk, and then back up at me. Finally, he shook his head.

"I never liked that desk anyway. I'm glad to be rid of it," he said. "Now that you've finished redecorating my office, what are you doing to do about Neha?"

"I'm going to do what I have to do to get her back," I said.

As soon as the words were out of my mouth, I realized I did not just mean get her back from the Sentinels. I also meant get her back into my life. Other than the Omega weapon, I had gotten something equally powerful from the Omega spirit's test: Crystal clear memories of my romantic life with Neha. As if the events actually had happened, I remembered us dating, me shopping for an engagement ring, me proposing, her saying yes, our wedding, our wedding night, the night our son James was conceived, the morning he was born, and so many other wondrous memories. Though they had not really happened, it felt like they had. I would cherish them until the day I died.

The memories of my married life with Neha reinforced to me that I loved her with all my being. I had been a fool to not reconcile with her before now. I would rescue her from the Sentinels. Then, I would make new memories with her. Real ones.

But first, I needed to tie up a loose end.

25

Antonio stirred a bit on the floor. Though his eyes were closed, I had been monitoring his pulse with my telekinetic touch. The rate of his pulse had just spiked. It told me Antonio was now conscious and just playing possum.

I reached out with my telekinesis and nudged him. He yelped in pain, rolled over, and sat up. From his perspective, the nudge likely felt like a swift kick to the ribs. I was sick of playing games and pussy-footing around. I needed to leave soon to meet the Sentinels.

Bleary-eyed and confused, Antonio looked around. He rubbed his side where I had prodded him. He had on faded blue jeans, moccasins, and a red plaid shirt. His too-tight shirt stretched out over his belly, making him look like he had swallowed a cannonball.

"Where the fuck am I?" he demanded in his surprisingly high-pitched voice. He had put on weight since I last saw him in his apartment what seemed like forever ago. The extra pounds appeared to all have landed in his belly. He obviously hadn't shaved his head in several days. There was a wide crescent of stubble on the sides and back of his head, and none from his forehead to his crown. Antonio must have gotten into the habit of shaving his head so people wouldn't know he was balding.

Though Antonio was as big and scary-looking as I remembered, it was hard to be intimidated by someone with male pattern baldness who looked pregnant. Harder still when you wore the Omega suit.

"You are in a place high up in the middle of the Himalayas," I said. "It's called The Mountain." Thanks to the Omega suit's malleability, I had fashioned a cowl that covered my head and features. I also had on a white cape. More often than not, a cape got in the way. Wearing one now seemed appropriate, though, like a judge donning his robe before presiding over a sentencing.

Antonio unsteadily got to his feet.

"How the fuck did I get here?"

I could have told him that I had flown from Astor City to the small village in Italy Truman had told me Antonio was hiding out in. With my powers augmented as they were by the Omega suit, the journey had taken me a tiny fraction of the time it normally would have. I could have said that I then located Antonio and knocked him out with my powers before he or anyone else spotted me. I could have told him that I then flew him from Italy to The Mountain. It had all been child's play thanks to the Omega suit.

I could have said all that, but why bother? Instead, I simply shrugged.

"I'm a Hero," I said.

"And who the fuck are you?" If you eliminated the F-bomb from Mad Dog's vocabulary, he likely would be at a loss for words.

"My name is Omega."

331

"And that's supposed to fuckin' mean something to me?"

"We've met before, though I don't expect you to recognize me. When we last met, I wore a ski mask." With a thought, the cowl slid off my head and melted into the rest of the Omega suit, like dry ground sucking up raindrops. My face was now fully exposed to Antonio. "My name is Theodore Conley. I was a friend and co-worker of your girlfriend Hannah Kim. My friend and I spoke to you in your apartment about her before you murdered her."

"Murdered? I didn't murder nobody."

I didn't need my powers to tell me he lied. It was written all over his face. My powers did confirm, though, that he was in fact lying. They told me his heart rate had shifted. It wasn't the reaction of an innocent man.

"It doesn't matter what you say," I said. "I know you killed her. Which is why you're here."

For the first time, Antonio seemed to realize that thick, transparent glass separated me from him. Antonio ran his hands over the glass, tapping on it probingly. Then he backed up and opened his mouth wide. He looked thunderstruck when nothing happened. I had put him in the Metahuman holding cell Isaac and I discovered during our earlier visit here.

"As you can see, your powers don't work here. I've placed you in a cell that neutralizes them."

Antonio pointed his open mouth at the glass several more times. He reminded me of a gaping fish out of water. Clearly he did not take my word for it that his powers wouldn't work. And here I was, a licensed Hero with a costume, a cape, a lair, and everything. Insulting.

Finally, Antonio gave up. He pointed a thick finger at me. "Let me out of here!" he demanded.

I shook my head.

"No."

"Let me out of here right now you little piece of shit. I got my rights!"

"Not here you don't. As far as I'm concerned, you forfeited any rights you had when you killed Hannah."

"I'm telling you, I didn't kill nobody."

"And I'm telling you I don't believe you. Besides, even in the unlikely event you're telling the truth, you still used to beat her black and blue. Plus, I know you committed a bunch of other crimes over the years you managed to escape punishment for."

"So what are you gonna do? Turn me over to the cops?"

"And have you or the Esposito family bribe you out of this mess?" I shook my head. "No. I'm not handing you over to the police. I've become less than impressed with the Astor City justice system. I'll take care of you myself."

"Take care of me yourself? What's that supposed to mean. Kill me? You say you're a Hero. Heroes aren't supposed to kill people."

"We don't." I thought of the Sentinels. "Well, most of us don't. Back when I was in Hero Academy, I was taught that a Hero shouldn't play the role of judge, jury, and executioner. I think my teachers were right. Heroes are too powerful to be allowed to take people's lives. So, as much as you deserve it, I won't execute you. I will happily be judge and jury minus the executioner part, though. Somebody's got to sit in judgment of people like you since the so-called justice system won't."

I took a breath. "For the crimes of the murder of Hannah Kim, the assault and battery of Hannah Kim, the rape of Hannah Kim, multiple instances of use of Metahuman powers by an unlicensed Meta, and various other crimes perpetrated on numerous people over the years, I hereby sentence you to life in prison with no possibility of parole. Your sentence shall begin immediately. Welcome to your new prison cell. It's got all the comforts of home. You'll see that I stocked it with canned foods that will last you until my next visit, plus bottles of water. That large can over there with the lid on it will have to serve as a toilet for now until I have a chance to install a proper one. Later, I'll bring you a change of clothes. Perhaps an orange jumpsuit. That all assumes I survive my encounter with the people I need to deal with after I finish with you. If I don't survive, since no one else knows you're here . . ." I trailed off. I shrugged. "Suffice it to say that in the event of my untimely demise, your life imprisonment will last as long as your food and water do. There are worse ways to die than starvation and dehydration. Having a hole blown through you by the man who professes to love you springs to mind."

I shook my head in disgust. I was disgusted with myself as much as I was with Antonio.

"I'll be honest with you, Mad Dog. Keeping you here is a punishment for me too. Me breaking into your apartment and attacking you led to Hannah's death. If it weren't for me, she might be alive today. Your presence here will serve as a constant reminder of the mistakes I've made. My mistakes can get people killed."

Antonio's pig eyes had grown wide with disbelief as I spoke.

"You can't keep me here. I've got my rights. It's . . . it's . . . it's against the law," he sputtered.

His chutzpah made me laugh out loud.

"You're one to talk about the law." I waved my fingers at him. "Hello pot. I'm kettle. Yes, what I'm doing is very much against the law. The problem you've got is that there are no cops or lawyers or judges up here to complain to. There's no clerk of court here for you to file a writ of habeas corpus with. There's just me and you. And believe me, I've been through too much, seen too much, and watched too many good people die for no good reason to give a rat's ass about your rights. What about Hannah's rights?" *And Dad's and Neha's*, I added silently.

I was tired of talking to Antonio. I wanted to get out of here and go face the Sentinels. To get Neha back.

I said, "Just between me and you, I'll let you in on a little secret: I'm not sure how much I believe in the law anymore. Too many people flout the law and get away with it for me to have a whole lot of faith in it. Sometimes I wonder if the law is just a smokescreen to keep the powerless out of the hair of the rich and powerful long enough for the powerless to be exploited and taken advantage of. My father never broke a law in his life, yet he had to struggle every day to barely make ends meet before a group of assholes put him into an early grave. Those same assholes are not only very much alive, they're free as birds and well-respected to boot despite breaking the law left and right. How great can slavishly following the law be if that sort of thing happens?" I thought of the Trials, my life in Astor City so far, and how corrupt so many people were. The Sentinels, Pitbull, Brown Recluse, the Astor City Police Department, Mitch and the flunkeys under him who dealt drugs on my street . . . the list seemed endless.

I cut myself short, realizing I was speechifying. A side effect of wearing a cape, maybe. If I put my fists on my waist and stuck my chest out, the pretentious picture would be complete.

I did not do that. Instead I said, "Even if my faith in the law is shaky these days, I still firmly believe in justice. Which is why you're staying here. So make yourself at home. You'll be here for a while. It's why I showed you my face and told you my name. I'm not worried about you escaping and exposing my secret to someone else."

I turned to leave. Antonio started pounding furiously on his cell wall. I looked back at him. His face was mottled with rage.

"Look at you, with your fancy costume and fancy cape and fancy words," he screamed at me. His spittle flecked the cell's front wall. "It all means nothing. I see what you are. You do what you want because you have the power to do it. Just like me. You act like you're better than me, but you're not. We're exactly the same."

I paused.

"You know what? You're right. Maybe I'm no better than you. But maybe that's what the world needs—someone in the muck, right alongside people like you, to make sure you stay in the muck where you belong, well away from innocents."

I had my fill of bandying words with this killer. I walked toward the portal leading back to Astor City.

Mad Dog's screams for me to come back fell on deaf ears.

26

I stood once again in the Situation Room with the Sentinels. Not everything was the same as the last time I was here. For one thing, the room was no longer pristine and glistening with shine. Now, much of the room was under construction. It gave me grim satisfaction to see all the damage I had caused when I was last here. Though the Sentinels had repaired some of it, they had not fixed all of it. All the monitors were dark as apparently Sentry was offline due to the damage. There was a huge hole in the ceiling, and one of the room's walls was partially collapsed.

The damage was merely a good start as far as I was concerned. If it were up to me, I would cave the entire mansion in on itself. The Sentinels who weren't psychopaths could then rebuild, this time hopefully without the murderous juju this place had.

The Bible speaks of how the walls of the city of Jericho were brought down by the Israelite army marching around it while blowing trumpets. And here I stood, wanting to tear these walls down, yet completely trumpetless. Maybe that part of the Bible was just a fairy tale, anyway. Along with the part that talks about the meek inheriting the Earth.

The second and most important thing that was different in the Situation Room now was the fact that Neha was here. She looked pretty much as she did in the video Mechano had sent me, fury in her eyes and all, except her bruises did not look as fresh. My relief at seeing her alive mingled with a fresh surge of white-hot anger at the Sentinels.

Seer, Millennium, and Mechano stood in front of their conference table. Neha, still bound, stood next to them. The same gold metal I had seen in the video was around her mouth, hands, and feet, preventing her from speaking or walking. Mechano in his nearly seven feet tall robot body towered over the rest of them. His hand was on top of Neha's raven-haired head, as a father might place his hand on his child's head. The major difference here was that, unlike a father, Mechano could squash Neha like a bug simply by pressing down on her with his super strong body. The tacit threat of his hand resting on her was not lost on me.

I wore the green and black of my Kinetic suit. Avatar's red cape was in my hand. I had just walked in, having been led through the mansion by Millennium's glowing ball much as before, only this time I had been brought on a more direct route. I stood far across the large room from the four, not willing to get any closer. I was grateful that the presence of the Omega weapon fouled up Seer's precognition. It was beyond annoying dealing with an opponent who knew what you were going to do before you did it. I wondered, not for the first time, if the Sentinels had allowed me to escape them the last time so I could retrieve the Omega weapon.

"It is not too late for you to change your mind and join us, Mr. Conley," Mechano said. "You still are the Omega. Together, we can do great things. We can protect the world. If you are sincere this time about joining us, we can forget about all the unpleasantness that has transpired between us."

My eyes darted to Neha's bruised face before returning to Mechano. I would say the gall of Mechano's offer amazed me, but frankly my amazement fuses had all been blown a while ago. I said, "Let's recap. You killed my father, killed a bunch of innocent bystanders, tried to kill me, and you kidnapped and hurt Smoke. Join you? I'll pass. You've lost touch with reality by living in that tin can for too long if you actually think I'd even consider throwing in my lot with the likes of you."

"Well you cannot blame a Hero for trying." Mechano's voice was disgustingly cheerful. He sounded like he thought the Sentinels were very much in the driver's seat. "All right then, let us get down to business. Give us the Omega weapon, and then we will give you your friend."

I shook my head. "No. You give me Smoke first, then you get the weapon."

"I am afraid I must insist." His huge hand resting on top of Neha's head shifted slightly. Neha's eyes met mine. She was unafraid. I was proud of her. The anger instead of fear I saw in her eyes strengthened my resolve.

"I said no," I said firmly. "If I give you the weapon first, you're liable to keep both it and her. I have no confidence in your good faith. I wonder why. Once you give me her, then— and only then—I will give you the cape. You have my word I will give it to you. Unlike you, my word actually means something. If you won't do as I say, I'll fly right back out of here with it. And good luck trying to stop me from leaving and trying to wrest the weapon away from me. You and I both know you would have your hands full taking the weapon by force. If you felt comfortable simply taking it from me, you would have already done so instead of using Smoke as leverage."

Mechano took a moment to respond.

"Do you really expect me to believe you would see your friend die over a simple matter of who goes first?" Curiosity mingled with surprise in his voice.

"I'm past caring about whether you believe it or not. But that's how it is, and how it's going to be if you want the weapon."

The room fell quiet for several long moments. Mechano's hand still lay on the crown of Neha's head. I had the feeling Mechano wanted to kill her just to show me I couldn't dictate terms to him. He wasn't used to that. He was accustomed to telling people what to do rather than the other way around. I was dead serious, though. I was tired of being pushed around. And there was no way I was going to risk losing both the weapon and Neha. I knew Neha well enough to know she was willing to die for a good cause. Despite the fact she had worn her cape only a tiny fraction of the time the Sentinels had, she was already more of a Hero than they would ever be.

I glanced at Neha. Her eyes met mine. There was no fear there. Just the same anger and frustration that had been there before. And perhaps a hint of pride toward me. Maybe that was just wishful thinking on my part.

Finally, Mechano took his hand from Neha's head. I let go of the breath I had not even realized I had held.

"I must admit, Mr. Conley, that the longer I know you, the more I am impressed by you. It is indeed a shame you will not come to your senses and join us," Mechano said. "We will do it your way. Take her."

I lifted a hand. Neha rose from the floor, a couple of inches up in the air. I levitated her toward me. As I did so, I scanned the gold metal that bound her, alert for any hint of an explosive. Based on the bomb the blonde had planted on me inside the bank in Washington, D.C. and the bomb Brown Recluse had planted during the Trials, Mechano seemed to have an affinity for trying to blow people up. I would not be caught off guard again.

Though I did not recognize the metal, it did not appear to be an explosive. Nor did I detect wiring or any other indications of an explosive.

I landed Neha by my side. I caught a whiff of her distinctive smell, a smell I had dreamed about all these months apart from her. A lump formed in my throat. I wanted to hug her, but it was foolish to take my focus off the Sentinels for an instant. "Are you all right?" I murmured to her.

She still couldn't speak, of course, with the metal gag in and around her mouth. Instead, Neha rolled her eyes at me, as if to say *I've been abducted, beaten, bound, and held captive. What do you think?* Yeah, it was a pretty stupid question. In my defense, I wasn't used to dealing with hostage situations. I hoped they never came up so frequently that I would get a chance to get used to them.

Now that I had Neha, I floated Avatar's cape across the room to Mechano. He plucked it out of the air. He stretched it out in front of himself. The red glow of his rectangular eye increased slightly, presumably as he scanned it.

"This appears to be an ordinary cape. You could have gotten this from anywhere," he concluded. "Millennium?" Mechano handed the cape to him. Millennium slowly waved a single gauntleted hand over the cape. As he did so, dim sparks flew off his hand, as if it were a sparkler.

"This is indeed Avatar's cape," Millennium said. It was the first time I had ever heard his voice. It had a rustling quality to it, as if he spoke while dead leaves were rubbed together. "Avatar's karmic signature is quite distinct."

"How do we activate the weapon's power?" Mechano asked impatiently.

"Unclear," Millennium said in his otherworldly voice. "That will require further study."

I had no intention of sticking around for all that. "I've upheld my end of the bargain," I said. "We're leaving."

"Of course, Mr. Conley," Mechano said. "We are not the unscrupulous monsters you seem to think we are. A deal is a deal. You and your friend are free to go."

He didn't have to tell me twice. However, there was no way I was going to wind all the way back through the mansion with Neha in tow, looking over my shoulder the whole time. So instead, with a force field around both myself and Neha, I shot up into the air. I burst through the hole in the ceiling of the Situation Room and through the reconstruction above it.

In seconds, we were outside the mansion and in the night air. I took off toward Astor City. The wind rushed past us. I scanned the air around and behind us with my powers. There were no threats I could detect. It appeared the Sentinels were letting us go.

I didn't trust it. This had been way too easy.

Despite a little voice whispering misgivings in my ear, I was so giddy I felt almost drunk. I had gotten away with tricking the Sentinels. I had not been stupid enough to hand the Omega weapon over, of course. The Sentinels had done too much to me and the people I cared about for me to think they could be trusted, either to uphold our deal to turn over Neha or to have possession of the Omega weapon. I had given the Sentinels my word that I would give them Avatar's cape. That was exactly what I had done—I had given them one of Avatar's capes from the mannequins in The Mountain. Though I had not technically broken my word, I had still pulled a fast one. Dad, who had taught me that without his honor a man was nothing, normally would not have approved of me playing fast and loose with my word. In this case, I thought he'd understand.

I had gambled the Sentinels would not be able to tell the difference between one of Avatar's ordinary capes and the real Omega weapon until I escaped with Neha. The costume I had on, though it appeared to be my old Kinetic costume, was in fact the Omega suit with its shape and color changed to replicate the Kinetic suit.

Even more important than retaining the Omega weapon, I had saved Neha. I held her in place right below me, with her facing me as we soared through the night air. Even with her face all bruised up, she was breathtaking. I loved her so much it was almost a physical ache. My heart raced. I was as nervous to be around her again as a teenager on his first date. This was the first time I had seen her in person since our falling-out shortly after the Trials.

———

It had just slipped out.

Now that the Trials were over and Isaac, Neha, and I temporarily stayed with the Old Man again in Chevy Chase, Maryland until we lined up what we were going to do with our new licenses, I had been waiting for the perfect time to tell Neha that I loved her and that I wanted us to be together. I didn't think us having sex in Neha's old room in Amazing Man's mansion in the middle of the night constituted the perfect time. Then again, I could think of worse times. Like in the middle of being shot at by a supervillain, for example.

I had just entered Neha when it slipped out of my other, supposedly smarter, head.

"I love you," I moaned, caught up in the heat of the moment.

Neha's body froze up like a cadaver's. She stared up at me. I stopped mid-thrust.

"I'm sorry, I didn't mean it. Well, I did mean it, but I didn't mean to say it," I said, mortified and flustered. "Not now. I was waiting for the right time. I guess the cat's out of the bag. There's a pussy joke in there somewhere. If Isaac were here, I bet he'd find it. The joke, not your vagina. Not that I'm saying it's hard to find. It's not like it's tiny." Neha stared at me silently, her face inscrutable. *Oh God, make me stop.* I sputtered, "I'm not saying it's huge, either. Goldilocks would say it's just right. Not that I'm implying we should invite another woman into bed with us. I don't even know someone named Goldilocks. What kind of nosy creep goes around eating strangers' food and sleeping in their beds, anyway? Unless you want to. Invite another woman, I mean. I've never done anything like that before, but I guess I'd be up to try it if that's what you're into. 'Up to try it.' Now there's a Freudian slip."

Shut up, shut up, SHUT UP! my mind shrieked at me. I bit down on my lip. I had just been about to joke that I couldn't stand Freud and his motherfucking complex. How come I could face a supervillain without gibbering like an idiot, but make me tell a woman how I felt about her and suddenly I was a nervous, prattling teen again?

Faint moonlight trickled in from the window, letting me see Neha's wide brown eyes and lithe naked body despite the otherwise dark room.

"I don't know what to say," she said. Born in India, she still had a hint of an accent.

Time seemed as frozen as my heart.

"How about, 'I love you too, Theo. I want to be with you. We should have some beautiful biracial babies together'?"

"I do love you. As a friend. As a best friend. But not like that."

"Do you let all your friends put their penises inside of you?"

"That's not fair, and you know it."

I pulled out of her. I collapsed onto the other side of the bed. I stared up at the dark ceiling.

"So that's all I am to you, then? Just a best friend with benefits? Isaac's your best friend too. Does he get the same special benefits, or are you saving him up until you're bored with me?"

"I know your feelings are hurt, and I'm sorry about that, but that's no reason to be mean. What do you want me to do, lie to you?"

The ceiling started to move, shimmering in my tears. I got up. I started to put my clothes back on.

"You know why I wanted to become a Hero," Neha said. She sat up in bed. "To stop my father Doctor Alchemy from trying to conquer the world. Until I do that, I don't have time for a relationship. With you, or anyone else."

The fact she was so calm and I most definitely was not calm really pissed me off.

I said, "Before the Trials you said you wouldn't even consider a relationship until after the Trials were over. Now they are. And you're singing the same old song. You're just making excuses. You don't feel about me the way I feel about you. That's fine. But don't pretend like it's something other than what it is." My fingers fumbled clumsily with my pants.

Neha sighed.

"Theo, I'm the first person you slept with. As far as I know, I'm the *only* person you've slept with. I wonder if maybe you're confusing love with lust and physical intimacy. It's easy to do."

A hot tear dripped off my cheek and onto the floor. "You're entitled to feel the way you feel. But don't you dare try to tell me how I feel." It was hard to not yell the words. Why couldn't I get these damned pants on?

"Theo, I was going to tell you this later, but I guess I should now: I'm moving to Chicago. I'm taking a job as the chief of security for Willow Wilde."

Stunned, my jaw dropped, as did my pants. "The reality TV celebrity? But you hate her. You always say that people like her with no talent or skill getting rich is a symptom of how screwed up society is."

"She'll pay me a lot. She thinks having a licensed Hero, even a new one like me, as her head of security will add to her fame. I can't say she's wrong. I need the money. Defeating someone like Dad isn't going to be cheap. I'm not rich like the Old Man. I don't plan to work for Willow for long. Just long enough to get the money I need."

I planned on moving to Astor City to go after Mechano once I found a job there. Isaac had already lined up a job there as an illustrator. Though we had never explicitly talked about it, I had just assumed Neha would come with us. The three of us had been inseparable ever since the Academy.

"How long have you known about this?" I demanded.

"I interviewed with her a few months ago. She told me then the job was mine if I passed the Trials."

"Months ago," I repeated, flabbergasted. "And you're just telling me this now?"

"I know I should have said something before. I just couldn't bring myself to do it. I'm closer to you and Isaac than I've ever been to anyone before. Telling you I was planning on leaving would make it all too real. Besides, there was no guarantee I would pass the Trials. You know how high the failure rate is."

My pants were pooled around my ankles. I stepped out of them and kicked them against the wall. The belt buckle left a dent in the wall. Who needed pants anyway? If Isaac or the Old Man saw me half-naked when I left Neha's room, I dared them to say something about it. I was in the mood to punch somebody.

I said, "So you've known you were leaving for months, yet you kept quiet about it and continued to fuck me anyway? God forbid you stop getting your jollies before you start partying with Willow. I guess you thought you needed to keep your privates loosened up for all those studs you'll be hooking up with alongside Willow. Just call me Theo, The Human Dildo. Sure, he's got feelings, but as long as he gets you off, who cares?"

"It's not like that." Neha was crying now. It was only the third time I'd ever seen her cry in three years. Good. I was glad I had made her cry. Misery loved company.

As I had forgotten all about sex, I was startled to see I was still erect and ready for action. It just went to show that mini-me had a mind of its own. I looked down at myself in disgust. Even my own body was betraying me. "I'll go tell Isaac it's his turn up at bat. Maybe darker meat will be more to your liking. Maybe you'll decide he's good enough for you. Obviously I'm not."

"Theo, don't leave like this. Let's—"

It was too late. I had already slammed her door behind myself. It sounded like a cannon going off in the otherwise quiet mansion. Bottomless, with my bobbing privates pointing the way, I stomped off to my old room.

That had been the last time I had spoken to Neha. She tried to talk to me in the days that followed my blowup in her room, but I ignored her like she wasn't there. I knew I was being childish, but I could not seem to help myself.

Later, once she moved to Chicago, Neha had called, texted, and emailed me. Literally not a week went by that she didn't contact me. Her calls I let go to voicemail. I deleted them without listening to them. Her texts and emails I deleted, unread. At first it was hurt and anger that made me do this. Later, stubbornness. Later still, just inertia and habit. She communicated with Isaac almost daily, though. Early on, after we had moved to Astor City, Isaac tried to intervene on Neha's behalf with me. He said me refusing to talk to her was stupid and breaking her heart. I told him to mind his own goddamned business. It was the biggest fight we ever had. Afterward, he did not bring her up much.

IN THE BACK OF MY MIND, I HAD THOUGHT I WOULD RECONCILE with Neha eventually. When the Sentinels kidnapped her, I feared I would never get the chance to patch things up and apologize for acting like a royal jackass. But now, flying back toward Astor City with Neha underneath me again, I had my chance. A second chance.

Though the memories I had of our marriage and son were but fragments of an Omega spirit-induced dream, I just knew I could make that dream a reality. Since acquiring the Omega weapon, I had learned that nothing was impossible. Surely matters of the heart were no different.

I knew Neha still didn't love me. Not the way I wanted her to. She had been clear about that months ago. That was the past. I had been a different person then. Now, I would *make* Neha love me. I would find a way. I was the Omega. I had moved the immovable neutronium spear, captured Hannah's killer, tricked the Sentinels, and liberated Neha. I could do anything.

How to begin? I had so much I wanted to say. I didn't know

how to say any of it. It did not matter. I was positively giddy being with Neha again, even under these circumstances.

I looked down at her. I felt myself grinning like an idiot. "So, how's everything since I last saw you? Anything interesting happen lately?"

"Mmmmm, mmmmmm, mmm," was all Neha could say through her metal gag.

"I can't. Sorry. Though I'm flattered, now's not the best time for that sort of thing. Maybe later, when we're in private. I can understand your eagerness to see me naked again, though. You're not the first woman to fall under my body's spell. You know what they say: 'Once you've had a taste of Theodore, you're always looking for more.'"

"Mmmm, mmm, mmmm, mmmmmm!" she said, more insistently this time. Her eyes flicked down to her metal gag, then back up at me.

"Sorry, I didn't quite get that last part. You'll have to speak up. On second thought, I take that back. Don't speak up. The quiet's kind of peaceful." I was so relieved I had gotten Neha out of the clutches of the Sentinels. I couldn't stop beaming from ear to ear. "You know what? I think I like you better this way."

Neha stared daggers at me. She looked like she wanted to hurt me almost as much as she wanted to hurt the Sentinels.

Intoxicated with relief and happiness, I laughed out loud. Neha had been wrong months before. What I felt was no brain chemistry trick, no side effect of mere horniness for the only woman I had slept with. I did love Neha. And I would find a way to make her love me.

Ungagging her seemed a good first step toward that. I'd had enough fun teasing her.

I reached out with my powers to probe the gag around and

in Neha's mouth. Careful to avoid hurting her, I applied tele-kinetic pressure, breaking the metal in several places.

My enhanced powers detected the quick flash of an energy surge from the metal manacles binding her hands and ankles together. I instinctively raised my personal shield. It was the same sort of automatic reflex that makes you pull your hand away from a hot stove.

The manacles exploded. Night became day. Neha and I were engulfed by a huge fireball that expanded like an exploding supernova.

If it hadn't been for my Omega weapon enhanced powers, I never would have survived the explosion. Since Mechano believed I had given up the Omega weapon, he undoubtedly thought the explosion would get rid of me once and for all.

He was wrong. I survived. Not only did I survive, but I flew away from the explosion without so much as a singed eyebrow. Physically, I was fine.

Emotionally, it was an altogether different matter.

Given even a tiny amount of more time, I know I could have done something. But there had been no time. There had been but a sliver of a fraction of a second between the metal's energy surge and the explosion. Enough time for my reflexes to kick in and protect me.

Not enough time to protect Neha.

The blast vaporized her. Not even her ashes were left behind. Believe me, I looked.

I had not even told her I was sorry.

For everything.

27

I slammed to a stop. The hard floor of the Situation Room cracked and cratered under me. I had already sliced through Sentinels Mansion like a bullet through paper after first swatting away the missiles and smaller projectiles the mansion's now active defenses had lobbed at me.

Taken by surprise by my sudden appearance in the room, it took a moment for the startled Sentinels to react. I targeted Millennium first. As an Omega-level Meta whose powers I did not fully understand, he posed the greatest threat.

Millennium raised his hands toward me, his fingers dancing in the air. With a downward flick of my wrist, an invisible force field exploded down like a guillotine, ripping through both of Millennium's wrists. Blood spurted, sweet-smelling and an inhuman sapphire blue.

Millennium screamed. The peculiar rustling sound of his voice mingled with a banshee's wail as his hands went flying, amputated from his arms far more neatly than any surgeon's knife ever could have done it. The gauntleted hands dropped like dead fish, plopping on the metal floor with a wet thump. Magical math: No hands equaled no spells.

With a dismissive wave of my other hand, Millennium went flying. His arms and legs flailed. His back and head hit a wall with a sickening crunch. I let him slide to the floor. He lay there on his back twitching, like a stepped-on cockroach, with ichor oozing out of his wrists.

Seer was on the move. She flew up toward the hole I had punched through the ceiling earlier. A rat fleeing a sinking ship. Though my suit blocked her precognition, you didn't need a crystal ball to see she and Mechano were no match for me in the Omega suit now that Millennium was out of commission.

I raised my hand slightly. I closed it, using my powers to grab and hold Seer like a fly in a clenched fist. She resisted me with her own telekinesis. Her efforts were like a child trying to break the hold of a bodybuilder. The temptation to squeeze harder and reduce her body to so much jelly was strong.

Instead, I flung her toward Sentry. The metal tentacles extending from Sentry's control panel rose to greet her, the helmet they were attached to ripping away at my mental command. The now free tentacles writhed like something alive. They enfolded Seer in an octopus' embrace.

A crossed wire here, a short circuit there, and the tentacles became electrified. Seer screamed. Her body danced in the tentacles' embrace like someone gripping an electrified fence.

I broke more wires deep within Sentry's innards. The electricity arcing through the tentacles shut off. Seer went limp. Unconscious, but alive.

Neutralizing Seer and Millennium took only a few seconds. Though they were no angels, I had saved the worst for last.

I turned my attention to Mechano. He stood far across the room, next to the Sentinels' heptagonal conference table. Avatar's red cape was spread out on it.

"You killed her," I said. The words came out in a hiss. Fury, cold and implacable, fueled me.

Mechano's single eye regarded me emotionlessly.

"You brought this on yourself. This cape is not the Omega weapon. It is a fake. You lied to us."

"You didn't know that when you planted those bombs on her. You planned on killing both of us the whole time. You wanted there to be no witnesses to what you had done. Dead men tell no tales to the Guild. When did you plan to kill Myth and Truman? Tonight? Tomorrow?"

I started to walk toward Mechano. His eye flashed red. A beam of powerful energy hit me in the center of my chest. I had a force field up, of course. Through it I absorbed the energy of Mechano's beam.

My own eyes burned. Beams of Mechano's redirected energy shot out of them. They sheared off his right arm, where a normal person's bicep would connect with his shoulder. The arm hit the floor with a clang. Thick gray lubricant sprayed everywhere. The arm bent and unbent, the fingers twitching.

Another beam from Mechano hit my chest, this one a different energy and frequency than before. It made no difference. I absorbed this energy too.

My eyes blazed. My eye beams cut off Mechano's left leg where it connected to his hip. Still advancing on Mechano, I shoved my hand forward, like I was pushing a door open. Mechano's one-legged heavy body fell backward. He hit the floor with a force that made the entire room rattle. His detached left leg, still standing upright, spurted lubricant like a geyser. The stuff smelled like burning rubber.

Hobbled, still on his back, Mechano tried to skitter away. He crawled clumsily backward with his remaining limbs. His metallic body screeched against the floor.

Energy blasted out of my eyes again. Right leg, gone. Left arm, gone. Lubricant gushed everywhere.

Mechano was now as immobilized as a dying beetle flipped on its back.

I stood directly over Mechano. He looked up at me. He made no effort to blast me again. He no doubt realized the futility of it. In the parts of his shiny torso that weren't soiled with lubricant, I saw a reflection of myself. My eyes blazed bright yellow with barely suppressed energy.

I felt no satisfaction in having the man behind Neha's and my father's death prostrate at my feet. Other than a block of icy fury that chilled the pit of my stomach, I felt nothing at all. The world seemed tasteless and gray. Nothing I could do to Mechano would bring either of them back.

Then, the strangest thing happened.

Mechano began to laugh.

It started as a chuckle. Then it became a belly laugh. It quickly transitioned to a full-throated, knee-slapping laugh, like that of a man who had seen something so incredibly funny he could not control himself.

I waited until Mechano's laughter played itself out. When it had, I said, "You think this is funny?"

"This is not," Mechano said, "but you are." Amusement was still in his voice. "Standing there like an avenging angel, looking like you're about to smite a sinner. I must admit that for a second I was worried. I thought almost a hundred and fifty years of towering technological achievements were about to come to an abrupt end. But then I remembered who the man standing over me is. The man your father taught you to be. The man we Heroes trained you to be. You are not going to kill me. It is not who you are."

I knew what he was doing. He was appealing to my better

nature, to manipulate me into not damaging him further. Just as he and the Sentinels had manipulated me and the people I cared about for years.

"There's no need to worry," I said. My voice was strangely calm. "I'm not going to kill you."

I raised a hand slightly. I pulled Mechano's various severed limbs toward us. I piled them on top of his torso, where they landed with a wet clatter. The stack of wet robot parts looked like a madman's art project. Mechano's head swiveled slightly in what would have been puzzlement on a real person.

I said, "I'm not going to kill you because I can't. To kill someone means to take their life. You're not alive. You're just a collection of circuits and servos that pursues its agenda with no regard for how it impacts real people. You are nothing more than the phrase 'the end justifies the means' in mechanical form. Seer and Millennium will go to MetaHold. But not you. MetaHold is where they imprison Metahumans. You're not human. You haven't been for a long time."

I gathered my will. I surrounded Mechano and me in a spherical force field.

"What are you doing?" I heard an emotion in Mechano's voice I'd never heard there before: fear.

"Taking out the trash," I said.

I triggered my powers, reaching deep down inside of Mechano.

Late one night, back when I had been in the Academy, I had felt the atoms of everything swirling around me, like an intricate dance set to unheard music. In my half-asleep state, the energy that had bound the atoms together seemed to cry for release. I had almost triggered my powers to unleash that energy, but fortunately had not. The next day I calculated I would have set off a massive nuclear explosion that would have incinerated the Academy, everyone in it, and taken much of Oregon with it.

That was what I did to Mechano now. All at once, I broke up the molecules and atoms that composed his robot body.

Mechano's body disappeared, replaced by blinding light. There was a roar, like that of countless erupting volcanoes. The energy unleashed was immense. Even with the Omega suit, I struggled to absorb it all. The nuclear explosions the Metahuman John Tilly set off in the Japanese cities of Hiroshima and Nagasaki to end World War Two paled in comparison to this one. If I hadn't erected the force field around us to contain the energy I had unlocked by breaking up Mechano's body, I would have released a destructive blast the likes of which the world had never seen before.

Now I am become Death, destroyer of worlds, came unbidden words to my mind. They were from the *Bhagavad Gita*, the Hindu scripture Truman had been reading in his office when I'd first met him. That seemed like a lifetime ago. It's weird, the things that occur to you and when they occur to you.

Finally, I sucked into my body all the energy released from Mechano's destruction. My eyes, burning with barely suppressed energy, probed where Mechano had been. Nothing of him remained. Every iota of him was gone, as if he had never existed. The bomb he had planted had left no trace of Neha. It seemed only fitting to do the same to him.

I dropped the force field around me. My entire being shook with the effort of containing all this energy. I was like an overcharged battery. I had to release this energy before my control of it slipped. During the Trials, when I had absorbed an explosion's energy for the first time, I had vented the excess energy up into the air to avoid injuring anyone. With the kind of energy I now contained, I hesitated to vent it like that again. It was possible I would set the Earth's atmosphere on fire.

I hesitated, tempted. With the woman I loved dead because of me, the world seemed empty and without meaning. Would it be any great tragedy to watch it burn?

I took a long, ragged breath. I shoved the selfish thought aside. I had sworn a Heroic oath. Unlike these three Sentinels, I intended to honor it. Mom was dead. Dad was dead. Neha was dead. My oath was the only thing I had left.

Before I gave into the dark temptation which threatened to seduce me like a whore's embrace, I sprang into the air. With all the power my body now contained, I punched through the solidly constructed floors of the mansion like they were mere soap bubbles. I rose in the night air, higher, higher, higher, and higher still, until I was well clear of Earth's atmosphere.

I turned away from the planet. Space was dark and cold as a tomb. I opened my mouth. The energy that had been Mechano vomited out of me. It raced into the lifeless void of space. The temptation to follow it until there was no air left in the force field surrounding me was almost irresistible.

I reluctantly turned my back to space and the thought. Earth glittered like a jewel. Despite all that had happened, it kept right on spinning. The sun would rise in the morning. People would wake up, kiss their spouses and kids goodbye, and go to work. Because I carried the Omega spirit and wore a Hero's cape, it was my job to make sure that what had happened to the people I loved did not happen to the people they loved.

I did not want the responsibility. Before Dad died, I had not wanted to be a superhero. I sure as hell didn't want to be one now. I just wanted to crawl into bed, pull the covers over my head, blot out the world, and dream of the people I had lost until I too was lost.

But, like it or not, I did have this responsibility. It was

clichéd, but true: With great power came great responsibility. Otherwise, you wound up behaving like the Sentinels had.

Though I did not want to, I would try my best.

Trying is all.

28

I stood on top of the UWant Building. It was late. I was wide awake and alert despite not having slept much in the days since Neha died. The Omega suit made it so I got along just fine on a few hours of sleep. It was a blessing. I did not much like going to sleep anymore. Neha awaited me in my nightmares.

I was perched on the roof's ledge. My eyes were closed. My hands extended in front of me, like a maestro conducting an orchestra. My telekinetic touch was so acute now thanks to the Omega suit that I could monitor much of what happened in Astor City without the bother of flying around on patrol. My silver-white cape flapped in the breeze. It matched the color of the omega symbol on my chest. It was a silly affectation, letting this cape sprout out of the neck of the Omega suit. The cape served absolutely no practical purpose. And yet, wearing it made me feel more official somehow.

It was a cold night. Colder than usual, even this high up where it was always cold. Local weathermen said this coming winter would be an especially harsh one. If only the weather were the least of Astor City's problems.

Dad is dead because I refused to train in the use of my powers, I thought.

Miles away, in Dog Cellar, five young men walked behind a shambling homeless man, whispering to themselves, egging each other on. The homeless man was dressed in rags, muttered to himself, and walked with a limp. He had nothing of value. The five following him must have known that. That did not prevent them from jumping him as soon as they all rounded the corner. My fingers splayed out. The men—no, the *children*, because that's what they were in all the ways that mattered—were flung off the homeless man, yanked into the air by my powers.

The homeless man cowered on the sidewalk. He looked up at the five in amazement through covered eyes, his eyes round through his fingers. The five hung in the air, yelping in surprise and confusion, their limbs sawing the air. Using a spray can from a nearby trash can, I quickly wrote a single word on the streetlamp lit sidewalk: *Run!* Then I smashed all five of them together like they were in a mid-air mosh pit, hard enough to rattle their bones. I shut off my hold on them, letting them fall heavily to the sidewalk. The instant they scrambled to their feet, they ran from the homeless man as if he were the Devil himself.

The homeless man stared at the retreating five in awe. He got to his knees. His face turned up to the night sky. His hands were clasped in front of him.

"Thank you Jesus!" he prayed aloud.

Hardly.

Hannah is dead because I was too naive to predict the consequences of using my powers.

In Shangri-La, a ritzy residential subdivision in the northeastern part of the city, a masked man slid open a window on the first floor of the house of a family of four. A young female and a young male were asleep in separate bedrooms. A man and a woman, presumably the parents, were asleep in the master bedroom. The masked man crept upstairs, into the dark bedroom of the young female. I had no idea how he knew which was her bedroom or how he had gotten past the house's alarm system. Perhaps he had been stalking her for a while now.

The man wrapped his hand around the female's mouth, waking her. His other hand held a knife to her throat. He was aroused. My stomach churned. The female had barely begun to develop, more girl than woman. She trembled in terror.

I flung the man off the girl. She screamed as the masked man sailed through the air and slammed into the opposite wall. For good measure, I rapped the back of his head against the wall a few times until I was sure he was unconscious. The parents were now up, getting out of bed. I turned on all the lights of the house at once. The parents rushed toward the girl's screams.

Neha is dead because I wasn't adept enough in the use of my enhanced powers to recognize the threat posed by the metal which bound her, I thought. I would never let something like that happen again. I would practice, practice, and practice some more until I was as well-versed in the use of my enhanced powers as it was humanly possible to be.

Darkness was approaching, both Seer and the Omega spirit had said. I planned to be ready. I would not fail someone again. Too many had already died thanks to me.

Downtown, not too far from the UWant Building, the Thug Three broke the high-impact front window of a high-end jewelry store. They clambered inside. They started smashing the store's display cases. They stuffed jewelry into their pockets. The store's alarm wailed, but it didn't deter the crooks. This was just a quick smash and grab. The Thug Three no doubt planned to be long gone by the time the cops arrived at the scene. I had encountered these three hoodlums before when I was Kinetic. They were low-level Metas who used their powers to make quick scores to fund their drug habits.

I threw a force field around the store. When the Thug Three tried to climb back out the window they had broken, they bumped against my invisible field. They were trapped like bugs in a glass jar. I would hold them there until the police arrived.

Beast, the super strong one of the bunch, tried to punch his way through my force field.

Yeah, good luck with that.

I sensed a presence land on the roof with me. After a while, with my eyes still closed, I said, "How long are you going to stand there staring at me?"

"You're perched up here with your arms out and your eyes closed like a zombie gargoyle," Isaac said. "I plan to stare at you until you become less creepy. I figure it might be a while."

I lowered my hands and opened my eyes. I turned to Isaac.

"The Guild have any luck finding Millennium?" I asked.

"No. No one's seen him since he somehow escaped from the mansion. Now that the other Sentinels are back from Peru, maybe they'll have better luck finding him. You've gotta hand it to him, managing to disappear despite what you did to him."

I thought of Millennium's hands lying on the floor of the Situation Room. "'Gotta hand it to him.' You can't help yourself, can you?"

"It's a gift and a curse."

"There still talk about arresting me for destroying Mechano?"

Isaac shrugged.

"You know how people are. Opinions are like assholes: Everyone's got one, and most of them stink. Half the Guild thinks you ought to be charged with murder and locked up in MetaHold, languishing alongside Seer and Brown Recluse until this whole thing gets sorted out. The other half thinks you should get a medal and a ticker tape parade for exposing the Sentinels' corruption. The only opinion that really matters in this situation is that of the State's Attorney. Laura Leonard, the attorney Truman recommended, says the law is murky in this situation as it's never come up before. It all turns on whether you can be convicted of murdering someone who's not technically human anymore. Laura says she can make a good argument that you can't be. Time will tell."

We were quiet for a while. I gazed out on the city, both with my eyes and my powers. I wasn't worried about what would happen to me. I was worried about what would happen to the world. Darkness was approaching. Seer and the Omega spirit were right about that. Maybe it was the Omega suit, but I seemed to feel the encroaching threat in my bones, like when you feel a storm brewing. A day of reckoning was coming. I didn't know from whom or from where, but it was coming.

I had to be ready for it.

With effort, I forced my mind back to the present. "What do you think?" I asked. "Do you think I did the right thing with Mechano?"

"I wasn't there. It's not for me to say. The more important issue is what you think. You're the one who has to live with your actions."

I nodded. His non-answer told me what Isaac thought.

I said, "I think that, despite the fact he wasn't flesh and bone, Mechano was a mad dog who needed to be put down. I don't regret it." Using the words "mad dog" made me think of Antonio, trapped in The Mountain. I had not told Isaac about that. Isaac would not approve. Just like he didn't approve of what I had done to Mechano, despite Neha being his friend too. Just like he wouldn't approve of me cheating during the Trials. He was a better person than I was in a lot of ways. But Isaac wasn't the Omega. I was. I had to do what I thought was best. Things looked different when the weight of the world was on your shoulders.

My mind had wandered. I realized Isaac was staring at me intently.

"If you don't regret what you did to Mechano, why do you look so upset?" he asked.

I hesitated, reluctant to admit the truth out loud. The cold, almost emotionless fury I had felt when I confronted the Sentinels had thawed when I heard fear in Mechano's voice for the first time. At the sound of his fear, my fury had transformed into something else. I remembered how I had looked, standing over Mechano's body. I had seen my distorted reflection in his shiny torso. There had been a grim smile on my face when I destroyed him.

I thought of what Mad Dog had said to me. About how I was just like him.

"I'm not upset because I destroyed Mechano," I finally said. "I'm upset because I enjoyed it so much."

The End

If you enjoyed this book, please leave a review on Amazon. Even a simple two word review such as "Loved it" helps so much. Reviews are a big aid in helping readers like you find books they might like.

ABOUT THE AUTHOR

Darius Brasher has a lifelong fascination with superheroes and a love of fantasy and science fiction. He has a Bachelor of Arts degree in English, a Juris Doctor degree in law, and a PhD from the School of Hard Knocks. He lives in South Carolina.

Email: darius@dbrasher.com
Patreon: www.patreon.com/dariusbrasher

facebook.com/dariusbrasher

twitter.com/dariusbrasher

amazon.com/author/dariusbrasher

Made in the USA
Monee, IL
01 March 2020